E. H. Johnson

Ezekiel Gilman Robinson

An Autobiography

E. H. Johnson

Ezekiel Gilman Robinson
An Autobiography

ISBN/EAN: 9783337121723

Printed in Europe, USA, Canada, Australia, Japan

Cover: Foto ©Raphael Reischuk / pixelio.de

More available books at **www.hansebooks.com**

EZEKIEL GILMAN ROBINSON

An Autobiography

WITH A SUPPLEMENT BY H. L. WAYLAND
AND CRITICAL ESTIMATES

Edited by

E. H. JOHNSON

SILVER, BURDETT AND COMPANY

NEW YORK . . . BOSTON . . . CHICAGO

1896

PREFACE.

IN the spring of 1893 Dr. Robinson was prevailed
upon to begin the dictation of an autobiography.
At the same time the contributors and the topics for
a memorial volume were agreed upon substantially as
they now appear. Dr. Robinson was urged to tell his
story with entire frankness, and equal frankness was
asked from the contributors; they were also assured
that what they might write, until it went to the publisher, would not come under any other eye than that
of the editor. A more candid memorial volume than
these plans have secured could hardly be found; yet
a less discriminating book would not indicate so fine
a reverence for him who is its subject. The Critical
Estimates are pervaded by a conviction that the impress made by Dr. Robinson upon the thinking and
the preaching of his denomination is the deepest that
it has received in a generation; the effort of the
writers has been to determine and to state the sources
and nature of an influence which, at the distance even
of many years, is still rated by those who came under
it as hardly less than prodigious. In such a case it
has seemed best to limit for the most part my service

as editor to a kind of secretaryship in behalf of the writers. This, I am aware, is to accept rather than to evade a responsibility.

The comparative silence of the autobiography and of the contributions with regard to Mrs. Robinson, to whom, as her husband over and over declared in public, he owed everything, is due to the restrictions which she herself imposed upon him and upon all who have had a part in the book; yet all feel that the tribute they would like to pay to her is indispensable to an understanding of him.

The supplement to the autobiography was prepared by Dr. Robinson's nearest friend. The list of published writings is due to the painstaking of A. G. Langley, A. M., the scholarly translator of Leibnitz's "New Essays," which are just coming before the public in English dress. The Index is from the skilful hand of Rev. Robert Kerr Eccles, M. D., of Ohio.

E. H. JOHNSON.

CROZER THEOLOGICAL SEMINARY.
February, 1896.

CONTENTS.

CONTENTS.

CHAPTER III.

THE ROCHESTER PROFESSORSHIP AND PRESIDENCY.

1853-1866.

CHAPTER IV.

IN EUROPE. — LAST YEARS IN ROCHESTER.

1866-1872.

CHAPTER V.

PRESIDENCY OF BROWN.

1872–1889.

THE CLOSING YEARS (1889–1891). — A SUPPLEMENT.

H. L. WAYLAND, D.D.

𝔓art Second.

CRITICAL ESTIMATES.

APPENDIX.

Part First.

AUTOBIOGRAPHY, WITH SUPPLEMENT.

AUTOBIOGRAPHY.

CHAPTER I.

CHILDHOOD AND EDUCATION.

1815–1842.

I WAS born, March 23, 1815, at South Attleboro, Massachusetts, about six miles from Providence, on a farm which had been in the family some four or five generations.[1] It was bought originally of the Indians. My father, Ezekiel Robinson, was the second of five brothers. The next younger brother than himself, Samuel Robinson, was a physician, who, having a pulmonary affection, removed to North Carolina early in the present century, practising medicine until about the year 1823 or 1824. Then he devoted his attention exclusively to mineralogy, exploring the localities of minerals throughout the then known United States, and collecting a cabinet of minerals[2] which afterwards found place at Harvard College.

---

[1] At a memorial service to Dr. Robinson held in Boston, the late Rev. Dr. A. J. Gordon stated that, in the course of genealogical investigations about his own family, he found Dr. Robinson to be a descendant of the Rev. John Robinson of Leyden. It is matter of record that his ancestor, George Robinson of the Plymouth colony, held lands by allotment in Rehoboth, after their purchase from the Indians. A part of these lands is still held by the family, and the subject of this memoir was born on the ancestral estate. — ED.

[2] This was really the nucleus of the cabinet of minerals at Harvard University, and was purchased by Professor Webster. My uncle published

My father, after the death of his father, who had left his
estate encumbered, removed from the farm to that part of
Pawtucket which was then within the line of Massachusetts,
becoming an innkeeper, and one of the sheriffs of Bristol
County. He died after a short illness in the autumn of 1819,
when I was four and a half years of age. My mother with
four children, of whom I was the youngest, returned to the
farm, where we continued to live until I was about eight
years of age. Desiring better opportunities for the education
of her children, she returned to Pawtucket. Of the schools
I attended prior to my eighth year not even the faintest
remembrance remains. Of struggles with words and of a
sense of victory in learning to read long before this, I have
a vivid recollection, but of teachers and schools all remembrance has vanished. The earliest recollection that I have
of being in a schoolroom goes back to the time when I must
have been nearly four and a half years of age. How I
happened to be there I cannot say; certainly not as a regular scholar, probably as a casual visitor with older sisters.
The recollection is not of anything studied or learned, but
of a great fright when the school had been dismissed, and

one of the earliest catalogues of minerals issued in this country. He died in
the winter of 1825–26 at St. Augustine. — E. G. R.

A letter from the late Professor J. W. P. Jenks shows the estimate in
which this uncle was held : " When I left for Florida in 1874, he [President
Robinson] requested me to look through the cemetery at St. Augustine to see
in what condition the headstone of his uncle's grave might be. . . . Instead
of a mere headstone I found a neat monument in a lot enclosed by an iron
fence, and on the monument an inscription to this import : —

" Sacred to the memory of Samuel Robinson, M.D., who attained great
distinction in his profession during a long residence in this city, and by his
public services and wise counsels greatly endeared himself to all his fellow-
citizens, by whom this monument is erected in grateful recognition of his
worth.

" These are not the exact words, but the meaning of the inscription I am
certain to have expressed."

the scholars had all left. It was in a late summer or early autumn afternoon, when, wearied from play, or lulled by the hum of the schoolroom, I had lain down on one of the long seats and had fallen asleep. Hidden by the desk from the eye of the teacher, and forgotten by my sisters, I had been left asleep and locked up alone. I awoke when all had left, and the alarm and wailing that followed have never wholly faded from my memory.

At eight my school days and education began in earnest.[1] I was sent to a large school kept by a Mr. Hill in Pawtucket. Here most of the scholars of both sexes were older than myself. Chief among many unprofitable tasks imposed upon me was the study of Lindley Murray's English Grammar. I was compelled to learn indefinite quantities of detail about "parts of speech," under the designation of " Etymology," and to commit to memory *verbatim* the twenty-two rules of "Syntax," and apply these in " parsing." Human ingenuity could hardly have devised anything more dreary and destructive of all childish interest. So desperate was the effort to master some of these rules that they have never ceased to haunt me with unpleasant memories. So far as any usefulness was concerned, any other English words arbitrarily combined would have served the same end. The weary months spent on that grammar were worse than wasted; they did me a permanent injury. I acquired the parrot-like habit of recitation, and of reading without taking in the sense of what I read. That study of grammar came near making useless the next few years of my school life. But there was one lesson learned by me at Mr. Hill's big school that has been invaluable to me ever since, — a lesson learned

---

[1] This account of Dr. Robinson's student life has been enlarged by incorporating parts of his article, " How I was Educated," which appeared in the "Forum " for December, 1886. — ED.

not from books but from a fellow-student, and from Mr. Hill's blind savagery of discipline. A youth named Lord, much older than I, sat directly in front of me, having, as all scholars then had, a " ruler," which he contrived in some way to thrust through the back of his seat for my special annoyance. I seized it, and on his trying to give it a wrench for my greater annoyance, it snapped with a loud report. The ever-watchful master, with rawhide in hand, — he was never without it in school hours, — was at once on the spot, demanding an explanation of the noise. With childish simplicity I told the story just as it was, which Lord vehemently denied, and denounced me as the offender. Older and bolder than I, he browbeat me into the weakened statement that " I thought he did it." The result was that for the first and only time in my life I tasted the qualities of a rawhide. The lesson, not to be frightened out of what I knew to be the truth, was worth to me all it cost, and has been more valuable in life than all I learned from Lindley Murray's grammar. I never shall forget the exciting interest with which, years after I had studied Latin grammar, I read an English grammar which seemed like a revelation. It happened one evening, and so absorbed me that I threw aside everything else until I had read it through from beginning to end.

When I was eleven years of age, my mother returned to the old paternal farm, which, with the help of hired men, was cultivated by my elder brother and myself. The spring-time, the open fields, the birds, the blossoming of orchards, the planting of gardens, banished all thought of school, and made life a genuine pleasure. Three or four years slipped away, my education being conducted chiefly in a country district school. The school was, perhaps, equal to the average Massachusetts schools of that day; but, as I now recall it, nothing in the way of teaching, so far as I was concerned, could have been more worthless. One winter afternoon, however, in that country school-house still lingers with me as one of the pleasantest of memories. Among the books used in the school was a reading-book made up mostly of extracts from well-known English authors. Among these was Johnson's "Hermit of Teneriffe." Something induced me to read it. I was absorbed; consciousness of my surroundings ceased. When the brief story was finished, the slanting rays of the sun seemed to have transformed the room. I was with the hermit on the slope of Teneriffe. It was my first conscious taste of literature. I had read "Robinson Crusoe," "The Pilgrim's Progress," and other books in vogue with boys; but nothing had ever interested me like this story. Why it so affected me I cannot tell, unless there may have been some mental mood to which it chanced at the instant to be specially fitted.

Little as these years of country life did for me in the way of mental training, they nurtured a naturally weak constitution into a strength that has since been equal to many a year of mental strain. About the time we returned to the farm an event occurred which had some influence on my after life: the old ancestral house with nearly all its contents was burned to the ground. In it were lost valuable papers and family relics that had been collecting for generations. The reflections caused by that fire enabled me afterwards to put out two fires which, but for immediate action, would have resulted in great loss.[1]

---

[1] In my first professorship at Covington the room in which I was teaching was suddenly darkened by a cloud of smoke outside the windows. We rushed to the attic; a huge hole had already been burned in the roof. I called for a bucket of water, which seemed absurd enough. I dipped in the

My farming experience extended till I was fourteen years of age, when I was sent to Day's Academy, as it was called, a well-known school of that time at Wrentham, Massachusetts. I then had no thought of going to college. My eager desire was to be a farmer. I was accordingly put to such studies as suited the convenience of the principal, and seemed to him not wholly unfit for a boy of my age and needs. With the exception of a mere smattering of mechanical principles, misnamed Natural Philosophy, and perhaps a perceptible shade of increase in mental discipline, the only real gain made at this school was in some slight knowledge, derived from "The Political Class-Book," of the constitution of our national government as well as of the governments of the several States of the Union.

Just how long I remained at Day's Academy I cannot now remember, nor precisely what followed my leaving it. I only remember spending another summer on the ancestral farm, with another trial of the country public school. The year came near proving a total loss educationally, though I made some progress in the knowledge of books. Physical mishaps,[1] disabling and shutting me up in the house, compelled me to seek recreation in reading. I was now sixteen years old, and it was necessary for me to decide on my future in life. The question then was, Should I go to college? I had rather by accident and aimlessly stumbled upon a preparatory course. My mother said, if there was any prospect of my amounting to anything, she would gladly

bucket an old pair of trousers lying on the attic floor, and in a very few minutes whipped out every trace of the fire. The class standing by said I acted like a frantic man. The other fire threatened the old presidential mansion at Brown University. — E. G. R.

[1] Dr. Robinson, while a boy, was easily poisoned by wild plants; and this fact weighed with his mother in deciding that he was not fitted for life on a farm. — ED.

have me go to college; but did not wish me to go there and come out a gambler and horse-racer, as Dr. —— had done, with whose parents she had been intimately acquainted. It must be admitted that all attempts up to that time to give me an education had been comparatively futile. They could hardly have been more ill-advised. Over-crowded schools, incompetent teachers, and the radical mistake of frequently changing schools, with intervals between the changes of long mental idleness, had borne their natural fruits. I was a boy past sixteen, with no desire for education, and with about the worst possible habits of study. But it was decided that I might, if I wished, prepare for college, and that for this purpose I should go to a preparatory school in New Hampton, New Hampshire, where my sister, six years older than myself, had spent the preceding summer at the woman's academy, under the tuition of Miss Haseltine, a famous teacher of that day.

It was past the middle of March, the snow had all disappeared from Southern Massachusetts, the robins had come, and the spring had fairly begun, when, with a full supply of clothing for a year, I was put on board a stage-coach for Boston, with the understanding that two and a half days' stage travelling would bring me to my destination. With less knowledge of the world than then belonged to the average boy of my age, that stage journey was itself distinctively educational. The landing at Wild's Hotel in Elm Street, Boston, the great centre for stage travellers of that day; the start at four in the morning for Concord, New Hampshire; the loud rattling of the coach-wheels over the cobble-stone pavement of the empty streets, in the cold darkness of that dreary March morning; the frightful state of the roads, prolonging the one day's drive to Concord into two; the exchange of wheels for runners on the fourth day from home, with the " seasickness " that followed, — all had their lessons for me. I reached New Hampton, the most forlorn and disheartened boy that ever dropped among merry school-fellows. The surrounding country at once interested me more than the school. I was made the room-mate of a soulless student, much older than myself, with whom it was impossible for me to have a particle of sympathy, and was set to work on Adams' " Latin Grammar," simply committing to memory its larger type, and its declensions of nouns and conjugations of verbs. My teacher, a middle-aged man, was, to speak truly, the most stupid person I have ever seen fulfilling the office of teacher. Nothing could have been more perfunctory than his instruction. If I recited the text *verbatim*, well and good; if not, he simply repeated the words for me, and nothing more. When the spring vacation came, I determined to quit Latin, abandoning all thought of college, and deciding to devote myself to such English studies as the school might offer. My sister ridiculed me for my lack of perseverance.

During the vacation there came to the school, from somewhere in Maine, a man who had several years before been prepared for college, but who through some family disaster had failed to enter. Having become a zealous Christian, he had resolved to fit himself for the Christian ministry, and had come to New Hampton to review his studies preparatory to entering college in the autumn. Becoming interested somehow in my welfare, and winning my confidence, he remonstrated against my purpose to drop the thought of college, and insisted on my resuming the study of Latin with him for instructor. And he knew by instinct how to teach. He was the first man that up to that time had ever enkindled in me a spark of enthusiasm in any study. He soon had me all aglow, and inspired me with a zeal that aroused me at four o'clock in the morning to continue the study of Latin. Till he left for college I was daily in his room, working with an eagerness to me never known before nor equalled since. Mr. Moses Curtis, the friend who thus saved me from a misstep, was a man of rare parts, of high endowments, and of warm sympathies. He left New Hampton at the end of the summer term to enter college. I saw no more of him for more than two years, when I entered Freshman, and he was a member of the Junior class. He died in his room at college from hemorrhage of the lungs. His death made a profound impression on the whole college, and on me, in particular, to whom he had especially endeared himself.

I remained at New Hampton for one year, when I returned home for some new clothes. On entering the house I was met with shouts of laughter at my appearance. I was a specimen of " the rising son " of the comic almanac. My trousers were too short, my coat too small and short-sleeved, and I was, altogether, a laughable object. But inwardly I had changed more than outwardly, and was now intent on a college education. I had then to decide whether I would return to New Hampton. It was not an attractive school ; at least, it had no attractions for me. A new academy had been opened at Pawtucket, under the principalship of Mr. Joseph Hale, a graduate of Harvard College. It was decided that I should enter it. At first I boarded in the family of a young and newly married physician near the academy; but as spring drew near to summer, an old yearning for the country revived with force. The distance between the academy and my country home was two miles, and I resolved to try the experiment of walking it daily. The experiment was a success. A fondness for solitary country walks was thus acquired, which has never forsaken me. The delight of the mornings and evenings in the orchards and woods, and among the birds, was incessant. The year passed swiftly by, and I made fair progress, under Mr. Hale, in the study of Greek, besides doing something in Latin. Some one suggested that I could enter college that autumn. I went to Brown University, and consulted with Professor Caswell. He received me kindly; but I was so self-distrustful and shy that my eyes filled with tears, and I choked in telling my errand. He advised me to wait another year.

But there was for me one serious drawback in the Pawtucket Academy: I had and could have no classmates. I needed instruction in three, if not four, distinct branches. As a single pupil the requisite time could not be given me. The New Hampton Academy, during my absence from it, had undergone a change; it now had younger and more competent teachers. There was a class of several young men who were to enter college in the fall, and I joined them. That summer school among the hills of New Hampshire was the happiest of all my school days; long strolls, pleasant companionships, and, withal, teachers superior to those I had previously known there, made me contented and joyous. These new classmates whom I found were all candidates for the ministry. I had myself no definite purpose in fitting for college. Association with these classmates had most likely much to do with turning my own thoughts toward the ministry. During a revival in 1829, when fourteen years of age, I had become a member of the First Baptist Church in Pawtucket. I became a member of the church with the crudest possible ideas of religion, and with a religious experience as unsatisfactory as it could well have been. Dissatisfaction with that experience was, for a series of years afterwards, a source of most painful anxiety. I had blundered blindly into the church. This has haunted me all my life, but has been of great service to me as a pastor and teacher. I stumbled purposelessly into a course of study. Of course the question was started with me, through association with my classmates, What was I going to college for? — a then unanswerable question.

On entering college I found myself about as poorly prepared for the work before me as any member of the class; and it has been to me a source of ceaseless regret that, instead of having picked up a fragmentary preparation for college at the hands of various and indifferent teachers, I could not have been sent either to Phillips Exeter or Phillips Andover Academy. It was the penalty of a lack of intelligent advisers. I entered college when I was nineteen. It was my good fortune to be a member of one of the most remarkable classes which Brown University has graduated. The most brilliant Latinist of the class died soon after graduating, — the brother of Chief Justice Ames of Rhode Island. In this class, numbering only thirty-two, were Chief Justice Bradley of Rhode Island; Chief Justice Morton of Massachusetts; Bishop Burgess of Quincy, Illinois; George Van Ness Lothrop of Detroit, afterwards minister to St. Petersburg; Judge Wilson of the Appellate Court of Chicago; the distinguished Thomas A. Jenckes, father of civil-service reform; Albert N. Arnold, missionary to Greece, and afterward professor of Greek in two institutions, with several others of only lesser note.[1] The majority of them had received the best possible training. I felt at once the inferiority of my preparation in comparison with theirs, and was disheartened. Severe illness almost at the outset drove me home; hence my first term in college was nearly lost time. The second was a great improvement on the first. Could the improvement have been progressively continued, the result

---

[1] For recollections by college mates, see note at end of chapter. — ED.

of my college life would have been different from what it was; but the memory of the first term haunted me: my courage and ambition sank to the verge of extinction. To add to my misfortune, the most intimate of my friends, though pure in their lives, and morally wholesome as associates, were low in their aims as scholars, satisfied with very little and very superficial work. They had been sent to college to prepare for the ministry, and were fair specimens of a class of men not yet wholly extinct. Selected, and aided by beneficiary funds, as " candidates for the ministry," they seemed to absolve themselves from the duty of high aims as scholars, and dropped into the wretched cant of " laying aside worldly ambition as unworthy the servants of the Lord."

But, on the other hand, it was my good fortune to be a member of a debating society composed of a very different sort of men from those who were my most intimate friends. Of the two great debating societies, candidates for the ministry were generally members of the Philermenian Society. Nobody imagined that the Christian ministry was thought of by me. I was supposed to be preparing for the law. I was a member of the United Brothers, which consisted of the rough-and-tumble element. But in direct education for the real work of life no influences of my college days were equal to those of this Society. It called into use and fastened in my memory what little I learned from text-books and in lecture-rooms; it prompted to inquiries and investigations that otherwise would never have been made; it stimulated the exercise of all my intellectual faculties, as the set tasks of professors never could. In many particulars the typical college of to-day is manifestly superior to that of fifty years ago; but in the societies of its students, for the cultivation of literature and skill in debate, its inferiority is too marked not to awaken solicitude as well as regret in the minds of all friends of liberal learning. Societies professedly literary, it is true, abound in the college of to-day, but they are societies in which social elements so predominate over every other that their influence on college life is to enhance its expensiveness, and to split its classes into rival cliques, rather than to quicken their intellects and to rouse them to high endeavor. Nothing yet devised has filled, or can fill, as a means of education, the place of the great debating societies, composed of representatives from every class in college, at once imposing and inspiring from their numbers, which were so marked a feature of the college of forty or fifty years ago. The Greek-letter societies were, about that time, introduced into college. At the end of my Junior year, when election of officers for the Brothers' Society was to take place for the following year, the bitter opponents of the Alpha Delta Phi fraternity, without conferring with me, made me their candidate for the presidency of the United Brothers. I was elected by a handsome majority. This result brought controversy into the Society. We fought like tigers, — an experience which materially helped to develop my debating powers.

Brown University, when I became a student of it, was not strong in its classical and its mathematical departments, which then comprised the larger part of its established curriculum. If a student became proficient in either of these studies, it was in spite of professorial influence. Latin and Greek could hardly, on deliberate purpose, have been more inefficiently taught. In my Sophomore year, however, came a great and radical change, comparatively a revolution, in the teaching of Latin. It came with the appointment of a new professor, young and enthusiastic, whose accurate methods and contagious spirit of enthusiasm put new life into all his classes, and were felt throughout the college. To this young professor, Horatio B. Hackett, afterwards known as one of the most eminent of American Biblical scholars, I owe a debt of gratitude such as is due to none other of my teachers of language. Rhetoric, when I entered Brown, was cultivated with marked success under the distinguished professor, William E. Goddard; but the class of which I was a member pursued that study under the tuition of the then youthful but no less skilful and since distinguished professor, William Gammell. By no means the least valuable part of my college education came from reading during my vacations, especially the long winter vacations, though it must be admitted that too much attention was given to the novels of Cooper and Scott.

The most profitable portion of my college life was its last year, under the instruction of President Wayland. He was then in the ripe fulness of his powers. His specialty as a teacher was moral science, though he also taught political economy. But the latter interested him only theoretically; the former, practically and intensely. His strong sense of justice and his profound love of truth made him a most impressive teacher of ethics, — the most impressive I have ever known; and his keen sense of humor, his quick wit, his appreciation of wit in others, always made his recitation-room a very lively place. He was no metaphysician; his moral science, even in its distinctively theoretic portions, was more practical than metaphysical, no part of it resting on any metaphysical system, avowed or implied. When I was his pupil, mental philosophy, even on its psychological side, had received from him only casual attention. His treatise on " Intellectual Philosophy " was written after I had passed from under him, and years after his views of moral science had become inflexibly fixed. Nor was he widely read in the science of ethics. Allusions in his lecture-room to authors whose views differed from his own were extremely rare. He had thought out his ethical principles for himself, and his conclusions were deep and strong, and rooted in the very depths of his being. Above all men whom I ever knew, he was himself the embodiment of what he taught. Clear and analytic in his own thinking, he insisted on analyzed and logical thought in his pupils. Possessed of a stature and a muscular development and a physiognomy that would have made him an admirable model for a Jupiter Tonans, and animated by a spirit that lifted him above everything selfish and mean, he succeeded beyond every other college president of his time, I suspect, in impressing himself and his sentiments on all who came under his instruction.

The class of which I was a member had the good fortune to be under Dr. Wayland in a year specially favorable for the best results of his teaching. It was the year in which he was writing and sending to the press his once famous little book on "The Limitations of Human Responsibility." His "Moral Science" had pleased neither the slaveholders nor the abolitionists. It had offended the former by going too far in its condemnation of slavery, the latter by not going far enough. He was between two raging fires. To defend himself, chiefly against the abolitionists, he wrote his "Limitations." Most of the positions taken, and of the principles defended, came up for questioning and discussion by our class. The teacher was full of his subject, encouraging and entering into the discussions with the liveliest zest. As our class contained an unusual number of bright intellects, the mutual stimulus of the class was no unimportant factor in our education.

I left college with perhaps an average knowledge of

Latin, Greek, and mathematics; of modern languages, history, and mental science I had learned nothing; of chemistry, physiology, and geology I had acquired a smattering; of "Butler's Analogy" and of ethics I had obtained a fair degree of knowledge. I had drifted aimlessly into college and drifted aimlessly through it, waking up only during the last year to see what I might and ought to have done.

About the middle of my college course the church at Pawtucket, of which I was a member, assuming that I was preparing for the ministry, invited me to speak before them for a license to preach. Without much reflection I consented to do so. An unused license was given me. In my Senior year a quiet but effective revival of religion occurred in college, which served to bring me to very serious reflection and to an earnest inquiry as to what I should do after graduation. No definite conclusion, however, was reached. As I was about to graduate, there came to me unexpectedly a proposition to accept an agency from the American Tract Society of New York City, then under the direction of the two distinguished secretaries, Rev. Drs. Hallock and Cook. In an interview with Dr. Cook, it was agreed that I should become agent of the Society to represent its work among the churches of Hartford County, Connecticut. My duties were to address the churches in all the towns of the county outside the city, giving an account of the work of the Society, and securing volunteer colporteurs in these churches to circulate and sell the works of the Society. I was to make one address each Sunday, keep an account of the books sold by the colporteurs, and return the proceeds to the Society in New York. The duties of this agency proved to be of great and unexpected value to me. They gave me a much needed self-confidence, relieved me from

a distressing timidity, besides widening my acquaintance
with men and business methods. I made many valuable
acquaintances among these churches and their pastors, such
as Dr. Porter, of Farmington, father of the late President
Porter of Yale, and many others. I had but one address,
which I learned by heart, and delivered before every congregation. I continued in this service until the beginning
of 1839, something more than six months, when I resigned
against the remonstrances of the secretaries. I felt that it
was time for me to decide as to my future course in life.
The Society, to my surprise, made me an honorary life-
member. There were a great many amusing scenes. I
remember one old Congregational minister who asked,
" Where have you studied theology ? " Well, of course
I blushed up to my eyes and said, " I have n't studied
theology." Many similar and embarrassing interviews
occurred during my continuance in that agency.

On resigning this service the question then occurred to
me, What shall I do next? I thought for a moment of
going to Newton Theological Institution, but speedily
abandoned the plan as impracticable at that season of the
year. Returning to Brown University, I secured and furnished one of the rooms, and became for six months a resident graduate. I began zealously the study of German with
my classmate, Bradley, then a tutor in the University, under
the tuition of Professor Hackett, then in the chair of Latin
at Brown. I have an indefinite recollection of having also
done something with Hebrew, but under whose instruction
I cannot recall. But my stay at Brown was of little profit.
There was no provision for graduate instruction. In the
following summer I was induced to write and deliver an
address on temperance in Seekonk, Massachusetts, which
was received with such favor as to give me considerable

encouragement. To my surprise the old Congregational church of Attleboro, where my ancestors for generations had worshipped, invited me to preach for them. I occupied their pulpit two Sundays. At this time, and for long afterward, the excitement of public speaking made me ill. That service seemed to solve the problem whether I was to be a minister of the gospel. At the end of summer the question arose whether I should study theology, and, if so, where. Dr. Hackett had resigned the professorship of Latin at Brown University, and accepted the chair of Biblical Literature at Newton Theological Institution. I decided to go to Newton, that I might be under his instruction.

At Newton I found myself member of a class of eighteen. Two or three only of these had been my classmates in college, all of whom dropped off before the end of our course. Our number was reduced to twelve before the completion of the course. With two of these my relations were very intimate. One of them was a South Carolinian, who had received a military training, and afterwards became a very successful theological teacher in one of the South Carolinian institutions,—James S. Mims. He was a noble fellow. And the other was Jacob R. Scott, a graduate of Brown of two years' earlier date than myself. He was a man of the finest qualities of nature, possessed of an exquisite literary taste, not inferior as an epistolary writer to Cowper himself. In personal appearance he was a reproduction of Henry Kirke White. Scott was the most intimate personal friend that I had in all my student life. Professor Hackett's instructions in my first year at Newton were in the highest degree stimulating. Under his tuition I did better work than I had done in any previous year of my life. He was, on the whole, the most stimulating teacher under whom I ever studied. When he thought his classes negligent in their work, he would drop his books upon the desk, and with flashing eye and both hands gesticulating, would so set forth and expatiate upon the value of Hebrew learning or a knowledge of the New Testament as to rouse some of us into a pitch of enthusiasm which would send us to our rooms with a purpose of doing the best we were capable of. I was more indebted to him than he became aware of till long years after, and especially when we became colleagues, in the latter part of his life, at Rochester Theological Seminary. At one period when Professor Hackett was despondent over his work, Dr. J. W. Parker of Cambridgeport took in hand to encourage him by telling him that Robinson, among others, had said he was more indebted to him as a teacher than to any man living. He querulously exclaimed, "Why did he never tell me that?" When Dr. Parker reported this to me, I replied, "Because he never permitted me to come within arm's length of him." This also was reported to him. Dr. Hackett took it good-naturedly, and I really think it made him more communicative with his students. In the intensity of spirit with which he himself worked, he thought very little of trying to stimulate his students by coming into personal relations to them.

In my second year at Newton I came under the instruction of Rev. Dr. Barnas Sears. He was then overflowing with German learning. He taught us Systematic Theology. His method of teaching was peculiarly his own. With a total absence of dogmatism he propounded and discussed theological questions with indefinitely numerous references to authors, especially the German, leaving each student to catch in his notes what he could. He rarely or never gave us definite and exact statements of his own theological opinions. The result was that we often left his lecture-room unsettled, afloat as to what we should definitely believe.

I concluded my course under him with no definable system of theological belief. There was not a single doctrine of which I could have given a satisfactory account.[1] But his teaching had roused in me a spirit of inquiry which was insatiable. The kindness of Professor Ripley was unparalleled. It was said of him, Nature had made him so kindly that there was nothing for grace to do. To the other professors of the Institution I was gratefully indebted for the special service they rendered. The library provisions at Newton when I was a student there were of the meagerest, and what the library contained was accessible to students only at intervals, — a complete contrast with the present provisions.

In the spring of the year that my course at Newton was to close I found myself in an uncertain state of health. The way it came about was that I sat at the head of the table and poured coffee for my two friends, Mims and Scott, breakfasting myself on coffee and a Graham cracker. I soon began to collapse. While I was thinking of a sea-voyage for the sake of my health, a proposition was made by a friend in the next class below me, who had been a teacher in Virginia, that, instead of a sea-voyage, I should accept an invitation to supply a pulpit during the spring vacation at Norfolk, Virginia. He insisted that a trip down the Chesapeake Bay and through Hampton Roads would give me all the benefit of sea-air that I needed. This invitation I accepted, spending the most of April and May in Norfolk. This preaching in Norfolk had no little influence on my subsequent life. My experience there was novel and of highest interest. It was my first acquaintance with slavery and

---

[1] My experience under the teaching of Dr. Sears would explain some of the peculiarities of my own method of teaching. I was determined that students should not leave my lecture-room without definite conclusions and convictions, and some sufficient reasons for holding them. — E. G. R.

Southern life. On leaving to return to my studies at Newton, I was surprised by a request of the church that I should accept a call to its pastorate. The request was not only a surprise, but gave me great anxiety. Four of the chief men in the church were extensive liquor-dealers. With the ideas of temperance then prevailing in New England, it seemed impossible that I could accept the invitation. Norfolk in those days seemed so remote from home, so unlike in climate and mode of life, so unlike everything with which I was familiar, as to make me reluctant to think of becoming a resident there. I returned to Newton by way of the historical James River, and it was a matter of intense interest to me, sailing up that river. The ruins at Jamestown, the famous old plantation residences, all excited the interest of a New Englander. I for the first time saw the city of Richmond; went to Washington, and had the good fortune to hear Henry Clay make his farewell speech when he resigned his seat in the Senate in 1842. That speech, though brief, made a lasting impression on my mind. The Senate itself was a most interesting study for a young man; but Clay at that moment was the chief figure in it. His intonation and clean-cut articulation at once arrested my attention, and gave useful hints for public speaking. On returning to Newton, my friend Scott and myself were accustomed to go into the woods, standing within ear-shot of each other, and practising elocution amid the rustling of the leaves. The hint from Clay's speech served as a guide in my part of the practice. The practice itself was of more value to me in public speaking than any amount of training I could have received from professional elocutionists.

The last term of my stay at Newton closed in August, 1842. As the time for leaving the Seminary drew near, there came the perplexing question, Should I accept the call from Norfolk? Meanwhile I had been invited to preach to the First Church in Springfield, Massachusetts. They requested me to visit them again; they wished me to become their pastor. I had agreed to come at a definite date to spend another Sunday with them. I decidedly preferred Springfield to Norfolk. On the day I was to go to Springfield several of my fellow-students gathered in my room; conversation abounded; I was delayed to the last moment in starting for the train, and came in sight of it just as it was moving out of the station. There was no way of reaching Springfield in time for morning service, and no telegraph to give explanation. Returning to the Seminary, I was shut up to fulfil a promise of reply to the call from Norfolk. Consulting with Dr. Sears, he advised me to accept the Norfolk call. The Norfolk call was accepted with many misgivings. Just the accident of those fellows chaffing changed the whole current of my life. If I had n't gone to Norfolk, I should n't have gone to Covington; if I had n't gone to Covington, I should n't have gone to Rochester. Perhaps I was a little superstitious about it, but I regarded my disappointment in visiting Springfield as an indication of Divine Providence that I should go to Virginia.

NOTE.

REMINISCENCES BY FELLOW-STUDENTS. *(See p. 13.)*

What manner of man Dr. Robinson was held to be in college days may be learned from fellow-students. His classmate, the Rt. Rev. Alexander Burgess, S. T. D., LL.D., Bishop of Quincy, writes : —

"I was the youngest of my college class, but eighteen at graduation. My home was in Providence. I studied at home, and went to the college buildings very seldom, except for prayers and recitation. So I had less opportunity than others of the class to associate with Robinson evenings and at students' meetings. . . .

"Robinson and I became close friends by his visits at my father's house and my driving him out to his home on Saturdays, about eight miles distant. He certainly was indifferently prepared on entrance. He was slow in his perception or thought, apparently. I may mention, as a proof of this, he sat in the class three above me. Between us were two of the least exact scholars. When a question was missed by one just above him, he seldom could collect himself sufficiently to answer immediately, and it became a saying, ' If Jenks fails, Burgess will be the first to stop the " Unprepared," ' that is the answer by him and the next two. With time to gather himself up, he commonly recited well, yet ended with a rank, if I recollect right, next to the middle. He did not show plainly the signs of the wonderful abilities which were subsequently developed. I was too young and immature to observe what was not plainly manifest in him. It should be noted that Dr. Wayland, twenty years or less later, said that 'the scholarship of the class was higher than any for ten or twelve years.'

"Robinson did not excel during college days in that which he afterward termed 'ability to think on your legs.' But he was positive and earnest in the few words he did say in debate. . . . His 'lack of polish and grace ' we students marked without criticism. . . . He was ever good-tempered, fair and just and without jealousy.

"Now that fifty years and more have passed and the history of each member of our class of about thirty-three has been put on record, he who showed low rank in scholarship and personality at the start, is acknowledged in advance greatly of most, and perhaps really of all, at the near goal. . . . If love and deep admiration and class pride were alone required to refresh memory and to paint the past as it really was, my paper would be all you could ask."

Another classmate, the Rev. J. C. Stockbridge, D.D., said in a memorial address : —

"I am sure I do my classmate no injustice when I say that he was not . . . a brilliant class-room student. . . . There were lines of study outside of the regular college curriculum in which he interested himself. We all recognized him as being a skilful debater on themes of popular interest. . . . Another of our classmates, the now Hon. George Van Ness Lothrop . . . was a member of the same society, fond of debate, and, if I remember aright, generally pitted against Robinson, and both alike the subjects of good-natured college criticism as to which

was the better and more skilful intellectual athlete in the Society
Rooms. . . .

"At length the time for graduation came. The part assigned to
our friend was a philosophical dissertation, its subject being ' The
Value of Metaphysical Speculations.' It was not among the highest
of the parts assigned, but it needed not a prophet's ken to forecast
what, if life and health were vouchsafed by kind Providence, would
be the future career of the speaker. . . . The youthful aspirant for
the honors of the University stood on the spacious platform, in front
of the pulpit, with his finely developed physique, and in that impassioned manner, which seemed so natural to him when he was thoroughly aroused, repeated those thrilling lines from Campbell's
' Pleasures of Hope' in which the poet dwells on the dreary fruits of
an unhallowed scepticism : —

> ' Are these the pompous tidings ye proclaim,
> Lights of the world, and demigods of fame ? ' "

A third classmate, the late Professor J. W. P. Jenks, wrote :

"I came to my present position in college in '71, he to the presidency in '72, I think. Not long after he came, as we were having a
social chat and speaking of our college days, he said, ' My whole career in college is a myth, as I try to recall it. I was troubled throughout the course with dyspepsia, and I never saw one well day in the
four years.' I was much pleased to hear that statement from his own
lips, — not that he was an invalid, but that his physical condition ac-
counted for his cynical disposition and tendency . . . to severe criticism
of the efforts of others. I never received the impression that he thought
himself superior to others, but he gave us reason to think he enjoyed
making us feel bad by sharp retort. . . . According to my experience
with men, such a disposition is apt to be a characteristic of dyspeptics.

" . . . As to his scholarship, he ranked just above the middle of the
class, if I remember rightly, and as far as I can recall never impressed
any of his classmates as possessing unusual talent.

" But what I am now to relate will be of interest to you. He graduated from Newton about a month before my closing a four years'
course of teaching in Georgia. Calling soon after my return upon
Rev. J. W. Parker, D. D., at Cambridgeport, he remarked, ' Do you
know that your classmate Robinson has impressed us all as being the
most acute metaphysician that ever graduated from Newton, surpass-
ing all his college classmates in the development of his intellectual
powers?' I replied, ' You greatly surprise me, as one of his classmates,

for I should have named half a dozen or more of the class that gave greater promise than he.' "

A contemporary in college recollects Mr. Robinson as "a young man of promising talents, but of much independence, strong, self-reliant, and not disposed to warm attachments with other students. I remember hearing the phrase 'the iron man' applied to him by some of the students. Whether they were his friends or not I cannot say."

This impression is interesting as coming from a warm-hearted Southerner who wishes to remain anonymous, and who belonged to a class enough lower to represent the current opinion of the college. As to the general bearing of Mr. Robinson in these days, one of the writers above quoted says that the words "awkward and shy" if used without emphasis would be fairly descriptive. Another describes him as in college "an awkward and immature country lad." But the powerful mind and energetic personality of the student broke away from these limitations so soon at latest as a definite purpose in life had been formed and professional study begun. Perhaps he did not mature early; but nothing more characteristic or more honorable could be said of any one than what President Weston says of Dr. Robinson, whom he knew from college days onward : —

"I met Dr. Robinson at intervals all his life, and always found that he had been growing. In later years he mellowed. It is probably an illustration of his growth that the awkwardness and shyness which his classmates speak of, had disappeared by the time he was a Junior, and I entered college. I remember those men distinctly; and while Robinson lacked the grace and suavity of some, he always seemed to me intellectually the peer of any."

Another acquaintance of a somewhat later period in his student-life declares that while he was never awkward, he was always shy. — ED.

CHAPTER II.

PASTORATES AND THE COVINGTON PROFESSORSHIP.

1842-1853.

IN the early autumn, packing up my belongings, I started to become pastor of the Cumberland Street Baptist Church at Norfolk. I was ordained in November, 1842, Dr. Jeter of Richmond preaching the ordination sermon. Everything in my new position bore the stamp of novelty. One of my first and somewhat embarrassing experiences there was at a funeral. I found myself, when starting for the grave, decorated with a long, flowing white sash, my hat bound around with a white band streaming far behind me, and with white gloves. I was placed in an open carriage beside the undertaker. It seemed to me that every eye was turned on me as a ridiculous spectacle. The undertaker assured me that every minister was so arrayed. My second odd experience was the baptism of a very low-born and low-bred white woman who had for a year or more been a standing candidate for baptism. The church had held her case in abeyance until it had a pastor. Baptism could be administered only at high tide. The tide would be high enough at six o'clock in the morning. With deacons and a few friends we started for the place of baptism. The poor woman was overjoyed at the fulfilment of her long deferred wishes. Emerging from the water at baptism, she bounded from my hands, splashing the water, shouting and screaming hallelujahs. Seizing and trying to calm her, I led her to the shore; but the one of my deacons who was to have received her, when he saw her coming, turned and fled.

Settling down to serious pastoral work, more than enough to fill my mind and hands at once presented itself.   I was disturbed at the selling of liquor by the leading deacon of the church and by three others of its prominent members. They assured me that I should have perfect liberty of speech on temperance or any other subject that I might wish to speak on, — a liberty which I was not slow to use.   I gave lectures to my own people on temperance.   After one of these lectures, an impetuous member of the church came to me and said, " Now, pastor, we understand you, and are ready for action.   We propose to exclude these liquor-dealers from the church."   My reply was, " My dear sir, you do not quite understand me.   I have faith in the power of truth and honest conviction much greater than I have in hasty church action.   Let us wait. These brethren are honest and faithful; we must wait till they see their way to abandon the traffic."   The peace and harmony of the church remained perfectly undisturbed.   In the church were several elderly widows who were true " mothers in Israel."   The coddling to which these dear old mothers subjected me in the first year of my ministry exposed me to perils of effeminacy from which I barely escaped.   The five to eight cups of Old Hyson tea of an evening gave a fillip to my nerves, from which they were long in recovering.   Take it all in all, the first year of my pastorate was as happy as it could well have been.·

In the spring of the first year of it I was invited to serve a year as chaplain at the University of Virginia, beginning in the following autumn.   It was then the custom to invite chaplains alternately from the four principal denominations of the State, — Episcopalians, Presbyterians, Baptists, and

Methodists. With my very brief experience in the ministry, it seemed risky to accept the position. On strong encouragement from others, I ventured to accept. It proved to me a very profitable year. With my slender resources I found very little time for attending to any department of study in the University, and was obliged to give most of my time to preparation for my work as chaplain. I was required to preach once on Sunday, and to lecture in the chapel each Wednesday evening. Fortunately for my after work I gave a weekly lecture on the Gospel of John, making the best use I could of such sources as were within my reach. The encouragement received from the professors gave me a self-confidence in which I was still sadly lacking. The University of Virginia was never manned by teachers more distinguished or able than some of those then in its faculty. Among these was the famous law-lecturer, Henry St. George Tucker, half-brother of John Randolph; also Professor George Tucker, the intimate friend and biographer of Jefferson; William B. Rogers, a very brilliant lecturer, afterwards president of the Boston School of Technology; Dr. William B. Cabell; Gessner Harrison, the distinguished professor of Latin, and father-in-law of Dr. John A. Broadus, with many others.

During my stay at the University occurred an event which has more materially than any other event affected my whole subsequent life. I was married to the lady whom I had known from her school-girl days, Miss Harriet Richards Parker, to whom I have been more indebted than to any one or all other persons whom I have known in life. At the close of the University year my wife and I made a trip to White Sulphur and other springs, to the Natural Bridge and to Weyer's Cave, thence by stage down the Shenandoah valley to Winchester, Harper's Ferry, and so on to New

England.   In the autumn we returned to Norfolk, and I resumed my pastoral duties, the church having been meanwhile under the care of a young student of theology, J. W. M. Williams, who has since distinguished himself in a life-long pastorate in the city of Baltimore.   I resumed pastoral work with redoubled interest.   Duties multiplied, and I began to be called on for outside work. In the month of August I was urgently requested to visit a church in one of the counties of the southeastern part of the State, on the borders of North Carolina.   They were kind enough to tell me while there that in no place perhaps this side of New Orleans malaria more prevailed than in their town.   I was obliged to take the train at midnight to return home.   Not long after, I had a serious attack of bilious fever.   It was the beginning of a malarial affection which has followed me all my life since.[1]

A call had come to me from a newly formed church in Old Cambridge, Massachusetts, to become their pastor.   The church at Norfolk made earnest remonstrances against my leaving there.   They offered to make my salary $1400, with a two months' vacation in the summer, which was a very generous offer for that time, and a much better one than came from the Cambridge church.   But the climate was evidently undermining my constitution; and, endeared as the church had become to me, and attractive as life in

[1] The author meant to give some account of the last meeting of the Baptist Triennial Convention before the Southern Baptists withdrew.   It was held in Philadelphia in 1844, and was attended by the youthful pastor from Norfolk.   The most notable scene was in a meeting of the Home Mission Society.   " I remember," writes Mrs. Robinson, " his graphic descriptions of the confusion and turmoil of the meeting, and of the futile efforts, both painful and ludicrous, of the poor, excited old gentleman who presided . . . to preserve order."   It was then that " Brother Jeter had the floor," and he held it for thirty minutes before he got a chance to make himself heard. See chapter xlvi. in Jeter's " Recollections of a Long Life." — ED.

Virginia in many respects was, to a New England man slavery was not one of its attractive features.

In the early autumn I became the pastor, the first pastor it had had, of the Baptist church at Cambridge. When I went to them, they were worshipping in a hall. Their house of worship was then in process of building on a site since bought by Harvard University, where now stands its Gymnasium. I seemed to have found an ideal place for a life-work. The surroundings and proximity of Harvard College and the library gave it special attraction. One Sunday there came into the service two men who bore unmistakable marks of being clergymen, one of whom was the Rev. Dr. Putnam, a Unitarian from Salem. They had evidently come to see what these Baptists were venturing to do under the eaves of Harvard College. Dr. Putnam, in a kindly, perhaps half-patronizing way, said to one of the deacons something complimentary concerning their pastor's sermon. Poor man! he took alarm, suspecting that the sermon which a Unitarian clergyman could approve must have some sad defects. This, added to the fact that I had previously been the pastor of a church many or most of whose members were slaveholders, gave him much uneasiness; but the great body of the church were as loyal and faithful parishioners as any young minister was ever blessed with.

I was happy in my pastorate; but as the summer was approaching, occurred an event that filled me with dismay, coming like a thunderbolt from a clear sky, — my wife was attacked with a violent hemorrhage of the lungs, from which she recovered slowly, having been brought very near to death's door. Our doctor said she must, as soon as possible, get away from the sea-coast, where the air was too stimulating for her lungs. My hopes of a long pastorate were suddenly dashed. Just then, one day our doorbell rang, when in walked Rev. Dr. Robert E. Pattison, once president of Waterville College, Maine, but then at the head of the theological institution which had been founded by Baptists of the Northwest at Covington, Kentucky, on the Ohio River, opposite to Cincinnati. He said he had just come from Providence, where he had been in consultation with Dr. Wayland, with the demand that I should go with him to Covington as professor of Hebrew. I told him of the condition of my wife's health, and that I could give him no answer without consultation with medical advisers. Mrs. Robinson went with me to the office of Dr. Oliver Wendell Holmes, then regarded as a specialist in pulmonary diseases, and also coming into notice as a poet, especially for Commencement occasions. I remember his little dingy office off Tremont Street. He then gave small promise to a casual observer of becoming the famous " Autocrat of the Breakfast-Table," or one of the foremost poets of America. He detected no disease of the lungs, but agreed with Dr. Wyman that we ought not to live near the sea. In answer to the inquiry about Covington, he replied that it was in the same latitude with Washington, and would do very well as a place of residence for my wife. It was decided that I should accept the professorship at Covington.

Our household goods were packed and shipped, by way of New Orleans and the Mississippi and Ohio rivers, to Cincinnati. My good and life-long friend, Henry R. Glover of Cambridge, insisted upon paying the expense of packing and freight. After spending nearly a month at my wife's home with Deacon Caleb Parker, secretary of the Board of Trustees of Newton Theological Institution from 1837 to 1854, we started for Covington on the first of October, — a journey of no slight difficulty in Mrs. Robinson's state of health. We travelled by boat and rail, by way of New York and Philadelphia, to Harrisburg. There we took a canal-boat, following the Juniata to the base of the Alleghanies. In a recent journey on the well-equipped vestibule train of the Pennsylvania Railroad, my wife and I traced the remains of the old canal, reviving the vivid memories of nearly half a century ago. One accustomed only to the spacious and elegant accommodations of the modern steamboat can have little conception of the stuffiness and confinement of canal passenger-boats. But it was leisurely journeying, amid magnificent scenery with its autumnal coloring, and afforded abundant opportunity for exercise along the tow-path. On reaching the terminus of the canal, the boat, which consisted of two sections, was drawn by a stationary engine up an inclined plane, and by the same process was let down the western slope into another canal, which took us to Pittsburg. We reached Pittsburg in the evening, a thousand open mouths of flame seeming to welcome us to the dingy city, — a weird picture, that still lingers in my memory. On the following morning I made diligent inquiries for a steamboat to take us down the Ohio to Cincinnati. Six days had already passed since we left Boston. The Ohio River was at so low a stage of water as to seem almost unnavigable. A solitary stern-wheeled steamer was advertised to leave that day. We engaged passage. We were assured that the boat, drawing only twenty-four inches of water, could easily cross the sand-bars. There was, for the little boat, a large crowd of passengers, among whom were several Southwestern planters, eager to reach their homes. On the afternoon of October seventh we started down the river. While yet in sight of the city, we came to a well-loaded keel-boat, which was fast aground. Our captain, with what seemed to me an astonishing degree of kindness, threw them a hawser to haul them off. It required but a few hours to discover that this keel-boat, which had been sent down the river ahead of us, was a part of our boat's belongings, to be towed to Cincinnati. For several ensuing days a large part of our time was consumed in getting aground and pulling off. Repeatedly our captain or first mate would leap from the bow with a hawser, wade ashore, and hitch to a tree or post, and then, by aid of windlass or engine, strive to haul off. Some six or seven days were thus spent in reaching Wheeling. We there met a steamer coming up the river. Our hot-headed Southerners, who for days had been on the verge of an outbreak, attempted to charter the upward-bound boat to take us to Cincinnati. After long and angry discussion, it was finally decided that we should all remain where we were. Copious rains seemed to promise that we could go on without further delay. We reached Cincinnati on the sixteenth of October, sixteen days from the city of Boston. Words fail to describe the relief and satisfaction with which at last we found ourselves in the hospitable mansion of Dr. Pattison at Covington. This mansion was the home of the owner of the large plantation which the Institution had bought, the rising value of which constituted the Institution's chief endowment. Near by stood the main building of the Seminary, containing recitation-rooms and dormitories.

The Faculty with whom I was associated consisted of Dr. Pattison and Professor Asa Drury. The classes I was to instruct had been waiting for my coming, and my work was to begin without the loss of a day. With fear and trembling I went to my lecture-room. I was thirty-two years of age, and with as meagre an outfit for the work I had undertaken as can well be imagined. My regularly appointed work was to teach Hebrew, though I spent all the spare time I could command in brushing up my Greek. I remember no period of my life in which I worked harder or with more satisfaction. In Hebrew I remember to have made written translations of earlier chapters of Isaiah and of the whole of Micah.

On reaching Covington I found that Dr. Pattison and various of his friends from Cincinnati had organized what was called the Walnut Street Baptist Church. It worshipped in the main hall of the University of Cincinnati. It was arranged that Dr. Pattison and I should preach for this church alternately,— he in the morning of one Sunday, and I in the afternoon; on the following Sunday I in the morning, and he in the afternoon. With the duties of my professorship I had, of course, no time for sermon-making, and simply fell back on what I had accumulated in my four years as pastor.

My second year at Covington, the third in the history of the Institution, opened with bright prospects and an increased number of students. But dark clouds were gathering about the horizon. The one disturbing and threatening element was slavery. The Kentuckians were dissatisfied with some of Dr. Pattison's utterances on this question, and during the year appealed to their legislature to amend the charter of the Institution by adding ten Kentuckians to the number of its Trustees. At the first meeting of this new board Dr. Pattison was summarily dismissed from office. A committee of six, with Rev. Dr. Dillard as chairman, Dr. Campbell, a Scotchman, president of Georgetown College, and four others, was appointed to wait upon other members of the Faculty. This committee came to my house with the question whether I recognized the authority of the new board. I replied that this was not one of the questions belonging to my chair as professor of Hebrew; that I had come from New England with definitely prescribed duties, among which, I was sure, was not an answer to that kind of question. A variety of similar questions was gravely propounded by the chairman, to which similarly evasive answers were given. As they grew impatient, I said: "There is a question, gentlemen, to which I can give a definite answer: it is whether I am willing to work in connection with, or under the direction of, men who are capable of what you have done. This, most definitely, in the negative. I have known something of violent abolitionists in the North, and by the grace of God have succeeded in keeping them at arm's length. All you have to do is to change places with that kind of men to change characters with them. I have no disposition to work with either class." I never saw six men jump more suddenly or more simultaneously to their feet. I was indignant, and they were not less so. That ended my connection with what was known as the Western Theological Institution of Covington, Kentucky. It was virtually the breaking up of the Institution; for, though the Kentuckians took possession of it with the purpose of carrying forward its work, very little, if anything, was accomplished.[1] What became of the property, which was regarded as a handsome endowment, I never knew. The buildings, I was informed, passed into the hands of the Roman Catholics.

Of the students who were at the Institution while I was there, several have achieved honorable distinction. Among these were Rev. Rufus C. Burleson, D. D., LL. D., for the past forty-two years president of Baylor University, Texas; Rev. William Ashmore, D. D., our well-known missionary to China; the Rev. John R. Downer, formerly professor in Denison University; and others successful as pastors.

While I was at Covington I heard, for the first time, the

---

[1] The Institute opened in September, 1845, with Dr. Pattison as president. He and Professor Robinson withdrew in June, 1848. Dr. S. W. Lynd was then made president by the new Board of Trustees. See Appendix II.—ED.

celebrated Dr. Lyman Beecher, and recognized the origin of certain peculiarities discernible in those days among the younger Congregational ministers of New England. One of them was a peculiar method of reading a hymn, striking the middle of the line with a peculiar ictus and pause. The glory of his earlier preaching had begun very perceptibly to fail.

My association with Dr. Pattison, whose ministrations I had attended at the First Church in Providence while a student in Brown University, was of the pleasantest. He was genial, warm-hearted, frank, a most agreeable colleague both as professor and as pastor. He never preached more effectively, with more unction and satisfaction, than during the two years that we served the Walnut Street Church. His mind, however, had a singular capacity for forgetfulness. As an amusing instance of this, he had a pet sermon which he preached on a given Sunday, and repeated two weeks afterward, wholly forgetting that he had previously delivered it. I would sometimes refer to a book which I knew that he had read, when he would reply that he knew nothing whatever about it. One book, however, probably more influenced him and his thinking than any other: this was Jonathan Edwards on the Christian Affections. He went from Covington to the professorship of Theology at Newton.

On the breaking up of the Institution at Covington the question came, What should I do next? The little Walnut Street Church, to which Dr. Pattison and I had ministered two years gratuitously, gave little or no promise of ultimate success. It lacked homogeneity, having been made up in a considerable degree of malcontents from other churches. In the way of its success stood another formidable obstacle: Dr. E. L. Magoon, then pastor of the Ninth Street Baptist

Church of Cincinnati, had, with his friends, initiated a movement for a new church to be constituted of members from the Ninth Street Church.   Just then I had an invitation to become pastor of the First Baptist Church in Rochester, New York.   I was greatly inclined to go, and had about made up my mind to do so, when a committee from the Ninth Street Church waited upon me, insisting that I should remain in Cincinnati.   The project of a new church for Dr. Magoon hung fire.   At that juncture he accepted an invitation to become pastor of the Oliver Street Church in New York for six months, during which his friends in Cincinnati were to complete their organization of a new church for him. The proposition for me was to become pastor of the Ninth Street Church.   The position was anything but an inviting one.   While the Walnut Street Church was to disband, the most of them going to Ninth Street, I was invited to become pastor of a church no small portion of which were simply waiting for Dr. Magoon to return from New York.   It required no little persuasion to induce me to accept the call.

An attempt on my part to follow Dr. Magoon seemed to promise nothing but disappointment and disaster.   His brilliancy as a preacher, his great popularity as a man, had given him a thronging congregation.   He was then at the height of his popularity.   I had known him from the day that I went as a youth to the New Hampton Academy, which he was just then leaving for Waterville College. Dr. Magoon was a man of remarkable natural endowment, possessed of poetic fancy, intense energy, a strong intellect, and, under proper discipline, might and ought to have been one of the most distinguished men of his day.   But from the outset of his education he had persisted in devoting his attention to such studies only as best pleased his fancy. He did this throughout his college course, as also at the

Newton Theological Institution. A voracious and indiscriminate reader, compiling tomes of extracts from all possible sources, he accumulated an almost measureless mass of chaotic materials, from which he was accustomed to draw freely in preparing his sermons. But to severe mental discipline, whether in mathematical, philosophical, or rhetorical studies, he seemed to owe as little as was possible for a man who could be said to have a liberal education. His power over an audience of untrained minds was at times simply prodigious. His success as a preacher when in Virginia was one of the marvels of the day. While abroad, in the interval between his life in Virginia and his coming to Cincinnati, he had made himself familiar with the French language, and had become a devout admirer of Lacordaire, the great French preacher at Notre Dame, in Paris. He had collected a large library of both French and English works. His preaching bore evident marks of his wide and varied reading; but I have scarcely known an educated man whose productions gave more striking evidence of an undiscriminating mind, either in thought or expression. In his public ministry he would sometimes soar to heights of almost unsurpassed eloquence; but the sentences following might be so marred by absurdities as well as grotesqueness of thought and bad taste in expression, as to make his audience blush and wish to hide their faces.[1] But with all these

---

[1] As an instance, I once heard him conclude one of his sermons on Republican Christianity, afterwards published, with a paragraph genuinely eloquent. It was in 1848, during the revolutions in Europe. He described the atmosphere of Europe as filled with the sound of falling thrones and of clanking chains stricken from the limbs of the enslaved. The discourse was followed by an abrupt transition to a prayer in which the shocking motto of French revolutionists, "A funeral pyre of the last throne, on which shall be burnt the last priest," was turned into a solemn petition to God, — the leader of the choir at the end striking up on his violin with one of the liveliest of dancing tunes. It was such a shock to my nerves that I got my head down in the pew and gave vent to hysterical laughter. — E. G. R.

defects Dr. Magoon was a wonderful master in the pulpit, besides being a man of the largest heart, genial in disposition and lovable to a degree. To attempt following such a man as pastor seemed rashness itself; and yet there appeared to be no alternative but to accept.

Thus, in the autumn of 1848 I became pastor of the Ninth Street Baptist Church. In the following spring we took a house on Mt. Auburn, then one of the rural suburbs of Cincinnati. It was embowered with trees in full blossom. It seemed an earthly paradise. We had bought a pet horse from Deacon Bevan, and a new rockaway. Our new home and equipments were all that could be desired. We were fortunate in being out of the city. In early summer the cholera broke out in Cincinnati with an alarming death-rate. By midsummer from a hundred and fifty to a hundred and sixty were dying daily. In driving down to the city in the morning the constantly multiplying crapes upon the door-bells, the burning barrels of tar, and the deserted streets filled one with a sense of desolation and gloom. But very few of my own flock fell victims. Though myself every day in the city and among the sick, I escaped with only a slight attack one Monday morning. A speedy application to a city physician by my neighbor and dear friend, Deacon Bevan, brought speedy relief, and I was well again.

The summer wore on, but at the end of the six months no sign appeared of the formation of the new church. With a winter's work before me we returned to a house in the city. I bent myself to the winter's work to the best of my ability. The spring came, and there had ceased to be any further talk about the return of Dr. Magoon to Cincinnati. The church was prosperous, but the situation was unsatisfactory. The church was large enough for its members to be in each other's way; but it was in vain that anything was said about colonization. In my congregation were enough men of education to stimulate any man to his best work. Among these, besides several other city lawyers, was Alphonso Taft, afterwards Attorney-General under the administration of President Grant, and later still minister to St. Petersburg. Besides several other ministers of the gospel was John Stevens, who had graduated with distinguished scholarship at Middlebury, Vermont, and had long been, as he was also at that time, one of the most conspicuous leaders among the. Baptists of Ohio, — a man of large and strong intellect, who, under other surroundings, might have attained to great distinction. He used to sit in the congregation with his eyes shut, apparently indifferent to all that was being said, and reminding me, as I used to tell him, of an old stone mill with its windows closed, but which kept on grinding its own grist in the dark. His answer was, " Pastor, I always hear what you say." The number of young men in the congregation who have since made their mark was proportionately large. At the end of the second year of my pastorate I made a list of fifteen young men with their wives, and fifteen unmarried women, mostly of middle age, to whom I submitted the proposition to join with me in forming a new church. Too well satisfied with things as they were, and timid from the failure of previous attempts, they hesitated to join in the undertaking.

During the third winter of the pastorate I set to work earnestly in the preparation and delivery of a series of discourses on Modern Scepticism. These discourses were received with unexpected favor, attracting large and intelligent congregations, including not a few avowed unbelievers. A request with many names called for a publication of the lectures, — a request to which, the lectures not having been written, I could not respond. The following summer gave me a much needed rest and recreation in New England.

The fourth winter of the pastorate opened, and my household was darkened by an alarming illness of my wife.   In the midst of this, my old friend, Martin B. Anderson, then editor of the " New York Recorder," made his appearance with an invitation to the professorship of Biblical Theology in Rochester University, then recently made vacant by the death of Dr. J. S. Maginnis.   The invitation was attractive from the outset; but there arose at once the question, What would be the influence of the climate of Rochester on the health of my wife?   Our family physician expressed a decided opinion that it would be beneficial.   This, of course, disposed me to accept the invitation; but the young friends to whom I had the year before proposed the formation of a new church, then came with alacrity to begin the undertaking at once.   I had, however, already become convinced that a pastorate was not the office in which I could do the best work of which I was capable.   My distaste for pastoral duties was unconquerable, while my experience at Covington had given me a preference for a professorship. I accepted the invitation with the condition that its duties should be begun in the following spring.   The breaking up of associations and friendships at Cincinnati was one of the painful experiences of life.

My life at Cincinnati and in Ohio had brought me many pleasurable experiences.   I was not wanting in sympathy with the efforts of the Baptists of Cincinnati and Ohio to re-establish, if possible, a theological institution on the Ohio side of the river.   A company had been formed and had purchased a farm of one hundred and fifty or sixty acres just outside the city limits, with the expectation of its rapid rise in value and of throwing it upon the market, thereby realizing a very handsome profit. Ten acres of the land, which had been designated as Fairmount, had been set apart for the new institution, and on this had been erected a handsome building for the so-called Fairmount Theological Institution. I was asked to become one of its professors, but could not persuade myself to accept the offer. The company purchasing the land had divided it into ten shares. Two of the company, over-anxious for profits, had assumed to carry two shares each. I became the purchaser of a half-share. Parts of the land, platted into house-lots, were distributed to the shareholders as successive payments were made on the mortgage, other lots being offered at auction to the public. The sales did not realize expectations. It speedily became evident that the members of the company who had assumed two shares each could not carry their loads. Payments on the mortgage were defaulted; foreclosure seemed inevitable. Desperately, but in vain, I sought to have my half-share released by paying my share of the original stock; but both mortgagors and mortgagees objected. The whole property, it was said, must be held responsible for the mortgage. The few thousands I had paid in seemed hopelessly sunk, to my own lasting embarrassment. The house and lot provided for the Fairmount Theological Institution were purchased by Germans and turned into a beer-garden and shooting-gallery. The closing up of the affairs of the company has been a complicated and almost life-long series of transactions.

NOTE.

METHOD OF PREPARING SERMONS.

If Dr. Robinson had found opportunity to look over his autobiography, he would have added to it at various points; and it was hoped that he would tell the curious story of how he first came to preach extempore. But he never found the opportunity. A letter from Mrs. Robinson makes good the deficiency at this point in a way that throws more light upon the habits of the Doctor's mind than his reticence would have allowed him to give. At the time referred to he was a student in Newton.

"I think Mr. Robinson was to go some little distance to preach, and looking for the sermon he was intending to take with him, found his whole collection — not a very large one, I fancy — gone. On inquiry he found that the other students had met with similar losses. The sermons had obviously been stolen, but no one ever knew who the culprit was. It is true that his success in the pulpit at that particular time encouraged other attempts to preach with only brief notes, and that finally even these were not taken into the pulpit, as his confidence in himself grew. But his habit of preaching without notes became fixed, not so much from confidence in himself, for he almost always apprehended failure, as from an inveterate dislike, which never left him, of putting into final shape what he was preparing. He liked the active mental exercise, the ' thinking out,' but he disliked the slow labor of setting his thoughts down; and he would postpone, on the plea that they still needed the inward work until it was too late to write and give them outward shape. Finally he resigned himself to the habit formed, and only wrote down heads for future use, writing these as often after speaking as before."

In another letter Mrs. Robinson shows with what care her husband prepared for the pulpit : —

" In his earliest days Mr. Robinson, besides the heads of a sermon, would write out the introduction, or perhaps the first head or a part of it, and have the manuscript before him in the pulpit; but he found the transition from the written page to unsupported direct address difficult and embarrassing, and he soon gave up writing anything except the skeleton, for pulpit use. His mind became ' hidebound,' to use his own frequent expression, when he began a sermon depending on his manuscript. But though he did n't *write* out, he *spoke* out his sermons while preparing them; not, of course, declaiming, but talking them over, thought by thought, as these came to him, and then as they arranged themselves or grew clear in the process of thinking. Almost invariably he went over the whole sermon, the heads and the principal points under them, before leaving the house for the church, where on entering he would often say in real anxiety of mind,

' I am not half prepared.' Of course this was not true of the more recent years, when, as a father with his children, he was intent only on instructing his congregation."

Incidents related by Mr. E. R. Andrews, the publisher of Dr. Robinson's "Theology," illustrate his readiness to meet an emergency when there was no time for special preparation. The first occurred at an early period in his Rochester life.

"The pastor of the First Baptist Church was to be absent for a Sunday, and had engaged Professor Raymond to supply the pulpit. The 'genial Professor' not only forgot the engagement, but also forgot to attend the morning service. A Quaker meeting was held until eleven o'clock, when, as the preacher had not arrived, Deacon Orren Sage went to Dr. Robinson, who was sitting in his pew, and asked him to occupy the pulpit. He cheerfully complied, and preached a sermon which was listened to with delight by the congregation.

"Another instance of a somewhat similar character occurred in 1865. In that year he preached the Thanksgiving sermon, it being the first after the close of the Civil War, to the united congregations of all the Baptist churches in the city, in the First Baptist Church. It was a broad, statesmanlike address, and was listened to with feelings of deepest interest and admiration, from its opening to its close. He was then asked to furnish a copy for publication. His reply was, 'Why, there is not a syllable of it written, and I have not time to write it out. I went home last night and sat down to select the hymns for the service, and went to sleep while doing it. The thoughts are not altogether new, but the only time that I had to arrange the address was while I was shaving myself this morning to come to church.'"

Another incident related by Mr. Andrews exhibits the Doctor's contempt for laziness and foppery. To help a beneficiary he gave him the job of mailing the "Christian Review."

"About an hour afterward the young man left, his work undone. A couple of days later the Doctor appeared and found the work unfinished. Straightening himself up to his full height, and with an expression of indignation, of which he is a master, he exclaimed, 'He does n't amount to anything; *he carries a cane !*'"

It is a question about which no small difference of opinion is found among Dr. Robinson's friends, at what period he exhibited his greatest power as a preacher. Professor Wilkinson regarded the sermons on scepticism, delivered shortly after Dr. Robinson became professor in Rochester, as the highest reach of his success as an orator ; but Dr. Sage, who heard the sermons when delivered to the Ninth Street Church in Cincinnati, thought them incomparably more effective than when repeated in Rochester. Another observer used to insist that the Doctor was never the same man after his typhoid fever in 1863, when he was at the age of forty-eight ; but some of the nearest friends of his long life declared that he had never before equalled the sermons delivered in Philadelphia when he was past seventy-five. Certainly they had rarely been so touching, and it is likely that never before in all his long experience the young people flocked lovingly around him at the close of the sermon as they did in those months of service for the Memorial and the Fifth Baptist Churches. It surprised him to be so received, and surprised some who looked on ; but the austere face wore a gentle look for the young folk who trusted him and thanked him. — ED.

CHAPTER III.

THE ROCHESTER PROFESSORSHIP AND PRESIDENCY.

1853-1866.

IN the spring of 1853 we packed our household goods and started for Rochester,[1] New York. We took a cottage with ample grounds and fruit-trees; and language fails to express the satisfaction and relief from the sense of care with which I found myself in my new home. My wife speedily regained her health, and I addressed myself with energy to my new duties. The very skies and the atmosphere, so unlike those of Cincinnati, inspired me with an ever-increasing exhilaration of spirit. My real work as a teacher could not then begin, as the academic year was on its last term. The most that I could undertake was a course of homiletic instruction to the graduating class in Theology. Dr. Conant had read to them during the year the manuscript lectures in Theology left by the deceased Dr. Maginnis; but they had received no homiletic instruction. I set the whole class at the preparation and delivery of sermons. The literary

---

[1] "He was thirty-eight years of age, in the full vigor and activity of robust manhood, although many silvery threads were even then gracing his head. He came upon the promise of a salary of $1200 a year, and a small addition for some special instruction; and such was the financial condition of the Seminary that as late as 1867, notwithstanding the high cost of living during the war, and his intense devotion to the interest of the Seminary, his salary had not been increased to more than $2000. I have said that $1200 was promised him; but much of the time it was not paid promptly, except in promissory notes, to be paid at maturity, or renewed, as the exigency of the time compelled." (From an address by E. R. Andrews, Esq.)

instruction they had received had by no means made them all master-workmen. The exercises, whether profitable to them or not, were specially useful to myself. They gave me opportunity to take a long breath in thinking of the work which I was to assume the coming autumn, and also to prepare what was absurdly called an Inaugural Address, to be delivered at the coming Commencement. It had been instilled into my mind by continuous iteration that whatever I should say in that address must be distinctively and pre-eminently orthodox. The jealousies created by the abortive attempt to transfer the institution bodily from Hamilton to Rochester had divided the churches into two opposing camps. Even a suspicion of heterodoxy, it was feared, would be fatal to the Rochester interest. I accordingly prepared an address on the need of Christian experience to a right understanding of theological doctrine. It was printed in the "Christian Review" under the title of "Experimental Theology," rather than "Experiential," as it should have been. That enabled me to steer clear of both Scylla and Charybdis. President Wayland of Brown University was one of the hearers of the address, which was not in disharmony with his well-known views. Whether from pity or from coincidence of view, the degree of Doctor of Divinity was conferred by Brown University at the following Commencement.[1]

When I went to Rochester, the Rev. Justin A. Smith, since then the so long and so distinguished editor of the "Standard" at Chicago, was pastor of its First Baptist Church. Unfor-

[1] The Doctorate of Laws was afterwards conferred by Brown, and again by Harvard University at the celebration of its two hundred and fiftieth anniversary. This was a very special occasion, and those who received the honors of the University were all men of note. All sat upon the platform, and each in turn arose as his degree was conferred. It was altogether an imposing array of American and European celebrities. — ED.

tunately, he soon resigned, and the church laid hold of me to occupy the pulpit. I had left Cincinnati for a smaller salary at Rochester, and a little income from preaching did not come amiss. But, unfortunately, when my real work as teacher of Theology began in the autumn, the demands on me as a preacher to the First Church added materially to the load I was carrying. The church had heard of the lectures on Scepticism at Cincinnati, and asked for a repetition of them during the winter. I was thoughtless enough to assent to the proposition, and, but for brief notes, which had been taken by a lady of the congregation at Cincinnati, the task would have been a severe one. I may add here that this foolish neglect of making notes for myself has been one of my grievous and life-long faults. But the delivery of these discourses, conjoined with the preparation of theological lectures, made necessarily a laborious winter. I had no theological system whatever. The doctrines to be taught were to my mind shadowy and indefinite. I began my theological lectures with discussions that to me possessed most interest, and about which I was best informed, the Evidences of Christianity. The views of Theodore Parker, published in his " Discourse of Religion," and of contemporary and corresponding schools abroad, presented inviting fields of inquiry. I discussed Christian Evidences and Inspiration *con amore*, wading in my personal reading neck-deep through the whole range of their speculation. The letters of Tholuck on Inspiration, growing out of the disagreement with the views of Scherer on the part of Merle D'Aubigné and others, and the brochure of Coleridge, " Confessions of an Inquiring Spirit," were just then attracting public attention. It was the first decisive beginnings of the great subsequent change of view on the doctrine of inspiration.

As I entered upon the special work of instruction in Systematic Theology, I was filled with constant solicitude as to how I was to teach the great doctrines of Christianity. There was no text-book which I could conscientiously use. My own views were uncertain, and in no sense constituted a system. There was no alternative; by the help of such books as I could lay hold of, American, English, and German, I set to work to clarify and settle my own views. Reading day and night as rapidly and widely as I could, I wrote only such brief propositions as I could venture to dictate to the class, often rushing from my desk to the class-room before the ink of the last sentence had become fairly dry. Around these propositions we indulged in ample discussion; but I was as much of an inquirer as any of the students. In all that was given, either in dictation or discussion, I was most distinctively and guardedly orthodox; but the question continually before us all was, not what is the orthodoxy of the sect, but what is the truth? The whole course in Theology was to be completed in a single year. Every day I flew to my lecture-room with nerves all in a tremor as to what was to be the result of the day's instruction. What was accomplished in that year's work in Theology comes back to me only as a very shadowy reminiscence. Some of the students whom I put upon the work of investigating and essay-writing very likely profited by the year's course; but I more than half suspect that they were not altogether certain as to the views of their teacher. It should here be stated, however, that, in the absence of all provision for homiletical instruction, it became my duty to train the class in sermonizing. To this work one day in each week was given throughout the year. This weekly exercise in sermonizing was an immense relief from the laborious formulating of theological doctrines. This first year I also taught Butler's Analogy to the Senior class in the University. It was a task that ought not to have been laid upon me, and which at the end of the year, in language somewhat vehement as well as explicit, I informed the trustees of the University that nothing could induce me to undertake again. As may well be imagined, the end of that year's work brought a sense of relief which no words can now express.

I entered upon the second year's work with less trepidation than upon the first. The burdens to be borne were considerably lessened. I was to give no undergraduate instruction in the University. My professorship in the first year had been nominally, but erroneously, regarded as a University professorship. The founders of the University, warned by experience in Madison University, had at the outset determined that, instead of a theological department, there should be a Theological Seminary, a totally distinct organization, under the direction of its own board of trustees and faculty of instruction. But the founders of the University, in raising money among the churches, had found it convenient to give great prominence to the value and need of ministerial education. On that plea the first and larger part of their funds were raised. The popular impression therefore was that the theological school was an organic part of the University. The confusion of ideas prevailed not only among the churches at large, but among the friends and faculty of the University. This confusion will explain the erroneous popular conception of the relation of the institutions at the outset.

I entered upon my second year's work with renewed zeal, ardent expectations, and buoyant spirits. My theological ideas were beginning to take some definiteness of form. Just then the whole intellectual atmosphere was vocal with discussion about the Hamiltonian doctrine of the relativity of knowledge. The application of this philosophical dogma to the doctrine of God was awakening the most animated discussion, which reached its climax only in years later, when Mansel had published his Bampton lectures on the "Limits of Religious Thought." Dr. Shedd's article in the "Christian Review," entitled "Sin a Nature, and that Nature Guilt," furnished material for liveliest discussions in treating of the doctrine of sin. These two questions among others gave special interest to my second year's instruction. In assigning to my class topics for investigation and criticism, I was myself obliged to read largely and rapidly in order to be fitted for an appreciation and discussion of the papers presented by them. It was a year of probably larger growth on my part than on theirs. At the close of a day's work, the floor of my study was strewn with books, as though a hurricane had been among them. I had also entered with redoubled interest on the work of homiletical instruction, inducing the students, so far as I was able, to turn their theological conclusions into a homiletical use. This practice had the beneficial result of prompting them to look at theological doctrines, not so much as abstract dogmas, as living truths to be brought to bear on the consciences of men. This attempted conjunction of a study of Systematic Theology with a homiletic use of it was, in these early days, one of the distinctive peculiarities of the Rochester Theological Seminary. Notwithstanding the wear and tear of nerves by this homiletic part of my work, necessitating the minute examination of not less than three sermons from each member of the class, the work, as a whole, was the most attractive of anything I had ever been engaged in. The crowding of all this into a single year did not leave me with a large amount of unused time; yet, as I now look back upon it, I remember that I was unwise enough to be drawn into almost continuous Sunday preaching.

In my third year I began work with a conscious increase of self-confidence. Theology did not seem so dark and unexplored a realm. The subjects engaging attention the previous year were increasingly attractive. The relativity of knowledge was re-examined in the attempt to find some determinative principle in classification of the Divine attributes. Among theological treatises there appeared to be no guiding principle, each author beginning with such attribute as apparently struck his fancy, or as seemed the fittest point of departure. In the doctrine of relativity I got the clew to a principle for the classification of attributes. The classification arranged the attributes according to the order of the relations through which a knowledge of the attributes had been obtained. These are the relations of God to space, time, the material universe, and man, according to which we discussed the attributes of immensity, eternity, power, wisdom, omnipresence, and holiness, whence genetically were derived all the moral attributes.

The doctrine of sin was examined more minutely as well as extensively, and special attention was given to the New England doctrine that sin consisted wholly in action. I am afraid, as I recall the work of that year, that we were too extraordinarily orthodox on the doctrine of original sin. We not only made sin to consist in a state, but as at times accompanied with a consciousness on our part of a responsibility for its Adamic origin.

The doctrine of atonement, which had been taught in the two previous years in a traditionally orthodox form, with a defence of the Anselmic theory, was brought under careful review in the light of the federal theory of Princeton on the one hand, and the governmental theory of Andover on the other. The class warmed to their work with a most gratifying interest, and did not fail to impart stimulus to their teacher by their questions, objections, and careful preparation of papers which embodied the results of their own reading and reflection. I had begun to get hold of the Neander Library, and to extract from it a much needed aid. Homiletic instruction became an increasingly absorbing part of my work, making a larger draught on nervous energy than lecturing on Theology. My custom was, after having the sermon read before the class for their criticism as well as my own, to require the student to re-write it, then submit it to me for private examination. I scrupulously read each sermon through from beginning to end, then sent for the student, and, in instances not a few, went over it with him, paragraph by paragraph, hatchelling, combing, and sometimes reconstructing the whole. I can recall instances of a two hours' sitting with a single student. Fortunately there were large numbers that required no such criticism.

During the immediately following years the work of instruction in the Seminary was largely a resurvey of the topics discussed in preceding years, — a readjustment of conclusions to one another, but still more largely an opening of new lines of inquiry. The doctrine of Christology was entered upon with a zeal the vivid recollection of which still survives. The helps and sources of information at that day were meagre indeed in comparison with what is now within the reach of every one. The humiliation of Christ became an inquiry of absorbing interest. Dissatisfied with any conception of it within reach, I set to work at the very careful study of the New Testament itself. It was forced upon my mind that the humiliation consisted in the limitations of the divine by its assumption of the human.

So thoroughly convinced was I of this explanation, that I made it the subject of a discourse delivered before the Society of Missionary Inquiry at the Commencement of Brown University in 1856. The view presented struck the audience as novel and questionable. President Wayland, who heard the discourse, thought it was " an important doctrine, if true. " The conclusions, however, which I had reached were in my own mind thoroughly settled, and determined to no small extent the whole range of my theological ideas. The Kenotist theory of Gess, Thomasius, and others, with which the theology of our day has made everybody familiar, had not then come to my knowledge. It was not until a later date that I adjusted this conception of the humiliation to what became my clearly defined view of the atonement.

At the end of the Seminary year, in 1857, my colleague, Dr. Conant, resigned the chair of Biblical Literature and Criticism to give his whole time to the work of translation for the American Bible Union. He had for some time before this been in their service in addition to his professorial duties. His retirement took from the Theological Seminary its most distinguished professor. His broad and accurate biblical learning, especially in Hebrew literature, was recognized both in this country and abroad. It was feared that his withdrawal might interfere with our prosperity. His going was the loss to me of a personal friend. It was also to me a matter of personal regret that he should leave the work of the Seminary for the service on which he entered; but it had been a life-long desire of his to put the Bible, particularly the Old Testament, into the hands of English readers in a much more accurate translation than was furnished in the so-called version of King James. This offer of the Bible Union seemed to him to afford the only opportunity for the realization of his long-cherished desire. To many of us it was a matter of serious regret, and, as we thought, financially a mistake, that he did not remain in the Seminary, proceed with his translation, and issue instalments at cheap rates to subscribers. We believed that such a translation would have an immense circulation. Against the Bible Union was a wide-spread and deep-seated prejudice, a dislike on the part of very many of the best minds in the denomination, for both its spirit and its methods. The ignorant and bigoted talk about " the pure word of God," by which large numbers of uninformed people were drawn to the support of the Union, we were confident could awake nothing but aversion in the mind of so clear-headed and enlightened a man as Dr. Conant. He was too well acquainted with the numberless variations in the original texts not to feel humiliated by this clap-trap talk of the managers and abettors of the Bible Union. Of the bitterness and bigotry of their spirit I had myself had experience before becoming a professor at Rochester. The scandal brought upon the denomination by the Bible Union among intelligent men, to say nothing of the reckless waste of funds, is one of the painful memories among those of us who have survived those days of noise, pretence, and fanaticism. It should not be forgotten as one of the warnings against unwise leadership.

The retirement of Dr. Conant required some reconstruction of the Faculty of the Seminary. My friend Hotchkiss, to whom I was more sincerely attached than he was ever aware of, was transferred from the chair of Ecclesiastic History to the chair of Biblical Literature, left vacant by Dr. Conant, for the duties of which he had special predilection. In the chair of Ecclesiastical History, thus made vacant, we placed a young man [1] who had just graduated from

[1] G. W. Northrup, D. D., LL. D. — ED.

the Seminary, and who has since made for himself a distinguished name as a teacher of Theology, and as the head of the Baptist Union Theological Seminary at Morgan Park, near Chicago, since become the Divinity School of the University of Chicago. The appointment of so young a man was regarded with distrust by some of the trustees; but his immediate success and his subsequent career fully vindicated the confidence of his instructors, who had recommended his appointment.

In one of the late autumns about this period I found my health affected by a distressing cough. In those earlier years my lecture-room in the old hotel building on Buffalo Street was but fifteen or sixteen feet square. To spend two hours at a time with fifteen or eighteen men in so small a room required an open window just at my shoulder, to keep us from partial suffocation. A succession of colds had fastened the cough. Our family physician took alarm, said I must quit my work and go South. He went with me to Baltimore. Ten days among my old friends at Norfolk, with abundant oysters and Southern atmosphere, speedily put me on my feet again, and within two weeks I was back and at work as well as ever, but in a more spacious lecture-room.

It is needless to say that with myself the horizon of theological thought was constantly widening and the atmosphere clearing. The inexhaustible doctrine of sin was still one of the living topics. It became clear to my mind that sin could be comprehensively discussed and clearly understood only under the triple conception of it as act, principle, and state. Sin, then, as I was accustomed to teach, may be comprehensively defined as follows: As an act it is a transgression of God's law; as a principle that determines the guilt of acts, it is opposition or hostility to God; as a state or nature, it is moral unlikeness to God. The meaning of the word " death " in the Pauline epistles, as well as in the Fourth Gospel, received special attention.   The position was maintained that literal death could not be held to be the specific penalty for sin, but that the term " death " was used by both writers in its metaphorical sense.

The doctrine of atonement was with all classes a subject of protracted discussion.   My own views had now begun to pass through a rapid transition.   Up to that time I had been a steadfast defender of the doctrine of substitution; but the Anselmic substitution had too much of the commercial tone for me to take it without large qualifications.   The federal imputation theory of Princeton was too mechanical and artificial to be endured; I had long before abandoned the whole conception of the decretive will of God on which the theory rested, as arbitrary and contrary to the Christian conception of the Godhead.   The governmental theory of Andover, so ably defended by Dr. Park, seemed to me superficial, and incapable of any just defence either on philosophical or scriptural grounds.   The Socinian theory of moral influence appeared to fasten its attention on the secondary effect of Christ's life and death, to the exclusion of that efficient principle which a right view of his death alone could supply, and which alone could secure the moral influence claimed; that is, by excluding a right view of his death it deprived the atonement of that moral influence which the theory ascribed to it.   The life theory just then coming into vogue, the first beginnings of what has since blossomed out into the New Theology, fastened its attention on the incarnation, making the death of Christ a means of communicating the life which he had brought into the world, rather than a propitiatory sacrifice, through which alone a participation in that life becomes possible.   To reach any clear and definite conceptions of the atonement, it seemed necessary to examine analytically and critically the fundamental principles underlying it. The chief of these were to be found in the scriptural ideas of the nature of God, of man, and of moral law, as expressing the nature of the relations between God and man.

For a series of years no question in my lecture-room took precedence of an inquiry into the fundamental conception of moral law. The older theories of the atonement all built upon the idea of law as either the decretive will of God, or as a statute made simply to secure some desired end. They conceived law as a statute whose penalty might be enforced or remitted as the wise will of God should decide to be expedient. With such an idea of moral law all modern science and all sound philosophy were hopelessly at variance. The realism to which all science and philosophy were converging made it necessary to conceive of law as constitutive in the nature alike of God and man. At this juncture familiarity with the writings of Neander, particularly with his account of the planting and training of the Apostolic Church, helped very greatly to clarify my own ideas. The more I read of various treatises on the atonement, the less I was satisfied with their ideas of moral law. Turning again to Neander, and from Neander to the conceptions of law presented in the treatises of scientists, I became thoroughly convinced that no idea of law was justifiable which rested in any decretive or legislative will, or was derived from any other source than the eternal nature of God, which had determined forever the moral constitution of the universe. Law is a constituent principle of moral being as such, whether that being be the infinite God or finite man. Thus moral law is as immutable as God himself, and its awards can no more be reversed than the nature of God can change.

The doctrines thus far referred to came naturally before

successive classes, but single doctrines occupied disproportionate attention with different classes, the special topics depending mainly on the philosophical training and abilities of the leading minds of the class. Different classes thus received different impressions as to what I regarded as most fundamental and important in a system of Theology. They did not always apprehend the relations to other essential truths of the doctrines on which they had longest lingered. They did not understand that I was myself steadily growing in apprehension of the logical relations of one doctrine to another, and was gradually forming the whole into a complete and harmonious system. It was only in the later years of my professorship of Theology that my mind became thoroughly settled as to the relations of the parts to one another. I never forgot, from the beginning of my Rochester work to its end, that I was myself a learner, and was ever open to the reception of truth, come whencesoever it might. This alone could explain the freedom which every student was encouraged to exercise in questioning and in discussion. We never were afraid of looking any opinion frankly in the face, and reverently and devoutly inquiring, under the teaching of God's Word, whether it was truth or error. It has always seemed to me that no greater wrong could be done to theological students than to require them to accept without scrutiny any principle or sentiment avowed by their teacher. They should, on the contrary, be encouraged, with an humble reliance on the Divine guidance, to inquire, think, and decide for themselves.

In one of the years between 1857 and 1859 occurred an episode in the history of the Seminary affecting its then existing status and its future. With this episode I was myself so connected as to make fit that there should here be an allusion to it, and an explanation of its occurrence. For several months the Seminary had failed to pay the salaries of its professors. There was a financial crisis in its affairs. The friends of the institution were invited to a conference on the subject. Our dear good friend, the Rev. Zenas Freeman, corresponding secretary and, in fact, financial agent of the New York Baptist Union for Ministerial Education, which had been organized to " sustain a Theological School," and which appointed the Seminary's Board of Trustees, made to the conference a report of the Seminary's financial condition. He began his report with a statement of assets. The two items with which he began were $50,000 of scholarships, and the money which had been given by Mr. Roswell Burroughs for the purchase of the Neander Library. At the close of his report I ventured to ask how it could be possible that we had an asset of $50,000, and there be no income for the payment of our salary. It then, for the first time, came to be understood that this $50,000 consisted of the first funds that had been collected towards an endowment of the University. As scholarships, every dollar of the income accrued to the University for the tuition and support of undergraduate candidates for the ministry, thus paying the salaries of University professors, while not a dollar of it was available for salaries of professors in the Seminary. How this $50,000 could be regarded as part of the Seminary's assets, or how money paid for the purchase of the Neander Library could be so designated, was incomprehensible. A mystification was immediately cleared up. Before accepting my professorship I had been assured that the Seminary had an endowment of some $60,000, the income from which at then prevailing rates of interest seemed ample provision for the salaries of Dr. Conant and myself, with our expected colleague. It could safely be anticipated that natural increase of the supposed endowment would provide for additional

members of the Faculty.   The result of the conference was a
dissipation of our imaginary endowment; the $50,000 never
again figured among the assets of the Seminary.   Unfortunately, this episode gave me the reputation of being the dis-
turber of an existing harmony.   The truth was it then
became clear to the public mind that the only provision for
ministerial education thus far made in the way of endowment was for support of undergraduates in the University.
This episode reached its climax a few years later, when it
became evident, on the death of Mr. Freeman, that the Seminary was absolutely bankrupt.   To meet the salaries of the
professors, the Rev. Mr. Freeman had borrowed money wherever it was obtainable.   He had advanced $1200 of his own
funds, taking, as security, a note signed by the responsible
officers of the Ministerial Union.   This note remaining unpaid, his widow had placed it in the hands of the distinguished jurist, Henry R. Selden, for collection.   There was
not a dollar in the treasury with which to pay it.   It was
quietly intimated to us that we should not be crowded for
payment, but that the widow was in great need of the
money.   There was but one thing to do, and that was for
me to go to New York and raise the $1200.   I left my class
in the hands of my colleagues, spent a Sunday with Madison Avenue Church, receiving a contribution of several
hundred dollars, and the remainder I picked up in various
places, hat in hand.   I found the lone widow in the upper
part of the city, paid her the $1200, and, taking the can-
celled note, returned with all haste to my work in the
lecture-room.   There were no stars in our heavens in those
days.   The future of the Seminary was problematical.   It
was a relief, however, to know our real condition, and what
alone could save us.   The real work of the Seminary went
on with unabated interest, no student, so far as I was aware,

having the remotest conception of the financial strait through which we were passing.

It was at about this time that the German department had become organized, and was in sorest need of some provision for the salary of Professor Rauschenbusch, its head teacher. I recall no service with more satisfaction than that of securing from the devout and large-hearted J. B. Hoyt, of Stamford, Connecticut, the sum of $20,000 as the basis of an endowment for Professor Rauschenbusch's chair. This was secured while we were also doing our utmost toward an endowment for ourselves; but I doubt if any money was ever devoted to a worthier object than that to which Mr. Hoyt gave his $20,000. The thirty years' service of Professor Rauschenbusch in Rochester furnishes part of one of the most interesting chapters in the history of American Baptists.

In the autumn of 1859 came a proposition from Mr. Smith Sheldon, the book publisher of New York, that I should revise Ryland's translation of Neander's " Planting and Training of the Christian Church. " A last and revised edition of the original work had appeared in Germany subsequent to Ryland's translation. The proposition was so to revise his translation as to incorporate all the modifications of the last German edition. It was soon discovered that this last German edition had been exhausted, and no copy of it could be obtained. A copy in two volumes was finally obtained from the library of the Rev. Dr. Hitchcock, of Union Theological Seminary in New York. A cumulative variety of duties, however, intervened to delay the appearance of the revision long beyond the time announced. First came from the same publisher in the winter of 1860 the proposition that Dr. Hotchkiss and I should edit the " Christian Review," of which he had become proprietor. This proposition we unfortunately accepted. The disordered state of the country, the alienation between the North and the South, made the support of such a review extremely precarious. The outbreak of the civil war cut off, at one stroke, every subscriber from the Southern States, and the overdue payments for past years. The minds of the Northern people were much more interested in the immediate prospects of the country than in theological or philosophical discussion. The outlook for a continued pecuniary support of the Review was dismal in the extreme. The Review was purchased by Mr. Ezra R. Andrews, of Rochester. I continued sole editor until 1863, when longer continuance of its publication seemed impossible, and the proprietors of the " Bibliotheca Sacra " became purchasers of its subscription list. I have called this an unfortunate service : it was four years of exhausting and unpaid labor.

In the meagreness of my salary as professor of Theology, it became a matter of necessity not to decline invitations to pulpit service. In 1860 came an invitation from the First Presbyterian Church in Rochester to supply its pulpit. Its congregation was one of the most intelligent and attractive that a preacher could desire to address. Its large proportion of liberally educated men, especially of the legal profession, furnished a stimulus to the fullest exertion of a preacher's powers. I accepted the invitation with the understanding that the service was to continue only until they could secure a pastor. It ran on for a year or more, covering one of the stormiest periods in our national history. The public mind was profoundly moved by the outbreak of the civil war. It was impossible that my preaching should not at times take a tone and coloring from what was in everybody's mind. One incident stands out conspicuously in my recollection : a single sentence in the course of the sermon so struck the congregation that, to my surprise and fright, they responded with a sudden outbreak of hand-clapping such as I had never heard at a religious service. For a staid Presbyterian assemblage it was not only a novel exhibition of feeling, but indicative of the feverish excitement of the public mind.[1] One of the peculiarities of this service was that a Baptist should preach on Sunday, give a mid-week lecture, preach a sermon preparatory to communion, and yet never appear at the communion-table. The incongruity was felt alike by the preacher and the people. With this exception the service was one which the preacher himself thoroughly enjoyed. While this service continued, my work as a theological teacher, instead of being in any degree slighted, was carried forward with ever-increasing interest. The ministrations of the pulpit reacted upon the work of the lecture-room to the stimulus of professor and students alike. The revision of Neander was held in' abeyance, and editorial work on the " Christian Review " was disposed of by me more summarily than it ought to have been. The unproductiveness of the Review made it

---

[1] The editor, who was present, well remembers the thrill that ran through the congregation when the preacher, yielding for a moment to the terrible strain of feeling which belonged to the early days of the civil war, invoked the judgment of God against the rebellion, and predicted that the besom of destruction would sweep the South. The effect was overpowering, and the spontaneous outbreak of applause a real relief. After Dr. Robinson had preached for this church a year, Judge Gardiner, a prominent member of the church, remarked to the writer that they must give up the services of Dr. Robinson, or they would never call a pastor. The " war speeches " of Dr. Robinson and Dr. Anderson were a notable feature of the meetings held at that period to encourage enlistments. When the news that Lincoln had been assassinated reached Rochester, " our citizens," wrote Frederick Douglass in his autobiography, " not knowing what else to do in the agony of the hour, betook themselves to the City Hall. Though all hearts ached for utterance, few felt like speaking. ... Dr. Robinson . . . was prevailed upon to take the stand, and made one of the most touching and eloquent speeches I ever heard." — ED.

impossible, in its closing years, to offer remuneration to the writers for it, and, accordingly, not many writers of the highest merit could be induced to become contributors.

In the summer of 1861 the Pearl Street Baptist Church of Albany was in a perilous condition through disagreement over the resignation of its pastor. They requested me to become stated supply of their pulpit until they could so far harmonize as to agree upon another pastor. Complying with this request, it became necessary for me to make a weekly trip to Albany. Sometimes I could so arrange duties and command my time as to take the Saturday morning train; not unfrequently it became necessary to take the train Saturday night, reaching Albany at four o'clock in the morning, giving me time for a morning rest before entering the pulpit. The congregation was all that one could desire. They were to the highest degree kindly and appreciative. This service continued for a year or more, but the draught on time and strength was too much to be longer protracted. In the summer of 1862 I recommended the church to send a committee to Jamaica Plain, Massachusetts, to hear the Rev. C. De W. Bridgman, with a view to calling him to the pastorate. He was immediately called, accepted the call, and after a most successful pastorate of fifteen years resigned, in spite of the earnest protestations of his church and parishioners.

In thus referring to Dr. Bridgman, I am reminded of one who graduated with him in the class of 1857, Abner Kingman Nott, the successor, immediately after his graduation, of the distinguished Dr. Cone as pastor of the First Baptist Church in New York. His ardent piety, his fine qualities of mind and heart, his winning manners, gave him at once the most extraordinary success. Almost at the beginning of a brilliant career, full of the largest promise, his life was suddenly terminated by drowning, in July, 1859, at the age of twenty-five. The vast concourse brought together by his funeral testified to both the depth and the breadth of the impression which he had produced, and to the tenderness of feeling which he had awakened. I had preached at his ordination, and it was a most melancholy service to officiate at his funeral.

In the beginning of the session of 1860 the Seminary may be said, in a sense, to have taken a new start. Up to this time its course of study had been limited to two years. Of necessity this compression resulted in incompleteness in every department. There was a growing feeling that we must have an additional year. How to effect this was a difficult problem. By many it was said, " It is best to let well enough alone. " To enlarge our course had been with me a long-cherished desire. From the time of the retirement of Dr. Conant no little responsibility for the work of the Seminary had devolved on me as senior professor. In 1860 the trustees of their own motion gave me the formal title of President. This act laid on me an increased sense of responsibility, as well as a feeling of obligation to the students and the public to extend our course of study. In addition to this was the inexorable necessity of a larger income, of a permanent endowment for professorships, and of a fund for the increase of the library. With the presidency came a multiplicity of duties and cares. Work inside the Seminary could not be slighted, and decisive measures for securing an endowment could be no longer delayed.

At the beginning of the session of 1861 the class which had entered in 1860 sent to the Faculty and Trustees a formal petition that their course should be extended to a third year. Their petition was granted without hesitation, and, accordingly, there was no class to graduate in 1862. All felt that a needed advance had been made, and the Seminary moved onward with freer breath and quickened step. The work of my own department was at once widened, as well as made more analytically minute. Classes in Systematic Theology now got clearer conceptions of the professor's views, and of the logical relations of part with part. My work was increasingly satisfactory both in process and re-sults. The department of Homiletics, which, from lack of funds to support a professor, I had never been able to trans-fer to the shoulders of another, could now receive attention more nearly commensurate with its need. Beginning with lectures on preaching in the Middle year, attention was continued to it throughout the remainder of the course.

In the spring of 1863 it became apparent in an unexpected way that there was a limit to human capacity for work which could not be passed with impunity. I was suddenly thrown upon my back by a violent fever. Our family phy-sician quietly said, " It is the result of overwork ; rest will speedily relieve you." But rest brought no relief. The fever had so firm a grip that it speedily developed into the typhoid type. Revision of Neander, editorial work on the Review, professorial work in the Seminary, and the raising of funds for an endowment were brought to a stand-still. What the result was to be I afterwards learned became to personal friends a matter of anxiety. I was myself unaware of danger, though impatient at the long interruption of what had come to be absorbing pursuits. While the class of 1863, a class in which I took special interest as being the first to whose course a third year had been added, were engaged in graduating exercises, it was a matter of uncertainty whether I should ever leave the sick-bed alive. The summer was far advanced before I could resume any serious task. My first public work, when I was barely able to stand on my feet,

was to preach the ordination sermon of the Rev. Wayland
Hoyt at Pittsfield, Massachusetts. The intervening weeks
until the opening of the next session of the Seminary were
spent in recruiting my strength. It was in this autumn it
became evident that, in the distractions of the country, the
publication of the " Christian Review" could be no longer
continued, and its publisher transferred its list of subscribers to the " Bibliotheca Sacra." With recovered
strength the long suspended revision of Neander was
resumed. Up to this time only fragmentary work had
been done on it. Then taking it in hand in earnest,
" copy " was soon on its way to the printers. Before another
summer had come and gone the task was completed, the
class of 1864 had been graduated, and hopeful progress had
been made in the attempts at endowment.

While engaged in prosecuting the work of endowment,
serious questions arose between the Seminary and the University proper, occasioning grave discussions which resulted
in decisions unacceptable to some of the friends of the University, and led to misunderstandings that may as well here
as anywhere be cleared up. Until now we had been occupying rooms in the old hotel building on Buffalo Street, and
paying rent for them to the University. Immediate friends
of the Seminary, including leading trustees, said, " If we
are to have an endowment, why should we not have a local
habitation as well as a name ? " It was decided that, instead
of paying rent to the University, of which we were popularly
understood to be a department, strenuous efforts should at
once be made for a building and a home of our own. The
grave question was, Where should it be placed ? The Trustees of the University, especially Baptist members of the
board, said, " Place it on the University campus." Drs.
Anderson and Cutting were especially earnest advocates of

this location. Their advocacy was seconded by Dr. Dean
and others.   It was claimed that, in accepting the grounds
for the campus, the right had been reserved to place on it
the buildings of the Theological Seminary; but when the
trustees asked for a deed in fee simple of the lot or lots on
which they should build, it was replied that this could not
be done, — the conditions on which the land had been
given precluding the right to deed it away.   But the Seminary refused to erect buildings on land which it could not
own.   In the unknown vicissitudes of the future, embarrass-
ments might arise, the risk of which the Seminary had no
right to incur.   It was decided to seek a site elsewhere.
This decision gave much dissatisfaction to the Baptist professors and trustees of the University.   The ruling idea of
ministerial education as the ultimate aim of the University
had been constantly presented among the Baptist churches
as a motive for its endowment.   To give to the Seminary a
distinct and separate location it was feared would diminish
the interest of Baptist churches in the University as such.
Up to this time many Baptists, under the illusion that the
Theological Seminary was an organic part of the University,
and the ultimate end for which it had been endowed, had
contributed moneys not a dollar of which, principal or interest, had gone to the support of either professor or student in
the Seminary.   To divert attention from the University to
the Seminary as distinctively theological would, it was
feared, work disastrously to the University.   Inevitably,
some coolness arose between the immediate friends of the
Seminary and those of the University.   As president of the
Seminary a little more than due share of odium fell upon
my shoulders.

As was natural, a shade of coolness arose between Dr.
Anderson, as head of the University, and myself, as head of

the Seminary. Our acquaintance and friendship had dated from 1840, when we were students together at Newton Theological Institution. It was also largely through his agency that I had become Professor of Theology at Rochester. In the earlier years of the work at Rochester our intimacy had been close and uninterrupted. Many a night, until the small hours, was spent by us in most animated and friendly discussion of topics in which we had a common interest. For theology he had no taste, and about its history and most fundamental controversies he had little or no knowledge. In many respects his mental constitution was widely different from my own. He could hold opinions and be subject to convictions that to my mind were not only inconsistent, but mutually destructive. His mind seemed to be constructed like a modern sea-going steamer, with separate compartments, one of which might be " stove in," and yet it sail right onward. Thus he could hold a scientific conclusion or principle that to me seemed destructive of Christian faith. With him, science and faith stood on independent grounds; with me, faith was crippled if science collided with it at any point, either in its premises or in its conclusions. He was a strict nominalist; I, in a modern sense of the term, was an equally strict realist. He was not by nature a metaphysician; but as teacher of philosophy he was extremely fond of philosophical discussion. His range of knowledge was very wide for a man of his age. As tutor in Latin, as also in Mathematics, at Waterville College, then Professor of Rhetoric and Lecturer on History, he was possessed of an unusually well-furnished mind. He was extremely fond, in our discussions, of free and wide excursions over the fields of knowledge with which his work at Waterville had made him more or less familiar. To this range of knowledge he had had occasion, as editor

of the " New York Recorder," frequently to recur.   As a
teacher and social disputant, all that he had acquired was
at his ready command.   His teaching accordingly was racy
to a degree.   As a companion in social life, he was full of
interest, and his visits were always more than welcome.
Between such old friends and companions the faintest air
of coolness was to me at least extremely painful; but the
interests of the University were to him supremely dear, as
were those of the Seminary to me.   He exercised his freedom in criticism of myself and the Seminary to others, and
to others I did the same respecting him and the University;
but never a word of angry dispute or of unkindness passed
between ourselves.   Our estimate of each other and of each
other's work remained as kindly as ever.   My estimation
of him as a man and as the executive of a college was of the
highest.   His habits of mind and ever-increasing range of
knowledge gave him a power as head of a college which has
rarely been equalled.   He would enter upon a new subject
of inquiry and push his researches with a fury until he had
made himself master of all its main particulars.   Continuing this for a year or two, he would drop the subject for a
new one.   Thus at one period he was absorbed in ethno-
logical inquiries under the guidance of such writers as
Prichard.   Discovering that comparative philology was
the most decisive of all tests, he dropped ethnology.   This
discursive habit he continued to the end of his career, concluding his life in the study of etching, engraving, and the
fine arts with absorbing interest.   Dr. Anderson, by his
tastes, his range of knowledge, and his fondness for
economic, sociological, and political questions, was pre-
eminently fitted for public life.   Rochester University is,
however, an enduring monument of a great life and of a
genuine self-sacrifice.   Effective as were his public ad-

dresses, Dr. Anderson, in my estimate, will be longest
remembered by his students for his chapel-talks, usually
on current events, and for his farewell words at the graduation of the several classes. He was a wise man in refusing
all invitations to leave his work at Rochester for any other
University.

While considering with anxiety how to secure an endowment for the Seminary, and means for the erection of its
needed buildings, as well as where they should be placed,
it seemed to me that, before proceeding further, one more
honest attempt should be made to terminate the scandal of
maintaining two rival theological schools, at Hamilton and
at Rochester, within the limits of a single State, both com-
peting for support from the same churches and on the same
pleas. In common with others who had had no participation in the original struggle which resulted in the founding
of Rochester University, I felt that one step toward healing
the breach that had been created might be taken in the
consolidation of the two theological schools. I accordingly
wrote an earnest letter to Dr. Dodge at Hamilton, proposing
that we should unite in a concerted effort to transfer the two
institutions to some Eastern city, either Albany or New
York, and build them up into a single institution of which
Baptists should have no occasion to be ashamed. I went so
far as to propose to resign my own position at Rochester,
without expectation of resuming it, and betake myself to
the States of New York, Pennsylvania, — the Crozer Theological Seminary had not then been founded, — and New
Jersey to raise an endowment for the new institution. This
seemed to me also to furnish a solution of the complicated
problem before us at Rochester. Dr. Dodge replied that
the proposed movement could not fail to be abortive, and
would, instead of uniting the two institutions, result in the

formation of a third.   The only alternative, so far as I could then see, was to take off our coats and go to work in earnest to put the Rochester Seminary into a home of its own, and to place it on a foundation where it could do its work more effectively than had been possible in its preceding years.

During the years 1865 and 1866 the work of collecting funds for an endowment was carried forward with encouraging success, though not at a very rapid rate.   Every day was given to it that could justifiably be spared from professorial duties.   All Seminary vacations and recesses were spent in New York and its vicinity, or in the States of Connecticut and New Jersey, soliciting subscriptions.   In addition to the endowment was the necessary provision of funds for the current support of beneficiaries.   From a variety of causes, needless here to explain, the Union for Ministerial Education, during these two years, had no corresponding secretary, one of whose chief duties had been to provide for the beneficiaries.   The care of them fell mainly to my lot.   Besides *bona fide* subscriptions, several very handsome amounts had been conditionally subscribed or verbally promised, and could not be counted upon beyond question for the endowment until certain contingencies in the future should be finally determined.

At the conclusion of the Seminary year of 1865 a colleague, Professor Velona R. Hotchkiss, with whom I had for eleven years sustained most intimate and most pleasant relations, sent in his resignation of the chair of Biblical Literature. His resignation gave me great pain, because tendered under misapprehensions which I was not then at liberty, though it was in my power, to dissipate.   I simply assured him that the time might come when I could explain to him what then seemed suspicious, and could give him conclusive evidence of the truth of my explanation.   That time came, thank Heaven! years before his departure from this earth. I not only dissipated the misapprehension, but referred him to the best of authority for its groundlessness. Dr. Hotchkiss was scholarly, genial, in the highest degree companionable, free from guile and all double-mindedness, a colleague from whom I parted with sincere regret. As an expository preacher he had few, if any, equals.

On the resignation of Dr. Hotchkiss, Dr. Kendrick of the University assumed the duties of the chair of Biblical Literature. Though professor of classical Greek, he had for many years been a most diligent and critical student of the New Testament. He was an acknowledged master in its interpretation. With the Hebrew he was not so much at home; in fact, he had only paid it the courtesy of an occasional and transient visit. He knew but little more of it than its alphabet. By daily acquisitions he kept ahead of his class; but the breadth of his knowledge and his masterly power of acquisition never permitted a soul among the students to suspect that he was practically a beginner in the study of the language which he was teaching. Such was his enthusiasm in the work that his class went forward with all the zeal and success of the pupils of a long-practised master. His duties were discharged alike to the satisfaction of himself, his colleagues, and his pupils. A long-cherished friend, a man of the greatest versatility and most varied acquirements, of poetic fancy, of rarest geniality, urbanity, and wit, he would have been gladly retained as a permanent member of the faculty in the Seminary, and was always a most welcome guest in our household.

CHAPTER IV.

IN EUROPE. — LAST YEARS IN ROCHESTER.

1866-1872.

DURING my visits to New York in 1865, I chanced to make the acquaintance of Mr. Coffin, who for many years had been at the head of the mailing department in the Post-Office of New York City. In conversation one day, having asked me if I had been abroad, he said, " Why don't you go ? " Replying that the expense of it, my duties as professor, and reluctance to be away from my family had combined to deter me from the thought of it, he at once said : " I can send you and your family to England without a dollar of expense to you. I have *carte blanche* from the Inman line of steamers to send abroad as free passengers any friends of mine to whom I may desire to show this courtesy. " And he added, " You will receive just as much attention from the officers of the steamer as if you were paying the highest price for your tickets. " His words were literally fulfilled. We· all had free passes both in going and in returning.

It was accordingly determined during the year 1865 that, as soon as arrangements of Seminary work could be completed, making possible a year and a half's absence, we would sail for Europe. Certain loose strings attached to subscriptions for endowment required to be carefully tied; one hundred dollars was to be provided for each of the beneficiaries during my absence; and, more than all, the course of theological instruction for the class which was to graduate in 1867 was to be completed.   A mountain of work lying in the way was to be removed before we could sail.   It was accordingly not till near the middle of December, 1866, that we found ourselves on board the " City of Paris " with faces turned toward the Atlantic.   Our commander was the accomplished Captain Kennedy, the commodore of the line.   He was extremely anxious to eat Christmas dinner in his own home, which was at Chester, near Liverpool. The full power of the steamer was accordingly brought into play, and we were at the dock in Liverpool before the middle of the afternoon of Christmas day.

It may not be out of place to tell of the somewhat amusing way in which I was welcomed to English soil.   Helplessly ill throughout the voyage, I had rarely appeared among the passengers in the saloon.   A canny Scotchman, who had lived long in Texas, was curious as to my identity, and discovered that I was some sort of professor.   While at the Queen's Arms in Liverpool Christmas evening, so many of the steamer's passengers as were at the hotel had met in the tap-room for a typical English Christmas evening over a punch-bowl.   A polite message was sent to our private parlor inviting me to come down to see some of my fellow-passengers.   As I entered the tap-room, two or three of them came forward with great cordiality, gradually leading me under the chandelier, which was decorated with mistletoe; when, quicker than a flash, a buxom bar-maid sprang from behind me, threw her arms about my neck, and planted a kiss upon my cheek.   Of course the maid was entitled to the usual forfeit, the price of a pair of gloves, and my fellow-passengers had their hilarious laughter at my expense.

On the morning after reaching Liverpool we took the

express train for London, and went to Faull's Hotel,[1] within a stone's-throw of Guildhall, and within easy distance of the Bank of England and St. Paul's Cathedral. It was a resort of college professors and other quiet and inquisitive people. Our stay of two or three weeks was improved by visiting old localities made famous in the history, both political and literary, of England. Our first Sunday we went in the morning quite a long distance to attend a service at which Archbishop Manning, afterwards Cardinal, was to preach. His sermon was an able discourse, skilfully constructed, and by successive steps leading up to and concluding with a justification of transubstantiation and the worship of Mary. It was a packed assemblage of Irish, with a sprinkling of some eight or ten other faces, into which the Archbishop was constantly peering throughout his discourse. He was then of middle age, spare and angular in person, with clean-cut features and restless, eager eyes. In the afternoon we went to hear the famous James Martineau. No two assemblages could form a more complete contrast than that which we saw in the morning and that with which we met in the afternoon. The number of substantial-looking men whose countenances bespoke education and refinement was surprisingly large. Dr. Martineau wore a silk gown, and his head was densely covered with raven-black hair. He was then about sixty years of age. Surprised at the color of his hair, I asked one of his regular hearers, with whom I chanced to be sitting, if he dyed it. As though the question were a reflection on Dr. Martineau, he replied with warmth, " No; he is not that kind of a man." The sermon was a disappointment; it was in no way equal to the author's published writings. It was on the

[1] A pleasant family hotel, then kept at No. 7 King's Street, Cheapside, by a retired Independent minister. — ED.

text, " As concerning this sect, we know that it is everywhere spoken against. " It was a defence of the Unitarian
denomination, and struck me as being strongly tinctured
with a kind of sophistry which a very ordinary man might
fall into in attempting to justify the existence of his
sect.

On the following Sunday we went, of course, to hear
Spurgeon.   I am sorry to say I have utterly forgotten both
his text and his discourse.   Like everybody else, we were
profoundly impressed by the vastness, the reverent attention,
and eager interest of the congregation.   The preacher impressed me, not by anything he said, but by the sustained
spirit and tone and easy energy with which every word was
uttered, and by his complete control of his audience.   The
discourse started in my mind a study of the preacher, which
was resumed on my return to London the following summer.
Shortly after this I made the acquaintance of Mr. Spurgeon
at a meeting of the London conference of Baptist ministers,
held in one of the larger rooms of the Tabernacle.   I was
seated next him at the collation which was usually served
at those meetings.   He was, of course, the central figure of
the occasion, and was called on for a speech.   What he then
said gave me a better idea of his versatility and the source
of his power than I received from any other one or all of the
sermons I heard from him.   I tried in vain during the supper to get him to talk about his theological college.   His
reply to my questions was, " I must refer you to my brother,
who knows all about it. "   A speech from " our American
brother" was, of course, called for.   The brief response consisted mainly in a defence of the Northern States for the part
they had taken in the great civil struggle through which we
had lately passed.   It was evident that not a few of the
company had no special sympathy with Northern sentiment.

The position of these English Baptists afforded a curious study for an intelligent Yankee. I am just here reminded of a remarkable misrepresentation made by some stupid person respecting this collation. I was not long ago accosted in the street by Rev. Justin D. Fulton, and inquired of about a dinner which had been given me in London, and at which there had been a copious supply of wines and liquors. He had, he said, a letter from some one whom he named who affirmed such a dinner to have been given. Dr. Fulton was specially anxious to know if wine was served at the collation above referred to. I could only assure him that I neither saw nor heard of anything stronger than water, tea, and coffee.

It was during this stay in London that I presented one of my letters of introduction. It was, so far as I can now recall, the only one of the many I carried which I used while abroad. It was addressed by Rev. Dr. Weston to Rev. Dr. Brock, a somewhat noted Baptist minister of that day in London. Soon after reading the letter, he stepped to his sideboard and asked which I would take, sherry or port. Declining both, we chatted awhile, and he proposed to call for me at my hotel on the following Monday, to take me to a public meeting of dissenting ministers, which had been called for some object, I now forget what. This was the only civility I received from Dr. Brock.

Of the London clergymen heard by us may be mentioned Dean Stanley at Westminster Abbey, whom I remember as following the beadle with his heels slipping up and down in over-large shoes, and as preaching in a drowsy and monotonous tone; and the once famous but then aged Dr. Melville, who preached in one of the chapels of St. Paul's a sermon which I was almost certain I had read among his printed discourses more than twenty years before. I recall also with great pleasure the delightful service we attended at the chapel of the Rev. Baptist Noel. The whole service, including the sermon, was refined in tone, truly Christian in thought, and winning in spirit. Of all the worshipping assemblies we saw in London, none could compare for apparent devoutness and intensity of interest with that of Father Machonochie at St. Alban's, High Holborn. It consisted to a very large degree of young men apparently from quite different classes of society. There was a baptism of infants during the service; I was amused at the skill of the good father in whipping over his stole, which was purple side up when he received the infant, to the white side at the instant of concluding the formula of baptism.

To any one accustomed, as we Americans are, to the complete effacement of down-town churches in our older cities, an interesting study is found in the parish churches which still survive in parts of old London, now almost exclusively occupied by business houses, — churches with rich endowments, well-salaried rectors or curates, but no parishioners. An intelligent and travelled physician of Queen's Street, Cheapside, told me he was the only gentleman resident in his parish. The curate, his personal friend, was required to hold a weekly evening service, provided there were any worshippers. The only person disposed sometimes to come to the service was one poor old woman, and she was hired to stay away.

Curiosity prompted me one week-day to go and partake of one of the famous fish-dinners at Billingsgate. I found myself in a spacious dining-hall, with clean sanded floor, a long table with a shorter one at the end, running at right angles. Standing at the angle was a sleek, clerical-looking personage, smooth-shaven, with a white cravat and a swallow-tailed coat, who snapped out a " grace," which served as a signal to the crowded guests to fall to and help themselves. I was seated at the end of the shorter table among older and much more substantial-looking men than were the majority of the diners. Four of my immediate neighbors soon discovered me to be a Yankee not long in England, and were not slow in plying me with questions about America and our terrible civil war. They began their dinner by each one ordering a glass of " 'alf and 'alf," a drink the nature of which they volunteered to explain to me. The dinner, which consisted of ten courses of variously cooked and different kinds of fish, was soon disposed of; but my four neighbors lingered long after the tables were cleared. Persistent in their inquiries about America, they remonstrated when I attempted two or three times to withdraw. Their potations amazed me, and I ventured to tell them that any one drinking in America as they had done would have been under the table. On leaving the hall, one of the four confided to me who they were; they were all intelligent and well-to-do men of the upper middle class. It was an odd afternoon's experience, and through it I got an idea of one sort of London life which could have been gained in no other way.

A snow-fall of some two inches in depth gave another amusing exhibition of London life. Cabmen demanded a pound for carrying one a distance for which they had previously charged but a shilling. The " Times " thundered away at the vestries for not shovelling up and carting away the snow. Such a snow would have excited no comment from either newspapers or pedestrians in New York or Boston.

From London we went to Paris, visiting Rouen, by the way, where we were well repaid by what we saw of provincial French life. Our stay in Paris was not protracted.

Reserving this city for a summer month, we hastened to Geneva, where we were to leave two of our children in the family of the distinguished historian, Merle D'Aubigné. From Geneva we proceeded directly to Italy. A single night's ride transferred us from a dismal evening snow-storm at Geneva to the bright and fragrant almond blossoms of Marseilles. The chill February air of Switzerland had been suddenly changed for the soft and soothing air of the Mediterranean. It was at Marseilles that we first saw stray glimpses of Oriental life. It was a queer sight to see customers served with milk from goats driven to their doors. The ancient city founded by Phœnicians, the earliest navigators and merchantmen of whom we have any definite knowledge, still abounded in Oriental scenes, notwithstanding all that France had done to modernize it. Our brief stay at Nice was among the pleasantest of our experiences; this place was at that time the terminus of the railway. The drive along the Corniche road brought us to Genoa. Here and at Pisa we saw what everybody sees. At Naples we employed for the first time, and also for the last, a guide to take us to such quarters as we described. He took us to one of the Neapolitan hotels, all of which were then recognized as disease-traps on account of bad drainage. He was evidently a hotel-runner. After being duly rated, he landed us at an excellent boarding-house on the second floor of a ducal palace which fronted on the famous Bay. A drive to Lake Avernus and the Sibyl's Cave, and to Baiæ, where we lunched on Lucrine oysters and Falernian wine, both execrable; a day at Pompeii and Herculaneum; drives to Puteoli, St. Paul's landing-place in Italy when on his way to Rome as a prisoner; to the extinct volcano of Solfatara, which then contented itself with innocent sulphurous smoke from unclosed crevices;

with frequent visits to various departments of the Museum,
filled up our two weeks' stay at Naples. I must not forget
to mention our visit to the famous Neapolitan Opera House,
and my first experience of an opera. One of the scenes
represented an eruption of Vesuvius, and the whole performance was to me imposing and impressive. The sudden
outburst of a stage-full of ballet-dancers in their gaudy
costume almost took my breath away. I had never before
seen the like. Our last glimpse of the real Vesuvius was
as we gazed back on it from the car-windows, and saw it
resting quietly under a mantle of snow.

On leaving Naples, we lost the only through train to
Rome. It was a Saturday afternoon, and we concluded to
go to modern Capua. Early Sunday morning we drove
to ancient Capua, two miles away, and there saw the uncovered substructions of the amphitheatre, of which the
Colosseum at Rome was a smaller copy. It seated one
hundred thousand people. The brick cells for wild animals,
surrounding the arena, were as complete and fresh-looking
as if less than ten years had passed over them. The vast
spaces occupied by the hundred thousand spectators were
then utilized as vegetable gardens. The few straggling and
forlorn-looking houses on the site of the once great city
suggested to the imagination a strange contrast with what
must have met the eyes of Hannibal and his victorious
soldiers during that winter of debauch which brought them
to ruin. Few of the thousands of travellers who rush through
Italy take the trouble of looking at old Capua.

The day before the carnival we reached Rome, where we
put in two months of as hard work as two vigorous people
could well endure. In the morning it was some ruin,
church, or picture-gallery, and usually in the afternoon St.
Peter's or the Vatican. Rome had not then become the

capital of Italy, and the whole city was filled with traces of mediæval Romanism. Priests and monks abounded. For the first time in my life I began to appreciate painting and sculpture. Michael Angelo's " Pietà " at St. Peter's disappointed me ; but his " Moses" at " St. Pietro in Vincoli " impressed me to a degree of awe while standing in its presence. For the study of the " Last Judgment " and the frescos of the Sistine Chapel, we had a quiet and undisturbed day. It is impossible to recount the vivid scenes recalled by memory of visits to the Mamertine Prison, to the Pantheon, to the Forum and the triumphal arches, to the ruins of the Palace of the Cæsars, to the Catacombs, to St. John Lateran, and to the Church of St. Clement. Around this last-named church we lingered with special interest, embodying as it does so much concrete illustration of ecclesiastical history. Itself below the level of the street, there is beneath it a complete church with beautiful marble pillars, erected doubtless in the ninth century ; and still beneath this are the remains of the oratory of St. Clement, without much doubt the Clement of Paul's epistle to the Romans.

We were with others introduced to Pope Pius IX. on one of his appointed days, and heard one of his fatherly addresses. We saw a good deal of his Holiness during Holy Week, which we diligently observed by daily visits to St. Peter's. On one occasion the Holy Father gave an amusing specimen of his unconsciousness of being observed by spectators. He was kneeling and praying near the head of the stairway which leads to the tomb of St. Peter. Resting in the midst of his devotions, and taking from his snuff-box a big pinch of snuff, he applied a huge red silk handkerchief to his nose with a report that sounded through the arches. He concluded the respite by clearing his throat with a loud " Ahem," and ejecting the contents of his mouth

in the direction of the stairway with an energy worthy of
a much younger man. The last we saw of the Holy Father
was when, from an elevated balcony in front of St. Peter's,
he sent forth his blessing upon the whole world, — a scene
which was impressive or otherwise, according to the faith
or imagination of the beholder.

One most enjoyable day was spent in witnessing a fox-
hunt on the Campagna. Many distinguished persons rode
out from Rome to witness the scene, among whom was the
famous actress, Charlotte Cushman, mounted on a very
English-looking bob-tailed nag. A profitable forenoon was
passed in visiting the gorgeously magnificent church of St.
Paul's without the walls, then just completed, — a memorial
of the Apostle on the supposed site of his martyrdom, but
with no surrounding population to worship in it. Another
day, now recalled with pleasant memories, was spent in a
drive to Ostia, where convicts under guard were uncovering
the ruins of an ancient temple, and in a return drive by way
of Pliny's Villa, where, in memory of his fondness for rose-
mary, which he specially mentions in one of his letters, we
obtained several sprigs of the plant and brought them back
to America.

In the growing warmth of April we bade adieu to Rome,
and turned our faces toward Florence, where the haunting
memories of Galileo and Savonarola marred the pleasure I
might otherwise have felt in its picture-galleries and splendid works of art. Space would fail me to tell what I saw,
thought, and felt on our way to Milan through the various
historic cities of Middle and Northern Italy. At Venice,
however, I may say we had the unexpected pleasure of
occupying one of the three thousand gondolas which were
massed together in the Grand Canal to welcome the arrival
of Victor Emmanuel on his visit to that city in May, 1867.

Our position in the immediate vicinity of his gondola gave us a fine view of his imposing and ill-favored Majesty. At Milan it was impossible to forget, whether within the cathedral or on its lofty height, the one great Church father, Ambrose, who, above all others that ever trod its streets, had made the city famous. I could say this, though standing in the presence of the imposing statue of Cavour, to whom is due the glory of having given to the Italians a united country. It was in Milan that an Italian gentleman congratulated me on the freedom of Americans, saying, "Here we are shackled by the domination of the priests over our women; they extract from our wives and daughters all our secrets, and tie us hand and foot, both politically and religiously." He had lived a good deal in England, and spoke English perfectly.

Our sail over the Italian lakes and our crossing of the Alps by way of the St. Bernard Pass were accomplished in the brightest of sunshine; but the ride by train down the Rhone from Brieg to Geneva, on the 3d of June, was through a snow-storm that would have graced a December day. .Vine-dressers in the vicinity of Geneva were in a panic on the following night, kindling great blazing fires in the vineyards to keep off the frost. The clergyman of the Anglican Church in Geneva preached a notable sermon the following Sunday, on the text, "Although the fig-tree shall not blossom, neither shall fruit be in the vines," etc. (Habakkuk iii. 11–18). A dismal frost on the 4th of June swept from Geneva to England, killing everything in its way, and in England blasting the apple-blossoms.

While we were in Geneva we were invited to take tea at Dr. Merle D'Aubigné's, or at Dr. Merle's, to employ the name by which he was usually called in Geneva. He came down from his library in a high state of mental exhilaration. He had just discovered that when Calvin was the guest of the Duchess of Ferrara, Titian, the great Venetian colorist, was there also, and was so moved by Calvin that he was on the verge of joining his fortunes with those of the reformers. The historian was in a most genial mood, but I learned very little from him of his work as a theological professor. He was too much engrossed with his historical studies to be much interested in anything else.

Lingering a week on our way from Geneva to Heidelberg, we remained at the latter place long enough to see and hear most of what was there attractive. I one day heard Rothe, then an old man whose lecture-room had once been thronged with hearers, lecturing to a class of thirteen, as ordinary-looking a set of young theologians as I had ever looked upon. A more complete absence of enthusiasm on the part of both lecturer and hearers could hardly be imagined. The professor rang endless changes on " das Absolut " throughout the lecture. I tried in vain to hear the then arch-heretic Schenkel. There were at that time in Heidelberg no brilliant stars either in theology or philosophy.

From Heidelberg we started for a July excursion through England and Scotland. Our route was by steamer down the Rhine. It was a German holiday; our steamer was overcrowded; hundreds stood at every stopping-place to rush on board; the vigilant officers of the boat would let on board only just so many as disembarked. We endured the crowd as long as we could, gladly quitting the steamer at Bonn. We had a pleasant stay at this old university town. While there we called on the commentator and theologian Lange, a typical German professor, diminutive in size, with an oval, benign face, genial in expression, who gave us a hearty greeting. He introduced his wife, whose very fingers bespoke the hard-working German housewife. His house showed plainly enough that he was not luxuriating on an over-large salary. From Bonn we made our way through Belgium and Holland, studying as diligently as we could the art of their galleries and churches.

Crossing the North Sea to London, our purpose was to go up one side of England and down the other. We accordingly proceeded without delay to Cambridge. I went, of course, on Sunday to worship in the old chapel made memorable by the ministry of Robert Hall in his palmiest days. It was a barn-like building, plain and unattractive. A very creditable sermon was preached by the Rev. Mr. Robinson, who was then its pastor, and whom I found to be both communicative and agreeable. It was vacation; none of the colleges were in session, and the professors whom I cared to see were out of town. The most that I could carry away with me from Cambridge were awakened memories of what I had read of its distinguished men in the past. Days spent in the cathedral towns of Ely and Peterborough aroused vivid thoughts of the differences between the England of to-day and the England of four or five centuries ago, when the cathedrals were erected, — piles of stone which no power short of the miraculous could erect to-day. Two or three days at Haworth, looking at its dirty village, the old historic church, the surrounding moors, gave an impression that no amount of reading could have given of the scenes amid which the brilliant genius of Charlotte Bronté found birth. We were not a little interested as well as amused at the garrulous communicativeness of the old landlady at the hotel, who was more than ready to tell us all she knew of the Bronté household.

Of an incident at Stirling, slight in itself, but of terrible possibilities, I still retain a vivid recollection. I had just been conversing with an American gentleman whom I had not seen since we parted in Italy; and in a fit of abstraction I was about stepping from the platform to cross the railway track, when a strong hand on my arm gave me a sudden arrest. It was that of a policeman, who saved me from stepping directly in front of an incoming train. A sight of the immediate peril escaped sent every nerve of my body into a quiver. I remained rather a silent man in that day's excursion. On returning the following day to the station and giving a suitable expression of gratitude to the policeman who had saved me, I was curiously questioned as to what I was rewarding him for, and first found courage to speak of my narrow escape.

What I saw at Melrose Abbey and felt at Abbotsford was only what everybody else sees and feels in visiting those localities. A visit to Dunblane, the seat and home of Archbishop Leighton, did not bring the satisfaction we expected. We saw his library, with its withered and worm-eaten bindings, carefully guarded in its locked and safely wired bookcase. His memory, so fragrant among the devout and studious, warrants more suggestive memorials of him than are furnished at Dunblane.

Two weeks at Edinburgh, in exalted apartments from which we had a fine view of the Firth of Forth, were filled with what are still the pleasantest of memories. At every turn in its streets we were reminded of the distinguished men who in former generations had walked them, and who by profound religious conviction, as well as by their philosophy, history, and fiction, had impressed and moved the whole English-speaking world. The spirit of Knox seemed still to pervade the atmosphere, though faintly; it was fast fading before the freer and less earnest though more enlightened spirit of our own day. Since the time of

Queen Mary and Knox, Hume, Adam Smith, Walter Scott, Sir William Hamilton, and others had contributed each his modicum of thought, out of which had sprung the Edinburgh of to-day, by no means now the epoch-breeding centre which it has so often been in the past. All that I saw of the great University of Edinburgh were its buildings and the interior of one of its chapels, where we attended a Sunday service.

From Edinburgh we made a memorable tour through the Trossachs, favored with most delightful weather and with full views of scenes made famous by the genius of Scott. Our stay at Glasgow awakened far less interest, and gave us far less satisfaction than our experience at Edinburgh. The first object seen by us from our hotel window was a drunken father led by a delicate little daughter across the public square. In fact, we saw more drunkenness in Glasgow in a single hour than we had seen in all our three months' stay in Italy. The squalor, drunkenness, and manifest signs of poverty and wretchedness, everywhere apparent, were a most intelligible commentary on the life of Chalmers, and his herculean efforts at charity organizations for the relief of misery among the lower classes. It was an amusing answer which I got from an intelligent Scotchman when I asked for an explanation of the abounding drunkenness everywhere visible: " Their unsubstantial diet of oatmeal," he said, " does not give them sufficient stamina to resist the intoxicating influence of even small drams. "

Content with what we had seen of the homes of Scotch metaphysics and Presbyterianism, and of Scottish writers of history and fiction, we betook ourselves to localities made famous by poets, both Scotch and English. With a jaunty dog-cart drive through Ayrshire to Dumfries, past the unpoetic Burns cottage, glancing at the ruins of the old kirk, at the " auld brig" over the bonnie Doon, we filled up the day, and freshened our memories of Burns and his poetry. Poor Burns, with his inimitable poetry, his gross life, and his sad ending, became to me a more real, living personality than he had ever been before. Delightful days were spent by us at Windermere. The days of the Lake poets had gone by; only the houses of those who had once made the place notable still remained. Rydal Mount, the home of Wordsworth, was to us the chief attraction. But I was disappointed in the unpoetic aspect of both itself and its surroundings. In contrast with the halo which my mind had thrown around the poet, the place had to me the appearance of being the home of a hard-minded and commonplace man. It was amusing to hear the old gardener speak of him as " a very near man," meaning by the Scotch term a man of penurious habits. A drive to Fox How warmed my heart anew toward the great teacher, Thomas Arnold, as I thought of the quiet enthusiasm with which he resorted hither to spend his vacations. A daughter graciously invited us in to look at a portrait of her father.

Chester, notwithstanding the great antiquity of the place and its Roman remains, failed to interest me, and we hastened on to Oxford. But, alas, it was vacation in this University town also, and we filled up our week's stay with daily visits to colleges, libraries, and whatever localities invited us and were open to inspection. We were told of an amusing instance of the antagonism then active between what was known as High Church and Broad Church. Merton College held its chapel exercises in what was also a parish church. The head of Merton was an extremist of the Broad; he would have only the baldest service permissible under the canon. The rector in all his services, Sundays and Saints' days, insisted on the use of all the ritual the canon allowed. One of the dreariest of services which I attended at Oxford was in a church then and for generations under the control of the Evangelical party of the Anglican Church. The sermon was but little above religious drivel; the congregation was small, and showed but little interest.

At Stratford-on-Avon, remembering what Hawthorne had written of Miss Bacon and her insanity while at work on her theory of the origin of the Shakespeare tragedies, we were interested in hearing from the person of whom she hired lodgings his account of her and her visits to the old church. At Kenilworth it was impossible for me, while looking at the ruins, to shake off the impressions made on me by Scott's novel, which I had read in the impressionable years of student-life.

It was a luxury to sit down in London for a day or two of rest after the hurried month of sight-seeing through England and Scotland. I spent one most profitable Sunday morning in going to Spurgeon's Tabernacle, not so much to hear him preach as to look at and study his congregation. An account of what I then saw I have furnished for Dr. H. L. Wayland's " Life of Mr. Spurgeon."[1] An afternoon in the

---

[1] [From Wayland's " Spurgeon," pp. 101-102.] Happening to be in London on a summer Sunday evening, I went to the Tabernacle, getting there designedly after the services had begun and with the purpose of looking at the audience from its rear. I looked in for a moment at the main entrance on the first floor, and then at the entrance on the second floor, where, from the junction of the great galleries, there was an imposing view of the vast throng of worshippers below; and then climbing a much narrower stairway, I went up to see what could be found above. On this third landing were two open doors, disclosing two triangular rooms, the base of the triangle opening wide toward the preacher, so that all in the rooms could have full view of him, and he a full view of them. Remote as these rooms were from the preacher (they covered the broad hallways of the first two floors), every word was distinctly audible. Every seat also was occupied, and apparently by young people employed in some kind of humble service. In a narrow

House of Commons offered little or nothing worth remembering except a study of the faces of Gladstone and Disraeli, as they sat near and opposite each other. An evening in the House of Lords was full of interest. The notables of both parties were present, — the then Earl of Derby, translator of Homer; the little sandy-haired Duke of Argyle; Lord John Russell, who had ceased to act with either party; Lord Stanley, the son and successor of the Earl of Derby; and others. There was an amusing discussion over the bequest of a certain Mr. Brown, who had bequeathed to the city of London some nineteen thousand pounds, to be available, after twenty years' accumulation, for establishing a hospital for sick animals. If the city of London declined to comply with the conditions of the bequest, it was to go to the University of Dublin. The twenty years had elapsed, and London was not complying with the conditions. The Bishop of Dublin made a very animated speech claiming the bequest for Dublin University. His Lordship was specially satirical in denouncing the scheme of a hospital for " sick dogs. "

We had arranged to spend the month of August in Paris for the study of the great city, its art, its churches, its historical localities, and its great exposition of 1867, then attracting to itself the attention of the world. We spent some pleasant hours there in re-reading Carlyle's " French Revolution," and in visiting the localities of scenes and occurrences so vividly described by him. We went, one Sunday morning, to a service at the French Baptist Mis-

aisle of one of the rooms stood one of the most forlorn and wretched-looking of human beings, a man in soiled and tattered clothes, with uncombed and matted hair, with a battered hat in his hand, unnoticed and unnoticing, but listening as if transfixed and nailed to the floor. It was the most touching sight I had ever seen in a house of worship. A more emphatic testimony to the preacher's power could not have been given. — E. G. R.

sion. The meeting was held in a small apartment, and baptism was administered in a decidedly novel manner. The candidate and administrator left the room where we were assembled, and passed through a door into an adjoining apartment. We saw nothing, but heard a voice and the splash of water. I was told, afterwards, that the candidate was immersed in a tub, the administrator standing outside of it. The impression made on me by all that I saw — the preacher, the assemblage, and the service — was that of a sad lack of good judgment and good taste. It was while in Paris that I first learned that Rev. J. G. Warren had been commissioned to see me about my becoming president of Brown University, and that he wished to know where we could meet for a conference. During our stay in Paris I preached several times in the American Chapel.

Leaving Paris, we made a dash into the Alps. Lucerne, Interlachen, Staubach, all left their impressions; but one red-letter day, hot and sultry in the valley, stands forth most vividly in my mind, — a day when, on the Wengern Alp, we had full view of successive avalanches from the Jungfrau, plunging and thundering into the abyss below. It was a most awe-inspiring spectacle. A cooling walk in the ice-cave at the foot of the Grindelwald glacier was a fitting conclusion to the day.

Early in September we were again at Heidelberg, on our way to Berlin, where I hoped to spend some months in study. We stopped at Munich, Leipsic, and Dresden. In the latter place we concentrated our attention on the art-galleries, and especially on the Sistine Madonna. No copyist and no engraver of that picture has ever yet succeeded in catching the Divine that looks out from the eyes of the babe. No photograph even speaks as does the original. Instead of the eight months' work at Berlin, which

I had looked forward to, I was limited to four by the necessity of answering the perplexing question suggested by the overtures of Brown University, — a question which could not be answered without returning home. Our leisure hours were diligently employed in the study of the language, guided by one of the best of instructors. Continuous study in connection with any one of the University professors did not seem to be the best use I could make of my time. I accordingly attended the lectures of those only who most attracted me, among whom I remember Hengstenberg, Dorner, and some of the younger and the less-known scholars. Hengstenberg, who drawled and bawled out his dictation from manuscripts conspicuously yellow with age, was one of the least inspiring lecturers I ever listened to, and his auditors gave as little indication of interest as I myself felt. Dorner's lecture-room was packed. He was at the height of his popularity. The students were anxious to catch every word. Any one making the least noise, by entrance or otherwise, was hissed. His quiet manner was in sharp contrast with the noisy restlessness of Hengstenberg. I remember spending one specially pleasant evening at Dr. Dorner's house, attending a meeting of a theological *Societät*, a small body of picked men, of whom Professor Briggs[1] was one. It was he who introduced me to Dr. Dorner. A few days after, Dr. Dorner called on me; we indulged in rather a wide range of conversation, touching on various theological questions in both their German and their American phases. There was little to choose between his broken English and my broken German. I recall also one delightful evening spent at the tea-table of Professor Piper, who had been an admiring pupil of Neander, and

---

[1] At this writing there is only one "Professor Briggs," — Charles A. Briggs, D. D., of Union Theological Seminary, New York. — ED.

was giving his chief attention to *Monumentale Théologie* and to the editing of a highly prized Almanac. Professor Piper was a bachelor, keeping house with an elderly maiden sister. We sat down at the tea-table a little past six in the evening, and left it at eleven. He was a most entertaining conversationalist, and was quite out of patience with me for not being eagerly desirous of visiting the Holy Land. He amazed me by his familiarity with the history of our government, repeating, without hesitation, the whole list of our presidents from Washington down to date. I have also a very distinct remembrance of an evening spent at a meeting of a theological debating society, where I was both amused and instructed by the German methods of doing things. The society consisted of the most brilliant and promising young men of the University, among them sons of Dr. Dorner, Professor Ranke, the historian, and other distinguished professors. The meeting was held in one of the rooms of a restaurant, which was a common resort of students. The members were seated alongside of dining-tables, and each one had his huge glass of beer before him. A paper was read, by one who appeared to be the youngest member of the club, on the doctrine of the Trinity, as taught in the Old Testament. The essayist stated and defended, with much skill and scholarship, the old orthodox position, which evidently did not command the assent of a majority of his hearers. A fellow-student, who was the appointed critic of the essay, had not half finished his first sentence when I was quite startled out of my gravity by a sudden and, to me, unexplained outcry from the whole assemblage. The critic, it seemed, was attempting to read from a manuscript in his possession. The rule was that the criticism should be strictly extemporaneous.

We had a novel experience in the celebration of our

American Thanksgiving, which was presided over by our American minister, Mr. Bancroft, and at which certain government officials assisted. Mr. Bancroft, in his introductory speech at the banquet, indulged indiscriminately in English and German, throwing in paragraphs of either language as the fancy struck him. It had been my fate to preach in the morning, at the American Chapel, a Thanksgiving sermon, after the true American style. We were all loyal to forefathers' custom in observing the annual festival. During our stay in Berlin the American Church dedicated a new house of worship. I was waited upon by Mr. Theodore Fay, formerly American minister to the Helvetian Republic, as chairman of a committee to invite me to preach the dedication sermon. But having given the invitation, he added, " Knowing you to be a Baptist, it is no more than just to say that at the close of the dedication we propose to celebrate the Lord's Supper, to which we are to invite all Christian people of whatever church, and even members of no church, if devoutly Christian. " To accept the invitation would place me in an awkward predicament, and, of course, I declined it, and did not attend the dedication service.

The urgency of friends at Brown University, and the still greater urgency of friends at Rochester that I should not leave the Seminary, made an earlier return home imperative. We accordingly turned our faces homeward. In Halle we enjoyed a Sunday evening reception at Dr. Tholuck's. Both he and Madame Tholuck were in their happiest moods. Much had been said in the newspapers about his coming to America to attend the Evangelical Alliance to be held in the following year. At his expression of a wish to come, Madame Tholuck, patting him on the shoulder, said softly, " Nein, nein ; " whereupon he laughingly added, " I am too much afraid of your democracy and your hot cakes. " That Sunday morning had opened with the most dismal of drenching rains; but before daylight we were awakened by a chorus of sweet male voices under our windows. Boys and young men from the Francke Orphan House, on their way to church, were singing their Advent carols. They were interesting to see as well as to hear, as they stood ranged along the curbstone in their " stove-pipe " hats, unprotected from the pouring rain. In the afternoon, when the sun came out, we went to a service in the old church where Tholuck had once preached famous sermons to thronging congregations. Sitting amid the meagre assemblage, I tried in vain to bring back in imagination the great preacher and entranced audience of which I had once read glowing accounts. I heard nothing from German pulpits corresponding, in any degree, to what I had read of the preaching of Schleiermacher and Tholuck.

At Cologne we, of course, filled our minds with all we could drink in of its great cathedral. It was our second visit to it, and the last that we were to see of the great cathedrals of Europe. We hastened to London, picked up the traps we had left there, and on Christmas day, just one year from the day of our landing, we sailed from Liverpool for America. The sixteen horrible stormy days of that passage home will never be forgotten.

On reaching Rochester I hastened to Providence in response to the invitation of friends of Brown University; and in spite of all that they could say in behalf of my taking the presidency, the conviction became clear and settled that duty required me to continue my connection with the Rochester Seminary. The very considerable amounts promised the Seminary would be likely to be lost by my withdrawal from it. Its friends had also given me a year of rest, and justice seemed to me to require that I should continue in its service. The decision to remain gave me a most welcome quiet of mind.

Finding myself back again in Rochester about the middle of January, 1868, with a clear conscience as to duty, I settled down to my work with the zest natural to a man whose appetite had been whetted by long abstinence. With the class graduating in 1867, and up to that time with the class of 1868, my instruction had been fragmentary, and to me, as of course it must have been to them, far from satisfactory. Theology as a department of knowledge never seemed to me more attractive than it did then, and I think I never saw more clearly the relation of its great doctrines to one another, or more need of a thorough grounding of religious teaching in a theology which should be both scriptural and philosophical. One abiding impression left on me in my European and particularly in my English observations was the inestimable value to a preacher of the gospel of a comprehensive theological training such as was furnished in our theological schools, and was not then furnished in any of the ministerial training-schools of England. The superiority of the average well-trained American preacher to the average English preacher was quickly discernible to any impartial observer. I felt a sort of divine call to persist in theological teaching.

When I came back, we had a broken faculty. During this year there was almost no working force. Professor Northrup had resigned the chair of Ecclesiastical History during my absence, to accept the chair of Systematic Theology in the Baptist Union Theological Seminary at Chicago. Hebrew was taught by the Rev. J. H. Gilmore, pastor of the Second Baptist Church in Rochester; New Testament Exegesis was in the thoroughly equipped hands of Dr. Kendrick;

the chair of Ecclesiastical History was vacant. The Seminary was, in fact, but little more than half manned in its teaching force. But before we could venture to fill vacancies, long strides needed to be taken toward completing an endowment. It seemed insane to invite professors, with no money to pay their salaries. Guardians and friends of the Seminary saw and felt the need of immediate action. John B. Trevor, Esq., of Yonkers, New York, came to our rescue in furnishing the means for a local habitation. The lot at the corner of East Avenue and Alexander Street was purchased, and steps were taken for the immediate erection of Trevor Hall, — a hall which, when completed in the following autumn, furnished dormitories for students, and rooms in which, though contracted, lectures were given. A fresh start was thus made, and contributions toward an endowment were more rapidly secured. This same spring Jacob F. Wycoff, Esq., of New York, came forward, and generously purchased a house to be occupied by the president of the Seminary, whose salary, also, the trustees had spontaneously raised to $4000. The purchase of this house proved unfortunate. Though sold by its owner at what he claimed to be considerably less than its value, a most desirable house, and on one of the choice streets of the city, it proved, through violation of every principle of sanitary drainage, a perfect malarial trap. A liability to malarial attacks, from which I had suffered before going abroad, now returned with redoubled frequency and force. The recurrence of these attacks seemed inexplicably mysterious until a too late discovery of the defective drainage. This aggravation of a long-settled disorder resulted in finally driving me from Rochester.

In the summer of 1868 it became imperatively necessary that steps should be taken toward filling vacant chairs in the faculty of the Seminary. Our most urgent need was an occupant for the chair of Hebrew; but where to find him was a question which brought back only an empty echo. I betook myself to Dr. Hackett at Newton Centre for his advice as to the fittest young man for the vacancy. He recommended as one among the fittest of his former scholars, Mr. George H. Whittemore, a gentleman of fine culture, a critical scholar, and a most painstaking teacher. He was still one of the members of the faculty when my connection with the Seminary ceased.

Entering our new home, Trevor Hall, with the opening of the session in the autumn of 1868, every one of us, instructors and students alike, felt ourselves called to fresh activity. For the first time in my Rochester experience the Seminary seemed to have a future. We got the Neander Library into a shape in which it would be available for daily use. We began to receive new books, for the importation of which I had made arrangements while abroad in 1867. The session of 1868–69 stands conspicuous, in memory, as one of the pleasantest and most encouraging of all my Rochester experience. It was the faint beginning in the realization of hopes long cherished, toiled for, and patiently awaited.

But the time had then come for prompt and vigorous efforts to secure the funds conditionally promised and before alluded to. The efforts were happily successful. We were then in a condition to fill the vacant chair of Church History. We were not long in finding a man for it in the person of Rev. Dr. R. J. W. Buckland, then pastor of the church in New York City, since made famous as the Calvary Baptist Church, under the ministrations of the Rev. Dr. MacArthur. In connection, however, with the election of Dr. Buckland, which had been greatly desired by friends who knew his worth, an addition to our endowment of

$20,000, on which I had confidently calculated, was lost to us through the inexperience and maladroitness of one of the Seminary's functionaries.

With a growing endowment there was also a growing desire to add to our Faculty men of the highest qualifications and repute. The full time and strength of my dear friend, Dr. Kendrick, whose New Testament expositions had been invaluable to us, were then urgently needed in the duties of his University chair. A renewed application to enter the service of the Seminary was accordingly made to the Rev. Dr. Hackett, who had previously resigned his position at Newton Theological Institution. To this proposition he assented, joining us in the beginning of the session of 1870. His coming gave new impetus to us all. Every student in the Seminary was anxious to be under his instruction. It was accordingly arranged that on certain days the whole Seminary should be brought together in the chapel for the study of the First Epistle of John, — an epistle which, on account of its difficulties, he said that through all his long experience he had hitherto abstained from teaching. The Professor himself, according to his own admission, was never happier in his work, or taught, as we know, with more complete satisfaction to his pupils.

It was during the session beginning in 1870 that I first felt at liberty to attempt anything in the way of post-graduate instruction. Four of our alumni, three of whom have since made a reputation for themselves as professors, avowed their desire to form a class for graduate study.[1] The only time alike possible for me and acceptable to them was the evening. We accordingly met evenings, in my study, beginning work as early as practicable after seven

[1] The names of these students are given in the contribution of Professor True. — Ed.

o'clock, and separating rarely, if ever, before eleven. Papers were presented by members of the class, on which free, full, and critical discussion followed.

No year of my Rochester life had, to myself, been equally satisfactory with this, and I think none had been more profitable to the students. The need for outside work in behalf of the Seminary had been greatly lessened, and there was the long-wished-for opportunity for a more full statement and defence of my own theological views. To the work of this statement and defence my last two years at Rochester were earnestly given;[1] and they were years which, on the whole, I am disposed to regard as the best of my life as an instructor; but they were years overshadowed by clouds of ever-recurring illness. Attacks came, often most inopportunely, making the fulfilment of engagements impracticable. A malarial affection had become so deep-seated as to resist all medical treatment, and to make uninterrupted labor impossible. The outlook for continued life in Rochester was of the dismallest.

---

[1] The revised statement was printed as far as half-way through the doctrine of Regeneration, and the printed sheets stored in the library of the Seminary. Since the death of Dr. Robinson Professor B. O. True, D. D., has compiled the remaining lectures from the notes of earlier classes, and the whole has been published by Mr. E. R. Andrews, of Rochester. — ED.

CHAPTER V.

PRESIDENCY OF BROWN.

1872-1889.

IN the spring of 1871 there came again a proposal that I should accept the presidency of Brown University. The proposal was not an enticing one. The duties of a college president were far from attractive to me. The change involved what seemed to me a descent to a lower and less useful sphere of labor. But the prospect of relief from malarial affections by a return to the climate in which I had been born and bred, had its weight. An immediate decision was impossible; my mind hung in suspense over the question of duty. In the summer of 1871 a committee, consisting of members of the Corporation of the University, followed me to the White Mountains, whither I had gone for recreation. They reasoned skilfully. Two of that committee, Dr. S. L. Caldwell and Dr. Heman Lincoln, have passed away. Dr. Hovey, the third member of the committee, still lives [July, 1893]. The summer ended without a decision. In the early winter the late Gardiner Colby, one of the University Trustees, desiring to try his hand at argument, invited me to meet him at the Delavan House in Albany, New York. I still remained in doubt as to what I ought to do; but a variety of considerations finally brought me to a decision. Funds long promised for the endowment of the Seminary had been secured. It was on a safe pecuniary foundation, and its future was assured. Nothing would be perilled by my leaving it. On the other hand, regard for health, obligation as an alumnus of the University to go to its aid in the hour of its need, whispered suggestions of unsoundness in my teachings, the moral certainty of a coming revolution in theologic thought, — all combined to bring me to the conclusion that I ought not to refuse acceptance of the unwelcome call. If I had foreseen the pain which my decision would give to the friends of the Seminary, and especially to my old teacher, and at that time my colleague, Rev. Dr. Hackett,[1] it would have been reached, if at all, even more reluctantly than it was. But the die was cast, and in August, 1872, my back was turned on the scene of more than nineteen years earnest and sometimes most exhausting labor. A three weeks' drive with a span of spirited horses from Rochester to Providence, across the States of New York, Pennsylvania, Connecticut, and Rhode Island, gave a most welcome opportunity for a needed and inspiring recreation. It also gave me a much better idea than I ever before possessed of the rural portions and populations of those States.

I found the University in a much less promising condition than I had hoped. The lack of enterprise on the part both of its governing Board and its Faculty gave me a most dispiriting impression. I could think of nothing but a heavily loaded team stalled in the mud. The Corporation was radically divided into two opposing parties, irreconcilable in aims and methods, and mutually jealous. It was no easy task to unite them on any single line of action. A bitter antagonism which had been developed a few years previously between an existing Executive Committee and the Corporation had resulted in the abolition of the committee. A forward step in any direction was accordingly impossible

---

[1] For Dr. Hackett's tribute, see Note D. at end of this chapter.

during the interval between one annual meeting of the
Corporation and another. My immediate predecessor in
the presidency, one of the most amiable and estimable of
men, from his long previous connection with the University
as professor was profoundly interested in its welfare; but
knowing that he held the office only temporarily, he did not
feel it his duty to take the initiative in any onward movement. In fact, the lethargy of the governing Boards gave
little promise of success, had he attempted it.

But whatever the lack of animation in the past on the
part of the authorities of the College, there was a sudden
disclosure of life and liveliness on the part of the students
which opened my eyes to an unexpected phase of the duties
of my new office. My experience up to this time had been
among students who had required no discipline and no over-
sight. The disclosure came on this wise: On going one
day into chapel for morning prayers, I noticed considerable
numbers of the students lingering in front of the chapel,
instead of immediately entering it, as was their custom.
I was too inexperienced to see any meaning in their delay.
But when the bell had ceased its tolling, and the chapel door
was closed, I was surprised to find only a portion of the
Senior class, and fewer still of the Juniors in their places,
while the seats of the Sophomore and Freshman classes were
almost wholly empty. The reading of Scripture was hardly
begun when loud shouts were heard outside, and immediately the clamor and tramp of rushing students filled the
air. Before the conclusion of the exercises the uproar had
died away into a distant murmur. But on leaving the
chapel a most comical scene met the eye. Under a steadily
falling rain the ground was covered with text-books, note-
books, coats, hats, waistcoats, fragments of shirts and flan-
nels, while from the lower end of the campus came two or

three bareheaded, half-stripped Sophomores, bearing in triumph the offending cane. Amid shouts by the victors, the discomfited Freshmen went about silently picking up their belongings as they could find them. This "cane-rush" was only one of a series of regular, or rather irregular, escapades to which the students, under the extreme leniency of my immediate official predecessor, had become accustomed. Cane-rushes at any hour of the day or evening, nightly bonfires with horn-blowing, an occasional hazing of a green Freshman, were established amusements. It was evident that the College was to be ruled by disorderly men, or there must be an immediate reform. How to effect this was a puzzle. Private remonstrance and appeals to a sense of honor and right feeling availed nothing. Suspensions and other penalties excited resentment as an unwarranted restriction of student-rights. A long-established practice of mock programmes at the Junior Exhibition reached a stage of indecency and blasphemy. Drastic measures became a necessity. In due time a healthier tone prevailed; and years before my withdrawal from office a more quiet and orderly body of students could not be desired.[1]

I found the range of instruction at the University narrower than that of most of the New England colleges. Its

---

[1] As to Dr. Robinson's methods as a disciplinarian, a member of the class of 1876 writes: "He aimed to do away with that state of affairs which made any extended discipline necessary. He tried from the very beginning to get into the students' minds that hazing and disorder of any kind was unworthy of them; and in this he was supported by my class, his first Freshman class, who in their Sophomore year simply refused in any way to annoy the Freshman class, and thus did what they could to abolish all remaining relics of barbarism in Brown University. After Dr. Robinson had been at Brown a few years, the whole tone of the college life in these respects, as well as in study and work, greatly improved. He frequently alludes to this himself in his Reports to the Corporation from 1878 on, especially in the last, that for 1889." — A. G. L.

only professorships in Natural Science were those of Chemistry and of Physics; under the latter term was included instruction in Light, Heat, and Electricity. It had no professorship of Modern Languages, instruction in French being given by a gentleman employed to teach it to the Sophomores a portion of the year. He found it extremely difficult to keep order in his class, and his instruction, accordingly, resulted only in an extremely imperfect knowledge of the language. German was taught to the Seniors as an elective by the senior professor of Latin. The only instruction in Geology was given in a brief course of lectures by the professor of Chemistry. The professor of Physics was saddled with the duty of teaching Physiology, a combination of duties more amusing than reasonable; and the professor of Rhetoric, who alone was responsible for all the instruction given in the English Language and Literature, had the additional load laid on him of teaching Logic. Any change in this distribution of duties seemed at the outset almost impossible.

The lack of professorships in the Faculty was more than equalled by the lack of buildings in which the work of the University could be properly performed. The professor of Physics had no laboratory; the damp, dark basement rooms of Rhode Island Hall, which he attempted to utilize as a laboratory, could be occupied by him only at the risk of his health and life. The apparatus which should have been at his command he had found scattered about, and much of it, from long neglect, scarcely fitted for use. He was discouraged, and talked seriously to me of resigning his professorship. The library was crowded into the dark room on the first floor of the chapel building, and was so crammed with books, two or three feet deep on the shelves, that only the librarian could find what was wanted. There were only two dormitories; and the rooms of these, to any young man coming from a well-furnished home, were uninviting and even repulsive. He could have but a single room, not over fifteen feet square, in which to sleep and to study; and ordinarily two were expected to occupy it. The older of the two buildings had been used as barracks for French soldiers at one time during our Revolutionary War. Its battered doors, its defaced walls, the gaping flooring of its hall-ways, and the unmistakable odor of decay pervading the building, made parents who came to select rooms for their sons, turn from the premises with ill-concealed disgust. The other dormitory, erected in 1822, had inside and out fewer marks of age, but was only a little less uninviting than the older building. The entries and stairways of the dormitories had never been lighted at night; students groped their way up and down as best they could. The introduction of gas was regarded by some of them as a curtailment of their nocturnal privileges; and when the mayor, at my solicitation, planted lamp-posts along the walks of the campus, there were grave discussions whether this was not an invasion of rights that should be resisted. When told that any one meddling with the lamps would be dealt with by the city authorities, they inquired of the mayor if this was true. His short, sharp, decisive answer gave them immediate pause, and not a lamp was ever meddled with. I may add here that the front campus was a mere hay-field, mowed once a year, just before Commencement Day. The grading of this campus and the introduction of the lawn-mower were regarded with a favor more than equal to the disfavor first felt toward the lamp-posts. The middle and the back campus were used as a cowpasture.

The University, after more than a century of its

existence, had for its work, all told, only five buildings: two dormitories, the chemical laboratory, the chapel building, and Rhode Island Hall, which had originally been erected as a chemical laboratory, but had been converted into recitation-rooms and a hall for portraits. Out of all the recitation-rooms three only could be regarded as even tolerably fitted to their uses, — two in Rhode Island Hall, and one on the second floor of the Chemical Laboratory.

There was, however, one encouraging feature in the aspect of the University's affairs, — it had a surplus income. The financial report of the year preceding my entrance on my duties showed a net balance of four thousand dollars. The University had been run on principles as strictly economic as any cotton-mill in the State of Rhode Island. The use that could be made of this surplus required no long deliberation. The provision of a laboratory for the professor of Physics was an imperative necessity. To meet this necessity an addition to Rhode Island Hall was proposed, and, after some urging, was accomplished. The slowness of movement in this and in immediately subsequent steps could be easily understood by any one who knew the composition of the Executive Committee, through whom the initiative was necessarily taken. The four leading men of that committee were past seventy years of age, and could not readily see why the University should not go on as it had been for a long time doing. More than once I have seen one or another of those elderly gentlemen during the committee meetings struggling hard with drooping eyelids to keep himself from nodding an involuntary assent to what was said.

The little physical laboratory was immediately recognized as a decided improvement, and gave me encouragement to believe that something further might be attempted. There were two wants which were an obvious discredit to a University of a hundred years' standing, — a deplorable need of new departments of instruction and new professorships, and an equally urgent need of new buildings for the use of these. Which of these deficiencies to remedy first was a question not easily answered. Neither one of them could wait till the other should be supplied. We were stifled and cramped for lack of buildings, and I was ashamed of the narrow range of studies open to our students, particularly in the Natural Sciences and in Modern Languages. The necessity was inexorable that we should strike at once for a widened curriculum and for new buildings. Fortunately, when the question was in suspense whether I would accept the presidency of the University, Mr. H. N. Slater, Sr., a member of the Board of Fellows, and one of the most liberal benefactors which the University had had up to that date, sent me word that, if I would accept the office, he would give twenty-five thousand dollars to be applied in such way as might be deemed best for the interests of the College. With his consent, this money, with its accumulated interest, was used in the erection of a dormitory, since known as Slater Hall, in which were suites of rooms in keeping with modern modes of living.

Mr. John Carter Brown, at his decease, had bequeathed fifty thousand dollars and a valuable plot of ground adjacent to the college premises for the erection of a Library Building. As soon as a cloud on the title of the ground, which Mr. Brown himself was intending to remove, had been lifted, and the sum bequeathed had become sufficient to warrant it, three architects were invited to prepare competitive plans. After mature deliberation, the walls of a new fire-proof home for the library began slowly to arise. The day on which the beautiful and commodious building was dedicated to its uses was one of great rejoicing to all friends of the University. The general satisfaction was enhanced by the announcement that the entire balance of the cost of erection had been generously provided for by Mrs. Brown, the widow of the donor. The books were now well housed, but professors and students were still suffering in ill-ventilated and incommodious lecture-rooms.

At this juncture Mr. William F. Sayles came to our rescue. His oldest son, a promising youth of manly spirit and bearing, a student in the University, had been suddenly stricken with an affection of the lungs, and, after a rapid decline, had passed away. His parents were overwhelmed with grief. Wishing to perpetuate their son's memory, his father proposed the erection of some kind of memorial to him on the college grounds. It required but short deliberation to determine the form the memorial should take. It was decided to erect a building of sufficient dimensions to contain a hall for alumni dinners on Commencement occasions, and some half-dozen lecture-rooms. Sayles Hall was a worthy monument to a worthy son. It was, still is, and bids fair long to be, architecturally the most satisfactory of all the University buildings. The solidity of the structure, its fine proportions and severe simplicity, along with the thorough sincerity of every inch of its masonry and carpenter work, insure its beauty and soundness for centuries to come. To the lasting credit of Mr. Sayles be it said, that, when the site for the Hall was selected, he foresaw the necessity of regrading the middle campus on which it was to front, and in his own mind he determined it should be done. Till then it had presented to the eye on its northern side, toward Waterman Street, an ungrassed and unsightly bank, and over the whole area its uneven surface reminded one of the recent days when it had been used as a cowpasture. On the completion of the building, Mr. Sayles insisted that the campus should then be graded and put in order. The result was one of the most beautiful spots in the city of Providence.

While in the humor of grading the middle campus, it occurred to some of us that, by the requisite grading and filling up of an unsightly swamp-hole, the eastern slope and terminus of the college land on Thayer Street could be transformed into much needed ball-grounds. The only perplexing question in the case was how to raise the necessary funds. One man only in the Faculty, Professor S. S. Greene, felt interest enough in the matter to give himself and his time to raising the money and superintending the work. Quietly, and without words, he took the work in hand, and persisted in it till the task was completed. It was a laborious undertaking, and to Professor Greene alone belonged all the credit of its successful accomplishment.

There still remained the old University Hall, both within and without an eyesore and a reproach. The grave question was, What should be done with it? The loud demand of many friends of the College was to level it to the ground, and to put up a modern structure in its place. A few of us were equally earnest in insisting that the old walls should stand, and the interior be entirely renewed. Minutest inspection could discover not so much as the sign of a crack in its walls. Renovation was resolved on, but the perplexing question was how to raise funds for the purpose. Fifty thousand dollars was the least it could be done for. The late Chief Justice Bradley was made chairman of the committee to superintend the renovation, and the fifty thousand dollars were soon raised by subscription. Few improvements made during my connection with the University gave more general satisfaction.

Some two or three years before this I had been waited on by a gentleman who desired a private interview. When quietly seated in my study, he pulled from his pocket a schedule of property which he estimated to be worth sixteen hundred thousand dollars. He said he would like to read to me portions of a will which he had had drawn up. The will bequeathed the sum of two hundred and fifty thousand dollars to Brown University, to be devoted in some way to scientific instruction. But there were other items in the will which I felt sure would prevent its getting through the Probate Court, and with all frankness I so told my friend. But he assured me the will had been so drawn it could not be broken. When he died, a wholly different will was offered for probate. Instead of two hundred fifty thousand, there had been left to Brown University a legacy of one hundred thousand dollars. Not all the causes of the change were disclosed, but in my own mind I was sure that one cause, by no means slight, was the fear, on reflection, that the aforesaid objectionable items of the will would result in breaking it. But there was a second and well-known cause. With the changed purpose a lawyer in Boston had been employed to draw up a new will. This lawyer, a graduate of Dartmouth College, told Mr. Wilson that two hundred and fifty thousand dollars was too large a sum to be given to so small a college as Brown University; that one hundred thousand dollars would suffice, and that he would better give fifty thousand to Dartmouth College for a Library Building. With the consent of Mr. Wilson's son, which the will required should be secured, the legacy was devoted to the erection of a Physical Laboratory to be known as Wilson Hall. Through a series of maladjustments and mistakes of the architect, Wilson Hall had risen no farther than its first story when I resigned my place at the University. From the facilities which the Laboratory should afford in the study of applied science, there were large expectations of increased attendance of students. It was a discredit to the University, on which I had for years been harping, that, as the only institution in a State wholly devoted to manufactures, it offered little or no aid to young men whose pursuits were to be outside the learned professions. A long-felt necessity of widening its courses of study was now to be supplied. The much-talked-of gymnasium was necessarily deferred. Subscriptions for the requisite funds came slowly. Mr. Lyman's bequest completed the needful amount, and the building was erected after I left. During my last Commencement dinner, in a conversation with Governor Ladd, who sat by my side, he authorized me to announce to the alumni that he would erect for the University an Astronomical Observatory. This ended my efforts to provide the University with its necessary buildings.

But while we had been earnestly striving for more and better accommodations, we had not been idle in striving also to increase our teaching force, and to enlarge our curriculum. It had become evident to me, soon after coming to the University, that several new professorships would have to be created. One of these was a professorship of Modern Languages; another, a professorship of Physiology and Hygiene; a third, a professorship of Geology and Paleontology; and a fourth, a professorship of Astronomy. A fifth professorship, that of Botany, was provided for by bequest of Mr. Olney, whose name the professorship now bears. Political Economy, which had been taught by the professor of History, was also made a special department, and, with a view to a future professorship, an instructor was appointed to teach it. A partial endowment of a chair of Natural Theology was slowly accumulating to a point at which interest enough could be derived from it to pay the salary of a professor. But how to provide salaries for the new professors was a most difficult problem. I proposed that the tuition fees of students should be raised from seventy-five to one hundred dollars.[1] A committee had this proposition under consideration for a year, and reported on it adversely. Meanwhile our invested funds from one source and another had been increasing, and I renewed with success the proposition to increase the price of tuition.

With the new professorship of Modern Languages came a new interest in the study of the spoken tongues of Europe. As elective studies, they perceptibly lessened the numbers who elected the classics, particularly the Latin. With the creation of the other professorships, there was throughout the College a manifest increase in the number of those who selected one or another of the branches of Natural Science. It was in the Natural Sciences that the University was most conspicuously deficient. But a start was made in the right direction, though somewhat to the discomfiture of the older members of the Faculty, who strenuously defended the old curriculum.

The progress thus made in buildings and in professorships is easily told, and to an outside observer it seemed to be of easy accomplishment; but the expenditure of time and thought in determining sites, style of architecture, interior arrangements, the procuring of necessary funds, the overcoming of prejudices, both inside the College and outside, so as to have everything move smoothly, formed a burden known only to him who had it to bear. The burden was all the heavier from the indifference of one or two of the older

---

[1] Dr. Robinson's annual reports to the Corporation are models of luminous and persuasive statement, and show how progressive and how sagacious was his policy from the first. — ED.

members of the Corporation. One especially, always most obtrusively active in the deliberations of the Corporation, was not only indifferent, but opposed to some of the most needed improvements. He could not see why the old rooms in University Hall should not continue, without change, to be occupied by students as they had been in past generations; nor could he see why the middle campus should be made sightly to the eye. For neither of these objects did he lift a finger or give a penny. It is a matter of grateful remembrance that, when the improvements were completed, every one was loud in expressions of approval.

The introduction of new departments of study and of new professors made necessary a readjustment of studies and a multiplication of electives. Naturally there was a jostling of old hereditary prejudices in behalf of certain studies which from time immemorial had taken precedence of all others. But science then got a foothold in the curriculum which it is never likely to lose. This wider opening of the doors of the University to the admission of the sciences pure and applied, made possible the rapid expansion and multiplication of courses of study which have since been so successfully achieved by my large-minded and enthusiastic successor.

A few years before the close of my connection with the University, a further advance was made in our course of study, in spite of a very strong opposition on the part of certain members of the Faculty. The strength of feeling against it, and against myself for proposing it, was a great and very unpleasant surprise to me. I had proposed a two years' course of study for graduates who were desirous to offer themselves as candidates for the degree of Doctor of Philosophy; and I had obtained from the Board of Fellows authority to institute such a course. It had been decided some years before to discontinue the practice handed down from time immemorial of conferring the degree of " A. M. " in course upon graduates of three years' standing, who might choose, on payment of a fee, to apply for it. The degree was supposed to be conferred on students who had been during the three years engaged in some regular course of study; and in the earlier days, when every student, immediately after graduation, entered a school of law, theology, or medicine, the degree was not unworthily conferred. But when men came to apply for it who had been engaged in no study, professional or other, the degree was in danger of losing all its significance. It was accordingly determined that, after a certain date, the degree should no longer be con-ferred " in course," but only after examination on a required number of studies. So that, when the time came for confer-ring the degree on this new basis, it seemed to me a fit thing to add to its requirements such further length and breadth of study as should warrant us in offering also the degree of Doctor of Philosophy. To this proposal, much to my surprise, two of the senior professors strenuously objected. The senior professor of Latin, an elegant scholar, and a deservedly popular teacher, thought the Faculty was already doing all that could be expected of them, and ought not to be burdened with additional work. The senior professor of Greek, along with this objection, also thought the degree would be cheapened if conferred on any such course of study as we could offer. These grounds of objection seemed to me insufficient. Of the other older professors, some approved and some stood aloof in apparent indifference. Most of the younger members of the Faculty assured me privately and confidentially of their entire sympathy with the proposal, and their readiness to do anything in their power to carry it into effect. The professor of History and Political Economy, afterwards my successor in the office of President, openly and emphatically avowed his readiness to furnish his quota of the requisite instruction. The plan was carried into execution, and to the course prescribed for the degree of A. M. another was added for the degree of Ph. D. The first [1] to receive this last-named degree, after an extended and thorough course of reading chiefly in Philosophy, was subjected to a written examination extending through parts of three days, after which he read to the Faculty a carefully prepared thesis. It was to me amusing that not a criticism nor a question was ventured on the thesis; but it was unanimously voted that the degree should be conferred. This closed what had been to me an unpleasant episode; but it was a new and important departure for Brown University, and has since become, under President Andrews, a noteworthy department of university instruction.

A change was also wrought during my connection with the University in the composition and temper of its governing Boards. As already intimated, these Boards were divided into two strongly marked and often bitterly antagonizing parties. The origin and grounds of the division were obscure; but this much was plain: during the closing years of the administration of President Wayland, a certain member of the Board of Trustees, who had been eager to be prominent in the counsels of the governing Boards, was obliged to take a back seat. On the retirement of Dr. Wayland, he sprang immediately into leadership, acquiring and maintaining it by awakening and zealously cultivating among Baptists a suspicion that their influence was not sufficiently recognized in the administration of the government of the University; that they were, in fact, in danger of losing their control of it. Diligent efforts were made by him to give the impression that another religious

---

[1] A. K. DeBlois, now President of Shurtleff College. — Ed.

body was desirous to acquire the control. By his manipulation of Baptist votes he succeeded in introducing into the Board of Trustees persons whose only recommendation to membership was their known hostility to just those members whom he charged with seeking to wrest control from the Baptists. This action, of course, gave serious offence to the persons aimed at. Partisanship thenceforward reigned in the governing Boards.

NOTE A.—BREAK IN THE AUTOBIOGRAPHY.

The last contribution to the autobiography was dictated but a few weeks before the death of its author. Like General Grant, taking up the task in hours of respite from struggle with the same formidable disease, unlike the military hero, he was not able to carry the story of his life to the period chosen, —the end of his presidency at Brown. Other work also pressed upon him, and he was prevented even from reading over more than a few early passages of the autobiography. It stands as he left it. — ED.

NOTE B. —CONCERN FOR RELIGIOUS LIFE OF THE COLLEGE.

A student in Brown from 1872 to 1876 tells something of what few but students could know, — the President's deep interest in the religious life of the College. Dr. Robinson frequently came into the general prayer-meeting of the students on Wednesday evening. Usually he said a few words, practical, simple, and to the point, or led in prayer. He showed his interest, and said he came as often as he could. With the alumnus whose statement is here closely followed, no memory of a special occasion comes up, but the general impression abides of "the Doctor's" active concern for the spiritual well-being of the students. He did not forget the influence upon his own character of a notable religious revival which occurred in the College while he was an undergraduate. He meant to add to the autobiography a notice of the part which President Wayland took in the revival, for he felt his own indebtedness to the fatherly counsel of that great teacher.

Dr. Robinson's sermons on the Day of Prayer for Colleges were better known to the public, and were deeply impressive. His daily prayers in chapel were so noteworthy in all that makes a prayer the vehicle and the inspiration of devout sentiment as to become a subject of admiring remark even among irreligious young men. — ED.

NOTE C. — SELF-RESTRAINT AND SENSIBILITY.

Those chapel exercises also furnish a curious comment upon the austerity with which he resented in himself any effusive emotion. One of his colleagues noticed that, after a particularly solemn or tender prayer by the President, Professor L——was the only member of the Faculty that ventured to walk off with him. And yet the reserve in which he wrapped his feelings was not altogether so native as to most persons it seemed. While a young man, he was so easily moved to tears as to find this a cause of frequent chagrin, and to set him at persistent effort to repress all show of the gentler emotions. He afterwards remarked that he had perhaps in the end carried this self-repression too far. It is certain that he rarely allowed in public any expression of pathos which he could repress. The peculiar controlled cadence of his voice seemed to mean, "I assure you there will be no scene;" but the real tenderness of his feeling not seldom suffused his eyes, changed the quality of his tones, and sent a look almost of pain into the grim face, making the involuntary appeal all the more irresistible from his own evident effort at resistance. This stoical reserve he extended to all show of enthusiasm. If betrayed into any marked exhibition of energetic emotion during the course of a sermon, he would linger in the pulpit, with bowed head, reproaching himself, and feeling, as he said, that he could never preach again, — as though he had demeaned himself by being so moved and so moving.

The sensibility which so few suspected in him revealed itself now and then to the surprise of some one. The Rev. T. G. Jones, D.D. of Norfolk, Virginia, writes : —

"With all his Puritan sternness, Roman solemnity and dignity, there was some softness of spirit and no little sentiment in him. Two or three years since, while the writer of these lines was in charge of the venerable old church [in Norfolk] of which Dr. Robinson in his youth had been pastor, he was surprised in passing up to his study to see a tall and very striking figure moving about the premises alone, and seemingly inspecting them with the deepest interest. It was Dr. Robinson. . . . He had come, after the lapse of half a century, to look once more upon the house of God in which he had commenced his ministry. . . . After looking about in the lecture-room for a few moments, he passed into the main audience-room, and, seating himself, long gazed, silent and absorbed, upon the fond, familiar scene unvisited but once before for half a hundred years. We could not disturb him, but withdrew to the study, where at length he joined us, and after an hour's delightful talk went on his way to his work on earth and to his rest in heaven."

The Rev. M. F. Johnson, of Middleborough, Massachusetts, recalls the following incidents, which are interesting less as showing what Dr. Robinson was than as showing what many thought he was : —

"When we were in Newton, Dr. Robinson gave us a course of lectures on preaching. One day he mentioned experimental sermons, but added, 'You young men cannot preach these yet.' And he stopped. As the men looked up to see why, they saw his blue eyes filled with tears; his lips quivered, and he said further, 'When you have stood by the open grave of your loved ones, you can preach such sermons to the great help of the afflicted.' One student who had spent three years in Brown said, 'That is a side of Dr. Robinson I never saw before.' It was a revelation to the whole class. I was relating this incident to a prominent clergyman, . . . and he expressed surprise, saying, 'I did not know he had shed a tear since the days when his mother chastised him.'

"His tenderness and his justice went together. I was once falsely accused by a college official. . . . He used very severe language, asserting that I was one of those pious devils that preach Sundays and break college regulations week days. . . . I went to Dr. Robinson and told him my trouble. No father could have been kinder to me than he was. He believed my story and comforted me, subdued my indignation, and told me he would personally investigate the matter. He completely exonerated me, and compelled the official to apologize for his accusations. I never forgot that kind act of the Doctor; and, however severe he might seem, I knew that a heart as tender as that of a woman governed that inflexible sense of justice which ever characterized his conduct."

There can be no doubt that the sorrows which fell so often upon his later years softened the asperity of Dr. Robinson's manner, while they never broke his spirit. He was strong, though gentler, to the end. The narrator of these incidents has properly connected the tenderness which he found in the Doctor with a sense of justice. Certain of his old theological students could testify that this sense of justice was as rigorous for them against himself, as his college boys seem to have thought it exacting for himself and against them. It was his unflinching sense of duty which prevailed in all cases alike. —ED.

NOTE D.—TRIBUTE BY PROFESSOR HACKETT.

When Dr. Robinson resigned at Rochester, Dr. Hackett paid the following tribute to his colleague and friend : —

". . . Most deeply do I sympathize with the friends of the Seminary that we see our President here to-day for the last time in his official capacity. I will not disguise it, I feel to-day a pride in recalling the fact that Dr. Robinson was one of my own early pupils, first at Brown University when I too was almost a boy (and that no doubt brought us so much the nearer to each other) and afterward at the Theological Seminary at Newton. To be able at this moment to look up and trace in our sky from that early beginning only an unbroken pathway of light, friendship, and kindly offices is to me a delightful spectacle. I hope it is also a gratification to him.

"It has been my lot (for I have led a somewhat vagrant academic life) to have been connected with the faculties of two or three different colleges and theological seminaries, and in at least two or three different Christian denominations. In these faculties have been some of the best scholars in the country; some of the most devoted, self-denying, earnest, as well as able educators in the land. I have known, therefore, something of the zeal, self-devotement, enthusiasm of our best men in their departments of intellectual and Christian labor. But I will allow myself to say, it is but truthful testimony to say, I have known no one, on the whole, that, in his devotion to his work, his spirit of labor, his enthusiasm, and power to awaken enthusiasm in his pupils, has surpassed Dr. Robinson. I do not feel it to be an extravagance to apply to him the words which John Foster applied to a well-known historic personage; Dr. Robinson has seemed to me to exemplify in the ways that I have indicated an intensity of soul in his work, 'kept uniform by the nature of the human mind, forbidding it to be more, and, by the character of the individual, forbidding it to be less.' We are sorry to have him leave us. We have done all we could to retain him. He acts, I am sure, under a rigid sense of duty in going from us; and we, his colleagues, wish for him from the bottom of our hearts God's benediction and every blessing in his new sphere of care and responsibility. He goes to add his name to a long line of honored predecessors. He will dwell there amid great memories, and feel the inspiration of great examples to incite him to a noble emulation. But I am sure of this: there is only one rival of whom he need have any fear, and that is — himself."

THE CLOSING YEARS.
1889-1894.

A SUPPLEMENT

By H. L. WAYLAND, D.D.

THE CLOSING YEARS.

MARCH 20, 1889, Dr. Robinson laid before the Corporation of Brown University his resignation. The resignation being unconditional, there was no course for the Corporation but to accept it. I cannot better express the sentiments of the Corporation than by quoting from the remarks of his friend and former instructor, Professor William Gammell, LL. D., one of the older members of the Corporation, who had been connected with the University in various capacities for more than half a century : —

" I can but recall at this time the honorable and successful manner in which President Robinson has discharged the duties of his office for the seventeen years of his incumbency. Any one who enters the college yard will notice the great changes and the marked improvements which have been made within that time. The grounds, which were plain and unadorned, have become a beauty and a delight. The number of new buildings and the important changes are without precedent in the history of the College. The John Carter Brown Library has been erected; also the Slater Dormitory, and Sayles Memorial Hall, the most beautiful and most costly building on the grounds. Also this ancient building, University Hall, has been renovated and made as good as any building connected with the College. The Metcalf Estate, of very great value, and a lot on George

Street, of great prospective importance, have been added to the college property.

[It might be added to the above that during his presidency means had been secured or promised, by gift or bequest, for the erection of the Wilson Laboratory, the Lyman Gymnasium, and the Ladd Observatory.]

" The funds of the University, which in 1872 were $552,430, were, in 1888, $960,411 [not including the gift of Mr. Duncan, $20,000, and a more recent gift of $20,000, and other gifts, which would make the total about $1,018,000]. The endowment has been very nearly doubled [not counting the Lyman bequest, from which $60,000 or $70,000 will be realized]. These gifts have come very largely from the community in which the College is located.

" For this prosperity we are greatly indebted to the judgment, the fidelity, the ability, and the diligence of President Robinson. During these seventeen years he has never been absent from a college duty, from a recitation, or from a chapel exercise, except when called away by public duties. This fact indicates at once his vigor of constitution and his fidelity to his duties. How few professional men have a similar record!

" Of his instruction I may speak with confidence, having had two sons under his instruction, and it having been my duty in various ways to know the internal condition of the College. The instruction has been of a very high order. He has done much to raise its standard; he has restored largely the spirit of the instruction of my old teacher, President Wayland, which had waned somewhat during the intervening period. I consider this a fair statement of the results of Dr. Robinson's instruction. He is entitled to high praise for these services.

" He has now left the position at a more advanced age than any of his predecessors had attained while in office. I cannot say that this step is unwise; it is surely better to lay down the office while one is in full intellectual vigor than to wait till a failure makes the step necessary. We do not, to-day, part with President Robinson; until we do so, we may defer such expressions as will be at that time appropriate. "

After his successor, President E. B. Andrews, D.D., LL.D., entered upon his duties, Dr. Robinson spent some months in and near Boston, where, at the request of Mr. Horatio N. Slater, he sat for his picture to the eminent artist, Grundmann.

In December Dr. Robinson came to Philadelphia, where he spent the greater part of the two following years. Dr. Wayland Hoyt of the Memorial Church having resigned, the church requested Dr. Robinson to supply the pulpit until they had secured a permanent pastor. Accordingly, he began preaching on the last Sunday in 1889, and continued until the close of September, 1890, when Dr. T. E. Brown entered upon his pastorate. The relations which Dr. Robinson held during these months to the Memorial Church were in all respects exceedingly gratifying. I doubt whether at any time his ministerial labors were more pleasant. His mind was at its best. He did not preach old sermons, but kept his powers in exercise by perpetual thought, study, and composition; and in all he said and did there was a tenderness and sympathy which his earlier days had hardly shown, although undoubtedly always existing. The church showed the utmost consideration and reverence. After the close of his period of service the church placed his portrait beside the portraits of Dr. Henson and Dr. Hoyt, and has always delighted in reckoning him among its pastors.   In his "History of the Memorial Church," given at its twenty-fifth anniversary, in 1893, Deacon Charles H. Harrison said : —

"The church owes much to the short ministry of Dr. Robinson.   His profound and original thought, his searching and exact analysis, his precise and elegant use of language, his lucid and able expositions of truth, afforded an intellectual and spiritual uplift which is not yet forgotten. It was an inspiration and joy to sit at the feet of this great and good man, whose hoary head and dignified bearing lent weight to the words in which he clothed the thoughts and experiences of his long and studious life. "

In April and May, 1890, he gave the Hyde Lectures on Foreign Missions, before Andover Theological Seminary, on the following topics : —

1. Christianity Designed and Fitted to be a Universal Religion.

2. Christianity provides for its own Extension.

3. Present Resources of Christianity amply Sufficient to secure its Universal Prevalence.

4. Manifestations of the Divine in Missionary Epochs and Progress.

5. Significancy and Favorableness of our own Time for Missionary Enterprises.

6. Connection of the Spirit of Missions, Foreign and Home, with Every-day Church Work and Life.

7. Methods, general and special, in Foreign Mission Work.

8. Kinds of Men and Modes of Training needed for Foreign Missions.

9. Subtle Hindrances to the Missionary Spirit and Enterprise.

10. Requisites for Keeping Alive and Active the Missionary Spirit in the Christian Ministry.

Professor George Harris, D. D., of the Seminary, kindly writes : " These lectures were given extemporaneously, with as much clearness, vigor, and interest as the Doctor ever showed. It was a delight to see, as well as to hear, a man of his age, standing, erect and commanding, to speak to a company of young men. During part of the time he was my guest, and a guest whom it was a privilege to entertain. At the time he was laboring under great anxiety on account of the illness of his daughter, who died, I think, soon after. But he was cheerful and deeply interested in the various subjects of conversation which arose. A kind of intimacy sprung up in those few days, as he opened his convictions and feelings. I found that his heart was as large as his brain. His sense of humor was charming. He was young in his feelings, and, I think, preferred the society of younger men to that of men of his own age. I felt the greatest admiration and affection for him, and look back on his visits and lectures with pleasure. I have been reading parts of his Theology, and am much interested in finding anticipations of tendencies of thought which became decided twenty or thirty years afterwards. The independence and breadth of his thinking are manifest on every page."

In October, 1890, he gave the same course on " Christian Missions " before Rochester Theological Seminary.

He constantly read with avidity and delight the most recent books in theology and philosophy, taking especial pleasure in Fairbairn and Bishop Lightfoot.

During this year clouds gathered about him ; but they mellowed, they did not obscure the rays of the sun. On the Saturday evening on which he heard of the hopeless illness of his only surviving daughter, the last of five, he said to me : " It does not seem as if I could bury another child."

The next morning he preached at the Memorial, upon " The Loneliness of Christ ; " to many who heard him the discourse was an era and a revelation. This engagement with the Memorial was a great blessing, giving him just the intellectual and moral occupation which he needed for the completest health.

In the spring of 1890 he gave a course of lectures at Crozer Theological Seminary, upon " Christian Apologetics and Evidences," which was in the highest degree appreciated. and prized. He gave a similar course at Crozer during the four following years, closing with the spring of 1894.

Naturally, the Commencement of 1890 at Brown University was marked by many expressions of regard for the ex-President. Touching allusions to him were made by many of the speakers. The Alumni poem, by Professor Walter Cochrane Bronson, contained the following : —

> " As leader of that host, a stately figure rode,
> With white head bared; the firm and upright carriage showed
> What power lay yet beneath those sunlit locks of snow;
> So moved he on, stateliest in that stately show.
> ' Who is he ? ' echoed the horseman at my side.
> ' Know you not him ? him the old Roman ? him the pride
> Of all these fellow pilgrims ? him whom robes of state
> And sceptre on the elm-crowned hill (resigned but late)
> Became so long and well ? Who — who can e'er forget
> That man in whom the Roman and the Christian met ?
> What though his outward badge of honor be laid down ?
> A king within himself is king without a crown,
> And such an uncrowned king is Robinson to Brown.' "

At the Commencement dinner the full-length portrait of Dr. Robinson,[1] before alluded to, was presented by Arnold Green, LL.D., in a chaste and felicitous address, the entire body of alumni rising as the picture was unveiled, and they

---

[1] A portrait by William Page is in Rochester Theological Seminary. — ED.

saw upon the canvas the striking, familiar features of the instructor at whose feet many of them had sat.

After the Memorial engagement terminated, he preached for a few Sundays to the Immanuel Church in Baltimore, whose pastor, Rev. A. C. Dixon, D.D., had just become pastor at Brooklyn. A few weeks later, the Fifth Church, Philadelphia, bereaved by the untimely death of the beloved Dr. Peddie, sought his services. He remained with them until the house was closed for the summer. After the settlement of Dr. W. T. Chase as pastor of the Fifth, for several months Dr. Robinson filled the pulpit of the Broad Street Church with his wonted power. In the spring of 1892 the Baptist National Anniversaries held at Philadelphia were preceded by the Baptist Congress. At one of these sessions Dr. Robinson felt that a word needed to be said. As his name was announced, and as he appeared upon the platform, he was greeted by an outburst of admiring enthusiasm such as rarely comes to any public man.

In April, 1892, he gave a course of lectures at Brown University, on " Modern Thought and Religion : 1. Science ; 2. Philosophy; 3. History; 4. Literature; 5. Religion and the Bible. " The very conception of this course, upon subjects so varied, notwithstanding their common relation to one central topic, illustrates the breadth and vigor of his mind, and the wealth of his resources. This course was afterward given at Crozer, of evenings, while he was lecturing during the day upon " Evidences and Ethics. "

In the fall of 1892 Dr. Robinson commenced his course of instruction in the infant but already gigantic University of Chicago, as Professor of Ethics and Apologetics. Of his relations to the University during these two years President Harper says, in his annual report for 1894 : " Dr. Robinson brought to us the best work of his life. His presence during these two years was a constant source of inspiration and helpfulness. "

The world looked with admiration when Sir Walter Scott, at the age of fifty-five, began what he called his *opus magnum*, the editing of his entire series of works. He achieved it, under the pressure of necessity and misfortune, but he fell, conquered, at the age of sixty-one. Robinson, at the age of seventy-seven, assumed the duties of a professorship which might well task the largest learning and the most vigorous powers. He still maintained his mental powers; his body, although it felt the weight of years, loyally answered the demands of his mind. The constitution which he inherited from his Bristol County ancestors, he had never abused or squandered. He lived somewhat sparingly; he exercised with system. He took long walks; and almost

> "To the last he had as light a step
> As any man in Ennerdale."

Like Francis Wayland, he delighted in his garden and in productive labor. During 1852 to 1854, when I was a tutor in the then young University of Rochester, he most kindly received me, an inexperienced stripling, to terms of friendship, and even intimacy. I recall, with pleasure and gratitude and sadness, the many Saturday mornings when I worked beside him in the garden of his earlier Rochester home, until far past noon; he bearing my horticultural and theological ignorance with the patience that is begotten of wisdom. He was through life a stranger to every enslaving and enervating indulgence.

February 23, 1894, a beautiful incident irradiated the fiftieth anniversary of his wedding. Many of his pupils and friends availed themselves of this opportunity to express their affection and gratitude by a handsome pecuniary gift; and the founder of the University of Chicago added an annuity to continue through Dr. Robinson's life. Dr. Robinson wrote to a friend who had taken some part in suggesting this action: "Your letter, with its list of names, seemed to fill our empty little parlor at once with a roomful of friendly faces. We should be glad to thank personally every kind friend who has joined you in this most gracious recognition of our golden wedding. Perhaps you will convey to them our warm sense of their kindness, and thus add another to our many obligations."

He was invited to give the annual address for the Robinson Rhetorical Society of Rochester Theological Seminary in May, 1894. He highly appreciated this invitation, but felt that he ought not to add to the engagements which he had already made.

Within the past two or three years disease admonished him; but it was mercifully withheld from inflicting acute pain, or dooming him to enforced idleness, which would have been a prolonged agony. His disorder was cancer of the right kidney, complicated with pleurisy in the left lung. His age precluded the thought of an operation.

He was never more delightful in conversation, never more master of his resources, than when he was under my roof, in the late spring.

He preached at Vassar College on the Sunday before Commencement, but the prolonged standing was a heavy tax. He was able to reach the home of his son in the vicinity of Boston, whence, at his earnest desire, he was removed to the Boston City Hospital, on June 10. Three days later, without a pang, without a struggle, with a single sigh, he ceased from among us. The sun vanished from our heavens to rise with unclouded glory upon another morning.   To him we may apply without change the words which he uttered at the grave of his teacher and friend, Dr. Hackett: " Surely, his was a fit ending to such a life. From expounding the words of the Divine Master and his Apostles, he was translated almost at once, to speak face to face with the Apostles, and with the Master himself.   The faithful servant, his work well done, has entered into the joy of his Lord. "

Two days later, on Friday the 15th, the funeral took place at Rochester, which had been for nineteen years his home, and where the great work of his life had been done. His friend and pupil, President Strong, was absent in the far West, and could not return in time for the service. Addresses were made by President Harper of the University of Chicago, and President Taylor of Vassar College; and then the hands of a younger generation laid his remains in the Mount Hope Cemetery, beside the five daughters who had preceded him.   On the following Sunday, a memorial service was held in the First Church in Providence, where for seventeen years he had been a worshipper.   Later, at the request of the Boston Conference of Baptist Ministers, an address was made by H. L. Wayland.   An address was given at Brown University by T. D. Anderson, D.D.   Rev. W. H. P. Faunce addressed the Boston Alumni.   Addresses were made before the Theological Department of the University of Chicago by H. L. Wayland and Professor George W. Northrup, D.D., LL.D.   A commemorative sermon was preached in the Memorial Church, Philadelphia, by Dr. T. E. Brown.   An address was also given before Crozer Theological Seminary, and before the Philadelphia Conference of Baptist Ministers.   These were but a few among the many expressions of regard and reverence for the great soul which had departed.

As I recall my intercourse with him during these past forty-two years, it appears to me that the leading feature in his character was reverence for truth, allegiance to truth, — an allegiance supreme and undivided. The love of truth was an instinct, was a passion. No other consideration seemed to enter; it was not a matter of question, whether truth should rule the hour. I cannot conceive that any motive would lead him to deliberate upon any other course than the quest of the truth. He did not any more ask, " Shall I abide by the truth ?" than a mother asks, " Shall I love my child ?" For the attainment of truth no price was too high. Hours of midnight toil, studies prosecuted through the dry and repulsive pages of mediæval theology,— all was nothing, if with it came the attainment of truth.

As I look back now, it seems possible that this supreme regard for truth made him negligent of some of the rhetorical arts by which men help to gain acceptance for the truth. He had less tact, less of the power of graceful little turns by which sympathy is enlisted, friends quickened, enemies conciliated, than any public speaker I ever knew. I think his idea was that the truth itself was its own sufficient commendation ; that if anything was *true*, it ought to be enough to set it before people, and that they ought not to expect to be won to the reception of it ; and he would have regarded any such device as a sacrifice of the dignity of truth.

Perhaps, also, there was herein a reason why he illustrated so sparingly, especially toward the latter part of his life. This feature of his style made him so difficult to report by any one not an expert. Most speakers give the reporter a chance to catch up every now and then, by introducing a metaphor, an anecdote, an illustration, for which a catch-word is enough, and which can be carried in the memory. But he applied the hydraulic compresser for himself : after he had condensed, there was no show for any one else. I imagine that the truth was so clear in his own eyes that he did not see any need for its being illuminated to the minds of others; and then he had within him so much that was demanding utterance that he could not waste his time on illustrating. But his clearness of thought was such, his addresses were so logical, and, not least, he roused those who heard him to such intensity of interest and to such attention, that he was understood without the aid of illustration. People knew when and wherein they differed from him. This same feeling toward truth in language actuated him in his relations to truth in action. He had not much patience with people who saw their duty and did not do it. Perhaps this gave rise to what people called his austerity of demeanor. Particularly his indignation was aroused by pretence or sham, in the pulpit or out of it. But if a man, however inexperienced, however young, really wanted to know his duty and to do it, to learn the truth and to speak it, he would not find in the whole world a kinder, more patient friend and counsellor than Dr. Robinson.

His real kindness of heart did not express itself in a universal, indiscriminate, diffused, diluted affability, which shook hands with equal fervency with everybody, and only wished that it were as highly endowed as Briareus, that it might shake hands with a hundred people at once; a friendship that means as much to one as to another, and nothing to anybody. But when there was a call for a kind word or a kind deed to one in need or in danger, it was not wanting. One Sunday evening there was a great congregation in the First Baptist Church in Rochester, gathered by the announcement that Dr. Robinson would preach on "Immortality." But somehow, though the audience was there, the preacher was not there. I never knew him, in the pulpit, to labor so hard and achieve so little. He seemed to be reaching after something which he could not lay hold on. As soon as the service was over, he asked me to see Mrs. Robinson home, while he darted off, I knew not where. I learned, the next day, that just before he went into the pulpit he had been informed that one of his students, a pious and promising young man, not largely dowered in the matter of astuteness, had become entangled in a very unsuitable engagement, which would have marred or ruined his future. For the hour the man dominated the preacher. His anxiety cost him his sermon. Before he slept that night, the foolish engagement was at an end; the young man was saved for a useful career, and for the missionary service, in which he subsequently died. To those who knew the facts, that pulpit failure did him more honor than the most brilliant success would have done.[1]

His mind worked with wonderful intensity, whether he was studying or thinking or composing. His habit of unwritten speech never led him into slovenliness; rather, it called for intense action alike in the first preparation of his sermon and in each repetition of it. A sermon preached the second or third time passed anew through the fire, and came hot from his mind. His mind was never in its shirt-sleeves. Perhaps this habitual intensity had much to do with keeping his powers up to the highest pitch to the very last. He was a standing protest against the saying of Macaulay: "It may be doubted whether there ever existed a human being whose mind was quite as finely toned at eighty as at forty." It was not more than a month before the close that I heard him give, in his course at Crozer, the lecture which forms, in his "Christian Evidences," Chapter III. of Part III. on "The Divine Origin

---

[1] See note on the character of Dr. Robinson on page 143. — ED.

of Christianity, as seen in its Self-Recuperative Power, its
Power of Self-Development, and the Expansiveness of its
Spirit." He spoke, sitting, for an hour and a half. Of
course there was not the tremendous vigor which marked
the meridian of life; but, on the other hand, there was all
the clearness and sequence, and there was a breadth and
sympathy which belonged emphatically to the hour.

It not seldom happens that breadth of intellectual sympathy is but another name for a want of definite convictions; but with him, the more he knew, and the wider
his outlook, the more clear and definite and positive his
assurances. In reading the account of the Parliament of
Religions at Chicago, he said, "They do not make enough
of Christ." While at Rochester, delivering his course of
lectures on missions, as he was walking with his friend
and former pupil, Professor True, the latter said to him:
"What do you think of the theory that Jesus Christ was,
like many great men, the product of his times?" With
profound emphasis, he said: "The times, the age, could no
more have produced Jesus Christ than the desert of Sahara
could have given birth to an overflowing fountain." To
him, Christ was the centre of theological truth, not less
than the centre of Christian devotion.

NOTE A.

The writer has spoken somewhat more at large of Dr. Robinson, in an address given before the Boston Conference of
Baptist Ministers, before the Theological Department of the
University of Chicago, before Crozer Theological Seminary,
and the Baptist Ministers' Conference of Philadelphia; now
issued as a booklet by the American Baptist Publication Society under the title, "E. G. ROBINSON, D.D., LL.D., by H.
L. Wayland.— H. L. W.

NOTE B.

ON THE CHARACTER OF DR. ROBINSON.

The lively and discriminating character sketch which follows is from the Memorial Address of Rev. T. D. Anderson, D. D., before Brown University: —

"The moral man is grander than the man of intellect, and the moral character of him whom we honor demands a higher admiration than his intellectual power. Faults there were; but the aim was high, the motives noble, the heart sincere, — in a word, the man was honest. Indeed, it was his honesty which gave prominence to some of his faults. . . . It is in recognition of this trait that many of his associates and acquaintances . . . have come to regard even the words which burned and blistered as sparks struck out by friction upon the surface rather than as bolts forged in the central fires. . . . In this exalted moral character a most prominent characteristic was tremendous power of will. The man's whole countenance betokened a dominant, imperious will. The strong forehead, the eye with its straightforward, piercing glance, the prominent nose, the firm lips with their scissors-like movement, and the full, prominent chin, all were indicative of high purpose and concentrated energy. It was this will which, to use language he himself might use, collared his mind and held it down to the grindstone; it was this that demanded a hard day's work every day; it was this that held the passions and appetites of the man subservient to moral law, and made the man bow in unaffected humility before the ideal of excellence which shines in the face of Jesus Christ.

"But this mighty energy was associated with a stern sense of moral obligation. This will was not prostituted to low ends. It was not self-will. It recognized a law to be obeyed, and it held the man in its grip until he rendered obedience. As in the tremendous energy of will we discover the centrifugal force, so in the high moral ideal we discover the centripetal force which determined the orbit of his life. The same will which showed its mastership in commanding all the faculties of the soul, manifested its true temper in its loyal submission to the moral ideal presented in the character of Jesus Christ. Dr. Robinson honored Christ. He found in him the most complete objective transcript of the nature of the eternal God; and to follow His teaching and to be swayed by His spirit was the deepest purpose of his heart. To be sure, it is what we may call the more masculine virtues of Christ that he honored the most and was most successful in imitating. Reacting from a sentimental conception of Christ, . . . he, in accordance with the bent of his nature, laid the greater emphasis on Christ's revelation of the unswerving justice and infinite holiness of God. His Christ loved, but that love was a moral, holy, transforming love. His Christ was a worthy ideal for a strong. completely developed man. . . .

"As in the life of Dr. Robinson we discover in striking combination tremendous energy of will and high sense of moral obligation, we also discover in that life a not unhappy union of pride with humility. Probably no human pride is virtue unalloyed. But there is a pride which savors more of virtue than of vice. Essential manhood is worthy of respect. . . . The great moral teacher of the ages inculcates self-respect as he instructs man to love his neighbor as himself. . . . In the philosophic, Christian sense, Dr. Robinson was exceeding proud. He had abundant self-respect; he had but little self-conceit. His pride was akin to the awe with which Kant reflected upon the moral law within, and differed heaven-wide from that Narcissus-like vanity which pines away in admiration of its adventitious and ephemeral beauty.

" This pride, however, retained its virtue, and was raised from the level of the stoic philosophy to the higher elevation of the Christian religion, as it was mated with humility. Humility, with him, was not cringing before one's fellows . . . it was not an undue depreciation of self; it was, rather. a just appreciation of another and a worthier, in comparison with whom self seems but little. Dr. Robinson bared his head before the Almighty. He walked humbly before his God. Often have we seen him at Commencement stand with academic hat upon his head while conferring degrees as president of the college, and then, in a moment, uncover his head, and with unaffected humility bow before the throne of the heavenly grace. That twofold picture was symbolical of his character. . . . His reverent humility was most strikingly illustrated in prayer. . . . His prayers were remarkable. Characterized by freshness of thought and variety of diction, they came forth, morning after morning, fresh as the sunrise, and rose as the out-breathings of an adoring soul." . . .

DR. ROBINSON AT THE AGE OF 39.

[From a daguerreotype made in Rochester, N. Y., in 1854, now in the possession of H. L. Wayland, D.D., Phila., Pa.]

Part Second

CRITICAL ESTIMATES.

———

I.

DR. ROBINSON AS A PASTOR.

By REV. A. J. SAGE, D.D.,
Cincinnati, Ohio.

AS A PASTOR.

THE pastoral experience of President Robinson was not an episode, an eddy in the current; it was a necessary part of his career, contributing volume, direction, and force to the entire movement. Without it he could not have exerted the powerful moulding influence on young students for the ministry which was the crowning glory of his life. Had he not himself been a pastoral preacher and leader of a church, he might have been an acute theological teacher, a stimulating intellectual force, but it is difficult to imagine him as inspiring scores of young men with intense enthusiasm for the work of the pulpit and the pastorate. A large part of his power in the theological seminary was acquired in his pulpit in Cincinnati.

Perhaps this last expression should be pluralized; for Mr. Robinson, not yet adorned with an honorary title, held, during five years or more, two pastorates in that city. While he was a professor in the Theological Institute in Covington, Kentucky, a church was organized, just across the Ohio River, in what is now the solid business portion of Cincinnati. The exercises at the organization of this church were held in the hall of the Cincinnati College, the sermon being preached by the Rev. William Hague. It was called the Walnut Street Baptist Church, and during its entire existence its services were held in College, Melodeon, and Apollo Halls, all still in existence, and all located within a block of one another. The second of these was of its kind at that time the most popular place of entertainment in the city. It was here that Jenny Lind, a few years later, gave concerts on her second tour of the country. At first Professor Robinson and Dr. R. E. Pattison alternated in the pulpit services. The contrast of styles in their preaching was interesting. Dr. Pattison was fervid, practical, synthetic in his method; Professor Robinson was calm, theological, analytical. As one of their hearers remarked, " Mr. Robinson began where Dr. Pattison left off." When, in 1848, the disruption took place in the Seminary at Covington, Professor Robinson became sole pastor of the church, Dr. Pattison being called to a professorship in the Theological Seminary at Newton Centre, Massachusetts. It was during this pastorate that a boy of eleven years discovered that the easiest way to dispose of the weary hour of the service was to listen to the sermon; and with Mr. Robinson's clear discourse and simple language this soon became an agreeable exercise. His delivery at this time was characterized by subdued strength, having something of the quiet tone of the lecture-room.

At the end of one year, in 1849, Mr. Robinson was called to the pastorate of the Ninth Street Church, whose pulpit had been vacated by the resignation of the Rev. E. L. Magoon. The Walnut Street Church was disbanded, and its membership was merged in that of the Ninth Street Church, thus making the second pastorate virtually a continuation of the first, on an enlarged scale. The Ninth Street Church was at that time recognized as the leading Baptist Church in Ohio. Its pastors had been men of eminence, Dr. S. W. Lynd and Mr. Magoon, both preachers of highly attractive qualities. Cincinnati was called the

Queen of the West. It had a pre-eminence which it has since lost through the rapid expansion of the great West and the growth of the cities of Chicago and St. Louis. It had literary men of high reputation and preachers of distinction. Considerable anxiety was felt as to the manner in which Mr. Robinson's ministry would be received, since his mode of preaching was so different from that of his predecessors. It was feared that his thoughtful, philosophical method might not be appreciated by a congregation which had been accustomed to highly popular preaching. It was not long, however, before this anxiety was thoroughly dispelled. The tall and vigorous form of the young pastor, just entering into the prime of manhood, his large and impressive features, his energetic manner, and especially his profound and commanding thought, expressed in the tersest and simplest diction, soon won for him the respect and the earnest attention of all his hearers.

The circumstances were such as to call out the ablest capabilities of the preacher. Solid men were in the pews, such as John Stevens, twice professor at Granville College now Denison University, the father of Professor William A. Stevens of Rochester Theological Seminary, and others, prominent citizens in their day, though now forgotten. One name, still remembered and honored, was that of the venerable Judge Taft, beside whom sat his son, Alphonso, a young lawyer, with a massive, intellectual head, destined to be a member of President Grant's cabinet, and Minister Plenipotentiary to two foreign courts. Charles Anderson, one of Cincinnati's brilliant lawyers, afterward Governor of Ohio, and Charles McMicken, founder of the University of Cincinnati, were frequent attendants on Mr. Robinson's ministry. Probably no one ever heard from him an expression which indicated that he was eager to acquire a wide reputation. Yet if he had such an ambition, this was his opportunity. His position was the most conspicuous that the West could afford in the Baptist denomination. But deeper than such motives, if they spurred him at all, was an intense moral earnestness, and what may be called an intellectual conscientiousness, which throughout his lifetime impelled him to bring forward the best products of his mind, clothed in the fittest expression of which he was master. He felt that he had a congregation fully equal to his best abilities, and all his energy of brain and body went into his pulpit and his lecture-room.[1]

Accessory to the service were a feature and a character which can by no means be passed without ample attention, — the finest choir in the city, led by its foremost musician.

[1] An incident which occurred during Mr. Robinson's pastorate illustrates a contrast in his character which not infrequently appeared. He seemed bold to the verge of recklessness, and yet at times he exhibited a sensitiveness amounting almost to timidity. One Sunday morning his attention was attracted by a stranger in his congregation of unusually impressive appearance. As sometimes happened, he was conscious of inadequacy in his preparation for the service, and in the broad forehead and dignified bearing of the stranger he at once discerned indications of an intellectual nature and a probable critic. Certainly this must be an eminent lawyer, or editor, or professor. Mr. Robinson toiled through his discourse, casting uneasy glances at the new-comer, and experiencing what ministers sometimes call "a pulpit sweat." The close attention paid by his hearer did not in the least relieve his anxiety. After the close of the service Mr. Robinson addressed one of his deacons: "Did you observe a stranger who sat in such a pew, and do you know who he is?" "Oh, yes; that's Mr. ——, the milkman." — A. J. S.

Once while preaching in the First Baptist Church of Rochester, the Doctor paused, stood speechless for some moments, and began to turn pale, to the no small alarm of his hearers, especially of his wife, who suspected what the matter was. He had forgotten altogether what came next. But with the readiness in extricating himself from an awkward situation that never failed him, he maintained the appearance of self-possession, and presently began to speak. As soon as his tongue was loosed the spell was broken, and the train of thought recovered. Afterward he asked whether he had talked wildly, for his mind, he said, had been an absolute blank, and he began to talk without the least idea of what he was saying. Yet no one perhaps except his wife and his friend, Dr. Kendrick, had divined what the trouble was. — ED.

Victor Williams, the chorister, was a Swede, born not far from the birthplace of Jenny Lind, with whom, during her two visits to Cincinnati, he established a cordial friendship. In personal appearance he closely resembled the French Emperor, Napoleon III., so that while travelling in Europe he became the object of much attention, through a suspicion that he was that distinguished person travelling incognito. Victor — for by that name he was commonly known — left at his death, in 1892, the remarkable record of having been for fifty years the leader of one church choir, that of Ninth Street, and, as he said to the writer of this chapter, having never had in it a singers' quarrel. In the slight foreign accent, which he never entirely lost, he said, " I hat but one rule; that was — Mint your own pizness. " [1]

[1] As Victor Williams was in those early days, with his violin, unquestionably Cincinnati's chief musician, no great local concert could successfully get on without him. To his latest day he loved to tell how, when the leader of Boston's Germania Orchestra became disabled by illness in Cincinnati, he was called upon to take his place, and how he successfully conducted the concert. It was his custom to organize a chorus and, after a due amount of drilling, to announce a performance of oratorio, the " Messiah " or the " Creation." All Cincinnati would be present. Cincinnati's choicest singers would be the soloists. Then Victor was in his glory. When he first took his place as conductor, with baton displayed, in response to the thunders of applause he would suddenly wheel upon his heels, front face to the audience, and perform an astonishing bow, bringing his body almost to an acute angle with its support, so that had his spinal column been a cannon, it might have fired his head through the midst of his audience. Then recovering his first position with the same alacrity, the baton would wave majestically on high, and the performance would begin. — A. J. S.

Mr. Williams related with great gusto how, when Jenny Lind gave a Saturday night concert in Cincinnati, he had with much difficulty persuaded his pastor, Mr. Robinson, to appear at a public entertainment just before the Lord's Day ; and how, when the great singer had rendered " I know that my Redeemer liveth," as she alone could, the pastor clambered over the seats and left the concert in precipitation, afraid, although he confessed he did not know one tune from another, lest the next number on the programme might mar the impression of that heavenly song. The next day it was touchingly referred to in the sermon. — ED.

Mr. Williams kept in constant training a choir of from forty to fifty voices, among which was some of the finest talent of the city. The expressive solos of the chief singers, the grand choruses in rich and stately hymn tunes or in majestic anthems, were features of the services expected with greatest interest and long remembered. There was no organ in the church, but accompaniments were supplied by the leader's violin, a 'cello, a double-bass, and occasionally a flute or other instruments. When, at the death of Daniel Webster, Mr. Robinson delivered an impressive memorial sermon, the choir sang a dirge, in which the impression was heightened by the muffled tones of a gong.

In his pastoral relations, Mr. Robinson manifested the same fidelity as in all else. He had little of that *bonhomie* which gives to some pastors easy access to the hearts of their people. To one of his members he said, " I wish I could approach people as some men do, shake hands heartily, and say, ' How are you, my brother? ' But I am naturally frigid and distant. I don't want to be so. " He did himself scant justice in this utterance. A gentleman whom he baptized still tells how, in Covington, as one of a group of children, he was sitting on a stile when Professor Robinson came along and talked to them so familiarly and delightfully that they never forgot it. A gentleman relates that as a boy, calling on Mr. Robinson in his study, he received suggestions as to his reading which were of great value to him during his entire after life ; and he remembers, with deepest interest, conversations with him on personal religion. Mr. D. G. A. Davenport, who was clerk of the church at that time, says that he had been accustomed to call on a pastor who, as soon as his business was finished, assumed a manner which suggested that it was time for him to go. Mr. Robinson, on the contrary, in the same circumstances, always kindly detained him for a few moments' chat. Years afterward, at Ninth Street, it was remarked how old women, poor and perhaps bedridden, recalled with fondness the faithful attentions of Pastor Robinson.

It has been said that he had no sense of humor. The truth is that his sense of humor, as in many other men of power, was subordinated to other qualities; but it was not wanting. " I met Mr. Robinson in the street to-day," said one of his church-members, " and what do you think he did ? He did n't speak or bow to me; he just lifted his forefinger and laid it beside that big nose of his in the most comical way." A young man called on him to say that a certain young lady professed a special interest in religion. The pastor, who knew the circumstances, inquired, " Is she interested in religion or in you?" The question opened the young man's eyes, and he is grateful to this day that he was saved from a misalliance.[1]

To one of such a temperament as Mr. Robinson's, the week-day meetings were sure to be something of a trial. He had not enough of the emotional or the evangelistic in his method to give to social religious services an easy and flowing movement. The attendance was not always as large, or the response as free, as could have been desired. A little disheartened at the result of his leadership, one evening he was heard to exclaim, " I put real bone work on that address. " At another time, after a long pause early in the

[1] At the dedication of the Theological Seminary at Fairmount, which was intended to replace the alienated institution at Covington, and perished after a career of four years, Mr. Robinson delivered the address on a platform under the trees. He selected Elisha's school of the prophets as the source of his theme, and in an amusing manner brought out of the narrative of the axe dropped into the pool of water a suggestion of the traditional poverty of theological students, based on the fact that the axe was a borrowed one. — A. J. S. [See note on page 158. — Ed.]

service, he arose and dismissed the meeting, advising the attendants to go home and pray. After that, on similar occasions, they were more prompt. A frequent attendant on these services was a young man of unusually fine presence, with a rich voice, who was destined to be an impressive public speaker of wide reputation; but at this time his part was that of a silent auditor. One evening he was startled by being unexpectedly called upon to offer prayer. Of course he responded, and this was the beginning of the public career of H. Thane Miller. In the mid-week services Mr. Robinson was at his best in expository discourse. His lectures on the Gospel of John were long treasured in memory by hearers whose inner life was enriched by them.

In the third year of his pastorate there was an unusual degree of religious interest, as a result of which twenty-one persons were baptized. Among the church-members was a young man, Joseph Emery, engaged in business, who exhibited considerable fervor of spirit and freedom of utterance. Under the encouragement of Mr. Robinson, he assumed the position of missionary for the Baptist churches of Cincinnati. After several years of this service he became a missionary for the city at large. The Rev. Mr. Emery still continues his work, and has done an amount of good in jails, hospitals, etc., which cannot be estimated. He speaks affectionately of the kindness Mr. Robinson showed toward him, and of his faithfulness to the sick while the cholera desolated Cincinnati in 1849, when whole families were swept away and seven thousand people perished. Says the venerable city missionary, " He was the friend of the poor. "

But it was in the pulpit that he made his most memorable record. To the work of preaching he devoted all his energy. His discourses showed the results of intense and laborious study. He was accustomed to investigate topics rather than to elaborate special sermons. Sometimes a labored manner in the pulpit indicated a more hurried or less felicitous preparation than was usual for him; but never could he fail to impress his hearer that he was drawing from wells fed by hidden veins of faithful and profound investigation. Said one of his hearers, " He was an omnivorous reader." In his most successful efforts he was an imperial preacher. Beginning in a deliberate and quiet manner, never having manuscript or even note before him, he expressed himself in short and pithy sentences. Erelong some striking utterance, remarkable for its thought rather than for any artifice of rhetoric, would catch the hearer's attention. His bearing at first might seem a little constrained, perhaps almost awkward. His theme, like all the divisions of the discourse, was announced in the clearest and simplest language. Then, as his thought became more fluent, he warmed into easier action; his words, never showy or ambitious, came more readily; his gestures, fashioned after no school of oratory, yet never mechanical, and often strikingly appropriate, became expressive and energetic, and he carried his audience along on a tide of discourse which called their intellects into liveliest action, stirred their consciences, and brought them into the presence of the grandest realities of eternal truth. When his topic called out his best resources, he rose at times into a passion of eloquence, his whole form swaying, his words flowing with torrent-like impetuosity, every gesture adding force to his utterance, and the sweep of his thought seeming to bear everything before it. According to his favorite definition, " Eloquence is thought on fire," he was at times supremely eloquent. A lad who sat in his congregation through nearly all his ministry in Cincinnati, afterward went East, eager to hear some of the star preachers, whose praises had so long been familiar to him, — Beecher, Storrs, Chapin, and others. To his astonishment, he discovered that nowhere in the land could he find a preacher with power to stir his soul as it had been stirred in the old church in Cincinnati. Said the brother of one of America's noted literary characters, " I can never think slightingly of the Baptist denomination so long as I remember that the most magnificent preacher I ever heard was one of her ministers, Dr. Robinson. "

Of course, such a ministry as this soon filled the pews; not, however, with a miscellaneous throng, — for Mr. Robinson was never, in the familiar sense, a popular preacher, — but with earnest and thoughtful hearers. At one time an amusing incident occurred. Attracted by the celebrity of the preacher, a Quaker, Mr. Marcus Mote, wished to attend one of the services. He was deterred, however, by scruples as to the wearing of his hat. He did not wish to attract attention by keeping it on his head, and he was not willing to remove it. His friend, Mr. William H. Corwin, a son of the distinguished Hon. Thomas Corwin, proposed to obviate the difficulty. It was done in this wise. Accompanied by Mr. Corwin and Mr. George R. Sage, now Judge of the U. S. District Court of Southern Ohio, Mr. Mote walked up the aisle through its entire length, wearing his hat. He took his seat in one of the pews of " the saints' corner. " After a few moments had elapsed, Mr. Corwin, in presence of the entire congregation, solemnly arose, and, placing a hand on each side of Mr. Mote's hat, removed it from his head and laid it on the window-seat. The conscientious Friend was then able to enjoy the service.

Mr. Robinson's preaching was in the style of a prophet rather than of an apostle. His main emphasis was upon the law rather than the gospel. To hold up a high, moral standard, revealing the eternal righteousness of God, seemed to be his mission. Sometimes he would lean over the pulpit and, in gentle tones of tenderness and persuasion, give utterance to the pleading and welcoming spirit of the New Testament; but after a few sentences, he would seem to recollect himself, and, rising into an erect attitude, he would resume his customary more rigorous manner. It was during the last winter of his pastorship that he announced a series of special discourses. He was to discuss ten phases of scepticism in twelve or more discourses. They occupied the Sabbath evenings of the winter, and were heard by crowded houses. In the masterly handling of the topics, the intensity of the interest which they excited, the deep impression produced, and the tremendous energy of the speaker's oratory, they undoubtedly marked the high tide of his career as a preacher. These powerful discourses, lifting the audience to the heights of thought and of moral feeling, thrilling them with impassioned eloquence, and followed in each instance by one of Mr. Williams's magnificent anthems, left the hearers with remembrances to be treasured for a lifetime. Those who heard them repeated in Rochester a year later got but a slight suggestion of the power with which they came from the orator when fresh from the forge of his brain and heart.[1]

At last, one Sabbath morning, in 1853, appeared in the pulpit the tall form of President Anderson, of the University

[1] The extraordinary impression made in Cincinnati by the discourses on scepticism was due in part to the preacher's avowal of a native bent toward scepticism. The intelligent inquirer felt that his own difficulties were not only candidly but sympathetically weighed.

It was a characteristic, suspected by only a few intimate friends, of that intellectual honesty which every one recognized, that Dr. Robinson not only deferred to facts which tend toward scepticism, but gave due weight to those which in some minds foster credulity. See Appendix I.: The Case of Ann T. Peck. — ED.

of Rochester. He and Mr. Robinson had been fellow-students at Newton Theological Institution. He had come to persuade his friend to accept the presidency of the Theological Seminary at Rochester. The church raised a unanimous protest. Entreaty and argument were used. But Mr. Robinson recognized the call to higher duty and wider influence; he resigned his pastorship, and accepted the larger career, in which he wrought so wonderful a work. The church testified its high regard for him years afterward by extending to him an ineffectual call to return to the pastorship.[1]

Mr. Robinson had not achieved large evangelistic results; but in deep impressions on character, in the quickening and intensifying of moral impulses, and in engraving upon many minds the profound principles of sacred truth, he did an immortal work. Many who came into the church during the following pastorship referred their religious experience to impressions received from Mr. Robinson's preaching.

NOTE.

ON DR. ROBINSON'S HUMOR.

No student of Dr. Robinson could suspect him of lacking wit, and his responses on Class Day at Brown showed that he had abundant humor too. The Rev. Dr. T. G. Jones, who was a student in the University of Virginia at the time of Dr. Robinson's chaplaincy, writes: —

"We well remember his bringing his bride home during his chaplaincy, and the ovation which the students gave them on the occasion,

[1] Forty years after the pastorate in Cincinnati ended, fourteen well-known citizens, his old parishioners, signed an address to Dr. Robinson, in which they congratulated him on "his new home and new field of labor" at the University of Chicago, recalled the "noble characteristics . . . and enduring value" of his pastorate, and lovingly expressed the "admiration and pride" with which they had followed his career. — ED.

and the speech they called out from him, in which, alluding to Paul's celebrated saying that he who married did well, but that he who married not did better, the young chaplain said that he was perfectly satisfied to 'do well,' and was vociferously cheered by the students."

His old students in theology will find quite in his manner the opening paragraphs of an article from his pen on "Migrations of the Clergy," which appeared in the "Independent" for November 21, 1891 : —

" Few subjects so rich in inviting materials have been neglected by the comic papers and the caricaturists as that furnished by the now prevalent migrations of the clergy. The words that could be truthfully put into their mouths as they soliloquize in journeying from one sect to another would divulge some strange secrets ; and the cajoling terms in which a pair of them might exchange salutations as they chanced to meet on the way each to the denomination the other had forsaken, would be instructive as well as amusing.

" Nor would there be any sacrilege in such caricature. Grant the clergyman all the immunities that can be claimed for the sacredness of his office, if he makes himself ridiculous in it he must expect to be laughed at and ridiculed. It saves the office from reproach when he who by trifling dishonors it, is stigmatized for his trifling."

In attending one of Dr. Robinson's lectures on Christian Evidences at the Crozer Theological Seminary, Professor J. M. Stifler heard a characteristic bit of the Doctor's good-humored drollery, which he reports as follows : —

"One day in review a dull student was struggling to reproduce something which Dr. Robinson had given to the class in the lecture of the day previous. The student started in on a long sentence, but broke down before finishing it. He made a second attempt, but with no better success than before. He tried a third time, and brought his sentence to a close, but in such a way that it utterly failed to reflect the Doctor's thought, or any thought. 'Mr. ——,' said the Doctor, ' when a man runs his plane back and forth so often, he ought to bring up a shaving.' "

Many anecdotes of Dr. Robinson used to be afloat in Rochester, and generally illustrative of his sardonic and sometimes almost surly wit. Professor H. C. Vedder, who was long a resident as well as a student in Rochester, contributes the following as a fair specimen : —

" It is said that on one occasion the elders of a Presbyterian church in Rochester (just then without a pastor) waited on Dr. Robinson and asked him to preach for them. The church in question is somewhat 'high,' has rather an elaborate form of service, and its minister wears a Geneva gown. The elders were a little nervous about Dr. Robinson's views on such matters, and after the invitation to preach for them some Sundays had been given and accepted, the spokesman rather hesitatingly said : ' I suppose you know, Doctor, that we have a form of service in our church to which the people are accustomed ; would you have any objection to using that ?' ' Not at all,' said the Doctor, but a trifle brusquely, as if he did not altogether relish the thing, yet knew not how to refuse. ' But,' proceeded the spokesman, still more hesitatingly, ' our-er minister-er usually-er wears a gown ; would you-er-er have any objection —' ' No, no,' cut in the Doctor ; ' preach in my shirt-sleeves, if you wish me to.' The reply of the elders to this is not recorded ; but certain it is that Dr. Robinson preached for this congregation some months, and in gown too ; and that this same man remarked to him at the close of the engagement, ' Dr. Robinson, if you were only a Presbyterian, this church would give you a unanimous call, and would n't take No for an answer.' "

II.

DR. ROBINSON AS A THEOLOGIAN.

By PRESIDENT AUGUSTUS H. STRONG, D.D., LL.D.,
Rochester Theological Seminary.

II.

AS A THEOLOGIAN.

IN attempting a sketch of Dr. Robinson's theology, I find myself unable to dissociate the doctrine from the preacher, the administrator, and the man. To my teacher and predecessor I owe more than I owe to any one else outside of my own family circle ; and since this indebtedness must color all my judgments, it will be best to state frankly, at the start, what the debt was ; the reader can then make what allowance he chooses for the personal equation.

Some of my earliest impulses to preach were determined by Dr. Robinson's magnificent bearing in the pulpit when, as a boy, I listened to him in the early years of his work at Rochester. He dealt with great themes, yet he was a master of extemporaneous speech. His lucid, intense, and thoughtful utterance, exact in expression, yet always simply and severely natural, keyed ordinarily to a high intellectual pitch, but tremulous at times with emotion, revolutionized all my ideas of oratory, and I desired to be a minister of the gospel that I might be a public teacher. When I left College, and had to choose a place of Seminary training, it seemed to me that no one but Dr. Robinson could teach me how to preach. I began my course full of literature and history, but with small thought of the greater problems of existence. In his class-room I found my intellectual awakening. His searching questions, and the discussions that followed, roused my thinking powers as nothing ever had before. It became the pursuit of a lifetime to know the truth.

Of dogmatic instruction in theology, in those years, 1857–59, there was little. His brief dictations constituted not so much a system as a series of suggestions to stimulate inquiry. Our teacher appeared to be feeling his way along, and his great anxiety seemed to be that each of his pupils should feel his own way. Nothing vexed him more than a lazy repetition of traditional formulas. He often challenged even a correct statement, in order to see whether the utterer understood what he was saying. Aside from the magnetic, inspiring, and transforming influence of his own personality, the greatest service he rendered us was that he taught us to think for ourselves.

As a theologian, he was at this time critical rather than constructive. He represented the tendencies of Brown and Newton, rather than those of Hamilton, from which his predecessor, Dr. Maginnis, had come. Dr. Maginnis, our teacher of Theology during the first two years of the Seminary's existence, was a Princeton theologian of the straitest sect. But Dr. Robinson at Brown University had been under the influence of President Wayland, who was partly educated at Andover, and was a great admirer of Professor Stuart. At Newton Theological Institution Dr. Robinson had been instructed by Dr. Irah Chase and Dr. Barnas Sears. Dr. Chase taught a theology so unlike that of Princeton that some of our extremely orthodox ministers refused to put their sons under what they regarded as heterodox teaching. Dr. Sears taught but little positive doctrine of any kind. His method was to suggest questions rather than to answer them. Scholarship and discussion were the main features of his class-room. No one of these teachers of Dr. Robinson had been strongly conservative. All had been men noted for independence as well as for thinking power.

Dr. Robinson began his theological teaching in a place where the traditions, though brief, were in favor of an old-fashioned theology. New England thinking was regarded as a sort of free-thinking. Dr. Shedd's realistic interpretations of the old orthodoxy were not yet widely known, even if they had been published. Princeton still claimed to represent the immemorial faith of the Church of God. There were elements of the Old-School doctrine which Dr. Robinson cherished as his very life. Neither Andover nor New Haven ever made a convert of him. He even seems to have tried, at the first, to use the traditional formulas of the theology of the Covenants. But it is clear to me that he felt the arbitrariness and externalism of the Princeton system, even though he had not shaken himself wholly loose from it. The lectures which he dictated at this time are cautious statements of the dominant orthodoxy, with its more mechanical features greatly softened down, and with the accompanying suggestion of new points of view which logically imply another and a better faith.

We must remember that he always taught homiletics side by side with theology, and that he deeply felt the responsibility of instructing men who were to repeat his views to all the world with an emphasis and exaggeration of their own. Therefore he made haste slowly. He was no iconoclast. He never intended to break with the old. He regarded theological terms as largely metaphorical, and his aim was to discover the substance that underlay them. He could have subscribed to John Bunyan's couplet:—

> "My dark and cloudy words, they do but hold
> The truth, as cabinets encase the gold."

He criticised with great severity the legal fictions of the Princeton school, but he had the deepest reverence for the reality which they sought so unfortunately to express. In fact, I regard the passionate bent toward reality as the central characteristic of his intellectual life. Shows and forms he had small sympathy with. He would get at the inner being. He censured all theologizing that did not go to the heart of the matter. He disdained all conduct that savored of pretence. When he spoke, he would say nothing, or he would say the truth. The truth, as he at the time conceived it, was often biting and galling to those whose views he antagonized. But Dr. Robinson did not spare on that account. Like Stein, the great German, he was proud toward man, but humble toward God.

From 1853 to 1872 he was professor of Biblical Theology in the Rochester Theological Seminary, and from 1868 to 1872 he was its President. During all the years of his professorship, as well as of his presidency, he was the one man who gave name and fame to the institution, and the one man who drew to it students and endowments. Drs. Conant and Hotchkiss and Northrup and Kendrick and Hackett and Rauschenbusch and Buckland were, in those early days, most able coadjutors, and their services were very great. But it is still true that to Dr. Robinson the institution at Rochester owes more of its character and success than to any other single man. The Seminary, which at the beginning of his administration in 1853 was absolutely destitute of property or endowments, had, in 1872, resources amounting to $224,000. This increase represents an amount of personal and skilful work on the part of one man which would simply challenge admiration, if it were not so pathetic and incongruous an expenditure of energy. That a thinker and teacher of such mark should have been compelled to turn aside from his proper work in order to solicit rich men's gifts, and to make his own living not by his week-day instruction but by his Sunday preaching, is pitiful enough. Yet such are the toils and trials that have gone to the founding of all our great educational institutions.

The institution prospered, — prospered so much that Brown University coveted its President, and at last succeeded in drawing him away to another sphere of labor. But this prosperity was purchased at a price. Dr. Robinson had not the time nor the strength which he ought to have had for the maturing and the publishing of his theological system. He was not a ready writer, and systematizing, with him, was a slow work. His critical faculty was always asserting itself, and was hindering the work of positive construction. But before his teaching at Rochester ended, his views had to a considerable extent crystallized, and he had proceeded a long way in the elaboration of his " Christian Theology." Three hundred and twenty pages of it were actually printed. He reached the subject of Regeneration; but there the work stopped. His new duties at Brown absorbed him, and theology was never taken up again. The loose sheets, with the exception of a few which fell into the hands of favored friends, have been boxed up for these twenty-two years. And so the work remains, like Aladdin's palace-hall, with only a window to add, but with no one to finish it.[1]

When I began my own work, as Dr. Robinson's successor, I deeply felt the overmastering influence of his teaching I knew that my ways of theological thinking had been largely shaped by him. I feared, if I made use of his

[1] Since Dr. Strong's article was written, the " Christian Theology " of Dr. Robinson has been published. — ED.

recently printed notes, that I should become a copyist. I resolved, therefore, to construct my own system *de novo*, without once looking at what my former teacher had written. In fact, the pages of his work have only, within a few months, been in my hands for careful scrutiny. Two things I desire to say with regard to the impressions which the reading has made upon me. First, I have a new reverence for the general weight and correctness of Dr. Robinson's theological·teaching. Here is a noble body of doctrine, grand in its leading conception, wrought out with singular originality, and in most of its lines true to Scripture. The quarter of a century which has passed since he began to print it has brought some new truths into prominence; if he could now write it over again, he would, doubtless, qualify some of his statements and make others clearer; yet it is still true that the work is even now one of great significance, and sure, if published, to attract the attention and respect of the theological world. Secondly, I am humbled to find how much of my own thinking that I thought original has been an unconscious reproduction of his own. Words and phrases which I must have heard from him in the class-room thirty-five years ago, and which have come to be a part of my mental furniture, I now recognize as not my own but his. And the ruling idea of his system, — that stands out as the ruling idea of mine; I did not realize until now that I owed it almost wholly to him.

Jean Paul says, beautifully, of the obscure teachers of village schools, that they fall from notice like the spring-blossoms, but they fall that the fruit may be born. Dr. Robinson's self-effacing way of pouring his own mind and will into his pupils, rather than of putting himself into printed books, has lessened his fame, but it has brought forth abundant fruit. Through hundreds of the foremost men of our Baptist denomination, he has been preaching truth and righteousness for forty years. I wish to be one of the first to put the praise where it belongs, and to say that the impulse to clear and manly utterance in the pulpit, the love of exact statement, the disposition to preach truth rather than tradition, which have of late years transformed our Baptist pulpit and brought it abreast of our advancing age, have been chiefly due, under God, to the teaching and the example of Dr. Robinson.

I have said that the passionate bent toward reality was the central characteristic of his intellectual life. He believed in reality because he believed in God. Yet many of his struggles and difficulties originated in a philosophy which obscured the testimony of our nature to God's existence and attributes. He had been greatly influenced by the reading of Kant. Hamilton and Mansel, who reproduced a part of Kant's doctrine, strongly attracted him. The relativity of knowledge perpetually discounted the things of faith. It is interesting to see how Dr. Robinson, while greatly influenced by this philosophy, made his way, notwithstanding, through it, and in spite of it, to essential truth both with regard to God and with regard to God's revelation. He was one of the first in this country to subject the common arguments for the existence of God to a careful criticism, after the Kantian fashion. Here, as well as elsewhere, he was the sworn foe to over-statement in doctrine, — indeed, he preferred to err on the side of doubt rather than on the side of dogmatism. Rational minds, he would say, cannot observe their own laws of thought in the contemplation of cosmical phenomena without believing in a primal and personal Force, lying behind all, and originating the universal whole. The world abounds in adaptations to ends; therefore the world must have been purposed; or, in other words, there is a personal Intelligence by whom it has been fashioned. Man, with his aspirations and cravings, can find an ideal only in God, while the moral distinctions which man is forced to make give unmistakable testimony to the existence of One who is at once man's Author and his ultimate Standard of right and wrong.

Although I do not find anywhere, in Dr. Robinson's chapter on God's existence, the phrase " immanent finality," I do find such an avoidance of the old " carpenter-phraseology " as to suggest that he viewed God's relation to the universe as not mechanical but organic. Yet while man, conscious of causality, intelligence, and responsibility in himself, is reminded, as he looks out into the universe, of a supreme and universal Cause, Intelligence, and Judge, no one of all the arguments can be said to be a demonstration. " The evidence of the Divine existence is not so much logical as moral; it is adjusted rather to the eye of the soul than to the logical faculty; if the eye be darkened, God is not seen in any evidence of his being." It is to man's moral consciousness, then, rather than to argument, that Dr. Robinson would appeal, while he still regards the arguments for God's existence as valuable means of stimulating this consciousness, and of calling attention to the revelations which God has made of himself.

There is a striking similarity between our author's method in speaking of Inspiration, and his method in speaking of the Existence of God. He treats God's revelation in his Word just as he treats God's revelation in nature. As it is not the fragments and petty details of the Universe that reveal the designing Mind, so in the Bible the argument for Inspiration is drawn from the book as a whole rather than from its separate parts. To inspire, he would say, was not necessarily to educate. The whole early Church was inspired, and the office of the Spirit in inspiration was not different from that which he performed for many ordinary Christians at the time when the New Testament was written. Inspiration was consistent with imperfect ideas in the minds of the Scripture writers, and the literary, logical, scientific, and historical defects which modern investigation has made apparent are only indications of a human element which the divine pressed into its service, or in spite of which the truth was progressively unfolded. The higher criticism had not become rife when Dr. Robinson constructed his system; but the principle and spirit of it, so far as it is theistic and reverent, are Dr. Robinson's own, and his whole conception of inspiration is surprisingly like that which has of late become so current. He did not regard the imprecations of the Psalms, for example, as inspired by God. Only the divine purposes and ideas were inspired, and the imprecations were but the drapery or the vehicle by which those purposes and ideas were necessarily interpreted to early times. As David's adultery was not commanded by God, yet was made the means of the descent of Christ, so human error was sometimes made the means of introducing into the world the revelation of the perfect God.

Yet Dr. Robinson declares the Christian religion " to be, in comparison with all other religions, in an exclusive sense, revealed," and its records were " made by men who were guided, as no other writers ever were, by an omniscient Spirit." He discards all theories of Inspiration, and " declines any attempt to state by what method the Spirit must have fulfilled the Divine will in the writing of the Scriptures." Each of the Scripture penmen, indeed, received and communicated the truth in his own way, and with such mingling of the human element with the divine that it is impossible to distinguish between the word of

God and the Scriptures through which that word has come to us. "The Bible can be properly understood only as a whole, as an organic growth of many centuries, all of which are necessary to be taken into account if we would see the consistency of its parts, the one with another; and though the writings of each age, Mosaic, Prophetic, and Christian, are now requisite to the completeness and intelligibility of Scripture as a whole, yet to each age its own revelations and writings, conjoined with all that had preceded, must have been absolutely authoritative, because it was as complete and explicit a revelation of the divine Mind as then was possible."

This view of the organic unity of Scripture, and the doctrine that Scripture, only as a whole, represents absolute truth, were views not common when Dr. Robinson began to teach. The clear statement of them, indeed, was wrought out only toward the close of his theological career. But the substance of them had lain long in his mind, and even his earliest students can remember the impatience with which he regarded the quotation of an isolated verse, as if it were a proof-text apart from its context and its historical setting. Hence he supplemented all other Biblical arguments by "the analogy of faith." For the Bible, as a whole, he had profound reverence. Though he did not assert that it was inerrant in unimportant matters of historical and scientific detail, he did believe it to be a complete and sufficient rule of faith and practice. Yet he did not deny that infinite wisdom has provided many helps to the study of the Scriptures. History, science, philosophy could even be called "collateral sources of theology." By this he meant that physical nature and human nature are themselves revelations of God, and that from them we are to learn all we can, though the "one direct and controlling source to which the decisive appeal must always be made is the Sacred Scriptures."

The attributes of God were defined by Dr. Robinson as "our methods of conceiving of him." Here I think he yielded too much to the Kantian and Hamiltonian relativity, and made it possible to regard the attributes as existing only in our subjective thought. But the further development of the subject makes it plain that he did not intend to be so interpreted. "Any argumentation," he says, "which will show that our conceptions of God can only be relatively true to us, and not positively true in themselves, will equally avail to overthrow the trustworthiness of all our knowledge, and can end only in universal scepticism. Our conceptions are inadequate, but not, therefore, untrue; they are limited because we are finite, but not, therefore, contradictory or false." This is sound and true. How, then, shall we interpret such *dicta* as the following: "The attributes do not represent distinguishable properties in the divine essence. . . . To suppose that we treat of essence when we treat of attributes is to confound God with our conceptions of him." I can answer my own question only by saying that Dr. Robinson was hampered here by a wrong philosophy. To him, as to Kant, the essence was always "the thing in itself," and could not be known. A more modern and more correct philosophy admits no such element of inherent and eternal agnosticism. Though essence can be known only through attributes, it is still true that, in knowing attributes, we know essence. Surely God is not concealed by his very manifestation. The reason why we cannot perfectly know God is that we cannot perfectly know his attributes; not that knowledge of attributes does not involve knowledge of essence. We do not fully know God's attributes because he has not fully revealed them, and because we are not great enough to understand them. But we do know them in part, and in just so far we know God. As in knowing phenomena we know the object, so in knowing God's attributes we partially know God himself. Attributes, therefore, should be defined, not as our conceptions of God, but rather as those objective characteristics of the divine Being which are necessary to the idea of God, and which constitute the basis and ground for his various manifestations to his creatures.

The slightly agnostic element to which I have alluded combined with Dr. Robinson's critical faculty to tone down his statements and to make them severely self-restrained. All the more strong and convincing were his teachings on matters where he had made discoveries or had invented new methods. We must give to him the credit for a new classification of the divine attributes according to the order of the relations that make them known: first, attributes related to space and time, as immensity and eternity; secondly, attributes related to the material universe, as omnipresence, omniscience, and omnipotence; thirdly, attributes related to moral creatures, as holiness, truth, love. But it is especially in his recognition of holiness, as the fundamental and supreme attribute, that I find his greatest originality and his greatest service to the theology of our time. When we remember how the New England theology was exalting benevolence, or the love of being in general, to the supreme place, and, by making holiness a means to an end, was denying to it any independent existence in the divine nature; when we remember how even Old School theologians defined holiness as the mere aggregate of the divine perfections, and so deprived it of any distinct significance, — we can appeciate the originality and the grandeur of Dr. Robinson's view, when he declared that " holiness should be our fundamental conception," and that "from it every other moral attribute may be synthetized or logically deduced."

Our materialistic and easy-going age has drifted even farther from the truth than it was a quarter of a century ago. Dr. Robinson foresaw the consequences to theology and to morals of a virtually utilitarian philosophy, and he laid the foundation of his system in the ethical being of God. What conscience declares to be highest in us must be highest in God. "Justice does not exist for certain *ends;* it is the expression of eternal right; it is the inexorable demand of related moral natures. Accompanying benefits reveal neither the grounds of its existence nor the qualities of its nature." Instead of holiness being a form of love, it is far more true that love is a form of holiness, "A pure being seeks the purity of others, and in so doing shows his mercy. Benevolence is only a generic and more comprehensive conception than mercy." This view of holiness as the fundamental attribute of God prepares the way for what was probably the most impressive and inspiring part of his teaching; I mean his idea of law as the expression of God's holiness, or the transcript of the moral nature of God. No man who sat under Dr. Robinson's instruction can ever forget the scorn with which he treated the vulgar notion of law as something devised or invented, a makeshift to meet an exigency, an arbitrary enactment for the good of the creature, founded in mere will, unmade as easily as made, suspended or abrogated by fiat even as mere fiat had given it birth. Nor can any student of his forget his sublime and perpetual insistence on moral law as the eternal and unchangeable expression of the nature of God and the relations between God and his creatures, — an expression so eternal and unchangeable that God himself cannot change his law without ceasing to be God.

By these conceptions of holiness and law Dr. Robinson

defined his position as an Old-School man, and made it impossible that he should have any other than an Old-School view of sin. For, observe that this law, which is itself the transcript of the divine holiness, is simply the demand in the nature of things that the creature within the limits of its own being should be morally like its Creator. Law requires conformity to God, therefore, not only in act and in disposition, but in the very state and substance of the soul. All lack of conformity to God is sin. Guilt is the obligation to suffer for such lack, and penalty is the natural reaction of the violated law. Is man unlike God in act, disposition, or state? Then, however he came into this condition, he is sinful, guilty, punishable. All men by nature, and from their first father down, are in this state of sin and guilt and punishment, and can be delivered from it, not by any effort or merit of their own, but solely by the grace and power of God in Jesus Christ. If we were to speak of Dr. Robinson's soteriology we might find something to criticise; but in our judgment his doctrine of holiness, law, and sin are worthy of all praise.

I have put these three things — holiness, law, and sin — together, although they are ordinarily separated in a theological system, and I have put them together in order to show conclusively that our author, in spite of peculiar views with regard to the method and the application of the atonement, cherished such conceptions as logically necessitated the deity and the propitiatory sacrifice of our Lord Jesus Christ. But before describing his opinions on these later points, it will be necessary to go back to his view of creation, preservation, and providence. Here we have another illustration of his refusal to dogmatize where he regarded Scripture as teaching nothing decisive, and of his earnest effort to reach reality beneath the forms of traditional statement. To his mind it was an open question whether the Scriptures teach the absolute *origination* of matter. The Hebrew word *bara* did not seem to him to settle the question. Yet he recognized in the organic *forms* of matter the embodied thought of a creative Will. " Even spontaneous generation does not preclude the idea of such a creative Will, working by natural law and secondary causes. Of beginnings of life, physical science knows nothing. Of the processes of nature it is competent to speak, and against its teachings there is no need that theology should set itself in hostility. "

I do not know how much of an attraction the idealistic interpretation of the universe had for Dr. Robinson. The mention of secondary causes above, and his declaration in another place that space must have existed before the universe, would seem to show that he sought no relief from the problem of creation in the thought that matter, as ideal, may also be eternal. But, in treating of preservation and providence, he seems to verge toward the idealistic explanation. Though he denies that law is simply uniform divine action, he also denies the so-called *concursus* of God with finite causes. Though he declares that " God's relation to the material universe is unknown and unknowable," he also declares that " matter and physical force are indissolubly one," that " all forces are modes of one force," and that " this force is personal force." " The natural is God's work. He originated it. There is no separateness between the natural and the supernatural. The natural *is* supernatural. God works in everything. Every end, even though attained by mechanical means, is as truly God's end as if wrought by miracle. " Here the more modern conception of the universe seems to be working in Dr. Robinson's mind, and to be coloring his thought. His readiness to recognize the working of God both in nature and in man, and his unreadiness to postulate a *Deus ex machina* where the " Spirit within the wheels " would account for all the facts, seem like an unconscious anticipation of the thought of God's immanence, which is so transforming the theology of our generation.

The definition of miracle as a " special sign from God, authenticating the claim of one of his messengers," is confessedly intended to exclude all dogmatizing with regard to the relation of the miracle to natural law and to second causes. If the signality of the miracle be maintained, then it matters not, even if natural law itself be the perpetual working of God. Mere outward wonder cannot certify to a divine commission, unless the teaching and the life of the worker commend themselves to the moral consciousness. The resurrection of our Lord, as a witness to Christianity, depends as much on the existence of the Church, as the Church rests for its foundation upon the resurrection of our Lord. The living Church is the burning bush that is not consumed. The church has the word " resurrection " written all over it. Its very existence is proof of the resurrection. Twelve men could never have founded the Church if Christ had remained in the tomb. Dr. Robinson would defend miracles, then, but he would not rest the whole weight of Christianity upon them. " No amount of miracle could convince a good man of the divine commission of a known bad man ; nor, on the other hand, could any degree of miraculous power suffice to silence the doubts of an evil-minded man." " The miracle is a certification only to him who can perceive its significancy."

As miracle involves no violation or suspension of natural law, so the ordinary providential government of God is conducted in such a way as to give full range to human freedom. Man's will as well as God's will can effect results without producing any jar in the system. I could wish that, in his treatment of the will, Dr. Robinson had more definitely set himself against determinism. He seems rather to intimate that Jonathan Edwards's argument has never been satisfactorily answered. The highest conceivable freedom, he says, is to act out one's nature. The will is the nature in movement. Will is self-determining, indeed; but this means, not that the will determines the self, but that the self determines the will. Observation and logic lead to necessitarianism. We have no consciousness of a power of contrary choice, for consciousness testifies only to what springs out of the moral nature, not to what the moral nature itself is. Yet consciousness testifies, in some sense, to freedom. Single volitions are often directly in the face of the current of a man's life. The will cannot be compelled; for, unless self-determined, it is no longer will. The consciousness of freedom must be trusted, even though we cannot reconcile it with our logic. So Dr. Robinson does not decide the philosophical question, though it is plain that his leanings are toward determinism. He declares that the will is as great a mystery as is the doctrine of the Trinity. As we do not know the nature of the human will, so we do not know the connection between human volitions and the divine will. But we do know, he says, — and this I regard as a most valuable and reassuring statement, — we do know that "the absolute certainty of events, which is all that Omniscience determines with regard to them, is not identical with their necessitation."

So the doctrine of Providence is connected with the doctrine of Decrees. "To the omniscient Mind, in which there is no succession, no events are contingent. Causes, with their conditions and effects, are alike and always known as indissolubly one. God's knowledge and purposes both being eternal, one cannot be conceived as the ground of the other, nor can either be predicated to the exclusion of the other as the cause of things; but, correlative and eternal, they must be co-equal quantities in thought." It might possibly occur to an objector to say that when God knows what he will do, his willing is the ground of his knowing, instead of his knowing being the ground of his willing. This is practically granted in other parts of the system, as, for example, where it is suggested that answers to prayer are consistent with the immutability of natural law, because the immutability of natural law has its only explanation and ground in the decrees of God; or where, under the head of Calling and Election, he declares that " in becoming Christians, men are moved, controlled, and transformed by a power of Will superior to their own, and that in transforming them the divine Will simply executes its eternal purpose." He justly prefers the Scriptural doctrine to that of the Positivists, who " disdain decree, but consign us to the iron necessity of physical forces," and to that of Pelagians or Arminians, whose system is " necessarily one-sided, and ministers ruinously to the pride of man."

But we must hasten to Dr. Robinson's anthropology. Here he diverged from the traditional view of man's original state, by teaching that the image of God in the first man did not imply moral perfection, but only the possession of those higher powers which distinguish man from the brute. " Christ," he says, " proposes to carry forward human nature to a higher point, not simply to restore what was lost." The phrase " very good," which is used to describe man's first condition, " does not imply moral perfection." Such perfection cannot be the result of creation, but must be attained through discipline and will. Man's original state was only one of untried innocence. I have no doubt that the old orthodoxy, which Dr. Robinson was here opposing, unduly magnified the powers and virtues of the first father of our race. When Dr. South declared that " Aristotle was but the rubbish of an Adam," he went far beyond Scripture. But it seems to me that Dr. Robinson went to quite the opposite extreme when he made the image of God consist in mere personality, and denied to the first man any, even a germinal, holiness of character. If, when God newly creates the soul in Christ, he gives a germinal " righteousness and holiness of truth," then in the original creation he could also impart a tendency toward the good and a love for himself. To deny this is to imply the whole Roman Catholic doctrine that man, being created destitute of moral character attains to holiness and earns God's favor by his own obedience.

There are two reasons, however, why I must decline to attribute this Roman Catholic doctrine to Dr. Robinson, and must regard him as protesting against an ultra-Protestant exaggeration of man's original excellence rather than against the substance of the Protestant view. One reason is that he grants man's possession, by creation, of " right spontaneities" or " a constitutional predisposition toward a course of right conduct;" and the other is that, in his own doctrine of regeneration, he so freely concedes that the original impulse and love of righteousness must come from God. So he appears to grant to the first man right *tendencies*, but to deny to the first man right *character*. At the same time, I could wish for a stronger affirmation than he has given us of man's original moral likeness to God. He describes him as " immature and untried at the outset, and consequently, at the best, only sinless." " His civil and social condition must have been of the humblest," he says. " But on the other hand, the supposition of an original savage condition, but little if any removed from the level of the more intelligent brutes, is a mere conjecture, unsupported by any decisive evidence, besides being wholly contrary to the Scriptures." One may question, however, whether the Scriptural argument against man's descent from the brute would have seemed to him so conclusive, if this chapter had been written a quarter of a century later, when the Darwinian theory is so generally accepted, and when evolution is regarded by so many theologians as the method of creation pursued by the immanent God.

It is easy to see that whatever view is taken of man's original state must profoundly affect one's view of man's fall. Dr. Robinson did not grant to man at the beginning any great height of virtue, even if he could be said to have virtue at all. But man was sinless; his state was one of innocence; he was "endowed with free-will;" he "could have resisted temptation and could have moved ever onward in normal development. Uninfluenced from without, he might, or rather, so far as any analysis of his actions for us is possible, he must, have remained an unfallen being." And our author goes on most admirably to say, "How, even under temptation, he could have so willed against his nature as by volition to have changed the nature itself, is absolutely inconceivable. But that he was capable of such volition, and by its exercise fell from his original sinlessness, is plainly taught in the Scriptures, and the reproaches of the individual conscience for personal obliquities, even amid the darkness and ruin of the fall, seem to be conclusive evidence of the same great fact." So Dr. Robinson transferred the whole blame of sin from God to man. And not only to the first man, but to all men; for "whatever befell the progenitors of the race, their descendants have inherited. By the fall there was lost an original righteousness"— here I call attention to the fact that our author had not entirely given up the idea of some positive tendencies to good in our first parents —" by the fall there was lost an original righteousness, which, but for its loss, would have been the birthright of every one of the race, and in its stead there were incurred certain positive evils which to every one have been a heritage of woe."

Dr. Robinson's doctrine of original sin cannot be understood without remembering that all lack of conformity to God is sin, and that no proper distinction can be drawn between penalty and consequences. "The distinction between penalty and consequences," he says, "between guilt and liability, so much insisted on in modern theology, can be maintained only by limiting our knowledge of moral law to the mere statutes of the Bible; by restricting human guilt to the violation of those statutes, and by so distinguishing between Nature and Revelation as most unwarrantably to separate them. But if God be the author of the constitution and course of Nature, if the office of the formal revelation of the Bible be to supplement and to supplant the earlier revelation of Nature, then all painful consequences of wrong acts must be as distinctly penal as if they had been formally threatened." Thus light is thrown back upon holiness, law, and sin : these are regarded as constitutional, not as matters of outward expediency or enactment. As all men, in consequence of the fall, lack the holiness which the law requires, they are sinners; as this lack is the fault of their common humanity, they are guilty; as it brings upon them pain and loss, they are under penalty and condemnation.

A definition of sin which covers all the facts of the case has always been a great desideratum. To say that sin consists in sinning is to confine attention to its most superficial aspect, while its deadly force is altogether ignored. Dr.

Robinson has probably given us the most comprehensive and exact definition of sin that can be found in theological literature, — namely, " As an act, sin is a transgression of God's law; as a principle that determines the guilt of acts, it is opposition or hostility to God; as a state or nature, it is moral unlikeness to God." He had no difficulty in concluding that the essence of sin, that in it which makes it to be sin, is neither sensuousness nor unbelief, but selfishness, or an inordinate self-love and self-seeking. " A certain degree of self-love is allowable. . . . But all love, to self or others, is legitimate only as it is subordinate to, and purified by, an intelligent and all-inclusive love to the common Father of all. All love becomes sinful, selfish, idolatrous, in proportion as its object is isolated from God. . . . Unselfishness is the soul of virtue, and selfishness is the vitalizing principle of every vice and of every variety of sin." Sin, then, in a true sense, is itself death, since it is the soul's voluntary withdrawal from God, the source of life and purity. While Dr. Robinson did not deny that physical death, or the separation of the soul from the body, is a consequence of Adam's sin, he held that spiritual death, or the separation of the soul from God, is sin's chief penalty. With separation of the soul from God, moreover, there has ensued a disintegration of man's own spiritual being. The real freedom of the will, which consists in the harmonious working of all the faculties, has been lost, and only that formal freedom which is a necessary condition of rational existence now remains.

As to the common guilt of the human race, Dr. Robinson was a believer in mediate imputation. Since his theology dealt primarily with conditions and not with edicts, he grounded the condemnation of the race not so much upon a common act of the race in Adam, as upon the more palpable fact of universal and congenital depravity. It is only through each man's depravity that we can impute to him guilt. Here, as it seems to me, our author diverged from the teaching of Scripture, became inconsistent with himself, and adopted a principle which burdened him greatly when he came to explain Christ's taking our penalty upon him. Dr. Robinson had granted that the consequences of the first sin are to Adam's posterity precisely what they were to Adam himself. But to Adam they were certainly first guilt, and then depravity. To Adam's descendants, also, the consequences of Adam's sin came in the same order. Jonathan Edwards saw this when he said: " The sin of the apostasy is not theirs merely because God imputes it to them; but it is truly and properly theirs, and on that ground God imputes it to them." And Edwards is only echoing Paul, who bases God's infliction of the penalty of death, not upon the ground that all are sinful, but upon the ground that " all sinned." Since the depravity is caused by the apostasy, we cannot be guilty of the depravity without first being guilty of the apostasy.

Dr. Robinson was a realist, but here, unfortunately, he did not consistently apply his realism. He should have considered that as Adam's act was condemnable apart from its consequences, so we, who were one with him in the transgression, have incurred guilt apart from the depravity which is a consequence of that act. A failure to recognize this leads him to mitigate the judgment which he passes upon the depravity itself. He says it is " condemnable and punishable, because it is in a sense sinful and guilty," and yet he concedes that " the words 'sin' and 'guilt,' when applied to an inherited nature, must necessarily have a restricted meaning as compared with that which attaches to them when applied to our voluntary actions. In the consequences of all voluntary wrong acts there is mingled an element of remorse, which can never enter into the penal consequences of a state or of a nature." When it is objected, however, that inborn depravity cannot be sin, if conscience brings no charge of guilt against it, he replies that, however true this may be of the nature in its passive state, it is not true when the nature is roused to activity. Then the " conscience traces guilt to its seat in the inherited nature." But guilt of nature Dr. Robinson does not explain. How we can be responsible for what is ours solely through the act of our ancestors, he does not tell us. His theology would have been more consistent if he had been more thoroughly realistic and Pauline, and had said plainly, " In Adam's fall we sinned all." It is unjust to hold us guilty of the effect if we be not first guilty of the cause.

But in spite of Dr. Robinson's unwillingness to press his principle to its logical conclusion, there can be no doubt that he believed in the organic unity of the race, and in its common guilt and punishableness. Even infants are born with a nature sinful, depraved, and condemnable, though they are in a salvable condition, and if they die in infancy they are saved. In their case the evil which has been involuntarily incurred is removed by a remedy which is provided equally without the volition of the sufferer. The explanation given of the method of their salvation is significant. " To destroy the germ of evil in the heart of an infant, it must, somewhere and somehow, as well as children and adults, be brought to a knowledge and love of Christ; in order to this knowledge and love, while as yet the evil is undeveloped into habit, Christ needs only to be seen; and if Christ, who, while on earth, said, 'Suffer little children to come unto me, and forbid them not, for of such is the kingdom of heaven,' shall receive the little ones

to himself on their entrance into another life, it certainly is
neither inconceivable nor improbable that the undeveloped
evil of their nature should give place at once to an implanted
and all-controlling love for him whom to know is life
eternal." I do not understand Dr. Robinson to be teaching here that, in the infant, mere knowledge can eradicate
sin, or that sin can be forgiven without atonement. I
understand our author to be describing simply the method
in which, in the case of the infant, the atonement is applied
and the heart is renewed by the Spirit of God.

As I have already intimated, Dr. Robinson was a strong
believer in the absolute deity of our Lord Jesus Christ.
But he also believed in Christ's complete humanity. His
conception of the relation between the divine and the human
elements in Christ is so essential to his system that we
must endeavor precisely to grasp it. He has the great merit
of being one of the first in America to unfold the doctrine of
the Kenosis, or self-limitation of the Logos in becoming
man. The old orthodoxy had made the person of Christ
unintelligible and incredible, by maintaining our Lord's
continual consciousness of his deity, and his continual
use of divine powers. This was either Docetism, a doctrine
of merely illusory humanity, or Nestorianism, a doctrine
virtually of two persons as well as of two natures. Our
author began his study from the oneness of Christ's person.
" The personal Logos was not so associated and conjoined
with a personal Jesus as to produce a kind of double personality ; " he rather " assumed, by supernatural generation,
from the Virgin Mary, a true human nature, though not, as
distinct from himself, a human personality. . . . Christ
assumed human nature, but he did not assume a human
person ; and the two natures were so conjoined as to constitute a single personality." He inveighed against sepa-

rating the two natures, and conceiving that our Lord spoke at one time as man and at another time as God. He maintained that this attributed unveracity to Christ, and held that our Lord spoke everywhere and always as the God-man, even when he declared that he was ignorant of the day of the end. I regard this doctrine of the single personality of Christ, and of the divine self-limitation in becoming man, as one of the noblest and most valuable parts of his teaching.

What human nature did our Lord take? Our author answers rightly: "He took the common nature of the race; not the nature of the unfallen Adam; nor yet a new-created nature, different alike from Adam's and our own; but the nature of those whom he came to save." But our race and nature were sinful; did Christ, then, in taking our nature, take a sinful nature, as Edward Irving taught? This Dr. Robinson denies. "Sin," he says, "is properly predicable only of personality; the hereditary depravity of man is derived by the natural descent of personal life from Adam; Christ did not derive a personal human life *ex traduce* from Adam, but took our human nature by a supernatural act, which cut off its hereditary guilt, though not the hereditary consequences of its guilt. . . . Hereditary depravity was in his case cut off from transmission by the supernatural manner of his assuming it. . . . No truth is more plainly, continuously, and variously taught, than the perfect sinlessness, the unapproachable moral perfection, of Jesus Christ; and his sinlessness was all the more conspicuous and marvellous that it was maintained under the load of a fallen nature and in the midst of a sinful race, with whom he had so closely identified himself. . . . Notwithstanding the nature he had assumed, and the race with which he had allied himself, he could preserve his sinlessness, because the basis of his personality was his divine nature and not the human. In becoming incarnate, he assumed human nature in its completeness, and yet so assumed it as completely to control it; whereas, in the birth of individual men, human nature simply assumes the form of personal life which it completely controls. Christ was conscious of the infinite purity of his own person because his consciousness was grounded in the divine nature which underlay and conditioned his whole personal being."

These extracts from Dr. Robinson's chapter on "The Two Natures of Jesus Christ" make it very plain that he did not regard our Lord as inheriting either depravity or guilt. And yet he inherits the consequence of guilt, — that is, penalty. This is our author's doctrine of the atonement. He insists that the necessity of the atonement is grounded in the holiness of God. "God, as holy, necessarily repels all sinners from his presence, and by the very act of repulsion punishes them. Whoever, therefore, should assume our nature, and take his place among us as one of our race, and take it for the express purpose of redeeming us from sin and reconciling us to God, would be under the inexorable necessity of so confronting the divine repulsion as to remove it, or he could not achieve our redemption. . . . He must bear our penalty, and, in bearing, survive it." But in addition to this: "The substitution which takes place in the intervention of Christ for the salvation of men must be of such a nature as to secure an actual personal righteousness on the part of the redeemed." Atonement, then, is, on the one hand, as respects God, an expiation of guilt, and as respects man, a means of reconciliation, renewal, and final salvation.

In criticising Dr. Shedd's theory that the atonement is

" an atonement *ab intra*, a self-oblation on the part of Deity himself, by which to satisfy those immanent and eternal imperatives of the divine nature, which without it must find their satisfaction in the punishment of the transgressor, or else be outraged," Dr. Robinson objects that " an atonement made necessary to balance the character of God could not be a gratuity to men. . . . Literal forensic substitution," he says, " involves a contradiction of the idea of absolute justice on which the whole theory rests. An absolute justice in God, which his mercy could satisfy or not, shuts us up to the alternative either of a one-sided nature in God, or of an atonement which is stripped of every vestige of grace." He has no patience with the representation of an " immutable justice which is so far mutable as to accept of a commutation both of persons and of punishments." We are obliged to grant that, to make Dr. Shedd's view tenable, another principle of identification must be introduced which Dr. Shedd has not mentioned; only the union of all men with Christ by creation can make Christ's substitution consistent with justice. Of this principle, which neither Dr. Robinson nor Dr. Shedd has recognized, I shall speak hereafter. I wish now only to say that Dr. Robinson does not seem fully to apprehend Dr. Shedd's position in the matter of the relation of the divine attributes. The latter's conception of justice does not exclude the possibility of grace, since but for grace Christ never would have " offered himself through the eternal Spirit without blemish unto God." As Dr. Shedd himself has said : " Where then is the mercy of God, in case justice is strictly satisfied by a vicarious person ? There is mercy in permitting another person to do for the sinner what the sinner is bound to do for himself; and still greater mercy in providing that person; and greater still, in becoming that person. "

But let us define more clearly Dr. Robinson's own doctrine. "Christ took our nature with its exposures and penal liabilities. He suffered the woes which but for him must have come on every member of the race." These woes are not to be conceived of as positive and external inflictions by God, but as the natural consequences of his assumption of human nature, the laws of nature being the laws of God, and all consequences being sanctions and penalties. He would have had to suffer what he did, even though no one else was saved. So far, we have something like Robertson's view, that Christ's sufferings were the necessary result of the position in which he had placed himself of conflict or collision with the evil that is in the world: he came in contact with the whirling wheel and was crushed by it. But Dr. Robinson held to a principle which never entered into Robertson's theology, — that the whirling wheel was not Satan's instrument of torture, but God's enginery of justice. "Christ bore his sufferings as the true penal sufferings for sin. In bearing them, he triumphed over them. To every one who has fellowship with him as a sufferer for sin, and faith in him as a personal Saviour from its power, it is divinely given to share in his triumphs. He exhausted and survived our penal woes; has so fulfilled the moral law and borne all the penalties of the race, that the believer finds his obligations fulfilled, his sins and their consequences taken away, himself put upon a new career of Christian living. Christ becomes our Saviour, not by imputation, but solely through the control which he exercises over us when we come to understand him as the one who has borne all our woes, and so borne them as to make full satisfaction to God, and to impart to all who believe an everlasting salvation."

The subjective element so predominates here, both in the

pains Christ bears and in the redemption the believer experiences, that we can easily understand how Dr. Robinson was regarded by many as holding to the Socinian or moral influence theory of the atonement. We must remember, however, that he continuously and vigorously protested against that theory in its assertions that God is primarily love rather than holiness, and that law is essentially decretive or a creation of will; while he maintained on the contrary that it was justice which made the atonement necessary, and that the sufferings of Christ were an expiatory sacrifice for the sins of the world. I cannot harmonize his view of the atonement with his view of the attributes of God, except by supposing that here, too, he was dominated by his impulse to reality, and that the idea of the immanent God was continually asserting itself in his thought. To him there was a holiness of God — which the Socinian or moral influence theory practically denied; but to him also this holiness of God expressed itself mainly, if not entirely, in the order of nature — which the Socinian or moral influence theory tried to recognize, though it called God only love. This explanation, I am convinced, will commend itself to us more fully when we have examined Dr. Robinson's views of justification and of faith, in both of which the subjective element is given what seems an overweening prominence, yet in both of which it appears certain that he intended to set forth what he regarded as the substance of the old objective theology.

Granting that God's holiness expressed itself in nature, however, it is still necessary to ask whether Dr. Robinson succeeded in reconciling Christ's sufferings with the orthodox premises from which he set out. I must be allowed to record my doubts. He fails to show that either law or justice has any claim upon Christ. And yet the foundation of the system is the holiness or justice of God, and the law as the necessary and unchangeable expression of God's nature. Justice simply renders to all their due, and penalty is but the correlative and consequence of guilt. We have already seen, however, that our own native depravity is visited with penalty although we have not originated it, and now we are told that Christ was visited with penalty though he had neither depravity nor guilt. If both depravity and guilt were cut off in his case by his supernatural conception, how can he justly suffer? Greg, in his " Creed of Christendom," speaks of " the strangely inconsistent doctrine that God is so *just* that he could not let sin go unpunished, yet so unjust that he could punish it in the person of the innocent. It is for orthodox dialectics," he continues, " to explain how the divine justice can be impugned by pardoning the guilty, and yet vindicated by punishing the innocent." I do not see that Dr. Robinson's scheme at all escapes Greg's criticism, or shows any consistent method of forgiveness. As, in the case of hereditary depravity, God's procedure in charging upon us guilt can be justified only upon the Scriptural ground that we were seminally and organically one with our first father in the transgression; so the visiting of the penalties of the race upon Christ our Lord can be justified only upon the ground that he, too, was heir with us to the same guilt and condemnation, even though depravity was cut off by his immaculate conception in the womb of the Virgin. And if any ask how thus becoming one of the race can load him with anything more than his portion of the common guilt of the fall, I answer that he was " the root," as well as " the offspring, of David," and that since all men, as well as all things, were created and upheld by him, there naturally and inevitably rested upon him who was their life the burden and responsibility of the sins of his members.

I think the way to such consistent realism as this would have been easier if Dr. Robinson had been able to attach more importance to the doctrine of an ontologic Trinity. That the Son and the Holy Spirit are alike and equally God, he gladly acknowledges. He grants also that " the terms Father, Son, and Holy Spirit, though derived from historical and economic facts, do nevertheless represent eternal, ontologic distinctions in the Godhead. " But he discards all theories of the relations between them, and contents himself with saying that " there is some ontologic ground for these names, though we do not know what it is. " He rejected the idea of an eternal generation, upon the ground that it implied an eternal subordination and dependence. He laid stress upon the fact that in John's first chapter Christ is carefully styled *Logos* until he becomes incarnate, and only then is called *Son of God*. The general tendency of Dr. Robinson's thought is to confine itself to the historical manifestations, and to avoid all attempts to interpret the ante-mundane mystery of the divine nature. We might well follow his example, if we did not seem to recognize in Scripture an effort to teach us something with regard to the pretemporal relations of the persons of the Trinity. Love and counsel are certainly ascribed to them, and the term " Logos " indicates derivation as well as union. There is a " larger Christ " whom recent theology is coming to discover, and this " larger Christ " is enabling us better to understand the work of the Christ incarnate. " The Lamb slain from before the foundation of the world" enables us to see in the sacrifice on Calvary the unfolding to human sight of a pain for human sin that had been undergone ever since sin itself began, in fact, ever since the decree went forth to create a world of which sin was to be an incident. Derivation does not necessarily imply beginning of existence, and subordination does not necessarily imply inequality of nature. Only when we regard the terms Father, Son, and Holy Ghost as intimations of a relation prior to all time, do we know anything of God's essential nature. Revelation is not revelation if it does not tell us something of what God is *in himself*, not simply what he is *to us*. The doctrine of the Trinity assures us that there is both eternal Sonship and eternal Fatherhood in God.

For the reason that Dr. Robinson's view of the Trinity was by preference the historical and economic, he does not discuss the doctrine in its ordinary place immediately after his account of the attributes of God, but reserves his treatment of it until he has considered the doctrine of sin and the person of Christ. The method adopted seems to imply that the Trinity is not so much the foundation as it is the result of the later doctrines of theology. As his thoughts of Christ centred about the manifestation of our Lord in the flesh rather than his work and dignity as the preincarnate Logos, so the idea of the believer's spiritual union with the Redeemer had no special chapter given to it in Dr. Robinson's system. He did not believe in what is commonly called the mystical union, and he regarded the parable of the vine and the branches as an Orientalism. The real truth was the influence of Christ *upon* us. Our union with Christ is a union of sympathy, of gratitude, of love. The term " union," like the term " substitution," is a figure of speech which expresses the result *in* us of his work *for* us.

And here, as I have already criticised Dr. Robinson's view of the atonement in its relation to God, and have been

unable to find in it any other than a metaphorical execution
of the justice which the atonement is supposed to satisfy,
so now, when I come to consider his view of the atonement
in its relation to man, I am unable to find in it any other
than a metaphorical bearing of the penalty of human sin on
the part of Christ, or any other than a metaphorical redemption of those who put their trust in him.   " The only sense
in which one's sins are laid on Christ," he says, " is that
one comes into such relations to Christ that he is saved by
him. . . . There is no transfer of guilt or penalty," for
" moral character is not transferable," and " the sense of ill-
desert cannot be handed over from one to another. . . .
Christ bears our penalty only in the sense that faith in him
gives us a sense of peace." Even this peace is not the
assurance that, now that Christ has suffered, we have no
penalty to bear.   He does not, by bearing penalty, free *us*
from the necessity of bearing it.   He rather, by his influence
upon us, " *enables* us to bear the penal consequences of our
sins, and so to bear them, through the saving faith and the
new affections he awakens within us, that we survive them
and escape from them as he did." In this way " penalty
is so inflicted on the guilty [sinner], in conjunction with his
Deliverer, as that by its infliction he shall be rescued from
his sin." Salvation is " a remedial or redemptive process
through which the effects of a law violated are overborne
and finally eradicated by the beneficent working of a new
law observed."

Certainly this seems very much like teaching that the
sinner, with the simple example and moral influence of
Christ, accomplishes both his own atonement and his own
renewal.   But since Dr. Robinson denied that he held either
the theory of Socinus or of Bushnell, I must believe that in
his own mind there was some principle of reconciliation

which was consciously or unconsciously working, though it was unexpressed. In one of his extemporaneous detached observations to his students he once said: " Salvation is the putting of a reconstructive principle into man's nature. But the subjective change does not come from man, but from God, through established methods." Here is again suggested the same possible principle of explanation which has occurred to us before. God in Christ is immanent in humanity. If all good in man is the work of Christ, then a seemingly subjective theory of the atonement may have an objective side or aspect. What before appeared to be simply man's work is God's work, now that we see all but sin to come from God. Unless some such principle be assumed, I find it difficult to acquit Dr. Robinson of inconsistency, and impossible to deny that the Old School doctrine with which his theology began evaporated, as he went on, in the fire of criticism. I am unwilling to grant that he was conscious of inconsistency. I prefer to say, therefore, that, like Jonathan Edwards, he unconsciously admitted to his system ideas which he did not himself work out to their logical conclusions. Jonathan Edwards intended to be an Old School man, but he unconsciously laid the foundation of the New School theology. Was Dr. Robinson in like manner building better than he knew, and preparing the way for a more modern theology ?

It is evident that a conception of salvation like this necessitates a new definition of justification. Justification has commonly been regarded as a change of attitude in God, not a change of moral character in the sinner. God acquits the sinner from penalty, and he restores the sinner to his favor, not because the sinner has become righteous, but solely because he is now joined to Christ by faith. Accompanying this justification, indeed, and giving rise to this faith, is the regeneration of the soul by Christ's Spirit. But Protes-

tant theologians of all grades have felt it supremely important
to deny that justification has in it any subjective element, or
that the beginning of a holy character was included in it,
lest man should seem to have the credit of his own salvation
and grace become a matter of debt.   In Dr. Robinson's
system, however, it was necessary that there should be no
merely external acts of God, no judicial decisions apart from
the beings upon whom they terminated.   To him justification
that had in it no element of subjective renewal was a mere
legal fiction.   Hence he made justification include not only
acquittal and restoration to favor, but the implanting of a
germ of personal righteousness.   He seems at times to
recognize that he is here introducing into justification an
unscriptural element, for he sometimes speaks of this last as
a " concomitant " of justification.   But at other times he
declares boldly that justification includes a moral change by
which the justified becomes personally just.   " Justification
and righteousness are the same thing from different points of
view.   Pardon is not a merely arbitrary declaration of forgiveness.   Justification is a transformation and a promotion.
Salvation introduces a new law into our sinful nature which
annuls the law of sin and destroys its penal and destructive
consequences.   Forgiveness of sins must be in itself a grad-
ual process.   The penal consequences of a man's sins are
written indelibly on his nature, and remain forever.   When
Christ said, ' Thy sins are forgiven thee,' it was an objective
statement of a subjective fact : the person was already in a
state of living relation to Christ.   We are saved only through
the enforcement of law on every one of us.   Justification
and sanctification are not to be distinguished as chronologi-
cally and statically different.   Sanctification differs from
justification only in degree, and both imply an agency of
God in different stages of operation. "   Justification then is

not only God's act *for* man, but also God's act *in* man. Our relation to Christ, which, so far as I can see, is only an external relation of gratitude, sympathy, and love, imparts to us a new religious life and a personal righteousness, which together make up the idea of salvation.

I wish to be more than just to my old teacher, but all my reverence for him cannot blind me to the fact that in thus making regeneration a part of justification, and in thus making the sinner's acceptance with God depend upon his possession of some beginnings of subjective righteousness, Dr. Robinson made dangerous concessions to Romanism, and paved the way for all manner of sacramental and High Church theories of Christianity. I am glad that the doctrine of regeneration, which follows that of justification in the system, is so markedly able and scriptural. Regeneration, he says, is the cause of conversion, and the latter follows the former. I interpret him as meaning that there is a logical, not a chronological, sequence here. In regeneration man is passive; in conversion, active. Man cannot and will not regenerate himself, — when he tries, the result is either Phariseeism or scepticism. Regeneration is ascribed properly to the Holy Spirit; but we are also " born again by the word of God. " The work of the Spirit is not on the truth, but on the soul; for the truth cannot be changed, while the man can be. Regeneration must first become conversion before it can be tested, and the best evidences that the change has been wrought by God are found in love for Christ, holiness of life, and Christian service.

There is much in Dr. Robinson's view of faith which merits attention and approval. He describes faith, in general, as an assent of the understanding combined with a consent of the heart. Saving faith is a crediting the divine declarations as true, and a confiding trust in Christ as a

personal Redeemer.   He distinguishes saving faith from the
faith of miracles, which he thinks have ceased, not because
faith has declined, but because the Holy Spirit has changed
the method of his manifestations.   Saving faith is neither
mere belief in historical facts, nor that full and all-compre-
hending confidence which is called assurance.   It is called
saving faith because it has for its end the saving of the soul.
" It is related to justification as means to end.   In dealing
with the self-righteous Jews, Paul urges simple trust in
Jesus.   But saving is more comprehensive than justifying;
and, in dealing with those who love sin, we must urge
surrender of the will to the holy dominion of Christ.   We
must not leave out the condition of an amended life. "
While we must not confound faith with love, or justification with sanctification, and while we preach the doctrine
of justification by faith without works, we must still make
it plain that a faith which does not bring forth good works
will never justify.   I am grateful to Dr. Robinson for this
recognition of the element of will in saving faith.   Faith
not only sees Christ, but it appropriates him.   It not only
takes Christ, but it gives itself; and without this element
of surrender it has no renewing effect.   All this is admirable, and I can only regret that it seems, in connection
with his doctrine of justification, to intimate that the
exercise of will in faith, instead of being simply the surrender of an empty soul to Christ as to one who can fill it,
is itself, somehow, the germ of a personal righteousness or
the faint beginning of a new obedience of our own, — which
would be only a more subtle doctrine of salvation by works.
I wish, moreover, that this thought of the will in faith, as
not only seeing, but appropriating the personal Saviour, had
led Dr. Robinson to the more spiritual conception of that
union with Christ of which faith is the medium.

In treating of regeneration we have seen that Dr. Robinson regarded the change in the heart of man as wrought by the Holy Spirit through the use of truth as a means. He regarded this uniform use of truth as shutting out the possibility of baptismal regeneration, and as rendering infant baptism an absurdity. Infant baptism, indeed, he called " a rag of Romanism." In his doctrine of the Church, therefore, we find our author a rigorous Baptist. Christ himself, however, founded a church only proleptically. In Matthew xviii. the word *ecclesia* is not used technically. The organization of the Church was the work of the Apostles after Pentecost, although the germ of it existed before. The Church was an outgrowth of the Jewish synagogue, though its method and economy are different. It is a mistake to regard it as a continuation of the temple with its priesthood and its sacrifices. It rather continues the prophetic office, and represents the progressive as distinguished from the conservative element of Judaism. The government of the Church is congregational. Three persons may constitute a church. Councils are only advisory; they have no authority. The diocesan Bishop is anti-Scriptural and anti-Christian.

The Church is organized to proclaim the truth of Christ and to induce submission to Christ, not directly to suppress vice or to regenerate society. Its aims are primarily religious and spiritual, not moral and social, and it has no right to abridge individual liberty, or to tell its members what they are to eat and drink, what societies they are to join, or what marriages to contract. Dr. Robinson regarded baptism as implying death to sin, resurrection to new life in Christ, and entire surrender to the authority of the triune God. Since we are baptized into the name of the Father and of the Son and of the Holy Ghost, we enter into the same relation to the Son that we sustain to the Father, and baptism can mean nothing less than the assumption of supreme allegiance to Jesus Christ.   Baptism is a prerequisite to the Lord's Supper, and no church has the right to celebrate the Lord's Supper with unbaptized persons.   The Lord's Supper is the sacred meal of the individual Christian society, and only those who are members of the society have rights at the table.   Each individual church, moreover, must determine for itself what is baptism, and any two churches essentially disagreeing as to what baptism is, cannot consistently commune with each other.   Yet no one can more earnestly or constantly than Dr. Robinson denounce the spirit of sectarianism.   While Christianity exalts Christ, he would say, the sectarian spirit elevates the Church above Christ.   He frequently used the word " churchism " to designate this Pharisaic and divisive tendency.   " There is not the least shadow of churchism in Christ.   Christ did not say, ' Blessed is he who accepts the Westminster Confession.'   Churchism is a revamped and whitewashed Judaism.   It keeps up the middle wall of partition which Christ has broken down."

In giving account of Dr. Robinson's views of faith and of the Church, I have not the advantage of his printed statements, and I am dependent upon the notes dictated to the last classes of his students in Theology.   These notes were not revised by him, and it is probable that they do not fully represent him.   In preparing them for the press, he would doubtless have explained and enlarged many points which are now very meagrely treated.   Yet the notes which I use were given after twenty years of study and of teaching, and they probably contain the substantial conclusions to which he would have subscribed at the close of his service as instructor in the Theological Seminary.   His teaching on eschatology is brief, but it is succinct and clear. The main thought of it is that the future is not separated from the present by any arbitrary line, but that it is the development and outgrowth of that which now is. "Eternal life begins here, and the second death is but the continuance of spiritual death in another and a timeless state of existence."

As to the conditions of personal immortality our author says, guardedly, in one place: "So far as we know, the soul exists only in connection with an organism, and a personal being cannot communicate with another except through external manifestation or through media. . . . We talk of disembodied spirits, but we do not know that there are any such in the universe." Yet he does not deny the possibility of bodiless existence in the intermediate state, but says, rather: "Man is not dependent for consciousness upon the possession of a bodily organization, and therefore will not find in the dissolution of the body a cessation of mental or spiritual existence." He believes that there is to be a personal coming of Christ, and yet he says that Second Adventism, probably including in this term the elements of definite prediction and of premillennialism that so often mingle with it, "stultifies the system and scheme of Christianity." He means that to depend for the progress of the Church upon Christ's visible and literal return is to discredit the dispensation and power of the Holy Spirit, which Christ himself declared to be better for the Church than his own bodily presence would be.

The doctrine of the resurrection is stated with great originality and suggestiveness. Here personality is the indestructible principle. Both at man's first creation and after death, personality takes to itself a material organization. It is a divinely empowered second cause. This refutes materialism and annihilationism alike. Materialism would

make the soul the product of the body, and with the breaking to pieces of the body the soul would pass into nothing-
ness.   But while science teaches that merely animal life is
a mechanical process, we cannot explain the facts except by
supposing that this very animal life is the effect and instrument of a personal power.   This organific power we call the
soul.   The body then reflects the soul.   When the process
of resurrection begins we do not know.   It may begin at the
moment when man becomes a Christian.   It may begin at
the moment of death.   However this may be, it is certain
that there is to be a future resurrection of the body.   Yet
we are not to regard the future body as necessarily containing any of the material particles that constitute our present
physical organisms.   The individuality only, the personal
identity, will be preserved.   It is simply a question of
God's power, and God will give to each a body such as
shall please him.   When a student asked Dr. Robinson at
this point, " But if Christ arose with identically the same
body that was laid away in the tomb, how can his resurrection be a type of ours ? " he simply answered, " The nature
of Christ's resurrection body is an open question. "

The same disposition to regard the beginnings of eternal
life and eternal death as manifest in this world appears
in his doctrine of the judgment.   " Judgment, " he says,
" begins here.   The searing of conscience in this life is a
penal infliction.   There is no *day* of judgment or of resurrection all at one time.   Judgment is an eternal process.
Man is being judged every day.   Every man honest with
himself knows where he is going to. "   I do not understand
Dr Robinson here to deny that there is to be a *culmination*
of the judicial process at some definite time in the future.
I understand him only to deny that divine judgment is
confined to the future, or that the word *day* is to be taken

in its literal and limited sense. And so with the doctrine of heaven and hell. " Heaven is not to be compared to a grasshopper on a shingle, floating down stream. . . . Heaven is a place where men are taken up as they are when they leave this world, and where they are carried forward. There is no intimation of that sudden transformation at the hour of dissolution which is commonly supposed. No sinners can go there, but men may enter there who still possess defects [in the sense of incompletenesses] of character " [and in the other world these defects or incompletenesses may be gradually removed]. If this is all that Dr. Briggs has meant by his phrase, " sanctification after death," we may concede its truth and regard him as advocating only what Dr. Robinson had advocated before him.

The same principles are applied to the doctrine of eternal punishment. The actual existence of sin and death in this world argues the possibility of the continued existence of sin and death hereafter. Punishment begins in this life, and is carried on in the next. Dr. Robinson does not deny that there are positive punishments in the world to come, though he regards punishment as essentially subjective, the reaction of natural law and not the infliction of arbitrary will. There does not need to be any whipping-post set up in the universe, in order to justify every word of Scripture threatening. It is better for us not to conceive of punishment as objective judicial infliction, but to remember, rather, that wherever sin occurs, there, by natural law, penalty is inevitable. " We have no right to say that there are no other consequences of sin but natural ones," but rather to say that " the eternal law of wrong-doing is that the wrong-doer is cursed thereby, and that harpies and furies follow him into eternity. . . . The fundamental argument for eternal punishment is the reproductive power

of evil, the reactionary power of a wrong elective preference, the reduplicating energy of sin. . . . Penalty in the
divine law enforces itself. We shall never be as complete
as if we had never sinned. We shall bear the scars of our
sins forever." As penalty is not reformatory, and as the
will may become obdurate in evil, there is no reason why
the sufferings of the finally impenitent may not be eternal.
Neither the justice nor the benevolence of God are impugned
by visiting eternal sin with eternal punishment.

As I close this account of the theology of a great teacher
and a great man, I find myself impressed anew with the
boldness and independence of his views, but also with the
fact that he represented consciously or unconsciously a great
movement of human thought, a movement of which the
Ritschlian School in Germany and the New Theology in
this country are later types and manifestations. Twenty-
five years ago Dr. Robinson probably taught in the Rochester
Theological Seminary a more modern system than was at that
time taught in any other evangelical Seminary of any
denomination whatever. His students can never blame him
for not being abreast of his time, for he was greatly ahead of
his time. In his love for reality and his determination to
rid theology of its ancient incubus of legal fictions, he rendered invaluable service to every student who came under
his influence. He had a large and free conception of inspiration, yet he considered the Scriptures as authoritative, and
from philosophy to Scripture as a whole, he was accustomed continually to appeal. The fundamental principles
of his system with regard to holiness, law, and sin were so
powerfully taught that even what seem to be his own aber-
rations from them failed to carry his students with him : the
nails had been fastened in so sure a place that he himself
was not afterwards able to pull them out. A philosophy of

relativity involved him in some ambiguities and inconsistencies. We are obliged to dissent from some of the later doctrines of his scheme, or to confess that we cannot un lerstand them. But even here it is possible that his views may be interpreted in the light of God's immanence in nature and in man, and be found to have in them less of paradox and more of truth than some of his critics have imagined.

He was himself a man of tolerant mind, and while he claimed the right to think for himself, he granted the same right to others. He was a genuine Baptist, in that he believed in soul-liberty, and he never thought the true interests of the Church of Christ could be subserved by withholding from any of its members the right of private judgment. His soul was stirred as by the sound of a trumpet whenever it was proposed to cast out of our ecclesiastical or Christian fellowship those who differed from us only in matters doubtful or unimportant. And so I give to him, what he freely gave to others — the recognition of his loftiness of mind, of his sincerity, of his eagerness to know the truth, of his bold advocacy of what he believed, even in the face and teeth of opposition. He has raised up a generation of thinkers and preachers who believe in manliness in the ministry. He has left behind him a body of divinity as stimulating and suggestive as any that had been written in America since Jonathan Edwards's day, and fully worthy to be classed with the works of Charles Hodge and of Henry B. Smith. All of his opinions are worthy of study, and many of them may yet prove the germs of progress in theology. May we who succeed him have something of his spirit, follow him where he followed Christ, improve upon his teaching where we can, do honest and independent work, as he did, in the building up of the fair and symmetrical structure of Christian truth! He was one who lived in and for his pupils; he cast his bread upon the waters, expecting that it would return to him only after many days; he did the sowing, and it has been ours to reap the fruit of his labors. God grant that we may all attain unto the unity of the faith and of the knowledge of the Son of God, and may enter at last, as he has done, into the presence of the great Teacher, where he who sowed and they who reaped shall rejoice together!

III.

DR. ROBINSON AS A SEER.

By PROFESSOR G. W. NORTHRUP, D.D., LL.D.,
DIVINITY SCHOOL, UNIVERSITY OF CHICAGO.

III.

AS A SEER.

[From an address at a memorial service held by the University of Chicago, October 3, 1894.[1]]

IN our denominational institutions at Rochester, in the earlier years of their existence, there were four men who rank among the most notable in the history of our people in this country: Dr. Thomas J. Conant, the first Hebraist of his day; Dr. Asahel C. Kendrick, then well on his way to that position which he has long held and still holds among those pre-eminent for scholarship in the Language and Literature of Greece; President Martin B. Anderson, the founder of the University of Rochester; and the great teacher, preacher, and leader, the memory of whose name we are met to-day to honor. No more stimulating and fruitful work in the way of education has been done in this country than was done in those days in the old hotel building on Buffalo Street, which contained for some years all the lecture-rooms, dormitories, and libraries of the University of Rochester and of the Rochester Theological Seminary.

[1] Dr. Northrup was invited to prepare an article for this volume, and declined "through misunderstanding of the time to be allowed for it." But when his address at the memorial service in Chicago appeared, it was found to be not only very just and striking throughout, but also to cover one of the most momentous parts of Dr. Robinson's service to his generation; namely, his foresight and provision for future theological development. The remarks of Dr. Northrup on this prophetic function are presented as indispensable to the understanding of Dr. Robinson's peculiar influence. — ED.

It is now forty years less one since I first entered the lecture-room of President Robinson. Upon the completion of my theological course I was honored through his influence with an appointment to the Chair of Church History in the Rochester Theological Seminary, which position I held for ten years, resigning it twenty-seven years ago to enter upon what was generally regarded as a premature and precarious theological enterprise at Chicago. Through my connection with Dr. Robinson, as a student, in the Faculty, and in social relations, — he was a member of my family for several months, — I came to know him well, — his powers of mind, views, spirit, and methods of work. . . . President Robinson was, in my judgment, the greatest teacher of this generation. He was a man of magnificent personality, of splendid presence, and powerful mind. He possessed, in kind and degree, all the prerequisites, intellectual and spiritual, for the most effective work as a teacher, especially in the higher ranges of truth, — extraordinary acuteness of perception, intense and rapid mental action, largeness of vision by which he took in at a glance all the aspects and relations of the subject in hand, ability to penetrate as by intuition to the heart of the questions discussed, a high order of analytic and constructive power, openness of mind to new light, a passion for freedom and truth and righteousness, and absolute confidence in their progress and triumph; and a mastery of the English language, and of the art of effective expression, which enabled him to unfold his thoughts in the most luminous and impressive manner. In view of the work which he did, and the quality, reach, and permanency of the influence which he exerted, we regard President Robinson as the foremost man that has appeared in our denominational history within the past fifty years. . . . During the long period of more than forty years' service as a teacher in the chief schools under our denominational control, President Robinson trained a great body of young men, hundreds of whom have held and still hold positions of power in the ministry, and in other spheres of thought and action, who will testify that, as regards their ideal of life and their equipment for its realization in labors and conflicts and sufferings and aspirations, they owe more to him than to any other man — possibly than to all other men. It is our conviction — one that we have repeatedly expressed — that through the men whom he trained, and by his splendid and almost continuous service as preacher and lecturer, he did more than any other man of this generation in raising the standard of preaching in the denomination to which he belonged.

But there is another fact, and it is one of the chief reasons, if not the principal reason, for assigning to Dr. Robinson the position of pre-eminent power and influence which has been indicated. He wrought in the line in which the Providence of God is causing his kingdom to advance. He was one of the greater prophets, a SEER of the first order; he saw the coming of, and did more than any other man among us to bring in, this movement of religious thought in which all share, even those who claim to be ultra-orthodox. No man of an observant mind, in looking over the history of the past thirty years, can fail to see not only marked changes of religious thought, but a growing freedom and independence in theological discussion in all denominations in this country, — at least at the North. It is impossible that theology, which is the apprehension and organization of the truths of the Christian revelation, should remain the same from age to age. " In the providence of God, and in the progress of men, the new wine is ever bursting the old bottles. Each age must fight its own doubts, and lay its own spectres, and formulate its own creed. "

The universe is the self-revelation of the infinite God which is one and harmonious, — all parts standing in definite and living relations to each other and to the whole. Science and philosophy, in the widest sense of these terms, are but the thoughts of God as slowly discovered by the growing mind of man. The revelation contained in the Christian Scriptures is not an afterthought with God, an excrescence on the original plan of the universe, but is an essential element — in fact, the fundamental, formative idea — of that eternal plan of which the universe is an endlessly progressive expression. To regard Christianity as standing apart from, as unrelated to, the other spheres of God's universal self-revelation, is a radical and confusing misconception. Since all departments of knowledge — science, philosophy, and history — are progressive, there is perhaps nothing incumbent upon the theologian of more importance than to *relate* theology, so far as possible, to the new learning of the age in which he lives.

The movement of religious thought, to' which we have referred, is due in larger measure to Dr. Robinson than to any other man among us. In one of his latest papers he indicated some of the marked changes in religious thought and pulpit phraseology that have occurred among evangelical Christians within the last thirty years. Among the changes specified we note the following : —

"The first chapters of Genesis are no longer quoted as a minute record of scientific or of historical facts, but as an Oriental and pictorial way of representing the great truths that God is the author of the universe, and that man came to his estate of moral disease and death through conscious violation of moral law. . . . Very few are now troubled about the imprecatory Psalms, recognizing that the office of the Holy Spirit was not that of sanctification; that in 'moving' men 'to speak,' whether Abraham, Moses, the prophets, or the Apostles, the Spirit used them as it found them, teaching them neither science nor philosophy, neither history nor logic, neither rhetoric nor grammar.

"The conceptions of God now most dwelt on are not those with which our fathers and grandfathers were made most familiar. To them God was presented more under the aspect of justice and wrath against ungodliness than under that of love. His mercy and forgiveness were won solely through the atoning work of Christ. Now the ever-recurring text is: 'God is love.' The conception of God which is coming to be dominant to-day is the Christian conception of him, — that conception of him which we get by accepting Jesus Christ as the true and full expression of the mind and heart of God, that he and the Father are one in spirit, rendering incredible the idea of a moral dualism in the Divine Being.

"Instead of the old doctrine that all things were made for the glory of God; that man by sin had dishonored God, and his glory could be secured only through the sacrificial death of Christ, we have the doctrine that the universe, including man, was simply an irrepressible overflow of infinite benevolence; that the resources of the world are subordinated to the welfare of man, to make the utmost possible of whom will be the consummation of all Divine purposes, creative and redemptive."

So also in the pulpit portrayals of the doctrines of grace: "The incarnation takes precedence of the atonement and overshadows it. The humbled Godhead, rather than the propitiating sacrifice, is made to appeal to us as a motive to repentance. It is to the second of Philippians rather than to the fifth of Romans that reference is most frequently made."

Not less marked are the changes in the pulpit representations of unrenewed human nature: "Depravity is now far less than total. Somewhere, amid the ashes of the natural human heart, lies a spark that needs only the motives of the gospel to fan it into a flame of holy love."

Theological theories are being discarded more and more; ultra-Biblical speculations — fictions logical, metaphysical, and ethical — which have burdened Christian theology for centuries, to its infinite injury, are rapidly giving way, and interest and emphasis are coming to be placed more and more on the great facts of revelation, — the eternal verities which constitute the substance of Christianity.

This movement of religious thought is not an eddy, nor a whirlpool, but is due to the action of causes similar to those which have operated from time to time all down the ages, among which great intellectual and religious personalities are chief in power, and is destined to continue till it shall shake all things that can be shaken, that they may be removed, "that the things which cannot be shaken may remain." This "shaking and removing" of theological dogmas of human invention is one of the most beneficent results involved in the progress of theology. Ecclesiastical dogmas which have had wide, almost universal, acceptance would, if now persisted in, "wreck the faith of the age." For example, such dogmas as the following: 1. That the atonement was made to satisfy the just claims of the devil. 2. That mankind are under a sentence of antenatal condemnation, based on the fiction of imputed guilt, — a sentence which, in the judgment of past ages, consigned to hell the great majority of infants dying in infancy, — one half the human race. 3. That the heathen have light enough to render their damnation just, but not enough to render their salvation possible. 4. That God made no provision in the atonement for the salvation of a part — apparently a very great part — of mankind. 5. That he arbitrarily elected some men to eternal life and others to eternal perdition, — there being between the individuals appointed to these infinitely diverse destinies no difference which even omniscience could discover as a reason for discrimination. 6. That the perdition of a large part of mankind — the non-elect — is *inevitable*, let them do what they can to secure eternal life, even in the way appointed in the gospel. 7. That God destinates men to eternal perdition in order to show forth his justice in the punishment of sin.

But we cannot multiply these points. Is it a matter of wonder that Christianity, burdened with such a mass of ecclesiastical dogmas, should make slow progress in the world, compelled to meet not only the powerful evil of the human heart, but the blazing hostilities of the human reason ?

And what are the things which cannot be shaken, and which are to remain ? Some of them have been indicated in the article of Dr. Robinson, already referred to, and in his last sermon published in " The Standard " : 1. The universal fatherhood of God. 2. " The universe, including man, an irrepressible overflow of infinite benevolence." 3. The humbled Godhead — God humbling himself and coming into the world in personal form, in Jesus Christ, to engage in a conflict with the evils which afflict mankind. 4. God's eternal purpose of love and mercy embraces in its scope every member of the human race. 5. Eternal life is within the reach of all men, and, to bring each and every man into the full possession of this transcendent good, God does all that he can do and remain God. 6. Man, though a prodigal son, is still a son of God, — the divine image in which he was made being defaced but not destroyed; his original divine constitution underlying the principle and habit of evil.   7. The brotherhood of man involved in the doctrine of the universal fatherhood of God.   8. The destined progress and triumph of the kingdom of God, which is a kingdom of freedom and truth and righteousness and love.

But we cannot continue this line of remark.   It was the firm belief of our departed friend that the changes of religious thought yet to come, like those in the past, " will not fail to bring the Church to a brighter future. "

When looking from my study window, in Cobb Lecture Hall, during the past two winters, I have seen now and then the striking figure of the departed President as he was coming to his work, through cold and storm, with the nervous rapid walk, or rather stride, which impressed me when I first saw him, forty years ago; and as I looked upon his tall form, still erect, though bearing the weight of fourscore years, and called to mind what an unresting worker (I might with justice say what a reckless worker) he had been through all his life, and remembered also how sharp and manifold had been the sufferings through which he had been called to pass, — I was at such times distinctly conscious of a strong emotion of moral sublimity, somewhat as I should have felt in looking upon a mighty battle-ship that had met and fought its country's enemies on all waters round the globe, entering the harbor with its sails full set, though bearing on masts and sails and flags and hull the marks of many a storm and many a battle.   In how many among us, young and old, pupils and teachers, has his presence awakened similar emotions? We thank God for Ezekiel Gilman Robinson, for his magnificent personality, for the largeness of his vision, for the courage and power with which he uttered his convictions, for that voice which has been heard for a half-century ringing out in the forefront of the battle for liberty and truth and righteousness. Of him may it be said with emphasis, that being dead he still speaks, — speaks in the men whom he inspired, in the writings which he left, and in the illuminating and liberating movement of religious thought, which he did so much to originate and strengthen and guide.

NOTE A.

ON DR. ROBINSON'S INDEPENDENCE.

Professor W. C. Wilkinson, D. D., calls attention to a trait, as distinctively moral as mental, without which, although Dr. Robinson might have foreseen, he would not have provided for, the theological exigencies of coming days. — ED.

" In theologic discussion, whether in the lecture-room or elsewhere, conducted whether with tongue or with pen, the strongest note with this great teacher was intellectual independence. Originality, I do not say; but independence. He liked freedom for himself, and he would not abridge freedom for others. Probably Dr. Robinson is as much responsible as any other individual force operative on minds within the limits of the Baptist denomination, for what degree of disposition exists among these minds to venture out, following new leaders in the fields of theologic thought. As long as he was professor of systematic theology at Rochester, he of course felt honorably bound not himself to depart widely in his express teaching, as indeed I do not think he felt inclined to depart, from the standards of orthodoxy generally accepted among Baptists. But he could not refrain, and he did not refrain, from giving impulses in the direction of freedom and difference. Within a year or so of his death, he said, in private conversation with the present writer, that the prospect for genuine religion in the world was never in his opinion so bright as now. He rejoiced in the movement of thought. This was instinctive with him, inevitable to him. It was an untamable revolt in his spirit against traditionalism, against cant. I remember his once saying to me, of a certain former student of his who had then already started on a course of some divergence from old paths and who has since followed that divergent course much farther, though remaining still within the pale of " evangelical " orthodoxy: " There is not a particle of *cant* about him." This was spoken warmly, as in the very highest praise. Cant, to Dr. Robinson, was an unclean spirit to be exorcised. He practised against it a relentless exorcism in all his theologic discussions. How his clear, incisive words, his often exquisitely chosen, though never finically chosen words, did cleanse the atmosphere where he talked ! I myself thought, when Dr. Robinson spoke with that sanguine optimism concerning the present outlook for religion, that, in his joy at seeing an old cant of verbal orthodoxy disappearing, he did not take sufficient account of an equally dangerous, perhaps more dangerous, new cant of freedom, of progress, of 'scientific' spirit, which was taking the place of that. To be at once free and genuine, on the one hand, and humble and reverent, on the other, is a difficult reconcilement in practice. But Dr. Robinson seems to me to have come as near as any one I have known, to achieving it. If he helped some to freedom whom he did not help to humility and reverence, that is a result which he would himself sincerely have lamented." — W. C. W.

NOTE B.

DR. ROBINSON'S LATEST VIEW OF THEOLOGICAL TRAINING.

Dr. Robinson repeatedly expressed the conviction that a new and much higher provision could now be made for ministerial training by taking due account of the fact that theological differences no longer strictly follow denominational lines. He held that every interest would be best provided for in an institution which selected its faculty with regard to their ability. and regardless of their denominations, except that the leading Protestant bodies should each be represented by a teacher of its views concerning the church. There are advances toward such a provision in various quarters, and his judgment in this matter is one more instance of the singular prevision of future conditions which marked his whole career as an educator. — ED.

IV.

DR. ROBINSON AS A TEACHER OF THEOLOGY.

By REV. A. J. F. BEHRENDS, D.D.,
BROOKLYN, NEW YORK.

IV.

AS A TEACHER OF THEOLOGY.

I N reviewing the thirty years which have passed since my
graduation from the Rochester Theological Seminary,
there are five things in Dr. Robinson's theological method
which have impressed me profoundly and permanently.
They are not connected with the discussion of separate doctrines nor with his theological system. The former was
not unfrequently fragmentary, and left many things to be
desired; the latter it is not possible clearly to trace. So
far as a complete and consistent system existed, it was present only in undeveloped form, and was more frequently
indicated by oral commentary than by dictated statement.
Of course, I must be understood as referring only to the
period of my professional study,— a period of which I
understand Dr. Robinson himself to have recently declared
that it had not witnessed the full and final development of
his views. It was my good fortune, therefore, as I regard
it, though some might regard it as a misfortune, to have
enjoyed his instruction when he was still hewing out his
theological lines. The notes in my possession bear upon
almost every page the marks of intellectual conflict. Sometimes the traditional exposition is given, at other times
all theories are freely and keenly criticised without any
suggestion of a substitute, and again a tentative statement
is presented, to which the lecturer was not quite prepared to
give his positive support. But the seeds of living thought

were everywhere deposited. Single sentences and parts of sentences lie embedded in my notes, which indicated a deeper view, and which only required thorough and consistent exposition to set the entire picture in a different frame. The most important statements do not always occupy the first place, nor do they always dominate the exposition. It would be easy to give illustrations from such chapters as those on inspiration, the moral attributes of God, the Divine decrees, the nature and guilt of original sin, — which latter phrase, by the way, is repudiated, — external and internal calling, the atonement, etc. Often, too, the slow dictation was dropped for an oral treatment, of which only snatches could be recorded and even remembered, but whose general tone gave a new meaning and force to traditional terms. I can, of course, speak only for myself; but doing this frankly, my tribute is that the numerous scattered and unconnected hints have been more productive and fruitful than the extended discussion of doctrines. I do not mean that the latter were not fresh and helpful, but the profoundest individuality of the man incarnated itself in the interspersed suggestions. I have perused the notes many times, and each successive scrutiny has revealed the inadequacy of the theological system as a compact logical and philosophical unity; while the scattered hints have served to bring more and more strongly into relief the fact that a closely linked system was struggling for adequate utterance. And yet, even here, the word " system " must be used in the secondary sense. Dr. Robinson never posed as the advocate of a philosophical or theological hobby; he was analytic and systematic, but he sharply distinguished between the systematic and the scholastic methods. To him the most sacred of all things was a well-established fact, and he insisted that no fact must be warped in the interest of a system.

The theological lectures which influenced me most profoundly, and which have left a permanent and salutary effect, were the introductory ones. At the time, they were studied with less care than was given to the subsequent expositions of doctrine; but as the years have passed, they have more and more secured the place of pre-eminence. Dr. Robinson's method, at all events, was fixed; and it is remarkable alike for its clearness, its comprehensiveness, and its caution. The goal was in sight, and the path by which it must be reached, though the strides were sometimes uncertain, and the clew was sometimes lost. The aim was a thoroughly rational construction of the contents of Christian revelation. Platitudes were always discounted and discarded. A reasoned and reasonable faith was the great desideratum. The very first sentences of the introduction brought that to the front, and in the front it remained. Theology was defined as the science of religion; and religion was traced to its root in convictions, by which the sensibility and the will were aroused, controlled, and made effective. Thus the discussion assumed an eminently intellectual character, and the eye was made to glow, the pulses stirred, and the will moved, only as great thoughts, clearly perceived and firmly grasped, made the soul captive. The intellectual atmosphere, however, was never permitted to become speculative and scholastic. He insisted that ethics and theology are inseparable, that doctrine and duty are always correlative, that the practical has its root in the rational, and that the rational must bear fruit in the practical. Theology had to do with moral character, and character was shaped by rational convictions. Speculative rationalism was discarded by this profounder view of the conditions under which the reason not only ought to act, but under which it always does act, when its action is not artificially restrained. The prerogative of reason was not limited to an examination of external evidences, nor to the construction of natural theology. It was accorded an infinite outlook, and it was never permitted to cease its earnest and enthusiastic search.

But in attempting to realize a rational construction of the contents of Christian revelation, great stress was laid in the introduction upon the manifold sources from which reason must draw. At the outset, the familiar distinction between natural and revealed theology was discarded; inasmuch as the source of revelation is also the author of nature and of man. Science and philosophy, therefore, may not be ignored. The moral judgments are authoritative in their sphere, and theology must take account of them. History, also, profane and sacred, is a revelation of God. The Scriptures, it was insisted, are invested with a primary and peculiar authority for the Christian theologian; but the Scriptures were brought into organic relation with the many-sided life of humanity, and with the constitution of nature. Theology could not be permitted to assume indifference, much less to foster hostility, to any department of research. The voice of God in theology could not contradict the voice of God which speaks in the stars of heaven and in the souls of men; and wherever the voice of God speaks, it is authoritative. The vexing question as to the source of religious authority was in this way so answered as to do justice to every witness for truth, without arbitrarily dividing the authority. The author of nature is the Father of souls, and by his Spirit has spoken to us through prophets and apostles, and with unique clearness through his eternal Son. Revelation has many channels; it has but one source. Science, psychology, philosophy, ethics, and history make valuable contributions to theology, — contributions which need to be carefully sifted, but whose established results may not be ignored by the interpreter of Holy Scripture and by the Christian believer. Theology, thus, with its clearly set task, became a comprehensive study, with living relations to every department of knowledge.

A third feature in the introduction to theology, upon which great stress was laid, was the limitations of the theological inquirer. Some of these limitations pertained to the inquiring subject, as created, finite, and dependent personality; others pertained to the nature of the themes submitted to his rational inspection. Every theological process must end in mystery. But this result was, in turn, justified as inevitable and rational, by an appeal to science and psychology. It was shown to belong to the constitution of universal nature. Matter cannot be defined. The relation between the soul and the body is a profound and insoluble mystery. We do not know what the soul is, and how it acts. Thus the rationality of the procedure was preserved, even though in every instance the result was a confession of ignorance. The ignorance was itself supremely rational, and it was not permitted to invalidate in the least such positive and partial knowledge as had been secured.

The inevitable result of this preliminary discussion was a critical attitude toward every great school of systematic theology. Dr. Robinson was profoundly and habitually evangelical; but he bore the stamp of no party, though in living sympathy with all great teachers. He was neither an Augustinian, nor a Calvinist, nor an Arminian. He served Princeton and Andover with equal severity. He was neither old school nor new school. The weak points in every system were mercilessly exposed in the interests of a rational construction, which would give due weight to every fact and to all the facts. Thus every system, as a system, was discredited; and no system was created to supplant them. As

I listened to the lectures, I seemed to be walking through a mass of theological ruins; and each successive perusal of them has only deepened the first impression. True, the necessity of system was emphasized, but the qualifying statement followed that the widely current aversion to systems of theology is justified by the refinements of Catholic and Protestant scholasticism. The plea for systematic theology was simply a call to clear and consistent thinking. It was not the advocacy for a rigidly logically concatenated scheme, reduced to ideal unity by the dominance of a single philosophical principle. Such an attempt Dr. Robinson did not make, though he believed in its existence; and his treatment of such systems as had endeavored to give it form was such as to act in the way of a wholesome check upon adventurous speculation.

Some may regard this as a severe and unfriendly judgment upon my revered teacher. They may think that they can trace a system in his theological lectures. I can discover no traces of it, except tentative and partial ones; and I can only say that while I thought that I had a fairly rational system of theology, which however I now see was an incongruous mixture of Lutheranism and Calvinism, when I came under Dr. Robinson's instruction, his sledge-hammer demolished the system which I had, and nothing was done to replace it. He never dreamed of the ruin which he wrought, and of the long years of mental agony by which it was succeeded. But the ruthless havoc was the greatest blessing of my life. It broke the chafing bonds of traditionalism; it drove me from the mud huts into God's free and boundless air; it made me docile and modest in my independence, averse to and impatient of speculative dialectics, adhering closely to what was known and could be tested, with an ever deepening eagerness to enlarge the boundaries of positive and practical knowledge. If at a later day than mine he wrought out a complete system, I am glad that I did not have the benefit of it; and I doubt whether such a system ever had with him scholastic definiteness and comprehensiveness. He must have been, from the constitution of his mind, a student and a critic to the very last. One of the best results of his influence upon me has been my deep-seated aversion to all strictly systematic theology, and my independent critical attitude to it. Of such theology I find no trace in the Scriptures, not even in Paul, who abounds in startling antitheses, which he never attempts to reconcile; and I have too keen a remembrance of what I have suffered from the systematic theologians, past and present, ever to take their yoke upon my shoulders. The door of liberty was opened to me by the hands of Dr. Robinson; and in saying this I pay him, in my sincere judgment, the highest praise which one man can give to another.

Yet the liberty was not license. Reason was not made to depend upon faith, nor faith upon reason; but both reason and faith were made subordinate to revelation, and revelation was made to cover every word and work of God. In other words, *facts* constituted the finality, to be accepted by faith, and to be interpreted by reason. Among these facts, the supreme place was given to the Holy Scriptures, and to Jesus Christ as the Incarnate Son of God. Prophets and apostles, when their meaning had been clearly determined, never came under the ban of criticism. Christ commanded a reverence which was never effusive, but always deep and absolute; and Christ held the central place as the key to Holy Scripture. The synthetic method was followed in the class-room, not the analytic, nor the christological. Yet the whole influence upon me has been to christologize every department of theological inquiry; to think of God and man, of sin and of redemption, as Christ thought of them; to search for his mind in the documents of our faith, and to surrender myself to that.

The five regulative principles which I have mentioned were made to fall under one comprehensive category, though this was not specifically named, — the general idea of law. This was the perpetual undertone of the discussion, and nothing was more frequently and earnestly insisted upon than that the first duty of a theological inquirer was a clear conception of law, and the rigorous application of the idea to all departments of theological study. The absence of a complete and thoroughly consistent theological system was supplemented by the presence of a vital systematizing principle. Nay, the system was incomplete because the principle was so searching and exacting. Physical, psychological, ethical, and redemptive law were not confounded with each other; their provinces were regarded and treated as distinct and separable. But the provinces were regarded and treated as concentric circles; they had a common centre. Law in every sphere was a transcript of the Divine nature; not the mere enactment of his will, but the disclosure of his reason. Law was more than observed order. The observed order, provided the ordered facts had been rightly understood, was the real and divine order. Its testimony was authoritative, which it was foolish and wicked to question or ignore. The order observed was the order which is, and the order which is was the order which cannot be other than it is, because the nature of a thing determines its ordered action. No one could get behind the observed order to study the nature of a thing, whether of matter or of mind or of God; but the nature of a thing was disclosed in its ordered action, and was discerned in the order as observed Accuracy and clearness in observation were therefore primary and indispensable. Analysis became the distinctive method of the theologian and the preacher. Rational order is the note of a Divine system, whether of creation or of redemption, a rational order disclosed in the facts of revelation and of Christian experience which are submitted to our inspection. From the facts there can be no appeal, but the facts can be understood only when their ordered action has been clearly discerned. Thus theology becomes scientific and systematic through the application of law to the facts of revelation and religion. It was a hard task to impose upon a student; but it was a tremendous spur to industry, and a call to independent, continuous, and profound reflection, under the guidance of keen and careful observation.

I have refrained thus far from any examination and criticism of Dr. Robinson's handling of definite doctrines. Others are better fitted for such a task than I am. Nor is it along these lines that my profoundest indebtedness lies. I owe to him the habitual endeavor to construe the facts of revelation and of religion in terms of rational knowledge, the recognition of the wide region which revelation covers, the constant remembrance of the inherent and insuperable limitations under which theological inquiry is pursued, a profound and ineradicable aversion to scholastic omniscience, a devout submission to the authority of Jesus Christ in Holy Scripture; and all this under the formative idea of law as affirming an inherent and eternal order or rational sequence in the revealed facts. These regulative principles have only controlled me more and more freely and powerfully during the generation which has passed since the time when I sat in the dingy classroom where Dr. Robinson trained his theological students. A theological system, determined by the idea of law as defined by Dr. Robinson, and consistently carrying that idea through to every minutest detail, has never been written. I am not sure that it can be written. He who achieves the task will be the pioneer in a theological revolution. But to have clearly grasped such an idea, and to have given it vitality in many minds, is a greater achievement, and indicative of profounder theological insight, than the publication of ponderous volumes on systematic divinity, in which conflicting and contradictory statements are left without any earnest attempt to reach and formulate the higher synthesis.

The idea of law is an eminently practicable and fruitful theological principle. Partially applied, as it was, by Dr. Robinson, the dominant phase given to it, and the secret momentum which it gave to all his discussion, have lodged it firmly in many minds as the simplest and the best method of theological science. Speaking only for myself, his theological influence upon me has been such that, while at many points I have been compelled to depart from his conclusions and his method of argument, I have in this very departure been controlled by the formative principles of his own thinking. In *fibre* I have remained his pupil, though, perhaps, in *form* he would not have cared to own me as his expositor.

NOTE.

REMINISCENCES OF THE LECTURE-ROOM AT COVINGTON.

Rev. William Ashmore, D. D., the honored missionary to Swatow, China, found in the young professor at Covington the same qualities that made him distinguished in later years. Dr. Ashmore writes : —

"When I went to the Western Baptist Theological Institute at Covington as a student, my attention was keenly awake to note the men who were to be my future teachers. Dr. Pattison and Professor

Robinson were there. I am to speak a word just now about the latter. He had us in Hebrew and Church History.

"I found myself confronting a tall man of commanding appearance, spare of build, with a stately, swinging tread, and a capacious spread of forehead. The most striking feature about him was a clear, sharp, penetrating gray eye. It had no end of various different expressions. It could be very mild and gentle, and it could bore like an auger; it could help along a hard-worked student in his perplexity, and it could make a pert one wince in his self-confidence.

"Things had to move briskly in the class; promptness, clearness, and exactness were found to be indispensable. We were encouraged to ask questions; but a question was almost sure to be followed by a question in return, sometimes by half a dozen of them. A student was often made to answer his own questions; still more often did he find his question 'referred back to the committee,' when he had to restate it in a more intelligible and pertinent form. Thus he was cornered and elbowed into a habit of looking at his subject on all four sides, and of making quite sure that he had got hold of the right end of his thought before he opened his mouth and 'spake unadvisedly with his lips.' When he chose to, and when the student was really modest and humble as well as inquiring, Professor Robinson could so handle the matter as to lead the man to feel that he had really thought most of it out himself; which was a great comfort to him, and wonderfully stimulating for the next time. He thought that the Professor was a man of fine appreciation.

"But the way Professor Robinson influenced us most was by his side talks along the line of the lessons, and sometimes not of things in the lesson, but pertinent to the situation. He was intense in his convictions, intense in his utterances, intense in his loyalty to logic and truth. We always felt his robust intellectuality, his robust manhood, and his utter contempt for shams. He would lash a sham with merciless severity. He was like a well-tempered die, and left his mark upon every one more or less, in some cases stamping them with an ineffaceable impress of his tremendous personality as a man, a teacher, and a preacher."

AT ROCHESTER.

It is agreed that Dr. Robinson was at his best in teaching Systematic Theology. He himself did not dissent from this opinion. Here he was free, imposing, and even picturesque. It is of special interest to know how, in the great work of his life, he impressed students of very different types.

We first quote from an unknown writer's contribution to the "Journal and Messenger," when Dr. Robinson left Rochester for Brown. The comments of Dr. Behrends add to its interest. He writes : —

"I do not believe that any one could have penned these paragraphs soon after his graduation. I know that, for myself, the spell of Dr. Robinson's personality completely captivated me. I was a Robinson-ite when I graduated in every fibre of my mental life, ready to do battle for his conclusions. But gradually, slowly but surely, the independent and fearless intellectual temper which made his teaching glow acted more and more mightily, until, in catching his spirit, I became independent of him, without abating one particle in my reverence for him."

The article from which the following quotation is made may be in some degree marked by the unshackled vehemence that it ascribes to Dr. Robinson : —

"He magnified his office above all others, and imparted to his students an enthusiasm for theological studies. Himself an independent thinker, having little regard for authority, a contempt for pretence and cant, an intense love for truth, an almost fierce delight in criti-cising opposing systems, a rare facility for terse, sharp statement, with little patience with mediocrity, none with dulness, and with withering scorn for laziness, he succeeded in convincing most of his students of the worthlessness of all their previous attainments in theology, and awakened in them an earnest desire for study, especially for discussion and investigation, and a bold, energetic, self-reliant spirit. His method, his spirit, rather than his teaching, told upon his students. Many of them never understood him, others did not accept his teach-ings, but all, in greater or smaller degree, felt the quickening influence of his vigorous mind. He was a great educator rather than a great teacher. Holding with tenacity to, and insisting with almost impatient vehe-mence upon, certain doctrines which he deemed fundamental, pushing them to extremes, with logic so relentless as to be illogical, support-ing them with props which he himself would have discarded save for the necessity for using them laid upon him by his system, holding fast to the formulas of the most rigid orthodoxy, striving with manly earnestness to find the basal truth in them which he could harmonize with his beliefs, yet growing more conscious each year that he taught of his divergence from the popular acceptation of these formulas ;

goaded by whispers, occasionally open to charges of heresy, he threw into his class-room discussions, which always accompanied the didactic lectures, a life and charm and fire and power which no student can ever forget, or ever cease to be thankful for. He was a most zealous worker himself, and kept his classes at work from the first hour of the session to the last; supplied them with new motives, and gave them new impulses to vigorous, manly, self-reliant labor, in comparison with which many found all the work done at college mere boy's play."

Rev. Norman Fox, D. D., says : —

" His power to stimulate the intellects of students was unequalled. The principal work in his lecture-room was not to force young men to accept ideas, but to arouse them to have ideas of their own. Often when he came into his room it was with the plainest signs of fatigue from travel or protracted labor. After the brief prayer, in a faint voice, came the usual inquiry whether there was any question on the preceding lecture. Some student would ask for further light, perhaps hinting some sharp dissent from the view presented, and instantly the tall form was erect as at the sound of a bugle challenging to battle, the signs of fatigue were gone, and there commenced a keen discussion, whose intense and exciting interest might last through the whole hour. Sometimes two or three days would pass without any advance to new topics, the time being wholly given to discussion of a contested point. . . . It was not his particular opinion on this or that doctrine, but his method of forming opinions, which impressed itself on the minds of the young men. Many of his former pupils are now professors of theology or eminent pastors ; . . . but it is safe to say that there is not one of them who in his methods of investigation, in the spirit in which he takes up a topic, is not still swayed by the method of inquiry which he saw continually before him in that lecture-room. . . . Again and again was the following scene enacted : A student had studied out something which seemed to him entirely to overthrow some ancient doctrine ; the next day in class he proceeds to state his point ; as he does it rather bunglingly, the Doctor interrupts him with, ' You mean so and so,' and the student assents, his confidence being at the outset well shattered at finding that not only has this wonderful idea of his occurred to others before him, but that the Doctor can state it much more strongly than he can himself. If in the discussion which ensues the student's difficulty is not entirely cleared away, the Doctor finally says, ' Well, think it over. You will come out all right.' In other words, the student sees that his instructor believes that honest investigation will never undermine Christianity."

The Rev. C. B. Crane, D. D., after stating, as Dr. Robinson's doctrine, that "in justifying a man God both declares and makes him righteous," adds : —

"What high and animated discussion we had in the class-room upon this teaching! . . . It was contrary to the traditional interpretation of the doctrine. We wondered, questioned, disputed, almost fought; and Dr. Robinson, like a radiant Apollo, accepted all our challenges, stripped for the combat, and with most of us came out victor.

"It almost maddened him to have his students 'play the boy.' He had a way of getting into the room almost as soon as he touched the door-knob. One poor fellow forgot this, and so came to grief. The Doctor had been called out for a moment, and our unfortunate friend . . . took his place at the desk and began a pretended dictation. In an instant the Doctor was in the room, and following with flashing eyes the student as he sneaked away to his seat. The rebuke was brief but blistering, and the victim never quite regained his standing with his teacher.

"We used to hand in anonymous plans of sermons for the Doctor to criticise, always hoping that we should not betray ourselves under torture. He was at work one day upon one of my own plans; and when the knife touched a nerve, I said, 'Is it not possible that the author may have meant it so and so?' 'Possibly,' said the Doctor; 'in which case my criticism will not hold.' A second time I winced, and asked the same question. The Doctor looked at me comically and said : 'I suspect you are the man who knows best of us all what the author of this plan meant.' The class shouted, and I collapsed. Sometimes he would toss a plan from him with the exclamation : 'One could make a hatful of such plans in half an hour.' Then the author would drop clean down into the hole of the pit."

Professor Lemuel Moss, D. D., says : —

"Perhaps the first thing that the pupil felt was the air of earnestness and eagerness which pervaded his lecture-room. One must be dull even to deadness who was not affected. Studying theology was not only a serious business, but an exacting business, from which there was neither release nor relaxation.

"Still more surprising was the matchless freedom which reigned in the class-room. The first personal impression that the student received was doubtless a sort of mental challenge. Dr. Robinson seemed in the student's initial experience unsympathetic, distant, austere, not to say haughty and exclusive; but the prickly burr was on the husk and not on the inner kernel. The teacher was positive, dogmatic, but not dictatorial; he guarded the rights of others as well as his own. Many a soul was born anew through these throes of discussion, and was grateful for a defeat which showed him how to conquer in subsequent conflicts. In these hand-to-hand contests Dr. Robinson rendered his supreme service to the students."

The Rev. R. S. MacArthur, D. D., writes: —

" But few men have ever taught a class of theological or other students, who could so stimulate them by his presence and his words. Tall and stately, with his clean-cut face, flashing eye, and white hair, he was a man to be noticed among thousands. . . . He anticipated a quarter of a century ago the trend of theological thinking with which to-day we are familiar. . . . He exhorted his students not to be alarmed when these discussions should come. . . . No one who sat under his instruction will forget his prayers at the beginning of each session. He walked masterfully and yet modestly into the class-room, put down his hat, bowed his head in prayer, talking often so low that only such expressions could be heard as ' O Christ, make us loyal to truth; make us love truth more than our prejudices, more than we love our systems, more than we love all beside. Thou art King in the realm of truth. May we joyously worship at thy feet.' Never will his students forget when he took his chair before the class, after the opening prayer was offered, and quietly asked, ' Are there any questions, gentlemen ? ' Then the questions were poured in upon him. Woe to the man who asked a foolish or a weak question ! Some of his comments on living and dead authors and preachers would make spicy reading. . . . His class-room was sometimes a field-day at examinations, when the good brethren came in to find out the heresy which some supposed was taught in the Seminary. He had a marvellous way of decapitating the brethren who accepted his invitation to ask questions and to scent heresy."

The suspicion that his views were open to challenge as heretical was no doubt due in part to the air of challenge with which he often announced them in lecture-room or in pulpit. When a controversy that made some noise in its day sprang up concerning his sermon, now published in the "Madison Avenue Lectures," on "The Relation of the Church and the Bible," he asked a waggish friend who was supposed to be a good judge of orthodoxy, whether he found anything heretical in that discourse; and the answer was: "No, I have heard you preach a great many times, and never heard you preach heresy; but you always give the impression of doing it. And I have heard a great many sermons from . . . [naming another professor of theology], and they are always chock-full of heresy; but no one ever notices it."

The Rev. Dr. A. J. Sage furnishes a reminiscence of lecture-room discipline : —

"Our class had one member, call him ' Lumley,' who had a propensity for asking questions which sounded as if they might mean something and might represent a real difficulty in the mind of the querist. When interrogated and followed up, he would persist in one blind statement or inquiry after another, until finally the whole matter would fade back into the fog from which it came. Dr. Robinson had several times followed these retreating and vanishing problems with a patience which astonished the class. One day, when the inquiry had been unusually protracted and elusive, and at last, as usual, had come to nothing, the Doctor closed the investigation by remarking, 'Mr. "Lumley," before you make another inquiry, be kind enough to ascertain that you have something clearly defined and important to ask about. It is somewhat disappointing to hunt down a stag and find that it 's a polecat.' The unanimous amusement of the class manifested their sense of the aptness of the illustration."

A noteworthy element in Dr. Robinson's power over students was that he never for a moment seemed ridiculous. His dignity was so unaffected yet complete that his exemption from ridicule has hardly seemed worth mentioning. With students his steady power and earnestness were always impressive. One does not laugh at a locomotive or a siege gun. And his rare command of terse, tense expressions kept alive the feeling that there was power in him. Early in life he was fascinated by Carlyle, and his habits of expression were no doubt much more affected by Carlyle than by Robert Hall, on whose style he afterwards sought for a while to model his own. He did not always hesitate to use against others the lethal weapons of denunciation and ridicule ; and like Carlyle he sometimes found the former, but never the latter weapon turned against himself. If any one laughed at Carlyle, he laughed at long range ; and Dr. Robinson met his students and his public at close quarters. Even his most playful moods in private showed the same quality of ingrained dignity. Something was no doubt due to his sense of the ridiculous, and his sensitiveness to ridicule. This kept him wary, instinctively, not studiously. And in close alliance with this should never be overlooked the gentle considerateness with which his endless task of criticism was performed. He was critical for his student's sake, and courteous for his own sake. The thoroughness of his work was thus made to seem, what it really was, thoughtfulness and fidelity in behalf of the student. — ED.

ADDITIONAL NOTE FROM COVINGTON.

Rev. Rufus C. Burleson, D. D., LL. D., President of Baylor University, Waco, Texas, furnishes a lively description of the Professor in the making : —

"Dr. Robinson became Professor at Covington in the fall of 1846. He was then thirty-one years old, over six feet tall, with high forehead and penetrating eyes. He was fresh from Cambridge, and had won fame as pastor in Norfolk, Virginia, and as Chaplain of the University of Virginia. No professor ever entered upon duties under more embarrassing surroundings. He was utterly unlike his predecessors, Professor Ebenezer Dodge and Dr. R. E. Pattison. They were mild, lovable, and forbearing as mothers; hence the stern, imperial bearing of Professor Robinson was chilling to the forty-two young preachers then assembled in the halls of the Theological Institute. His contempt and sneers for all shams and superficial thinking, and for such expressions as 'It is about that way,' 'It rather seems to me,' 'as it were,' caused the students to dread the new professor. He demanded that the student should grasp every point profoundly and explain it clearly. Dr. Pattison, with the loving heart of a mother and the profound wisdom of a philosopher, grasped the situation, and at the proper time and place explained the peculiar nature and history of the new professor. He said : 'He was born and reared among

New England farmers, who have a great contempt for all hypocrisy and outward demonstration of feeling. But often under cold and icy appearances there glow hearts full of love and tenderness for friends, and of devotion to God and native land.' He said Professor Robinson was exacting in his demands because of his love for profound thinking and investigation, and his burning desire to see all young preachers thoroughly rooted and grounded in the faith, so as to be able to meet and demolish all the superficial scepticism of this age, and lead the people of God to higher attainments in divine wisdom and knowledge. We all soon rejoiced to find these views of our beloved President were eminently true, — that under an apparently cold countenance there glowed a noble, pure, and loving heart, and that his rigid requirements resulted only from his profound conviction that nothing would save this generation from scepticism and heresies but the rearing of young preachers 'called of God as was Aaron,' with heads and hearts all on fire. We were more deeply penetrated with these convictions when we met him in the prayer-meeting, the mission-concerts, the sick-room, and when we listened to his profound and burning words from the pulpit of Ninth Street Baptist Church. In all these relations we saw he had the simplicity of a little child, the purity of a saint, and the wisdom of a Christian philosopher. Though I was born in the extreme South and the son of a large slaveholder, I soon regarded him as one of the noblest, grandest men of earth; 'and time has that impression deeper made, as streams that channels deeper wear.' Whatever success I have attained as President of Baylor University for the last forty-five years, in instructing over eight thousand young men and young ladies, I owe largely to Dr. Robinson and his sainted co-laborers; and my beloved classmates Rev. Dr. Wm. Ashmore, Rev. Dr. Wm. Moore, Rev. J. R. Downer, Rev. R. H. Taliaferro, and others have all been inspired and girded for noble deeds by the same holy influence."

V.

DR. ROBINSON AS A LEADER IN POST-GRADUATE STUDY.

By PROFESSOR B. O. TRUE, D. D.,
Rochester Theological Seminary.

V.

AS A LEADER IN POST-GRADUATE STUDY.

AFTER fourteen years of constant and conspicuous service as Professor of Theology in Rochester Theological Seminary, Dr. Robinson, with his family, passed a large part of the years 1867 and 1868 in Europe. In the early autumn of 1868, invigorated by the change and stimulus of his European experience, he resumed what many of his theological students persistently believe was the great work of his life. During those last four years of theological instruction, from 1868 to 1872, he was in the prime of life and in the full exercise of his superb power. A large proportion of his students at that time were mature men. Not a few had been soldiers in the civil war. They brought the unwonted earnestness, heroism, and devotion of the battlefield to the work of the ministry. Many had delayed the completion of their college and seminary training on account of the war. They were men of rare spirit, large experience, mental discipline, and versatile talents. Younger students caught the enthusiasm of the older men, and quickly learned the power of definite, persistent, and consecrated purpose. Dr. Robinson seized the opportunity, and magnified his office. His long and successful experience, intensity, devotion, and acknowledged ability gave him, at the very first, an unquestioned mastery. In the class-room, as on the street, he might easily have passed for a military commander in citizen's dress. His type of mind and method precluded the treatment of high themes in an elementary or a commonplace way. His work was never formal or perfunctory. The spirit of earnestness and reality impressed every pupil from the first to the last hour of his course.

Whatever he was to other men or elsewhere, by the five successive classes to whom he taught theology with tireless energy and boundless enthusiasm from 1868 to 1872 (including the class which graduated in 1873) Dr. Robinson was considered equal to almost any mental effort, however difficult or impossible it might be for ordinary men. Beyond a doubt, those were great years, even for him. The reputation of the Seminary was established. The present grounds were purchased, and in 1869 Trevor Hall was completed. The number and quality of the students had never been more satisfactory. Dr. Robinson fairly revelled in his work. He was at his very best everywhere, and nowhere more easily than in the class-room, where he worked with the greatest efficiency. By many those days are recalled with inexpressible gratitude; to some they furnished the opportunity of a lifetime.

As a preparation for work of a high order, in 1862 the earlier two years' course of the Seminary had been lengthened to three years. Later Drs. Kendrick and Hackett were successively induced to devote their ripest powers to the New Testament department. At Dr. Robinson's solicitation, one of the rarest young men of the land,[1] in both

---

[1] Samuel Emmons Brown was born at Portland, Maine, February 27, 1847, graduated at Phillips Academy, Exeter, 1867, at Harvard, 1870, and at Rochester Theological Seminary, 1873. He studied three years at the universities of Leipsic and Halle, 1873-76. He was Acting Professor of New Testament Exegesis in Rochester Theological Seminary during the scholastic year 1876-77, and gave abundant proof of his remarkable ability both as a scholar and an instructor. His character commanded general admiration, and with

scholarship and character, destined to be removed by death after a single year of service as professor, was selected and specially prepared to become Dr. Hackett's assistant and possible successor. All work in the Seminary was of a high order, and promise of future advance had never been brighter.

In those last years of theological instruction Dr. Robinson's entire theological course had come to be practically post-collegiate work. It presupposed in students the mental discipline and reflection of a full collegiate training, and with scarcely an exception the students at that time were college graduates. Naturally the scope and method of theological instruction were adjusted to these conditions. All sources of enlightenment were sought, and all truth was welcome. Discussion, if adequate and relevant, was never curtailed, because difficult and complex. The results of Old and New Testament interpretation, sometimes illustrated microscopically by the examination of a single word, sometimes telescopically by the argument or chief purpose of an entire epistle, the established conclusions and promising hypotheses of natural science, the philosophy of history, ancient and modern, and the most notable phases of philosophical thought, furnished constant contributions to the instruction of the class-room. The relations of theology to the whole realm of truth were clearly recognized. The suggestion of a four years' course, or of a fourth year for supplementary theological study, became distinct and emphatic. This was a favorite hope of Dr. Robinson, and provision for some proper system of advanced work by prepared men was his cherished purpose. The material equipments

<hr>

his natural ability and exceptional training gave promise of distinguished usefulness; but he was suddenly stricken with typhoid fever, and died in Lowell, Massachusetts, August 5, 1877. — B. O. T.

of the Seminary were sufficiently modest, but students felt that in the heart of the institution was a thousand-horse-power Corliss engine, and that by impulsion, propulsion, or expulsion *something would be*, and, if men remained long under Dr. Robinson, *much must be* done.

Other professors of theology gave more attention to authorship. Dr. Robinson gave his best strength to his pupils. As a direct result of that course, several members of the Class of 1870 proposed to return to Rochester after their graduation, for another year of study, under the guidance of Dr. Robinson. To this proposition he gave the most cordial encouragement. Three members of the class — Professor Wayland R. Benedict, now Professor of Philosophy and Dean of the University of Cincinnati; Rev. John T. Beckley, D.D., pastor of the Epiphany Baptist Church, New York; and the writer — met Dr. Robinson regularly, during the scholastic year of 1870–71, not simply for post-collegiate, but for post-seminary theological study. Dr. T. J. Morgan, the present Corresponding Secretary of the American Baptist Home Mission Society, a graduate of the Seminary in the Class of 1868, though prevented from regular attendance and full work with the class on account of his duties as Corresponding Secretary of the New York Baptist Union for Ministerial Education, was frequently present, and shared the work of the class. Somewhat similar work, though in closer imitation of the German *Seminar*, had been done by Henry B. Smith, but probably by few, perhaps by no other, professors of systematic theology in America at that time. The members of the graduate class represented four different colleges in four widely removed sections of the country. Twice every week, on Tuesday and Thursday evenings throughout the Seminary year, from September to May, the class met in Dr. Robinson's parlors.

Mrs. Robinson was always present, and keenly interested. She was accustomed to relieve the sessions, often three hours in length, by a gracious hospitality which can never be forgotten; and her contributions to the discussions were always discriminating, suggestive, and welcome. The work consisted of special reading, with the preparation and full discussion of papers upon subjects of vital and paramount interest to students of theology.

Among my own manuscripts of that date I find papers on "The Historical Books of the Old Testament," "Christian and Heathen Morality Compared," "The Testimony of Paul to Christ," and "The Sensational School of Philosophy." The details of the paper on "The Old Testament" were doubtless crude enough to make a modern student devoutly grateful for the progress of the last twenty-five years; but the free discussion of the dates, composition, and design of those Old Testament books, with special reference to the objections to their trustworthiness, under the searching analysis and discriminating guidance of Dr. Robinson, was an invaluable preparation for the progress of recent thought. The phrase "Higher Criticism" was not then common, but much which it involves was largely anticipated. In like manner I gratefully recall, as the result of that year's work, impressions of Spinoza's philosophy, of his influence upon later thought, especially in Germany, and of the striking alternative which he proposed, — the rejection of either Scriptural miracles or his own philosophy, — an alternative which led to the famous cry, "Spinoza or Christ?" Those long evenings when precious time was lavishly and willingly bestowed upon pupils eager in their search for truth, would most certainly have been succeeded by similar work, had Dr. Robinson continued to teach theology. The next and last year of his work at Rochester was absorbed by the extra labor of preparing and printing the larger portion of his " Christian Theology. " Every paragraph of this book is a protest against superficial or commonplace work, and a testimony to the author's superior fitness for the highest order of theological instruction.

Had Dr. Robinson declined the presidency of Brown in 1872, as he had once done at an earlier date, and had he remained at the head of the Theological Seminary, he would have made speedy provision for the continuation, in a more permanent and systematic way, of the supplementary theological work which was done in 1870 and 1871. There are those who believe that such provision in the leading scholastic departments of the Seminary, with suitable prescribed work as a prerequisite for admission to advanced classes, would be vastly more satisfactory to teachers and students, and would secure far better results than either an exclusive system of prescribed studies or the option of multiplied and confusing electives from the beginning of a theological course.

No man was better fitted to direct such an advance in theological education twenty-five years ago than Dr. Robinson. There was then no Baptist Seminary better situated to enlarge and develop its facilities than that which he had so firmly established. But after serious hesitation and unfeigned reluctance, for what appeared to him to be sufficient reasons, he went to Providence. Any disposition to disparage or undervalue his great work at Brown University would be ungracious and unjust. That work has been compared with the influence of his own famous teacher and friend, Francis Wayland; and it is certain that, whatever the merits of others, Brown University has had two great presidents, Wayland and Robinson. Yet there were many of Dr. Robinson's theological pupils, who, because they knew that he was especially fitted to give instruction of a high order, and that he would be content with no other type of theological teaching, greatly regretted a change which inevitably compelled him to restrict his daily instruction to men at an earlier and less mature stage of mental development than was the case at Rochester. There are those who, while grateful beyond words for what Dr. Robinson has done for many men at Brown University, cannot overlook the fact that his long experience, fixed habits, and mental characteristics fitted him to teach men rather than youth. Such cannot think without sadness of what might have been, if, with twenty more years devoted to theological education, and with such suitable support in men and money as he deserved and might have received, he had developed, upon the broad and firm foundations which he did so much to establish, a really great and adequate Baptist Theological Seminary, proportionate to the increased wealth, intelligence, and needs of the denomination in the Central and Eastern States.[1] Had he continued to teach theology, he would certainly have aimed to produce such an institution, and he would have chafed like a caged lion had his purpose been thwarted. Truth compels the acknowledgment that, after a quarter of a century of unparalleled material prosperity, such an institution does not exist, even in hopeful promise. It is impossible to estimate the immense influence of such a Seminary, amply provided with needful facilities, and or-

---

[1] Provision was made by the founders for the separate corporate existence of the Theological Seminary and the University at Rochester, with the distinct anticipation that the future removal of the Seminary to New York might be highly desirable. This is clearly shown by an extant letter of Dr. Maginnis, in his own handwriting. At one time Dr. Robinson earnestly advocated this removal. The great advantages of the proposal were recognized by the local trustees, but strenuous objection was made by the officers of the University, especially by Dr. Anderson, and the plan was not consummated. — B. O. T.

dered by such a man. It is not easy to imagine with the nineteen years of experience behind him, what more than twenty years of additional service as a theological instructor might have accomplished; but it is safe to predict that if such had been his career, with spared life and health, among his contemporaries he would have had no equal in America as a teacher of theology, and no superior as a theologian.

What Dr. Robinson was, as a leader in post-graduate work, is abundantly understood by those who at Crozer Theological Seminary and the University of Chicago received his instruction in the maturity and ripe wisdom of his later years. He taught " Christian Ethics " with the interest and power of Wayland and Hopkins, and, what was best of all, he illustrated his theme by his own high and almost ideal realization of his constant obligations to God and to men. He taught " Christian Evidences " with a preparation not primarily designed for public utterance, but as one who had " felt out, fought out, and thought out " every phase of the subject for his own satisfaction, and for the peace of his own soul.

Dr. Robinson was a leader in higher professional education from personal conviction and not merely by the circumstances of his position. Fifty years ago, when many superior men, notably Dr. Wayland, gave only a qualified support and sympathy to theological seminaries, Dr. Robinson heartily believed in them, and no man in the Baptist denomination did more to justify their existence and to demonstrate their great value. Twenty-five years ago, when there was a general demand among Congregationalists and Presbyterians for more practical training and for practical men in the ministry, Dr. Robinson cordially and wisely encouraged men, who had the inclination and opportunity, to prolong their special theological studies, and, if possible, to anticipate the urgent questions of the future by earnest preparation for their solution.   The result is, that few of his pupils have been surprised, and none dismayed, by the inevitable transitions and changed formulas of current thought. They have been men with their faces towards the sunrise, welcoming light, but unwilling with indiscriminate haste to put darkness for light and light for darkness.   They have not mistaken the restatement of old errors for new truth, neither have they contentedly closed with the conservative *dictum*, "what is true is not new, and what is new is not true."   For the happy *via media* between conservatism and radicalism Dr. Robinson's theological students owe to him an incalculable debt.

His faith in prolonged preparation for professional work remained firm to the end.   It was abundantly manifest in his remarkable adjustment at seventy-five years of age to unaccustomed conditions, and in his helpful co-operation with the novel plans of younger men.   Perhaps he was never a typical professor, after the order of the schools, because he rose above the petty conventionalities of smaller men.   But this gave him special fitness for exceptional work.   He was a willing and persistent stranger to perfunctory professionalism, both in the class-room and in the pulpit.   Hence he was particularly adapted to render those ready, incisive, correct judgments which are constantly demanded in the higher instruction of advanced students.   Certainly more than any man of his years, and perhaps, without any qualification, more than any other man, he illustrated at Chicago that high type of post-graduate instruction which he anticipated at Rochester twenty years before.   The conditions were very diverse, but the work was essentially the same.   No variations of time, place, or circumstance were allowed to diminish the fidelity and thoroughness of his instruction.   As a consequence, the best qualified men sought Dr. Robinson's instruction, and often selected their previous studies with reference to his work. At Chicago, with famous professors in the prime of life, no students were more profited than his pupils, and no instruction was more eagerly sought than that of the man who, though nearly fourscore years of age, taught with a vigor and efficiency unusual in most men of middle life.

Dr. Robinson fully believed that the responsible care of property, life, character, and destiny was sacred work, and that it should not be undertaken lightly or unadvisedly. No price could be too great, and no vigilance too constant, in the preparation for such work. Therefore he taught men to study as ardently as they prayed or preached. He believed in prolonged and persistent search for truth, " as for hid treasure." " Buy the truth and sell it not," was the exhortation of his life. Yet he constantly recognized the limitations of human thought, and turned from other and inadequate sources of authority to the revelation of nature, of man's moral constitution, and of the sacred Scriptures, with grateful, reverent, and discriminating faith. There were *lacunæ* in his system of theology. He often paused in silence before questions of " doubtful disputation," when there was no possibility of credible utterance. His emphatic recognition of the necessary limitations of human knowledge, no less than the power of his positive affirmations, fitted him to be a marked leader of men.

It is yet too early to estimate the place which will be accorded to Dr. Robinson as a systematic theologian; but as a religious teacher his place is assured.

The elder Hodge was doubtless more learned in the historical theology of the reformed churches; but no man could imagine Dr. Robinson boasting, as did Dr. Hodge, that no new idea in theology had ever been hospitably entertained at Princeton Seminary throughout its entire history. Dr. Park was a master of language, plausible in argument, and skilful in the art of expression. Henry B. Smith was more familiar with German philosophical and theological thought, more appreciative of its excellences and more discriminatingly sensitive to its dangers, than any American theologian of his day. His service in theological instruction was invaluable. But as an independent thinker, who induced others to think, of all his contemporaries perhaps only Horace Bushnell should be compared with Dr. Robinson. But Bushnell's thought, always stimulating and vigorous, was critical and one-sided rather than symmetrical and constructive. Both Bushnell and Robinson were acute, intense, alert, broad-minded, reverent. Neither was held by the external authority of confessions and great names, as was the elder Hodge; neither cultivated the polished rhetoric of Park; yet both were masters of a unique and vigorous style. Neither was, from early life, so widely conversant with the details of German thought as was Henry B. Smith; but as thinkers who sought beneath customary formulas for the "eternal verities," who demanded as immovable supports of their faith essential realities, Bushnell and Robinson were not unlike. If at one time Bushnell seemed more radical than Robinson, it must be remembered that Bushnell became conservative with years. And however radical Robinson may have seemed, he was never dazed with mere novelty. He was discriminating and courageous. He strove to prove all things, and to hold fast that and only that which is good. He did not acknowledge the authority of any uninspired teacher. However he may be regarded as a theologian, his place as a great teacher of theology is assured.

He has impressed himself indelibly upon hundreds of living men.

Were I obliged to express in two words the secret of his remarkable power, I would say fitness and fidelity, or, possibly, ability and duty. His loyalty to moral convictions, to great spiritual realities, joined to his great ability, gave him supreme mastery over his pupils, and lifted him far above ordinary men. Only One was his Master. There was no divided allegiance. His earthly work is finished, but the influence of that work is deathless. " Being dead, he yet speaketh. "

VI.

DR. ROBINSON AS A TEACHER OF HOMILETICS AND AS A PREACHER.

———

By REV. WAYLAND HOYT, D.D.,
MINNEAPOLIS, MINNESOTA.

AS TEACHER OF HOMILETICS, AND AS PREACHER.

WHEN I was student in the Rochester Theological Seminary, both the chair of Theology and the chair of Homiletics were filled by Dr. Robinson. It is needless to say that he *filled* both of them, and the last as splendidly as the first. The Rochester Theological Seminary was then a school with meagre endowment and equipment, compelling much doubling of work on the part of the few professors. I never got anywhere such notion of *shouldering* various, and even sometimes apparently antagonistic, duties as I did in those days from Dr. Robinson. He was in the very prime of his rare manhood, at the full blooming point of his physical and mental vigor. He was almost everything to the Seminary, — at once its engine and its engineer. He was general scurrier for funds for it, presiding officer over it, teacher of Theology and of Homiletics in it, editor of the "Christian Review" also, and almost every Sunday preacher somewhere, — frequently stated supply for some church in Rochester or in Albany or in New York. The absolute tirelessness of the man made upon me profound impression. The marvellous ease with which he wrought so constantly and so variously was also as evident as the mass and weight of work to which he set his hand. And the wonderful freshness of him, — never a trace of exhaustion, never the least lagging from high ideal of finished duty, never a bit of slouch or shabbiness, never the suggestion of an excuse for doing anything slightingly because so much was given him to do. Well, the sight of him to me was like the vision of the strong sea, which no commerce can overweight; and contact with him was as when one catches the tonic of the salt-breezes.

When, then, on each Wednesday afternoon, which was always Homiletic day, Dr. Robinson turned the attention of his class from the study of Theology to the study of the making of sermons, there was no relaxing of his high energy or ceasing in his scrupulous and manly thoroughness. Prince of theological teachers, as he was, and doubtless looking at that as his main function, there was no evidence of side-play feeling when he turned toward Homiletics; he was as princely here, as nobly serious, as inspiring, as stirringly magnetic.

The core of the teaching-system of Dr. Arnold of Rugby was to show the pupil how to do it himself, and to make him do it. This was pre-eminently Dr. Robinson's method of teaching Homiletics. He would insist and keep on insisting that the fellow do it himself. He did not, therefore, so much deliver formal lectures on the subject of sermon-making. He rather kept giving informal hints and suggestions, taking his departure from the production of some student. Through the distances of years comes to me the memory of his emphasis on *plan*. No clear, orderly, conclusive, persuading speech without distinctly imaged plan for such speech in the mind of the speaker, — this was his fundamental *dictum*. The bones of the thing must be exact and precisely articulated before you proceeded to wrap the flesh around it. How remorselessly hostile he was against all aimless and merely padding speech! How quickly, and severely even, he would strip it off, hunting for the real and sustaining skeleton of thought beneath; and when, as often happened, there was no such skeleton, how evidently he made the emptiness of the whole thing helplessly gape before you! For a large part of the first year in which one came under Dr. Robinson in Homiletics, he held his students to making plans. "Tut!" he would say, glancing through some careless and unthoughtful plan, and flinging it aside in a way which once seen could never be forgotten, "one could make a hatful of such plans in half an hour." Then would follow some strong, clear instruction on the absolute necessity of plans, on the right method of fashioning one, — on introduction, statement of theme, argument, application, peroration. How living, incisive, shocking into vigor as with an electric battery, his speech would be! How his words burned themselves into the memory! What glimpses he gave one of the nobility of preaching! With what shame he whelmed one at the thought of undertaking so lofty a function except in the most honest, thoughtful, sincere way! How he caused the ideal of real preaching and the real preacher to flame and glow! How he fascinated into the pursuit of it! How he made one feel like a racer stripped for the race, and intent on reaching the shining goal! Mere professionalism in preaching, — withering was his scorn of it. But the essential manliness of preaching and the need of manhood in the doing it, — how he would lay hold of you with this idea, catch you with it, impel you toward it, make you vow in your innermost soul you would achieve it! The contagion of his enthusiasm, — how it would sweep through that class! One might as well try to be listless whirled in a cyclone. How I have seen attention stretch and strain until one forgot to breathe, in the presence of some of his masterful utterances about preaching!

But severe as Dr. Robinson was toward a careless and

shiftless thoughtlessness, no mother could be kinder toward a child than he toward any real thinking, or attempt at it, even though the thinking might be faulty. Said Dr. Arnold of Rugby, of a pupil not bright, but grandly toilful, " I would stand to that man hat in hand." I rarely think of that sentence that I do not think of Dr. Robinson as illustrating it. If any one ever called him cold or hard, such did not know his inner heart. He would brood over some poor plan, but with real attempt and thought in it, as a June sky does over laggard flowers. He would so delicately praise and so stimulatingly; with such kindness suggest better method; put such courage into the man who really tried. And when the man had produced a better plan, he would so graciously recognize it, notice so painstakingly the steps and elements of advance.

After such drill in plan-making would follow equally careful drill in sermon-making. Now, having analyzed the parts of sermons, and carefully studied in this live way the several divisions of them, you must synthetize the components, — put them all together in a finished whole. Here came in the study of exegesis for sermons, proportion of contents, language, etc. Woe to the man who did not do his best! What summer for the man who did his best, though that best were ideally poor! No clearer, keener, truthfuller, at the same time really kinder atmosphere of criticism ever reigned in any lecture-room. And what infinite pains he took with your production! You read your sermon before him and before the class; you were to take note of all the criticisms to which himself and the class, after free discussion, gave consent; you must then rewrite your sermon, taking heed of all these criticisms; you must then visit him in his study, and Dr. Robinson would again go through the whole thing with you in the carefullest way.

How much he taught you thus! You had done it yourself. What you had learned of sermon-making was thus indestructibly your own. I used to wonder how he could get time for it all; but he did. The impulse I got from sermons produced in this way, while I was his student, has never passed; is as fresh and forceful and helpful now, as when, years back, I would leave his study-door.

I think Dr. Robinson, at least in the Baptist denomination,— nor would I limit it there, so great was the widening and reflex influence of his work,— plainly introduced a new era of preaching. He lifted the level of it, he enlarged the function of it, he enriched the quality of it, he strengthened the sceptre of it, he ennobled the idea of it.

Of extemporaneous preachers Dr. Robinson was the foremost. And of Dr. Robinson himself, as preacher, what better description can be given than by these sentences, culled from the concluding lecture of his own Yale lectures on preaching? He says: " Rant and rhapsody and declamation and rambling garrulity, sometimes known as extemporaneous preaching, are a disgrace to Christianity, and always offensive to people of discernment. The first thing always is clear and just thought, with its appropriate expression." How clear and just his thought, how appropriate his expression, what severe and noble freedom from any rambling rant of mere harangue in him!

" Choice language is not like a dress-coat that can be put on or off as occasion calls; it must come, if at all, from within, and to be natural and effective must come without effort. The best language, like true gentlemanliness, has its seat in the depths of the soul, and cannot be put on as we change our apparel." And who ever listened to Dr. Robinson, who did not feel that the fibre of him, even to the last shred of it, was thus strenuously cultured ? " Please banish, therefore, from your minds all notions of great sermons on small preparations. Impromptu thoughts and deep emotions cannot be safely expected to come just when wanted. The only inspiration that any man who is to extemporize can rely on with safety, is that which springs from being filled with the thought and spirit of his subject. " You could not get rid of the impression, when Dr. Robinson was preaching, that his theme thralled him, that he was not thinking of himself, but was only eager to make you know the truth he himself, through study, prostrate prayer, earnest reflection, and sincere experience, had come to know.

" In an age like ours, of great apparent penetration, but of shallow emotion, there is no means of protecting one's self against error, and no resource in battling against it or in enforcing the authority of truth on others, like that of a complete surrender of soul to the control of the personal Christ. Let his Gospel do its full work in moulding your characters after his divine pattern ; then will your words be instinct with a life no eloquence can impart, and carry with them something of the authority with which the Gospel was first spoken to the world. "

And Dr. Robinson spoke with the authority and the eloquence and the vitalizing power of a soul in complete surrender to the control of the personal Christ.

Like a waft of wondrous music, hushing all discordances, and binding with an imperial peace, and opening reaches of awing truth, and lifting into rapt communion with the Unseen Holy, abides with me the memory of those prayers of his in the Seminary chapel, when the day's work was done, and he led us and waited with us in devotion before the personal Christ.

NOTE A.

ON DR ROBINSON'S PULPIT MANNER.

From the Memorial Address before Brown University, by Rev. **T. D.** **Anderson, D. D.**

It was in the sermon that the powerful personality came into fullest manifestation. So potent was the personality of the man, and so strong his personal magnetism, that his whole manner, though unconsciously observed, is clearly photographed on the memory. Leaning over the desk, and resting his hands on either side of the Bible, he slowly and distinctly reads the text; then, removing his eyeglasses and assuming an erect position, with shoulders thrown back and chest expanded, after a brief silence, in slow and measured tones he gives utterance to some short and pithy sentence. Having taken firm position, he slowly continues his march of progress until the proposition is announced and the analytical discussion begun. Thus far the preacher seems to have been feeling his way. Apart from the physical effort of articulation, the mind is wellnigh the exclusive factor in the discourse ; the orator has not yet been aroused ; gestures have been few ; the left hand has again and again toyed with the button of the trousers' pocket, but the preacher is still conscious of proprieties and restrains it from entering. But as the discourse advances and the thought unfolds, the manner becomes more and more animated ; and occasionally at some one point in the discourse, as the man becomes profoundly interested in his theme, and the orator thrills under the magnetic response of his congregation, the soul takes fire and carries the body with it in its mighty onward rush. The left hand, no longer under restraint, is thrust deep into the pocket, the right hand is in vigorous action, the voice rings out clear and distinct in the upper register, and sometimes the curiously arranged locks of hair are dislodged and fall in confusion about the head of the preacher. It is quite possible that those who heard the preacher in his latter days only may never have seen this display of energy, or felt the immense personal magnetism of the orator; but those who remember him in the early days of his presidency, when he filled with a deeply interested congregation the "aching void" of the First Baptist Meeting-House, will bear testimony both to the energy and magnetism of his pulpit oratory.

But while the manner of the preacher was striking, it was the matter of his discourse which made him pre-eminent. . . . He was pre-eminently an instructive preacher. Not infrequently were his sermons packed with the results of the thinking of months and years. On special occasions he appeared a veritable giant in intellectual power. He chose the extemporaneous method of delivery. . . . But the extemporaneous method did not exempt him from careful preparation. . . . It was only through the most exacting mental discipline and the most patient literary cultivation that he became the consummate master of unwritten discourse that he was. . . .

His sermons in general were characterized by comprehensiveness of thought, by keenness of analysis, by sharp discrimination in definition, by clear, forceful, and elegant diction, by honesty and earnestness of purpose, and on occasion by tremendous power of appeal. Those who heard his first baccalaureate sermon from the text "Christ, the wisdom of God," will not deny his power of impassioned utterance; while those who heard his sermon on College Fast Day from the text "So they are without excuse," will bear witness to the overwhelming force of his pathetic appeal.

One other characteristic of his preaching . . . was what might be called his intellectual honesty. His moral honesty was shown as, shunning all hypocrisy, he preached level with his convictions. His intellectual honesty he illustrated as, guarding against prejudice, he preached level with his thinking. At times the critical hearer, following a masterly discourse to its conclusion, might think the whole had not been told; questions might suggest themselves which the preacher had not answered. On second thought the critic would discover that some of these questions the preacher himself had started by his own relentless thinking, and on still deeper thought he would discover that frequently the failure to answer was not

due so much to the poverty of the preacher's thinking as to
the limitations of human thought. He thought as earnestly
and as far as he could, and very few thought farther; but
where his thinking stopped, there his sermon stopped also.
. . . He knew but in part, and he was honest enough to
prophesy but in part.

NOTE B.

DR. ROBINSON'S PREACHING IN PROVIDENCE.

The following notice of a special period of pulpit service in
Providence is furnished by an alumnus of Brown, Professor
B. C. Taylor, D. D., of Crozer Theological Seminary: —

" When Dr. Robinson became president of Brown, Dr. Caldwell had
just resigned from the pastorate of the First Baptist Church, and for
about a year the new president was called upon to fill the vacated
pulpit, part of the time preaching each successive Sunday, though
occasionally, to the regret of the audience accustomed to listen to him,
another would take his place. There were certain features of the
audience room of the First Baptist Meeting-House that probably had
a good deal to do with the habitual condition of the congregations
accustomed to assemble there. The pulpit was one of those box
affairs perched up against the wall high enough to be nearly on a
level with the galleries, and thus decidedly above the heads of most
of the audience, and in this the preacher was expected to shut himself
off from his hearers; and the distance between the two was ordinarily
very great.

" Then, too, the pews were so constructed that their backs were
high enough to reach with convenience the heads of most persons, so
that when the regular worshippers had entered their own pews and
carefully shut the doors, they had no fear of being disturbed by any
intruders, could put themselves in a very comfortable position, and
as a general thing slept soundly.

" The students of the University, being allowed to worship where
they wished, preferred generally to go to some other church.

" When Dr. Robinson began his service with the church, all was
changed at once. The house, both main floor and galleries, was well
filled with an audience made up of those representing the intellect of
the city; and none of them slept. Though the sermons were not
especially intended for the students, these were evidently prominent

in the preacher's thought, and they did not fail to go to hear him. The audiences consisted largely of men from the professional and business classes ; and while the sermons challenged the powers of trained intellects, they were yet presented so simply, clearly, and powerfully that none could fail to be moved by them.

" Dr. Robinson's services were sought by other churches, both of his own denomination and of others, the Congregationalists and the Unitarians ; and he never lacked a large and appreciative audience." — B. C. T.

VII.

DR. ROBINSON AS PRESIDENT OF BROWN UNIVERSITY.

By PRESIDENT E. B. ANDREWS, D. D., LL. D.,
Brown University.

VII.

AS PRESIDENT OF BROWN UNIVERSITY.

THE last great piece of his life-work Dr. Robinson accomplished as head of Brown University. His teaching, while in this position, also his mental, moral, and religious characteristics at large, are reviewed elsewhere. It is proposed here simply to set forth his record as the chief administrative officer of the University.

Dr. Robinson began his presidency at a time (1872) which was in certain important respects favorable for his success. President Sears had resigned in 1867, and the years between this date and 1872 formed a kind of interregnum. For one year Professor George I. Chace was president *ad interim*, and then followed the four years of Dr. Caswell's presidency. Each of these gentlemen did for the University all that it was possible for him to do under the circumstances. The teaching in Philosophy and Ethics, continuing the entire five years in the hands of Dr. Chace, did not suffer; and Dr. Caswell had no little success in soliciting funds. Still, as it was universally understood that this *régime* was temporary, all were ready to welcome a president whose views and power might be expected to impress the development of the University for many years.

Moreover, Dr. Robinson came to the University with fame, as her most distinguished living son. Many remembered the high rank which, while in college, he had attained as a student and a speaker. His writings, the numerous positions of prominence which he had ably filled, and especially his high reputation as a thinker and a teacher, permitted none to doubt the wisdom of the Corporation in choosing him to direct the affairs of the University.

In one point, indeed, the promise of his success was less complete. In 1872 the Corporation of the University, besides being exceedingly conservative, contained conflicting elements, the result of ill-feeling and contention engendered in previous years. Each of its factions seemed at times more intent upon carrying its own point against opponents than upon advancing the welfare of the University. A bold and progressive policy on the part of the President bade fair to be extremely difficult. Whatever measure or line of measures he might adopt, some one was likely to think that he had sided with a party, and to oppose him in consequence. As a matter of fact, this infelicity did beset President Robinson through almost his entire administration, making his success the more remarkable and the more to his credit. What still further heightens the merit of his achievement is the fact that to the end of his term he personally performed the whole work of instruction in the department of Philosophy with the single exception of that in Logic. Devoted teacher that he was, he felt himself imperatively called to this work, and was unwilling to relinquish any part of it to allow himself proper time and strength for the consuming task of administration.

Besides his obvious duties as an executive officer, the administration of rules and regulations and insistence upon order, fidelity, and progress in the various parts of the work intrusted to him, a college president must also be a business manager, an educational manager, and a disciplinarian. As business manager, he has to provide and conserve facilities for training minds. He thus comes, through his trustees and otherwise, into relation with the public, testing his tact, popularity, and influence. As an educational manager, he is called upon to supervise the use of the educational provision placed at his command. He must, in conjunction with his colleagues, determine the order and nature of the subjects taught, and he ought to have much influence over the methods of teaching, though he cannot dictate these. There is thus put to the test: (1) his abstract knowledge of educational problems and of their proper solution; in other words, his comprehension of the task to be accomplished; (2) his skill in the use of his means, for he must make them go as far as possible; (3) his influence with the faculty; and (4) his intellectual and moral power over his pupils in general, — those, that is, who wish to do well and need only to be shown the way. As a disciplinarian the college president has to deal with idle, vicious, and refractory students, in particular. The best educators often fail here, as the best disciplinarians often fail in teaching.

How well Dr. Robinson bore himself under each of these three great demands of his office, the following paragraphs will indicate; and they will show that, in spite of the obstacles which he found in his way, he was enabled to see his labors for the University crowned with gratifying success. If any one will contrast the condition of the University in 1889 with its condition in 1872, he will see clear proof of President Robinson's leadership; for the changes of these seventeen years were the results, not of natural growth, which must have come at any rate, but of growth under strong propulsion and guidance.

In the material resources of the University his administration witnessed an increase greater than ever occurred in the same length of time at any preceding period. He wanted for the University more in buildings and endowment than it received, and made vigorous efforts to get more. He constantly emphasized the absolute need of large sums in order to the proper development of the work in his charge. Still, everything considered, that he obtained so much is more wonderful than that he did not obtain the whole amount sought.

The material advance made under the Robinson administration is illustrated by the increase between 1872 and 1889 in the University's funds, and its property in buildings and grounds. In these years the new Library Building was erected, costing, with the land on which it stands, over $110,000. Slater Hall, Sayles Hall, and Wilson Hall also all date from this time. The Lyman fund for the Gymnasium was received during these years, and most of the fund for supporting instruction in it raised. Rhode Island Hall was greatly enlarged, and old University Hall renovated from top to bottom, making it in effect a new building. The valuable Metcalf estate was acquired, and the money promised by Hon. Herbert W. Ladd, which subsequently went to erect the Ladd Observatory. In all, the University's material resources were enlarged during President Robinson's seventeen years by not less than nine hundred and twenty-five thousand dollars. In this computation no account is taken of the increase in books and apparatus continually going on, but so difficult to estimate. The President introduced a great many new provisions for the daily comfort of the students. He improved the external appearance of the grounds by grading them, and placed and kept the buildings in better order every way than had ever characterized them before. Some part of the emolument thus sketched the University would have realized under any administration; yet a very great proportion of it certainly resulted from the President's efforts and influence.[1]

Dr. Robinson had no special fitness, of a positive order, for the business of securing funds; in some respects quite the reverse. He was naturally reserved and dignified. His thinking was upon high and abstract themes. He could not gossip familiarly with men occupying the ordinary plane of mental life. When he tried to do so, he usually failed. On the other hand, most of his words and acts were very discreet. His utterances on religious subjects, though positive, were always catholic. He was no partisan in politics, and was fortunate enough to have no offensive hobby touching any social reform. Being thus, perforce, without prejudice against him, the public was open to the favorable impressions which Dr. Robinson's sterling character, as also his appearance and address, was calculated to make. His dignified presence and his strong yet elegant speech, whenever he came before an audience, did much to bring friends and resources to the University. In a platform talk, in formal public lecturing, and especially in the pulpit, the President was peerless, — an ornament to the University which cannot but have exerted a powerful attraction in its favor. Students of other institutions, and many, besides, often remarked: "How fine a thing it must be for a college to have such a man at its head!"

The teaching force was greatly strengthened during the Robinson Presidency. The Hazard Professorship of Physics was established and filled, also the Professorship of Zoölogy and Geology, and that of Botany. The instruction in English, in Mathematics, and in Modern Languages was materially broadened and improved. History and Political Economy, for the teaching of which the same professor had

<hr>

[1] See Note on page 278. — ED.

18

hitherto been responsible, were divided, and assigned to separate hands. A similar division was made between Astronomy and Mathematics. The old office of Registrar was made into two offices, one of them filled by a competent mechanic, able to supervise the buildings and grounds, — an arrangement that still continues, and has proved most wise.

Recognizing that " new occasions teach new duties," Dr. Robinson was always advocating extension, enlargement, and enrichment in the curriculum; such changes and additions as would give the University the best attainable life and efficiency in view of new demands upon it, while retaining all that its past history had proved permanently worthful. He pressed not only for better efficiency in the departments already established, but for new departments, larger facilities, more science with the laboratories necessary for teaching it well, broader and higher instruction generally. Especially did he desire the best possible training in English, the fullest mastery and the purest use of our mother tongue.

Dr. Robinson earnestly insisted that it was the University's duty and privilege to undertake graduate instruction so fast and far as the strength of the Faculty might warrant. To this end he wished not only increased resources for teaching, but foundations for fellowships, to support graduate students either in residence at Alma Mater, or, when necessary, to supplement Alma Mater's instruction at some University abroad. For many years before the policy was actually introduced, he urged that (save when honorary) the degree of Master of Arts should be granted only after examination. Upon such candidates as it could prepare for it, he wanted the University to confer the degree of Doctor of Philosophy; and it is pleasant to remark that the two gentlemen who were the first to be crowned with this degree from Brown University, both now in prominent educational positions, bear diplomas signed by President Robinson and received by them from his hands.

Graduate and extension teaching owe in considerable part their present development at the University to President Robinson's example and encouragement. Professors Chace and Diman had long been accustomed to lecture before classes of intelligent people not members of the University; but such work received new impetus from a course of weekly lectures on philosophical subjects which Dr. Robinson delivered in 1878–79 to a class gathered by Messrs. John H. Mason and Alfred G. Langley. This course was followed the next year 1879–80) by one, very popular and largely attended, on the History of Philosophy, for which careful reference lists were furnished by Mr. W. E. Foster, Librarian of the Providence Public Library. During the same year (1879–80) several other members of the Faculty began to lecture in this general way, each delivering one or two lectures a winter. These lectures occurred evenings, and were open to citizens as well as to students.

President Robinson's high record as an educational leader, like that which he made in the business control of the University, sprang more from his powerful intellectual and moral personality, with the general influence which this exerted, than from any special skill, art, or policy characterizing his efforts. His vigorous thought and great personal influence never failed to impress any with whom he had to do. His success was the direct result of his great intellectual strength, which commanded admiration; of his high moral character, which gained him respect; and of the essential and far-reaching wisdom of his ideas, some of which were not at once accepted because enforced in a pugnacious rather than in a tactful way.

The Faculty with which President Robinson allied himself on coming to Brown University was a very strong one, which it was no easy matter to lead. A number of its members had seen decades in the University's service, and as teachers and authors had won national reputation. Such men, and perhaps no less their younger colleagues, naturally had positive convictions touching the proper development of the University, with some of which the President could not sympathize. Dissidence of view not infrequently thus arose, sometimes, though rarely, generating friction.

While the President's ideas in such cases were nearly always sound, tending to life and progress, and being opposed to mere routine, dead tradition, or pedantry; yet they did not always prevail, and they often prevailed, when they did so, only against more or less protest. The cause of this has been already suggested. Himself conceiving clearly, in all its reasonableness, the good end sought, the President lacked the patience necessary to show such as had not considered it the desirableness of what he proposed; and if, therefore, his scheme proved unacceptable, instead of biding his time and setting to work to convert its opponents one by one, he was too apt either to scold, thus defeating his purpose, or to relinquish his purpose altogether, expecting others to bear the blame. It was largely in consequence of this habit that at the end of his presidency Dr. Robinson did not receive from his Faculty the support which every college president must need. It would not, however, be just to lay the responsibility for this entirely upon him.

The President's writings contributed not a little to that personal influence of his which stood him in so good stead. His pupils wish that he had left more of his thoughts in permanent form; but he disliked to write, and was never satisfied with anything which he was induced to put down on paper. The matter which he did commit to print, elsewhere spoken of in detail, was of a high order, an honor to the University as well as to its author.

With his students Dr. Robinson seems to have been less popular at Brown University than at Rochester. Spite of the generous aid which young men in college continually received from him, often out of his own pocket, and though not a few of his pupils were admitted to a warm and genial friendship with him which they will forever cherish as among the richest results of their life at college, the majority even of those under his immediate instruction regarded him more with awe than with affection. This was doubtless due in part to the President's rather stern way of dealing with students. He was an autocrat, accustomed to command and to receive obedience. He seemed to feel it his duty to teach collegians subordination, and to hold them at some distance. His most enthusiastic college pupils agree that this habit greatly hindered his success in drawing ingenuous young men near to him in order to mould their thinking and purposes, in which, however, he grandly succeeded with many.

The habit likewise balked his efforts at discipline. He had slender natural aptitude for this duty, and had enjoyed no training for it. He expected in the students of Brown University the same docility and attention to duty which he had found in his theological pupils at Rochester. With boyish pranks he had no patience whatever, and was unable to think of them as innocent. He was thus often surer of an accused student's guilt at first than the sifted facts warranted. Yet, terrible as he was in laying down the law, his heart was very tender. He could never withstand a mother's tears. In fact, he as often inflicted too light as too heavy penalties for students' misdeeds; and any hard sentence imposed by him was almost too sure to be mitigated on evidence of the culprit's deep penitence. It should be said, however, that President Robinson encountered few, if any more difficulties in discipline than most college presidents had during the transition period in which his presidential service fell. Students had not yet learned that their own highest interests and greatest happiness lie in promoting the best college order.

NOTE.

ON IMPROVEMENTS AT BROWN.

The following summary of the improvements secured for Brown University by President Robinson is from the Rev. Dr. T. D. Anderson's Memorial Address. — ED.

"The College showed greater material advance during the administration of Dr. Robinson than at any other period of its history. The grounds were greatly improved. The front campus was transformed from a hayfield into an attractive lawn overshadowed by its beautiful elms; the middle campus was graded, sodded, and paved; and the field of athletic sports was transferred to the lower campus, which had arisen out of a swamp. The University came to be much better housed and equipped. Rhode Island Hall was extended; University Hall was renovated; the Library, Sayles Memorial Hall, and Slater Hall were erected; Wilson Hall was begun; the Ladd Observatory was promised, and the money for the Lyman Gymnasium was in hand; and while this better equipment was secured, the funds of the College had been increased, speaking in round numbers, from $550,000 to $1,000,000. When we reflect that all this was done in spite of the President's confessed lack of tact in dealing with men, and in face of obstructions raised by a divided Corporation, we find in these gratifying results abundant evidence of the persistent purpose and unflinching fidelity of the President, and a substantial expression of the respect and confidence which his abilities and character inspired in the community at large."

VIII.

DR. ROBINSON AS A TEACHER OF PHILOSOPHY.

BY ALFRED G. LANGLEY, A. M.

VIII.

AS A TEACHER OF PHILOSOPHY.

PRESIDENT ROBINSON was Professor of Intellectual and Moral Philosophy in Brown University from 1872 to 1889. During this entire period he gave instruction to the Senior class throughout the year,—the first term in Psychology and Ontology, the second term in Ethics. Near the close of each academic year he added a few less formal lectures on the outlines of Natural Theology and the Evidences of Christianity. Beginning with the session of 1879–80, he gave, during the second term each year, a course of one hour weekly in the History of Philosophy as an elective, making it a two-hour course in 1888–89. In addition to these courses he gave, by request, in 1878–79, a weekly course of nineteen lectures " on some of the more difficult and controverted questions in Metaphysics and Ethics," including five lectures on " The Philosophy of the Atonement," to a class composed of a number of recent graduates and others interested in these topics, and attended by a considerable number of ladies and gentlemen, not regular members, who by their presence manifested their interest in and their indorsement of what may be termed the beginning of graduate instruction in the University. An immediate outgrowth of this course was the series of sixteen public lectures to graduates and others on the History of Modern Philosophy delivered the next year (1879–80) in Manning Hall before large and interested audiences, which were very instructive and successful.

While President and Professor at Brown, Dr. Robinson gave a series of lectures on " The Relations of Philosophic to Christian Ethics" at Boston University in 1877–78, and afterwards repeated the course in Philadelphia, as the " Samuel A. Crozer Lectures," for 1883, before the Crozer Theological Seminary, with the title " The Relation of Christianity to Ethics."[1] Early in 1879 he lectured at the Newton Theological Institution on Homiletics, — the professorship in that department being vacant,— accompanying the lectures with private work in the construction and criticism of sermons. In January and February, 1882, he delivered the " Lectures on Preaching" to the Students of Theology at Yale College. In 1883 he gave a course of twenty lectures on Theology at the Andover Theological Seminary. These lectures, as being either philosophical in character or in the method of treating their subject, or both, deserve here passing mention as, in the broader sense of the term, a part of his philosophical instruction.

The ground covered by the Senior course throughout his professorship can best be given in the words of Dr. Robinson himself, in his Annual Report to the Corporation, June

[1] Of the lectures given at Boston University President Warren writes: " Despite the pressure of his daily duties in Providence, the necessity of journeying daily to and from the city, he carried his elaborate critical review of historic men and systems and periods from stage to stage with admirable clearness of thought and charm of expression. As a specimen of attainable possibilities in the line of extemporaneous exposition I think I never saw it surpassed, unless it was in the ancient church of St. Mary's at Oxford, when in 1887 I listened to the Bishop of Ripon (a) as he delivered his course of Bampton lectures without having written a single page in advance.

" President Robinson well deserves the crown which loyal disciples and admiring friends are weaving for him. The undersigned desires to be counted among those who revered and loved him." — A. G. L.

(a) Rt. Rev. William Boyd Carpenter, D. D., D. C. L. The Bampton Lectures are entitled " The Permanent Elements of Religion." — A. G. L.

26, 1873, page 19: " In Intellectual Philosophy the attention of the class was directed to so much of psychology as pertains to the science of mind, and to the fundamental principles of ontology, or metaphysics proper; in Moral Philosophy, special attention was given to theoretic ethics and to those questions which underlie the whole science of morals, though practical ethics were not overlooked." The usual method of instruction was the lecture, " in which brief but comprehensive statements of principles were dictated and accompanied with explanations and illustrations, which the class were at liberty to take in their own way, but which all were required to retain so far as was necessary to a full exposition and recitation of what had been dictated."

Dr. Robinson's dictations were prepared with very great care. The matter had been thoroughly thought out, and was expressed with the utmost clearness, in a style exceedingly terse, forcible, and compact, in which it may, perhaps, be said without exaggeration that there was scarcely a single word that was superfluous or that could be dispensed with without essentially marring or vitiating the thought. These lectures of Dr. Robinson to his classes in Brown University are a model in every respect of what a lecturer's syllabus or notes for class use, whether dictated or in type, should be. Any one who will carefully read his lectures in Ethics, published under the title of " Principles and Practice of Morality," will find the above statement no exaggeration.

The character of the work done may, perhaps, best be seen by a description of an average class-room exercise. The Doctor usually began at once with the remark: " Any questions, gentlemen?" Then often questions were asked, and there followed a very earnest discussion of the points at issue between the professor and the students. The sparks flew, and the intellects of the students participating in the

discussion were aroused and stimulated into such action as
till then they had never known or even dreamed of; while
those who merely watched the contest could not but get
their share of the intellectual awakening and life. The
student had to strike out for himself and defend his positions, or go to the wall. The weaker ones fell. Some were
too timid to try it again, and some too timid to try it at all;
but those who realized and appreciated their opportunities,
and braced themselves for the encounter, reaped the priceless advantages and permanent increase of power which
resulted therefrom.

But although at Providence in Philosophy, as previously
at Rochester in Theology, discussion with the students
formed a distinct and very important feature of his instruction, it could not be so prominent a feature or so fruitful in
results in the University as in the Seminary. The students
were much younger, their minds less mature, their knowledge more limited, and their capacity for participating
in and deriving benefit from such discussion correspondingly less. Furthermore, the students in theology were
almost all intending to devote themselves to the work of
the ministry, or to teaching involving the knowledge and
use of the study they were pursuing. The students in
philosophy, on the other hand, were, many of them, taking the course simply as a part of the required work of the
college curriculum, with no prospect of using the knowledge gained therein or desire for the same, and in many
cases with a positive dislike, if not a total want of capacity,
for the subject. The Doctor found it difficult — as he told
the writer some years after he had passed out from his instruction — to adapt himself to these younger and less
mature minds, many of whom were just beginning to
think at all, and especially on such subjects as the

lectures in Philosophy discussed. Notwithstanding all this, there was, during at least the first two-thirds of his professorship, a good deal of discussion, and profitable discussion too. The Doctor was not only always ready for it and welcomed it, but sometimes, especially if the men seemed indisposed or reluctant to enter into it, put forth considerable and varied effort to induce them to participate. The very positive, and at times seemingly dogmatic, manner in which he set forth and argued for the positions he advanced, challenged the better and more earnest men to the combat. At times he made statements in a form which seemed designed to provoke dissent and awaken discussion.

But, according to the competent and trustworthy testimony of some of his best students, discussion gradually fell off during the last four or five years of his professorship, till there was scarcely any whatever, and his teaching became " increasingly and extremely dogmatic." This absence of discussion is so strange, and so .unlike anything known of him by those who were acquainted with the splendid work in this direction of his earlier years at Brown, and previously at Rochester, and so seemingly contrary to all his theories of education and to his hitherto uniform practice, as to demand some explanation, if we are to attain a just and adequately appreciative account and estimate of his work. The youth and mental immaturity of many of the students, and his own difficulty in adapting himself thereto; the presence of men in the class-room having little or no interest in the subject or particular capacity for it; the indifference of these and others to discussion and criticism, and their unwillingness to participate therein; the irrelevancy and comparative superficiality of much that was said by honest, well-meaning, and even able students; the growing strength and positiveness of his own convictions, each

and all may have had — doubtless did have — their influence
in bringing about and continuing the change in question;
yet the true explanation seems rather to lie in the considerations herewith following. Throughout his professorship, and especially during the last four or five years, Dr.
Robinson was burdened with an immense amount of constantly increasing administrative detail, which helped to
exhaust the vitality so essential to enthusiastic teaching,
and, to one of his nature and temperament, became more and
more irritating, the more so as much of the work might just
as well have been done by any ordinarily competent person,
leaving him free to give the bulk of his energies to the
work of instruction and the more important matters of
administration. He had, furthermore, throughout his
presidency, in all his efforts to advance the College, to
contend with adverse conditions and forces that never
should have existed, and with a corporation too many of
whose members were altogether too inert, ultra-conserva-
tive, short-sighted, narrow-minded, and slow,[1] — difficulties
still further aggravated by his own lack of tact in advocating and carrying out his plans. All this seems to have
reacted upon him to an extent sufficient to affect, though
no doubt unconsciously, his teaching. He grew increas-

[1] The statement in the text is strictly true, and is made solely in a spirit of
justice and fairness to Dr. Robinson, with no reflection whatever on the
motives of those who for any reason opposed his vigorously progressive
plans. Dr. Robinson has been criticised with considerable severity for not
accomplishing more in the development of Brown than he did. The plain
fact is that he was as wide-awake, far-sighted, and progressive a president as
teacher, and indisputably far too radical and progressive for a large number
of the Corporation as well as of the Faculty of the University. His Annual
Reports to the Corporation furnish abundant and convincing evidence of the
truth of this statement, and should be carefully and thoughtfully read by
any and all who desire to get any adequate idea of his educational and
administrative views. They contain succinct and valuable discussions of
almost all questions affecting higher education in our day. — A. G. L.

ingly weary of the long and hard struggle to push the University forward to the position he knew it ought and must take, if it was to hold its own and advance to its rightful place and influence among the institutions of our land; and this weariness showed itself in an increasing irritability at any manifestation of criticism or opposition in the class-room.

Finally, there were personal trials and worries adding their weight to the already overtaxed and weary life; but the nature, brave and strong and self-respecting, kept them to itself, and bore them in the secret and silence of its own depths.

But to return to our description. Sometimes the discussion took the whole hour, so fierce was the struggle, or so important, fundamental, and far-reaching the subject under discussion. After the discussion came the recitation, which the Doctor almost always had, if there was sufficient matter on hand, and on which he laid great stress. Recitation in his presence was no mere formal repetition of so much memorized lecture. The men must know what they were saying, and the Professor was quick to discern whether they did or did not know. He was wide-awake, alert, and let no statement pass unchallenged. The student reciting was met at every turn with question after question going right to the heart of the subject, and sifting and testing thoroughly his knowledge of it. He was made to realize his knowledge or his ignorance. Even when the statements made were wholly correct, the Doctor would often require the student to explain and justify them in his own way, in order to be sure that he had mastered them, and to make the student himself aware of that mastery. He would occasionally help a student whom he had good reason to suppose was honestly and earnestly trying to do the work to the best of his ability; but he was by no means like his contemporary, Dr. Porter of Yale, of whom it is said that he would never, if he could help it, allow a man to fail in class, making his questions easier and easier until the student could not help answering them. A careless, superficial, slovenly recitation called forth at once a sharp and stinging rebuke or withering sarcasm, which the student did not forget, even if he did not profit by it; and sometimes, though perhaps more rarely, a serious, sober, and kindly reproof, designed to remind the student that he was wasting his opportunities, and of the sad and irreparable loss that must inevitably follow such misuse of time and powers. In every possible way he put men on their mettle, compelled them to think, and to bring out and develop all that was in them.

After the recitation, which also very frequently included more or less discussion, came the dictation of the new matter forming the next portion of the course, accompanied with the necessary exposition and illustration. Here, as always, the Doctor's expositions were brief, logical, and to the point, " his explanations of the most profound things extremely childlike and simple," and his illustrations, drawn from every available source, — science, literature,[1] history, and life, — often homely but fresh, apt, and forcible, illuminating the truth and fixing it in the mind forever.

[1] Dr. Robinson in his earlier student days, especially at Newton, devoted a large amount of time to a systematic reading and study of literature. Occasionally in class and frequently in private conversation he spoke of certain authors as especially worthy of careful reading and study. In his later years most of his reading of literature was done in the long summer vacation. Then, as he once told me, he gave himself up to the reading of novels and other forms of literature for which he had no leisure in term time. His method of reading, like all his work, was critical. He noted everything about an author, — his subject and manner of treating it, plot, characterizations, style, general attitude towards all the problems he touched or hinted at, methods of reasoning, explicit or implied. — A. G. L.

With one class he sought to provide for debate [1] in his own presence; but the experiment was a failure.

Incidentally, in his Senior required courses, Dr. Robinson gave, throughout his professorship, more or less on the History of Philosophy by way of exposition and illustration. What was here done incidentally was done in a more systematic and extended manner in the elective in the History of Philosophy, given each year from 1879–80 to the close of his connection with the University. The course covered in very brief outline the chief names and systems in modern philosophy, usually beginning with Descartes and extending to Kant, and one year (1888–89) to Hegel. For the three years (1886–89) the course also included the History of Greek as well as of Modern Philosophy. He had a very remarkable and extraordinary, almost preternatural,

---

[1] In his Annual Report to the Corporation, June 22, 1862, pages 6–7, Dr. Robinson thus speaks of college debate: " It has often been the subject of remark and regret among thoughtful men, who are familiar with the existing interior life of our older American colleges, that so· little attention is now given by students to voluntary and systematic practice in extemporaneous debate. The old debating societies that forty years ago were so prominent a feature in college life, have now very generally ceased to exist. They have given place to numerous smaller associations, consisting of numbers insufficient to arouse the interest and enthusiasm necessary to such results from the practice in debate as used to be attained in the older and now extinct societies. That the young men of liberal education, who are now entering public life, show far less skill in extemporaneous speech than their fathers possessed at the same age, is frequently remarked. . . . Among a people living under a free government like ours, the value of such training to our educated men can hardly be overestimated. That would be a grievous mistake in the education of the American college, if ever, in a blind imitation of universities that work under other forms of government, the neglect of practice in debate, now so general, should become established and universal. If the educated men of our country would fit themselves for the kind of leadership in our legislative assemblies, state and national, to which their education should entitle them, we should hear far less than we do now of lament over the indisposition of the educated classes to participate in the political affairs of the nation. The training that is to fit one for public life should begin not later than his college days."— A. G. L.

insight into truth and into the heart of the various systems, a firm grasp of their essential features and fundamental principles, and an almost equally rare power to set them forth in a wonderfully clear, forcible, and often elegant manner. He had always been interested in philosophy and its history, — a fact evidenced among other ways by his library, which was largely philosophical, — and at some time in his life made a careful study of the chief periods and systems. It should be remembered that he did all the work in philosophy done in his time, constantly increasing its amount throughout his professorship, — work that is now distributed among four professors. To him more than to any one is it due that Brown University does in Philosophy the noble work she does to-day.

In his graduate work Dr. Robinson followed his old-time method of freest and absolutely fearless criticism and amplest discussion.[1] The following account of it, together with some reference to the undergraduate work as he knew it, has been kindly furnished by Rev. A. K. DeBlois, Ph.D., President of Shurtleff College, Upper Alton, Illinois: —

[1] Regarding the work at Chicago, Professor George S. Goodspeed, Brown, 1880, in response to my inquiry, writes: "It appears that Dr. Robinson's custom in the work in Ethics at Chicago was to assign a section in his book 'Principles and Practice of Morality,' for recitation. Ordinarily the recitation of this took fifteen minutes. Then the door was thrown wide open for discussion. The utmost freedom was allowed, and all sorts of objections, arguments, suggestions, received a fair hearing; only prolixity and irrelevancy being mercilessly choked off.

"My informant tells me that it was a most stimulating exercise; the Doctor was full of electricity, and the sparks and shocks were frequent. The students were above the average in maturity and ability, drawn as they were from all departments of the University. They called forth Dr. Robinson's best, and he gave it in full measure. He seemed to enjoy the hour to the utmost.

"I was not able to get any special incidents which would illustrate the methods and characteristics of Dr. Robinson; but it was perfectly clear that he had gone back to his earlier method of which you wrote."— A. G. L.

" I spent two years in resident graduate study at Brown University, and one year in non-resident study, while I was taking my Junior year in the Newton Theological Seminary. These were the last three years of Dr. Robinson's presidency at Brown. During my first year of residence at the University I attended the classes in Psychology and History of Philosophy, which he had with the Seniors in the undergraduate department, and I also did special work in Psychology, Ethics, the History of Philosophy, and the Philosophy of Religion, meeting Dr. Robinson for recitation and examination on the work pursued. Usually he assigned me some author or authors to read during the week, and on Saturday evening I took tea with him at his home, and after tea we adjourned to his library, where he gave me a thorough examination on the work which I had pursued during the week. As soon as we were seated in the library, he would turn to me and say, in his decided tone, ' Well! what have you done since we last met?' I would then plunge *in medias res*, and give in as succinct a manner as possible a review of the authors which I had read, emphasizing their special characteristics and the noteworthy features of their work, explaining, criticising, and at the conclusion giving a rapid survey and summary. This was not altogether plain sailing. Dr. Robinson would sweep down upon me again and again in the most abrupt manner, requiring me to outline some theory which I had stated, demanding an explanation of some statement which I had made, gathering up what I had said into some general truth, or asking of me an original criticism of some minor point in the discussion. These interruptions coming unexpectedly, and in a stern and commanding voice, did not serve to increase my repose of manner, although they were undoubtedly helpful from a disciplinary point of view.

Dr. Robinson would often break in with some broad and brilliant criticism of his own, and would explain and illustrate his issue clearly and forcibly.

"I never found out whether or not Dr. Robinson had a system of his own. He was keen, thorough, earnest, suggestive, and stimulating, but in all my work with him I felt that there was a lack of positively constructive principles. As we went on week by week and month by month examining author after author and philosophy after philosophy, I wondered when the time would come in which the Doctor would build a system of his own, or outline the system which he had already built. I must confess that I was disappointed when, at the close of my period of study, no fair system rose to greet my anxious vision. The genius of the teacher had discovered the flaws and faults of all other systems, but had failed to bring forth a system of its own. In a general way, and emphatically, he was a realist; but of his special views and opinions, as parts of a complete system, I was always in ignorance. Although his students were compelled to seek elsewhere the positive system that they desired, or manufacture a system for themselves, the inspiration and power which they could not fail to receive from listening to the words of Dr. Robinson became a permanent possession of their lives. In the department of Ethics the full force and value of the Doctor's teaching were most clearly seen. Although here also his method was destructive rather than constructive, all the fundamental principles were outlined with a resoluteness, freedom, and independence which were admirable. No one could go from his class-room in Moral Philosophy without feeling the grandeur and beauty of the teachings which had been set forth. During my first year at the University I took the elective course in the History of

Philosophy. About eight of the students, all Seniors, were in the class. During the first half of the term we used Zeller's History of Greek Philosophy as a text-book. The Doctor supplemented the text with lectures of his own. These were delivered extempore, and I think impromptu, and the students took what notes they could get. In the last half of the term we used no text-book, but took notes at the Doctor's dictation. Here, as always, a rigid adherence to ' the letter of the law' was required. In the regular class-room work I never knew Dr. Robinson to be otherwise than extremely positive in statement. His views, and especially his criticisms, although rationally grounded in all cases, were uttered with an emphasis that debarred question. There was no free discussion, and the student who offered suggestions or criticisms of his own was made to feel that it would have been far better for him to have kept silence. This was very different from his method in the private work which I took with him. In the latter he invited original criticism; in the former he seemed anxious to avoid it. I considered that *all* of his teaching was helpful. He seemed to understand thoroughly what he was teaching. In the History of Philosophy he concerned himself with general outline rather than with detail. It seemed to me that he had at some time made a minute and comprehensive study of the various systems, and had embodied the results of his inquiries in certain sweeping yet clearly defined criticisms and estimates. The details and the minutiæ dropped out of his memory, but the results remained.

" At the same time he never seemed to be behind the age. He quoted constantly from the most recent works, and was familiar with the latest drift of thought. There was a freshness and vigor about him that was indescribable. He was always alert, always strong, always clear and forcible. His stern personality, his fearless denunciation of all forms of error, and his logical habit of mind gave a stimulus to my intellectual life which has been far-reaching in its effects. The influence which he exerted upon me, and the inspiration which I received from my association with him, I appreciate more and more fully as the years go by. Over the tea-table and in private life the naturally rigid and rugged disposition of the man relaxed into a kindness which was delightful. I respected him as a teacher, and, as time went on, I came to honor and to love him as a man of true and wonderful nobility of character. At the same time the glimpses I got of the inner life of the man intensified the admiration which I already had for the great teacher. He was not a favorite with the students, and I think became less and less popular toward the close of his administration. I believe that there was a change in this respect after he left Brown. Although few of the students loved him with a personal affection when I was at the University, there was hardly one, I think, who did not revere him as a prince among teachers and a hero amongst men. ”

Of the philosophy he taught it is impossible here to give a detailed account and criticism. The account here presented gives the more attention to his Psychology, chiefly because it represents, so far as may be, the philosophical foundation of his ethical and theological views, and thus of the entire character and influence of his instruction. It would perhaps be more accurate to designate his course in accord with the title of his professorship, with the general custom of the time and with his own co-ordinate usage, by the old name Intellectual Philosophy. Though endeavoring to cover the entire field in outline, he chiefly concerned himself with the problem of knowledge,[1] — *Erkenntnisslehre*,

[1] Consciousness, which he regarded as one of the most important and vital topics in Psychology and on which he laid especial stress, because of its philosophical importance as the immediate source and ultimate ground of our knowledge of the individual self and of its existence, and as the sphere in which all truth must vindicate itself as such before it can be accepted as the ideal and controlling force in life, he thus sets forth : " It cannot be correct to define consciousness as ' the soul's knowing that it knows,' or ' the power by which the soul knows its own acts and states,' or ' the power to know that it is itself that knows.' But consciousness is rather *the soul's actual knowing with itself that it knows ;* that is, is that relation to itself into which the ego is brought by cognition of any object other than itself, is the ego as subject communing with itself as object through the mediation of some object distinct from itself. It is not a power of the soul, but is a state, a condition, a function of the soul which always necessarily accompanies any normal or voluntary exercise of the soul's powers. Speaking figuratively and popularly, it is the mind's illumination of itself by its own action. . . .

" When we make consciousness an object of attention and analyze it into its component parts, we find it always to consist of three distinguishable elements : namely, the ego cognizing, the object cognized, and the communion of the ego with itself in the cognitive act ; that is, we find the soul communing with itself in the act of knowing something which is not itself. But these three elements when themselves analyzed reveal the existence of but two distinct quantities or entities, the ego and the object of its knowledge. Out of these two factors, subject and object, carefully analyzed, come directly or indirectly the entire materials of mental philosophy."

The doctrine concerning perception is as follows : Perception is " the mind's act of apprehending, cognizing, knowing external objects." . . . From a " brief survey of what are called the five senses there seem good reasons for believing that neither one of them by itself alone gives us direct knowledge of an external world. Each one gives us a direct sense-perception of the bodily organism as extended and as distinct from the perceiving ego, but it is not certain that it gives us anything further. That the five special senses combined may give it, is possible ; that it is given through the five senses as aided and directed by the sense of muscular resistance obtained through exercise of the locomotive energy, there is no good reason to doubt. . . .

" It is agreed among philosophers that our knowledge of what is in the mind is immediate and indubitable, but how we can be assured that the external world of things is as we apprehend it or imagine it to be, is a matter of persistent dispute. . . .

" The following statements may be regarded as safely made : —

" (*a*) As the initial of perception is at the instant that sensation is local-

— its processes and results, and their validity as against Agnosticism or the Philosophy of Nescience, · maintaining the reality and trustworthiness of our limited knowledge

ized as an affection of the bodily organism, so this localization is a perception of the bodily organism as something distinct from the ego that perceives it.

"(b) This initial or primary perception is related to sensation, not as a natural physical sequent, an effect of which sensation is the cause, nor yet is it an inference which the mind draws from sensation as a precedent fact ; that is, there is no interval of time between the sensation and the perception, but the perception is an immediate apprehension or knowledge of sensation as an existing affection of the organism, and the perception continues only while the sensation lasts. The sensation exists for the ego only while the ego perceives it, and the ego perceives it only while it exists.

"(c) This sensation, while giving us primarily only a perception of the affected bodily organism, yet in giving it enables the ego to come into direct and immediate cognitive relation to the external object by which the sensation is caused. The ego perceives the object immediately in the sensations received from it. Whatever may be the agency or the process through which a knowledge of externality is first obtained, — whether each sense organ can give it, or whether two or more combined give it, or whether first given by muscular resistance obtained by locomotion, — one thing is certain, and that is, that contactual relation of healthy sense organs to external objects gives to the mind an immediate or intuitive and assured perception of them as external and real. To what extent, if at all, the mind is helped in this by its recognition of the principle of causation, or whether the perceiving ego directly intuits in and through the sensation the object causing the sensation, it may not be easy to say. Whatever the process may be, the ego is incapable of practical doubt that external objects are immediately apprehended, and that they are just what they are by all men apprehended to be.

" (d) If to these statements it be objected that the qualities of the material objects perceived and the attributes of the soul that perceives are so totally dissimilar that there can be no resemblance whatever between material objects and our ideas of them ; that the ego as spirit, though capable of immediately cognizing itself and its processes, cannot immediately cognize matter, — it must be replied that man as conscious and cognitive is physicopsychical, that he is both spiritual and material, that he is in fact a tangential point between the two realms of matter and spirit, and as such is capable of cognizing at once the attributes of spirit and the qualities of matter. The methods by which external objects are cognized may differ widely in kind from the method of self-cognizing, and the ideas formed in either case may have no resemblance whatever to the objects themselves, may differ as widely as the qualities of matter differ from the attributes of spirit, and yet the perceptions, the actual cognitions, in both cases be equally decisive and complete." — *Lectures on Psychology, MS.*, §§ 23–28, ed. 1884.

and its continual and progressive growth and expansion; and with the vindication of an idealistic realism as against the widely prevalent materialism of the day, maintaining the existence of the soul or spirit as superior to and underived from matter and essentially distinct therefrom, itself weaving continually its body from the material elements of its environment, and leaving these again to depart to their own place and conditions when the soul or spirit has no further use for them.

The Lectures on Psychology always keep in mind the bearing and significance of modern physical and physiological science in its relations to the science of mind; and the statements of principles and the argumentation in support of them always shape themselves in view of the ascertained and proved facts, as well as the mere theories of modern scientific investigation. Dr. Robinson, as a teacher of Theology, was the first in this country fully to appreciate and take account of physical science in its relations to theology, and as a teacher of Philosophy he manifested the same sense of its importance as a modifying factor in the formation of the concepts, and in shaping the methods and argumentation of Psychology and Ethics. "Physical science," he said, "is knocking down many an old crockery god!" His philosophical instruction in this, as in other respects, was thoroughly abreast of the times, progressive, and with a very definite and positive outlook towards the future. His classes were made familiar with the English Associational and Physiological Schools and with psychology as treated by them from the side of physiology; and his lectures and discussions took account of all real contributions to the science from their investigations, while at the same time subjecting to merciless and generally successful criticism their arbitrary assumptions or hasty and inadequate inferences and generalizations. There was also considerably frequent reference to German thought, especially to Kant and his followers down to and including Schopenhauer and Von Hartmann; and in general the latest views and theories of all schools received as much consideration in the expositions and discussions of the class-room as time and other circumstances allowed. That he did nothing with the so-called " Physiological Psychology," " New Psychology," or, more properly speaking, Psychology as an experimental science, is explained and justified by the fact that, at the time he was nearing the end of his work as Professor of Philosophy, the subject in this form was but just coming into prominence, and investigation just beginning to any extent in this country in the direction in which now nearly all the work is done.[1]

Dr. Robinson was in general an intuitionalist and a realist. He was an intuitionalist in his view of consciousness as the final source of appeal, and as the sphere in which all truth must and does vindicate itself as such by its own inherent self-evidencing power. To this self-evidencing power and consequent authority of truth, consciousness at once responds. He was a realist in his

[1] The first Psychological Laboratory was established by Wundt in Germany in 1879. The first American Psychological Laboratory was founded by G. Stanley Hall at Johns Hopkins University in 1881, and existed five years. A second period of activity opened in 1888 in the founding of the three laboratories at the Universities of Pennsylvania, Wisconsin, and Indiana, followed by three more in 1889, the year which marked the close of Dr. Robinson's professorship at Brown. After this time laboratories multiplied quite rapidly, until in 1895 there are more of them in this country than in Europe. The laboratory at Brown University was founded by Professor E. B. Delabarre in April, 1892. The "American Journal of Psychology" dates from 1887. Cf. an article by Professor Delabarre of Brown University in " L'Année Psychologique," 1894, pp. 209–255. For more detailed account cf. Baldwin, " Pyschology, Past and Present," in the " Psychological Review," vol. i. p. 364. — A. G. L.

doctrine of perception and knowledge, in his doctrine of the
relation of the concept to reality, and in his doctrine of the
intuitions. In reply to a question from some member of
the class of 1876, as to which of the three views—realism,
nominalism, and conceptualism — he thought the true one,
he said: "There is a root of truth in old realism. Nominalism throws two or three pebble-stones into the cog-
wheel of thought which continually make some cracking."[1]
Of the intuitions as related to realities, he said: "We prefer
to regard all our really intuitive ideas as springing from an
immediate beholding of realities, — realities our knowledge
of which is as trustworthy as that which we obtain of the

[1] That phase of realism which held so important a place in Dr. Robinson's theology, especially in his theories of depravity and atonement, and
which used to be the theme of pressing inquiries in his lecture-room, received
from him at Brown a more explicit statement than he gave to it while at
the Seminary. This statement is furnished by Mr. Langley, and is offered
to the students of Dr. Robinson's theology as, with the possible exception of
his kindred idea of law, the most significant and fruitful of the doctrines which
he derived from any other immediate source than the Bible. — Ed.

"Modified by modern thought and by new theories in physical science,
the question of realism and nominalism is being revived under new forms.
To a modern intellect the theory that all concepts are representative of
universal realities seems absurd; but that they are all merely arbitrary
names of what has only an individual existence, or of what has only a mental
existence, the later teaching of physical science will hardly justify us in
believing.

"Extreme positivists, in imitation of Comte, who, like Hobbes, explicitly
affirms the theory of nominalism, are ultra-nominalists. But evolutionists
who recognize a directive and moulding power, a plastic force, a *vis vivida*
which inheres in and works in and through typical forms, if logically consistent, must also recognize a somewhat that underlies and runs through and
determines every individual of the type. That plastic power or somewhat is
the same in each and all of the class to which it belongs, and each and all alike
partake of it. A common participation in this somewhat necessitates a kind
of theory of realism.

"That the concept cannot be conceived or made real to the mind except in
an individual is indisputable, but that concepts representing such classes of
objects or attributes of objects as are endowed with an inherent power of self-
perpetuation do represent universals of essence, there seems to be no good
reason for doubting." — *Lectures on Psychology, MS.*, § 40, ed. 1884.

external world through use of our senses (Lectures on Psychology, MS., § 44, ed. 1884). Knowledge he " proximately, though very imperfectly, defined as a conscious apprehension of relation and distinction between self and a somewhat that is not self, a conscious communion of self with some object distinguishable from self as cognizing. . . . The knowledge of objects in the material external world comes through the phenomenal reports they make of themselves by sensation in consciousness. The personal ego that knows these objects comes through use of the bodily sense organs into direct and immediate relation to them, and thus knows them directly and immediately in the sensations as material objects; but it is spirit knowing matter, and knowing it only through the medium of the bodily organism. This knowledge differs in kind, if not in degree, from that which we have of ourselves and of other beings. "

" Opposed to the Kantian-Hamiltonian view of knowledge," — which, " in the hands of Herbert Spencer, becomes agnosticism (philosophy of nescience), "— " it is maintained that the phenomenal and the noumenal, qualities and essence, are not separable in fact if they be in thought; that the notion of a somewhat that cannot appear, that has no qualities and sustains no relations, is self-contradictory; that the very idea of phenomenon is that a somewhat and a real object appear, and that the appearance is a veritable and reliable revelation of both reality and essence. "

Dr. Robinson's greatest omission in Psychology, as in Ethics, was a discussion of the sensibility. He discussed the subject, it is true, briefly and incidentally in his Ethics, where [1] he gave his reasons for the omission, which was conscious and purposive, of a full and separate treatment; but from the point of view of system it was a defect. In Psy-

---

[1] Cf. Principles and Practice of Morality, pp. 19–21.

chology the omission was probably due, in addition to the reasons given in the Ethics, to the fact that the problem of knowledge seemed to him the most important and vital, and, the time at his disposal being limited, this problem, therefore, claimed his chief attention.

Towards the latter part of his professorship the classes began to manifest a lessening interest in his instruction in Psychology. This in the case of the best men was at bottom probably due to the growing sense and conviction of the need of a more thorough and minute study of details before we have scientific warrant for affirming any positions or doctrines, even though the positions or doctrines affirmed and taught were on the whole correct. The feeling itself, though a part of the current movement of thought, was in his classes largely caused by and greatly intensified and furthered by his own critical spirit and method. Some one has said that " philosophy is psychology, and psychology is a question." The statement is to a certain extent true, and no one felt its truth more deeply than Dr. Robinson. He recognized the importance and value of the modern methods of experimental research and study, and the bearing of their results on the dark problems of the science of mind. He often alluded to the work needing to be done, and the aid that we might legitimately expect therefrom in the clearer understanding and statement, if not the solution, of these problems. He always looked forward to the future, and fully believed that it would some time bring us further light at least than we now possess. The results of psychological investigation and experimentation have as yet thrown but little light on the ultimate problems. They have cleared up to a certain extent many obscure points, but thus far have not overthrown, or at least proved false, the old views. How through sensation the mind comes to

a knowledge of the external world has not yet been discovered, and the "soul" is still the most rational theory
of the inner life. For the purposes of Psychology, as now
understood and studied, it may perhaps be superfluous and
unnecessary; but philosophically the need and substantial
truth and reality of the soul are as great and as firmly
established as ever. Thus far the philosophy taught by
Dr. Robinson stands firm; and his students may rest upon it,
and work on till the present twilight breaks in clearer day.

In psychology, and I think in his ultimate philosophy
as well, if he had any, Dr. Robinson was a dualist.
"Dualism," he said to the class of 1883, "is the only
tenable position." In his Brown teaching Dr. Robinson
did not go into speculative philosophy, strictly speaking, to
any extent. He distinctly stated to some classes that he
should not do so. His reason for the course adopted was
probably the immaturity in power of thought and philosophical attainment of the students, and the lack of sufficient time for such discussion. Had he done graduate work
to any extent, he would doubtless have given a course in
speculative philosophy. In private conversation with me
I have heard him say that, while he recognized the impulse of reason in the direction of monism, and the tendency of present philosophic thought in that direction, yet
he felt, as in the case of dualism, its difficulties, chief of
which was .that it necessitated pantheism. He could conceive of no monism that did not involve pantheism; and
pantheism, from the point of view of ethics and theology,
he considered a false philosophy. This at least was true in
the present stage of our knowledge and experience. What
the future may have in store for us is known only to God.
In his own good time he will reveal it. Meanwhile it is
our duty to study and to wait. It is wholly useless with

our present data and insight to attempt to construct a final and complete system of philosophy. Such a system would be worthless if made. Teach, then, he would say, what we know; investigate as far as we can, but leave the edges as ragged as the facts necessitate; and never for the sake of system arbitrarily force facts into the mould of a philosophical theory, the product of mere abstract thought.

It is generally admitted, and I think correctly, that Dr. Robinson's work in Ethics was greater and more thoroughly satisfactory than that in Psychology, and that the course in Ethics was the best he gave at Brown. This was perhaps due partly to the fact that, great as was his ability and interest in speculative thought, his interest in the realization of ideal character and its philosophical foundations was still greater. With all his splendid intellectual insight and ability, he was both by nature and by habit preeminently a prophet and preacher as well as a speculative thinker.

In Ethics Dr. Robinson considered the most fundamental questions, especially at the present stage of ethical discussion, to be "those of conscience, inclusive of the moral judgments, and the ultimate ground of moral obligation. All ethical questions resolve themselves, in the last analysis, into the question of conscience and the final ground of its decisions."[1] Conscience, "the. most decisive characteristic of personality, . . . the foremost factor in a philosophy of ethics," is "the moral judiciary of the individual soul, the judge and the arraigned being one and the same person, . . . the reason passing judgments on acts with distinct consciousness that the acts judged are one's own, . . . the soul's inquisition with itself. . . . It is that rational power by which the soul, with inwardly

---

[1] Principles and Practice of Morality, Preface, p. viii.

responsive emotions, and in obedience to an inward and inexorable necessity, judges itself and its own acts the instant the character of itself and its acts is disclosed." It is distinguished from the moral faculty, " the soul's power to judge all kinds of moral acts, by whomsoever performed. . . . The difference is not in the nature of the faculty, but in the function performed, and in the emotional results that follow. . . . In the emotions awakened by a judgment on one's own bad acts, there is an element that never enters into the emotions from a judgment of the acts of others,"— namely, remorse. The real function of conscience is to enforce the moral law accepted as such by the whole mind; and its judgments, though necessary and certain in view of this accepted law, are dependent for their accuracy upon the accuracy with which the other mental functions have performed their tasks. Conscience is supreme, because, enforcing what the whole mind has accepted as law, it " simply expresses the highest authority the soul can know." Its judgments are always according to one's present apprehension of moral truth, and " the very conception of authority as contrary to truth, or as superior to it, is subversive of the foundation of right and justice, and consequently of all obligation; . . . no external authority, whether of the parent, the state, the philosopher, the priest, the Bible, or experience and utility," being able to " reach the ruling power of the soul," save through that " personal conviction of duty which it is the sole prerogative of the self-judging faculty to enforce." A denial of its supreme authority is " to deny the possibility of religion, and to withdraw from morality its essential principle."

In his discussion of the origin of the conscience, Dr. Robinson exhibited most clearly his appreciation of the truth, influence, and worth of the Derivative school of

Ethics (Evolutionists, Sensationalists, Experientialists, Historical Ethics). Maintaining that conscience " as the soul's demand and capacity for moral distinctions, and for moral judgments with responsive emotions, is an integrant part of human nature as such, and is as universal as the human race," and that, like any other faculty, it can by practice and training be educated to the better performance of its functions, he also maintained that the derivatist " assumption that conscience is the product of education and training . . . confounds the faculty of conscience with its products, — with its judgments and the resulting emotions." It is the soul's conception of the moral law or ideal, the standard by which conscience judges, not the faculty that judges, that is given and changed by training and experience; and, further, " there can be no emotion, call it by whatever name you will, without thought; and there can be no thought without a faculty for thinking."

" There is no solution of conscience apart from moral law." According to Dr. Robinson, moral law is the point of contact between the intuitionalists and the derivatists. The intuitionalists are right in affirming that conscience is an original endowment, and moral law an essential and constituent part of moral being. But the derivatists are right in asserting that a knowledge of the law by which conscience judges, and its education in strength, facility, promptness, and accuracy in performing its function, come largely from experience.

Moral law exists as subjective principle and as objective rule or precept. As a subjective, constitutive principle of the personal being, it is " that requirement or series of requirements in the moral nature of man which he must strictly comply with, or there can be for him no realization of the moral and ideal perfection of his being." "As objective precept, rule, or formal statute, moral law is simply the statement in words of what the indestructible properties or attributes of personal being are and inexorably require one to do and become if he is to attain the best type of manhood. . . . If man bears the image of his Creator, — that is, embodies in his personality the same constituent principles of moral being as the Supreme Being," — moral law is at once "a transcript of the Divine nature," and "a picturing in words of the moral nature of a perfect man." Moral law, therefore, "is not a something made for an end," but is simply revealed. The "sanctions of moral law are the natural sequences of moral actions. . . . The morally innocent cannot be morally punished, nor the morally guilty be by fiat absolved from penalty. The essence of moral penalty lies in self-conviction of ill-desert," and there will be active penalty so long as there is active evil. "The penal sanctions of moral law, falling as a blight on the personal being, can be removed only by a remedial agency in which the beneficent results of some new law observed shall counteract and obliterate the penal consequences of other laws that have been broken. . . . No remedial agency can so far obliterate the effects of penal sanctions as to restore one completely to that state to which he could have attained had he not transgressed." Moral renewal is a reconstruction of personal being and character through the agency of moral and spiritual ideas and forces. These are centred in the "archetypal and Divine Man, who alike unfolded the fulness of moral law in his teachings and illustrated its absolute perfection and its sanctions in his own person and life; and who for all who will know him and trust in him as Teacher and Deliverer, will translate objective precept back into subjective principle, bringing the action of the will and the requirements of moral law into an ever-increasing accord."[1]

The exposition and discussion of moral law, especially of its nature and sanctions, exhibits most clearly the influence of physical science in clarifying, deepening, and enlarging the conceptions of ethics, and in removing from them all traces of externality and arbitrariness. It shows the moral life to be the normal and natural life for every man.

Dr. Robinson's most original work in Ethics was done on the topics of conscience and moral law. His discussion of these subjects, especially the latter, is undoubtedly his most permanently valuable contribution to ethical thought. His treatment of the will and of virtue and its theories is masterly; his classification of the theories of the ultimate ground of obligation clear and for the most part accurate, and their discussion and criticism acute, searching, and in the main just. He held to the freedom of the will as " a necessary condition, an essential principle, of rational being as such," and as " a harmonious working of all the powers of the personal being; " and found the ultimate ground of obligation " in the immutable moral nature of an infinitely perfect archetypal Being. "

In passing from the account of the philosophy taught by Dr. Robinson to the final summary and critical estimate of his work as a teacher of philosophy, we must constantly bear in mind not only his qualifications for the work, but

---

[1] The foregoing account of Dr. Robinson's doctrine of Conscience and Moral Law is purposely given for the most part in his own language. It confines itself to a brief statement of the chief characteristic points, and for the thorough comprehension of the nature, development, and grounds of his doctrine needs to be supplemented by a careful study of his "Principles and Practice of Morality."—A. G. L.

also the conditions under which it had to be done. These conditions may be briefly summarized in the statement that he was both President and Professor, charged with the heavy and increasing duties of administration with their infinitely numerous, petty, and irritating details, consuming an immense amount of time and energy, and leaving a correspondingly less amount of both for the duties of instruction; and that he came from a graduate school to a college where he had to deal with students less mature intellectually, some of whom had little capacity for the study of philosophy, and many of whom had no interest therein.

The philosophy he taught was a rational philosophy, and not one founded on authority. His method was always positive, increasingly so as the years passed by, and latterly at times verging very closely on the dogmatic; but, strictly speaking, it was never dogmatic. Never in his thinking or teaching was he dogmatic in the sense of assertion on authority simply, or of effort to induce or to force the student to accept a statement or doctrine on mere authority. He was the very last man to do anything of this sort. His whole life of thought and instruction was totally opposed to such a method. In the formation of his views it was his habit, as I know from his repeated statements to me personally, and from the critically constructive character of all his work, to give as much, if not more, consideration to what could be said by way of objection to a given view, than to what might be advanced in its support.[1] He always wanted to know the worst that could be

---

[1] In the lecture on "Faith and Authority," in the Graduate course of 1878–79, Dr. Robinson said: "In past years, when a professor of theology, I felt it my duty to read a vast amount of sceptical literature. A Presbyterian minister talking with me said he should not have dared to do it. I replied: 'I don't dare not to do it.' But I would not advise one to do too much of it, or any save in a humble spirit. The result of all is that the Person of Christ

said against a position to which he was inclined, as then he knew the real strength of his own side and the real value of his own views.

Ever learning and ever coming into a larger knowledge of the truth, he taught a progressive philosophy. He was always revising his dictations and bringing the latest facts and theories into the class-room expositions and discussions, and could not understand how so distinguished a philosopher as Sir William Hamilton could read or have read to his classes the same lectures without change for twenty years. That there were great and at present unsolvable problems, he was too wise to deny and too honest to conceal. Insisting on certain fundamental truths which he considered thoroughly well established in reason and absolutely essential to any real progress in philosophy or life, he occupied himself chiefly in teaching his students philosophy and its significance for life at the present stage of both. He held that the universe of mind and matter was an expression of God's thought and energy; therefore we must push bravely on to such results as the Providence of God makes possible, joyfully accepting all new facts and insight, and modifying our previous constructions accordingly.

He did not teach or attempt to teach a " final philosophy." This he thought wholly beyond the power of man with his present limitations as to data and powers of insight and interpretation, and he regarded all attempts to construct

and the New Testament are to me absolute authority. And this is not irrational; there is no decree about it; the truth vindicates itself." In the second lecture on " Final Cause," in the same course, he remarked : " It has been my lot to have read more than was probably healthful of the most bitter, blasphemous, and fearful writings against our holy religion; and while I feel the force of the objections brought against it, yet I cannot look out on life and the future and not feel assured that God is behind it all."

such a philosophy or even to determine the complete body of principles absolutely essential thereto as pretentious and vain. For system-making in itself considered he had little concern. He never seemed anxious, therefore, to construct a completely ordered system for himself, and I doubt if he had such a system, even a tentative one. If he had, his students never found it out. Certain fundamental elements of such a complete system he taught with tremendous emphasis and with generally convincing power. But he was more intent on arousing his students to think for themselves, to ground them in the essentials of a true philosophy and ethics, leaving them to complete the work than to furnish them with a ready-made system. He realized only too well that if a man has a real and genuine system of thought, it must be the product of his own thinking, the outcome of his own reflection on the facts of the universe, including his own life and experience, and that only thus could it at all satisfy his reason or control his life. Aside too from these considerations, and behind them all, he was by nature and training stronger in analysis than synthesis, — though by no means lacking in synthetic power, — a man of insight rather than a systemizer; and this trait, emphasized by an intense love of truth and an earnest desire to attain it, led him to the most searching examination of all facts and theories claiming acceptance as truth. I have called his work critically constructive; but the emphasis should on the whole be on the " critical " rather than on the " constructive. " He synthetized and constructed as far and as fast as he was able; but the critical in fact hindered the constructive, and systemization was correspondingly slow.

As a critical thinker on broad fundamental principles, Dr. Robinson was a master. For minute details he had little taste and small patience. The vitally essential points of a theory or principle he grasped with great rapidity, and in general with accuracy, and presented them with remarkable clearness and power, while his own criticisms of principle or theory were set forth in a manner even more acute and forcible.

In his criticism of authors or theories Dr. Robinson confined himself mainly to their rational grounds, such as the lack of a basis of fact, faulty interpretation and construction of fact, arbitrary assumption, and rational inconsistency. Frequently he pointed out clearly their practical consequences as legitimate considerations in estimating their truth and worth. But he never reflected on the motives of the authors of the theories in the sense of reflecting on their honesty, though he might and often did question their intellectual acumen and grasp. On the other hand, he often commended for their good points views with which he did not and could not agree; and he repeatedly tried to find and point out the idea or thought underlying, in the minds of those holding thereto, a given theory or practice which he could neither sanction nor approve.

The full effect of his otherwise magnificent teaching was lessened somewhat by his failure to secure the sympathy and affection of a large number of his students. This failure to secure sympathy was due largely to his natural reserve, emphasized by the well-nigh habitual repression of the emotions. But the fires of deep and powerful emotion burned within, gave vitality and intensity to all his life and work, his thought and utterance, and occasionally burst all barriers, and revealed themselves with a force and splendor that made itself felt, and was all the greater because rare and unexpected, and for this very reason more deeply and enduringly impressive. A man of profound and powerful convictions, the product of the heart as well as of the intellect, he impressed in a masterful way, both in and out of the class-room, in spite of his lack of sympathy, a very large number of his students.

This lack of sympathy probably partially accounts for his failure always fully to appreciate the difficulties of his students.   His own mind working in long familiar fields with great rapidity and intensity, he was at times too impatient with the slower minds, because they did not at once or more rapidly see the truth and arguments presented.   " If you can't see it," he would say, " God help you, for I can't. "

Intellectually intolerant at times he seemed to some to be.   Perhaps he was ; but if so, he was nowise different from other great and profound and independent thinkers, and I doubt if his intolerance, if such it was, ever involved any personal animus towards the person or persons holding the views from which he differed.   He reminded one of Carlyle in his denunciation of what he thought wrong or a sham. In calmer moods, when out of the intense fires of class-room discussion, he was, in large part at least, certainly modest in regard to his own views, free from prejudice or intolerance, and considerate of the views of others.

In point of time and in a sense he belongs to the older generation of philosophical thinkers and teachers, when the study had not the importance and rigidity of method it now has, especially in the scientific direction, deducing its principles from a much wider range of patiently observed and critically interpreted and systemized facts.   In reality, however, he was fully abreast of the time, and indeed in some respects very much beyond it, especially in his firm insistence and constant emphasis on facts rather than theories, in his penetrating and exhaustive criticism and patient construction, and in his marvellously rapid propheti-

cal insight into the real significance and tendencies of new
and current phases of philosophic thought, and into the
heart of the pretentious and sophistical assumptions and rea-
sonings of physico-metaphysical and ethical theories, with
their inevitable results in the moral, religious, and social
life, and on the ultimate philosophy necessarily following
therefrom. Long before the thinking world reached certain
phases of thought, he saw they were coming and pointed
them out, and as far as possible prepared his students
to understand and, so far as was necessary, to meet them.
Rather than force a closed system, let us leave things at loose
ends, and hold firmly only to that which thus far seems
indisputably true and rationally coherent with all we now
know or seem likely soon to know. Other than this, wait
and search. Such was the spirit of his philosophical thinking and teaching throughout his life. More than one student
owes to him all the rational faith he has.[1] He saved many
from utter scepticism, and he did this by the very things
just mentioned, — solid foundations in essentials, fairness
in admitting and treating difficulties, in accepting what was
valid and worthful in views opposed to those inculcated,

[1] Professor Benjamin Ide Wheeler, Ph. D., of Cornell University, writes:

"I can never fully acknowledge the debt I owe to Dr. Robinson's preaching and instruction. He restated for me the old faith. I am not aware that
he changed it, but he restated it in terms which enabled me to co-ordinate
my religious thinking with my other thinking. When I came under his
instruction in 1874, I was in rebellion against the faith of my boyhood. The
old formulas had lost their meaning for me. My religious life and religious
thinking had not grown with my growth. I was getting to be ashamed of
them, as a youth is of his childhood's playthings. Dr. Robinson's teaching
all tended to make a man approach the problems of the religious life with
an openness and fearlessness that engendered confidence and rebuked the
thought of shame, and best of all led to the construction of a faith that could
hold a natural and constituent place in a man's whole thought and view of the
universe. His teaching was suggestive and stimulating rather than systematic. It inspired his men to build their own houses and not to live in rented
tenements."

refusal for the sake of systematic completeness to assert beyond our knowledge and on the ground of mere abstract theory, and openness of mind to light that might come in the future. He not only taught these things, but was himself a living exemplification and illustration of his teaching. Through the broadened and deepened thinking and life of his students he exerted a powerful and permanent liberalizing influence, which still continues, on and in American ethical and religious thought. Both directly and indirectly much of the present movement in philosophical and religious thought and life is due to him.

His dignified and impressive presence, indicative of philosophic mind and noble moral character, was an important element in his power and influence as a teacher and a man. His dignity was not haughtiness, and his seriousness was not austerity. His reserve and apparent distance were elements of character more fully appreciated as men grew older; and his fearlessness before men and reverence before God called out the same qualities in his students. His eye, when at rest, was quiet and deeply meditative, like Hegel's, indicating a mind that sees deep and far into truth and reality. When aroused, that same eye, like Sir William Hamilton's, could flash forth fire, penetrate to the very centre of the soul, and look the looker through and through.

To those who never knew him in the class-room it is wellnigh impossible to convey an adequate and satisfactory idea of his power as a thinker and teacher. By such his special excellences as a teacher of philosophy will be most clearly seen in his spoken and written style, the outward expression of the inward thought. In fact, by such they can be seen only here. His style exhibits the conspicuous merits of most keen and penetrating analysis, remarkable precision and accuracy in definition, with the additional and often rare merit of abiding by the definition given throughout the discussion; lucid, terse, incisive, and forcible statement of principles; exposition clear and discriminating in quality and quantity; and a logic, including the justification of the premises as well as the argumentation thence proceeding, masterly and generally convincing. It is a philosophical style at once simple, lucid, compact, strong, and attractive, with none of the diffuseness and mistiness which characterizes so much of the philosophic writing of the present day. He was indisputably superior to the large majority of thinkers in exact thought and expression.

Doubtless greater in theology than in philosophy, his work in philosophy both as thinker and teacher was great and powerful, of permanent and abiding worth, both in spirit and substance an essential part of our country's work and heritage. Certain fundamental doctrines, such as that of consciousness in Psychology, and those of conscience and especially moral law in Ethics, have been more clearly set forth and more firmly established by him than ever before.

He was a magnificent example and illustration of the essential character of Brown University training as it always has been in the past, and as I trust it always will continue to be in the future. This training aimed to develop the acutest and strongest intellect, but at the same time to make it subordinate to the purest sensibility and the noblest will. The aim and spirit that ruled in all the past history of the College was identical with that of its late President and Professor of Philosophy. It was said of him when he left Rochester for Brown: " He was a great educator rather than a great teacher. " I should prefer to say that he was a great teacher, but a greater educator, and that he was both because he was a great man. The best students always appreciated him. His work was great and worthy work, — worthy of the splendid personality that did it, and of priceless worth to the students and the university in and for whom it was done. It was the transfusion of intellectual and moral energy, the continuous begetting of new and vigorous life and personality. It will be an irreparable and fatal loss, if all our colleges and universities do not in the future possess at least one great teacher like him, who will pour out their lives into the lives, and impress their characters on the characters, of their pupils, charging them with the vital force of their own personality, — a force which no stress of labor or trial in life's battle can wholly destroy. If we have not such men, then, as President Andrews once said, " we must grow them," or others as nearly like them as the changing conditions of life and civilization make possible. Such was our loved teacher to very many of us. Some of us can truly say, with full appreciation and gratitude to all our other teachers, that his work with us and in us was the greatest and best we have ever known.

IX.

AS COLLEAGUE AT THE UNIVERSITY OF CHICAGO.

By PRESIDENT WILLIAM R. HARPER, PH. D., LL. D.

IX.

AS COLLEAGUE AT CHICAGO.

IT is with great hesitation that I undertake to represent, even in outline, the work of Dr. Robinson during the last two years of his life, while professor in the University of Chicago. The hesitation is due to a feeling that, however minute the statement may be, it will inadequately describe these crowning years of his life and work. The influence which he exerted, as indeed is every influence of the highest order, was one which could be felt, but not described.

When it was proposed one Sunday morning at Vassar College to Dr. Robinson that he should join the Faculty of the new University, an institution which at that time was still a dream, he manifested the greatest possible interest in the work proposed, but evidently hesitated to accept the proposition, because of his age. With characteristic modesty he feared that he might prove a burden to the new university. In those earliest days, when the attitude of mind in reference to the new undertaking was almost universally that of doubt, and in not a few cases that of suspicion, the heartiness of Dr. Robinson's words, his strong faith in the future of the institution, and his kindly personal disposition did more to encourage some of us than any other one element in the situation. In my conversations with Dr. Robinson at Vassar College, where it was my good fortune to meet him more than once, he would enter into the most minute details of the organization, and discuss the new departures proposed with an interest and a freshness almost beyond description. His vast fund of experience and his kindly appreciation of new features combined to furnish help of a most important character.

The work proposed in connection with the Department of Philosophy — namely, a course in Christian Evidences and a course in Christian Ethics, each of which should continue through six months — appealed to him very strongly, and he entered upon the work with the enthusiasm of a young man.

The thought has often suggested itself to me, how great the contrast must have seemed to him between the old institutions at Rochester and Providence to which he had given so many years of his life, and the new institution which he now entered at a time when, under ordinary circumstances, his life work would seem to have been finished. The work of the first year in the University of Chicago will never be forgotten by those who participated in it. With a great Faculty, most of whom were strangers to each other, and a body of students coming from more than a hundred different institutions; with a plan of organization wholly distinct from anything with which any of the Faculty or students had experience, and no traditions; with a lack of many necessary facilities for doing work; with all of the confusion growing out of the near proximity to the grounds of the World's Columbian Exposition, — it is difficult for any one who was not a part of the institution to realize how entirely strange must have been the situation, especially to those who had been connected with institutions long established, in which rigid routine existed, and in which the life and work had taken on a fixed and formal character. Through all this period Dr. Robinson worked quietly, regularly, and enthusiastically. No lectures were more highly appreciated, and none aroused a more general interest. Again and again a student has come to me with the statement that he regarded it as the greatest privilege of his life to have come in contact with Dr. Robinson in the class-room. The fidelity with which he performed his work was an example to every member of the new Faculty, young and old. The very fact that a man of such reputation, whose work had been so marked, could, at his time of life, take up so cheerfully and so energetically a new work, in a new city, in the midst of new surroundings, in a new faculty, the great majority of which were young men, occasioned surprise, and at the same time exerted a peculiar influence upon all.

It is true that Dr. Robinson did not attend the Faculty meetings. Before the opening of the University he came to me and raised the question whether it would be best for him, compelled, as he was, to husband his strength, to take an active part in the administration of the University. It was, of course, evident that such expenditure of his time and strength would not be to the best interests of the University. But no important questions were discussed, and no important action was taken, in reference to which his advice was not received; and on many occasions he most kindly and generously made suggestions which were most helpful with reference to questions of a particular character, as well as questions of a general character. When I remember the many occasions on which he permitted me to consult him, and the many occasions on which unsolicited he came forward to offer his suggestions, I realize how deeply interested he was in the undertaking, and how, notwithstanding his age, his mind occupied itself with the problems of the new situation. There were not a few delicate questions concerning which it was important that right action should be taken from the beginning. In every case his experience and his great fund of practical wisdom furnished material without which it would have been difficult to act.

A few days before the opening of the second year, he sent for me to announce that in all probability he would not be able to take up the work of the year, his physician having notified him of the disease which later was to prove fatal. He wished to know whether, if he recovered his strength sufficiently, notwithstanding the physical difficulty which had come upon him, it might not be best for him to continue his work. The courage of the man at this critical point, and his eager desire to carry out the announcements which had been made for his classes, gave me a new conception of the vigor and energy of his spirit. When the opening day of the year came, Dr. Robinson was at his post, and through the entire year, without a single omission, he performed the duties of his chair, being conveyed to and from the University in a carriage on days when the weather was particularly inclement. Toward the end of the year he saw that the time had come for the further organization of the Department of Philosophy, and, fearing that his presence might be an embarrassment to such reorganization, he placed his resignation in my hands. This resignation was never accepted by the Board of Trustees. With the new plans for the department he was in hearty sympathy; and when he left Chicago for the East in April, it was his desire, and at the same time the purpose of the University, that he should return and continue his work. If his life had been spared two or three years more, it is impossible to conceive how much greater his influence among the students would have become, for they were just beginning to realize the value of his work and appreciate its helpfulness.

Providence ordered that he should not return. Short, however, as was his stay with us; hampered as he was, especially during the last year, by his illness, — Dr. Robinson's connection with the University left an impression upon its organization, the members of its Faculty and its students, which will never be forgotten. I consider it to have been, perhaps, the greatest single advantage of the early history of the University, so far as concerns the Faculty of the institution, that in the Providence of God it was possible for him to live and work with us during these years. Personally and officially, I wish to make acknowledgment of the many and great benefits which accrued to the University from his residence.

NOTE.

ON DR. ROBINSON'S RESPECT FOR AVERAGE MINDS.

There is no rumor that Dr. Robinson ever showed special favor to any undergraduate; but it has been suspected that he held in contempt students of only average intelligence. Certainly he treated pretentious dulness with scorn; and he did not love a question of which the student ought to find the answer for himself. "Doctor, which is the right pronunciation, Gennésaret, or Gennesarét?" "The Sea of Galilee." If the story is not true, it is well invented. But the testimony from Brown University is explicit that he was careful to encourage all modest and faithful men. How he bore himself at the University of Chicago is testified by the Dean of the Divinity School, Professor Eri B. Hulbert, D. D. — ED.

"It fell to my lot to register most of the students who took Dr. Robinson's lectures. The fame of the man and the importance of his topics made the students eager to take his courses. By a rule of the University only advanced men, in limited numbers, are admitted to Seminars; while men of lower attainments, and to the number of thirty, may be received into the lecture classes. I had no difficulty in selecting men for the Seminars, but the lecture courses troubled me. I was aware that Dr. Robinson's heart warmed toward brilliant students; but what was I to do with ordinary men, having no claim to brilliancy, who were eager to enjoy his instruction? In my perplexity, I submitted the question to the teacher himself. With some warmth he instructed me not to draw this distinction, assuring me that he would find peculiar satisfaction in aiding those whose sole commendation was plodding fidelity. He seemed almost hurt that I should hesitate. I enrolled men of high and low degree, women, and foreigners. So the work began and continued. Frequently the Doctor came to my office to tell me of the progress inferior men were making, and to assure me of his patience and painstaking with mediocrity and dulness. His kindly interest in ordinary students as well as men of conspicuous ability revealed to me a new trait in Dr. Robinson's character, which trait endeared him to all who were fortunate enough to be numbered among his pupils."—E. B. H.

X.

DR. ROBINSON AS AN ORATOR AND A MAN OF LETTERS.

By PROFESSOR W. C. WILKINSON, D.D.,
UNIVERSITY OF CHICAGO.

X.

AS AN ORATOR AND A MAN OF LETTERS.

DR. ROBINSON was in every respect — physically, mentally, morally — a striking personality. This will of course have been said many times elsewhere in these pages; but that is no reason why it should not be said additionally here. The fact that exists can in no other way make its due impression than by repeated restatements of it made from different personal points of view. One comes to associate so inseparably the physical aspect and impression of a man with that man's peculiar type of mental and moral character, that it is perhaps not often safe in any given case to say that there was from the beginning an inherent and inevitable " pre-established harmony " between the one and the other. But certainly, if to say so be in any case whatsoever safe, then it would seem to be safe in the case of Dr. Robinson.

His tall form, not always erect, but always capable of erecting itself, and upon fit oratoric occasion frequently doing so with commanding effect; his habitual carriage, naturally dignified and decorous, but of a character betokening it that of a person who scorned to be finical, and who might surprise you with a sudden manly breach of the conventional; his gait, the stalwart stride of a man intent on getting forward, while in will, as in locomotive equipment, amply able to get forward, and that with speed, too, such as would put you upon your mettle to keep up with him;

his voice, a mint of the clearest-cut, freshest-stamped utterance, given forth in tones keen, incisive, insistent, penetra-
tive, tones fond of the high key natural to a mind consciously
pressing to a point perfectly well perceived ahead, but ready
at times to bottom out into a solid, hearty, rich, vibrant,
pectoral quality, — all these outward traits in Dr. Robinson
you felt to be but the reflex of the manner of man that he
inwardly and essentially was.

Have I seemed to describe a man in whom the challenging, the aggressive, the belligerent, spirit predominated?
Well, complaisance was undoubtedly not the chief note of
Dr. Robinson's character.   Still, there was fineness in him,
as well as strength.   His heart was tender and true when
you got to it, although he was indeed far from wearing it on
his sleeve.   And running all through his intellectual con- ·
stitution was a vein of the genuinely imaginative and
poetical.   I can testify to the fact that when, in his fresh
manly prime, he first came from pastorship in Cincinnati
to Rochester as teacher of theology, and there immediately
began to make himself felt as a preacher of extraordinary
power and brilliancy, one of the traits in him that gained
him the adhesion and admiration of the most cultivated
and the choicest among the students, both of the seminary
and of the college, was the openness, the hospitality, that
he displayed to the influence of the poets, and the occasional
gleam, as of original poetry, that lighted up his eloquence.

It seems to me now, as I recall the cycle of discourses
which he delivered on the then current phases of religious
scepticism during the autumn and winter of the first year of
his memorable work in Rochester, that he never afterward
surpassed the triumphs of that period of his pulpit achievement.   I know of a circle of young men — friends they
were in perpetual council as to things of the spirit — among

the Rochester students, who used as often as possible to
meet after each one of the evening discourses now alluded
to, and discuss it in a prolonged symposium of mutually
exciting and excited admiration and delight.   The writer
of the present contribution, then a college freshman, but
admitted by special privilege to quasi-equal fraternal rela-
tionship of intellect with certain choice spirits of the
theologues, was one of this, alas! now long since unsoldered
round table.   He taught a district school fifteen miles away
from the city during a part of the time covered by the
delivery of those memorable discourses.   This prevented his
hearing the whole series.

There was one signal occasion, however, which he, though
so far away, felt that he could not miss.   After preaching
himself twice that Sunday sermons prepared under pressure
of a sudden call, in the midst of a week filled to the brim
with six days' teaching (six hours each day), he walked
those fifteen miles to Rochester, that he might hear Dr.
Robinson on Theodore Parker.   (This lover of pulpit eloquence had in addition previously walked two miles out
and two miles back between house and church to do his
own preaching.)   I mention this incident to illustrate the
enthusiasm aroused by Dr. Robinson's pulpit eloquence of
that time.   The particular demonstration described was no
doubt a specimen of individual youthful extravagance; but
it was such extravagance as was little likely to have occurred
without a surrounding atmosphere of contagious enthusiasm
to support it.

The discourses thus recalled were, like Dr. Robinson's
discourses in general, from the beginning to the end of his
conspicuous career, delivered *extempore*.   And now I must
say something which, save to the most thoughtful, will
seem like derogation from the praise that I bestow; to some

it will seem, on the contrary, enhancement, rather than diminution, of eulogy. Brilliant then, as those discourses were, and powerful, they yet fell something short of that decisively triumphant effect in oratory of which the speaker all the time tantalizingly seemed capable. This was, I think, the case with Dr. Robinson's public discourse generally. There was a certain lack of *abandon*, a certain self-checking refusal on the part of the preacher to trust himself wholly to the sweep of the inspiration that was perpetually swelling within him almost, but not quite, to the volume and the head that would burst every barrier and pour forth eloquence in an irresistible torrent, in an overwhelming flood.

I account for this just missing, on Dr. Robinson's part, of the supreme achievement in oratory, chiefly by two considerations: one pertaining to the personal constitution of the man, and the other incidental to the occupation of his life. Dr. Robinson was primarily a teacher, and but secondarily a preacher. His habit in utterance was formed and was controlled by the practice of the class-room rather than by the practice of the pulpit. He thought in brief, rapid " swallow-flights " of the mind, rather than in long, continuous, sustained voyages to a goal far off, but clearly perceived and definitely aimed at. He seemed to challenge and invite interpellation from his hearers. This he often secured in the class-room ; and then it was that he appeared in the full glory and power of his extemporary eloquence. He perhaps needed such perfectly sensible and unmistakable reaction on the part of his audience, to bring him out in the plenitude of his incredibly swift and ready play of intellect and of imagination.

" To that, three things may be replied," was almost a formula with him, when a student would state an objection

to some point made by the teacher.   "In the first place,"
and Dr. Robinson would launch himself full speed at once
in reply, with lightning-like celerity and infallible precision
of aim.   The effect was incalculably enhanced by an unsurpassed, unsurpassable clearness, accuracy, emphasis, momentum, of articulation and utterance, sufficient in themselves
to have produced a complete illusion of the intellectual
quality corresponding, even had that quality been, as it was
not, wanting.   The chances were even that the second and
third of the " three things " would not be reached.   To me,
as pupil, it was often in some respectful doubt whether the
" three things " were as clearly present to my teacher's mind
at the moment of his venturing to assert their existence, as
in his own confident conviction they were at least potentially
available, and safe, at need, to be depended upon for yielding themselves up to the quest of that imperious and impor-
tunate intellect of his.   In truth, and though it be a thing
paradoxical to say, Dr. Robinson's habitual manner of challenge and self-confidence appeared to me the unconscious
self-rallying expedient of a nature sincerely modest, even
timid, much more than that outward expression of overbear-
ing spirit in the man, which by the casual observer it might
easily be mistaken to be.

This leads naturally to the stating of the second one of
the two considerations which to me chiefly account for Dr.
Robinson's not being in fact quite the supremely triumphant
orator that he seemed in almost all respects so capable
of being.   Notwithstanding his high, half-haughty, half-
scornful outward air of audacious self-assertion, Dr. Robinson was at bottom too modestly doubtful of himself, or, if
you please, he had too much wise disdain of pretending to
be, where he knew he was not, altogether sure of his ground;
in a word, he was too much a thinker, pure and simple,

with the thinker's circumspect speculation and misgiving, to be the bold mere *voice* that the popular orator has need to be.

It is hardly a third consideration, though it admits of being named as such, the fact that Dr. Robinson's equipment was too predominantly of the intellect, rather than of the heart, to constitute him the ideal orator. "Rather than of the heart," I say. But it is of what I may call public, not private, heart that I speak. Toward his friends, and especially toward his kindred, the people of his home, Dr. Robinson, I should do him wrong not also to say, had a capacity of the most exquisite, the most costly, affection. Yet it remains true that, although for personal friendship and for the intimacies of the hearth, thus choicely and richly endowed, he was comparatively wanting in that broad, that genial, that common, quality of temperament which seems often to inscribe the elect popular favorite's heart, *Pro bono publico*, and offer it freely for daws to peck at. But this very characteristic in Dr. Robinson helped make him, helped keep him, the teacher, in his kind not easily equalled among his coevals, that he was universally acknowledged to be.

Apart from the orator and the educator that he was, Dr. Robinson was potentially a literary man of a very high order. I have just now been re-reading the inaugural address delivered by him on occasion of his being inducted into his office as professor of theology at Rochester in 1853. Dr. Maginnis, a clear and venerable name in Baptist educational history, had, not long before, died while occupying the place in which Dr. Robinson now stood as his successor. Here are the sentences with which the inaugural address begins. I invite any qualified critic of literature to name a single point at which, for brevity, simplicity, sincerity, measure, fitness — and I might almost add, as to turn of expression, felicity and grace — these sentences are wanting. The buried Wordsworthian quotation and allusion in them takes on a value not less really poetical, and distinctly more substantial, than that belonging to the lines of the original : —

" The service that has brought us here this evening cannot but turn the first thoughts of most of us to one who a twelvemonth ago was in life and among us, but who to-night sleeps with the dead. And, surely, it is fitting that in passing to the evening's reflections, we take his resting-place in our way. The thoughts that are to engage us will take a sober coloring from eyes that have but glanced at the tomb, especially the tomb that conceals from us so much of intellect and piety. It might be profitable even to linger here in our meditations. It would strengthen our courage to look steadily at the example of one who, while compelled, his life long, to defend himself against the attacks of disease with the one hand, could yet with the other accomplish so much for the Master.

" But he needs no memorial at our hands; and, least of all, in this place, where genius and sanctified friendship have already presented one inimitable in its beauty and eloquence. [The allusion is, I believe, to a discourse pronounced by Dr. William R. Williams, but modestly withheld by him from print.] Indeed, he had engraved a memorial for himself on the spirits of his pupils. He had erected to himself a monument in every mind that had felt the power of his influence. The monuments of his worth and witnesses of his toils are here, and are scattered throughout our land. His works will be still praising him.

" But to stand in his vacant place, and take up his work where he left it, is certainly no idle undertaking. You know how sad and solemn is the task laid on him who is made to lift, with untried hand, the staff that dropped from the hand of such experience.   Your sympathies and prayers, I am confident, may be relied on for the future; for the present, your kindly attention is bespoken, while a delineation is attempted of the need and the advantages, in our day, of what, for the want of a better phraseology, may be denominated Experimental Theology."

Something like the same awe, as in the presence of the noble dead, that inspired the foregoing exordium, usurps now the present writer's mind in concluding this very inadequate tribute to the memory of Dr. Robinson.   If former students of his suffer themselves ever to recall that the teacher whom they so much admire sometimes indulged, to a degree beyond what was wisest and best, in a certain disdain as toward fellows of his, perhaps less gifted, or even less elevated in character, than he was himself, then those students will be irresistibly reminded likewise that as toward ONE personage at least, that lofty, that imperial, spirit always uncovered himself with a reverence and an awe that was as unreserved and as absolute as it was unquestionably sincere.   There is no image of my revered teacher in theology dearer to memory with me, none spiritually more helpful, than the image of that noble head, silver in advance of its time, declined in reverence before the invisible Christ, while the repressed manly voice vibrated out its rich, sweet tones in prayer, amid the gathering glooms of the twilight-tide, at the close of the daily two-hour session of the classes, in the little upper room where we met in the Seminary at Rochester.

Whatever else fail from my mind of the memory of Dr. Robinson, let that august, that pathetic image of him, adoring, abide!

NOTE.

ON DR. ROBINSON'S ELOQUENCE.

(From Memorial Address by Rev. W. H. P. Faunce, D. D.)

"His last public discourses were his best. He had found subterranean foothold and rootage in the realms of truth, each year adding new diameters to his girth, and unfolding new ramifications of thought and life. At fourscore there was not the slightest mental decrepitude. He stood umbrageous and prolific when many a sapling was in the sear and yellow leaf.

"We students knew him as a speaker and preacher long before we came under his instruction in the senior year. As a preacher, he was logic on fire. He thought on his feet, not repeating sentences carefully conned in the study, but actually going through the thought process in the presence of his audience; and we had the same pleasure in hearing as in watching a powerful engine in resistless and serene movement. We shall never forget his sermons on the Day of Prayer for Colleges or his thrilling baccalaureates. He always chose great themes, and treated them greatly. . . .

"As a speaker he cared nothing for the adornments of showy rhetoric. He had no artifice of speech; he never got into the period of 'anecdotage.' He was like a builder so intent on getting massive timbers into place that he had no eye for stucco and fresco. The stripling preachers of our day, whose chief effort is to collect stories with a moral, may well remember how this man worked. He stood out on the platform with no device save that of truth and personal character. The strength of his blade would not have been aided by any petty carving at the hilt. He hewed to the line in pithy, straightforward speech, and at every blow cut away some tangle of mental underbrush. Probably no man in this country possessed a finer extemporaneous English style. Like his own body, it was flexible and muscular, the perfect vehicle of his burning thought. He was absolutely simple and lucid. One might disagree; he could not misunderstand. Fogginess he hated. His style was like a morning atmosphere in which each object stands out sharp and bold.

"Hence he had immense power to carry conviction to an assembly. As he proceeded he kindled, until his voice grew clear and resonant, the eyes gleamed dark with scorn of falsehood and evil, the gestures grew more swift and awkward, until at some critical moment his left hand was thrust into his pocket! Then came the lightning and the thunder. The hand in pocket was the unfailing sign that the preacher had been totally swept away in the torrent of his own conviction. His Yale lectures on preaching outline his own method, and in some degree disclose the secret of his power."

XI.

DR. ROBINSON AS A TRUSTEE AND A FRIEND.

By PRESIDENT J. M. TAYLOR, D. D., LL. D.,
Vassar College.

XI.

AS A TRUSTEE AND A FRIEND.

AMONG the services Dr. Robinson rendered to his generation, probably none is more likely to be lost sight of by most who knew him than his trusteeship of Vassar College. The office is so frequently perfunctory, and its responsibility so divided among many, that the real service of a trustee to education in general, as well as to his institution, is likely to be forgotten. Dr. Robinson was chosen by Matthew Vassar, the founder, as a charter trustee of the institution he was about to build. It was a time when but few efforts had been made for the higher education of young women, and when public opinion was either indifferent or antagonistic to the conception of Mr. Vassar. There was a call, therefore, in the new board, for a wide experience in the organization and administration of educational institutions, for a liberal conception of educational policy, for the balance of judgment which should meet new conditions with new and liberal views, and yet not antagonize the conservative instincts of society with a dreaded radicalism. It is difficult for any one to-day even to recall the critical conditions in which the trustees undertook their new work.

Probably no injustice will be done the many wise workers in this cause if it be said that in those early years Dr. Robinson was one of the chief formative influences at Vassar. His active service continued till the end of his life; and indeed his last public service of any kind was rendered in the chapel of Vassar, on May thirteenth, a month before he died.

He brought the rarest qualifications to this work. Himself an able administrator, he saw clearly the danger which threatened the new administration, and gave to President Raymond his powerful support and sympathy. Down to his latest years, — and he served the college thirty-three years, — he kept his interest in the questions bearing on the responsibility and power of the executive, and was himself instrumental in bringing about the latest changes which made for the unification of the various powers of administration, and hence for their efficiency.

In questions of the curriculum, again, he proved himself not only the experienced, but the born educator. He kept his mind open to every new suggestion, as was·his wont in theology, philosophy, all truth; but he was not driven of the wind and tossed. Certain definite lines in education were clear. A teacher by nature, whose very throne was the class-room and the pulpit, he stood for an educational policy which should promise thoroughness, the development of individuality and independent thought, breadth, fearlessness, and efficiency in action. The questions of the relation of prescribed and elective work he settled for himself on lines promising first thorough foundations, and after that a broader, liberal outlook. He avoided extremes in discussing the vexed question of the relations of graduate and undergraduate work in the college, and as at Brown as president, so at Vassar as trustee, he stood for whatever could be done honestly, thoroughly, and efficiently.

Of how much value his counsel has been in these last years, it would be difficult to speak too strongly. In his advice about teachers, in his clear views of a wise, progressive policy, in his counsel regarding questions of curriculum and administration, he was always sure of an eager and respectful attention from his colleagues; and in his lectures on ethics, and in the sermons he delivered in the chapel from time to time, he won as well the interest and the admiration of the students.

Reference has already been made to his last sermon. It was a presentation of the claims of the truth in its appeal to our consciousness, in contrast with the claim of external evidence, — " though one rise from the dead." With the energy of earlier years the speaker most impressively urged the appeal of the Spirit to our spirits, and with such freshness, and grasp of all recent speculation, as led a student to remark afterward, " It was the sermon of a young man." She could not know that no young man could have preached it, that it was the product of years of thought, and, what is more, of deep experience in things spiritual.

To speak of Dr. Robinson as a counsellor is to bring into view the qualities which made him so fast and firm and helpful a friend. To many this side of his character was little known. Certainly to those who, as students, never came to know him well, his appearance may be said to have been stern, cold, intellectual, rather than sympathetic, cordial, and fatherly. He was of a reserved nature, not given to the display of his feelings, and even holding them in check by his great self-control. It was inevitable that most who only knew him in the class-room should so measure him. Many never understood how abiding was his interest for them all, how he followed his students in their careers, and how he rejoiced in their successes. Those who came to know him well found more. They saw that the feeling of which the public gained an occasional glimpse — as when his emotions overcame him in his address at the obsequies of Lincoln — betokened a condition, and not an incident. His heart was as strong as his head. His distinguishing intellectual qualities were set in an emotional and affectionate nature marked by the same characteristics. Those who saw him in the more intimate hours of his home-life will recall the many evidences of his tenderness of heart. The writer recalls a Christmas evening in Providence when he was found in his library, and his talk of the lessons of a holiday to a household already broken, and how affectionately he talked of a little girl whom he had buried many years before. Nor will this seem singular to those who knew him in his latest ministry in Philadelphia, when his afflictions and the mellowness of age seemed to lead him to allow more of this tenderness of his nature to shine through his preaching and his other ministrations. How deeply he felt the occasional word which came to him from some student who had learned the debt he owed to his teaching! Exceedingly modest in his estimate of the value of his work for men, these occasional testimonies seemed to bring to him a genuine joy.

This side of Dr. Robinson's nature must be dwelt on if one would understand his character. "The old man has a heart," he said a little while since, "if he does not wear it on his sleeve." He was not merely intellectual, as some thought, though his intellect was of remarkable keenness and force. His interests were not primarily speculative, though he felt the fascination of speculation in the mine of truth. His moral and intellectual enthusiasms were touched throughout by deep feeling, restrained, often unmanifested, but giving after all the peculiar note of power to his work in the class-room and the pulpit. Indeed, no one could have been the orator he was whose thought was not instinct with feeling.

The great outlines of the character which made him so

stimulating and inspiring, so revered and loved, as a friend, are easily sketched, though their combination was his own deep strong character.

He set *truth* before him, in thought and life, as his ideal. His love of it was apparent to all who knew him. No one could associate with him, and not feel impelled to seek as he sought. "Gentlemen," he would say in the theological class-room, " if we live in a house of cobs, let us down with it." No consideration of comfort or policy blinded him to his duty to seek the simple truth ; and his influence on those who knew him well was thus to stimulate all love of truth and hatred of all sham. His students will never forget that question which so often probed their general statements, " Precisely what do you mean by that ? "

His *fearlessness* in pursuit of his ideal was another most prominent characteristic. It went hand in hand with his love of truth. He was singularly free from the bond of traditional belief, while holding the balance of mind which kept him from rationalism and radicalism. This quality gave a certain polemical turn to his teaching and his thinking. In the years when he was followed rather closely because of the views he was teaching regarding the Atonement, — views which, in their essential lines, have become common beliefs to-day, — his examination days brought out many a keen discussion. " Look out, gentlemen," he once said, as some examiners were pressing a student with questions bearing on this point, — " look out; they scent a heresy. " But on the platform, in private conversation, in the most friendly relations at home, one was sure that Dr. Robinson would never hide his views nor trim them to suit the demands of any man or any body of men. As was said of the Puritans, it might be said of him, " He feared God and nothing else; " and the man who knew him and was privileged to enter into friendly relations with him must have felt the influence of that mental and moral courage which shone out of his very presence.

Combined with these qualities was a great *breadth of human interest.* To many a student he seemed pre-eminently a metaphysician, a theologian abstracted from the world by the deepest issues of thought. But nothing human was foreign to him. His prime interest was in man living, and then in all that concerns his life. Political life intensely interested him. He was a true patriot, but never a partisan. Rochester cannot forget his eloquent efforts for the country in the time of the war. But his view was broader still. When Japan was a new object of curiosity to our world, with its wonderful awakening, it was Dr. Robinson who introduced the subject to the public in a lecture replete with fresh information regarding the young nation. When Whittier was honored in Providence, Dr. Robinson's address, abounding in quotations as characteristic of the speaker as of the poet, was one of the most suggestive of the day. But all these tell of the student only. One could not walk out in the country with Dr. Robinson without being impressed with his interest in the farm and garden, the country habitation, the cattle, the horses. One friend remembers his surprise, when a student, at discovering that the theologian knew about potatoes, and discoursed on them, on a suitable occasion, as freely as he discussed the doctrines of grace. In short, he was never what he was so often judged to be, — a recluse, a mere student, an abstract thinker. Everything interested him that had real significance in life, but pre-eminently man.

The great strength of his character, however, was in his *simple faith.* Theological subtleties never blinded him to the fatherhood of God and the brotherhood of Christ. It was natural that one of his temperament should see, first of all, in his reflections on God, a *Holy One.* Indeed, the strength of his soul and his power largely grew out of this conception of righteousness as first, last, everywhere. None the less the tenderness of his heart was nourished by the thought of God as his Father. It was with him no general truth. We who followed his prayers day after day — those prayers so wonderful in simplicity, variety, and spiritual inspiration — knew that to him that Presence was real, vivid, and that he lived in it. No one who ever heard him speak of Jesus Christ, his character and work, could doubt where the foundations of his own faith and hope were laid. An earnest, careful student of the whole New Testament, with a spirit in him which made him so akin to the great apostle that the thought of Paul aroused him to many an eloquent burst in the class-room, he yet turned more and more to the Gospels, and he said again and again, " As you grow older and read your Bible more and more, you will find yourself turning to the Gospels as the source of your inspiration and your hope, in the life of the Master they portray. " Jesus Christ stood out for him as a vivid personality, and he bowed to Him as his Lord, and worshipped. He stood for the righteousness that stood first in God, and the tenderness that he sought in a Heavenly Father.

It was such qualities that won the regard and reverence of his students, and that, seen in the nearer light of friendship, will prove an undying inspiration to those who have felt toward him as toward a father, and who, because they *knew* him, loved him.

APPENDIX.

APPENDIX.

I.

THE CASE OF ANN T. PECK.

OFTEN quite as much courage is required to accept as to reject evidence. An illustration, recalled with almost tender interest in his later days, occurred during Mr. Robinson's pastorate in Cincinnati, and deserves mention because so unusual as to be almost beyond belief. The facts were fully recounted in a book published by the Congregational Sunday School Society of those times under the title "Religion as It Should Be." Ann Thane Peck, a devout and intelligent girl of eighteen, a week or more before her death from pulmonary consumption, experienced an ecstasy, not uncommon in such cases, the remarkable peculiarity of which was that she not only believed she saw the Lord and heard the angels sing, but that her face and pillow were for some hours suffused with light from no external source. Mr. Robinson repeatedly had the story from Ann's father, a physician of Cincinnati, who could see in the event only a recurrence of the supernatural light with which the face of Moses shone as he came down from the mountain of the law. The phenomenon was witnessed by several, including her pastor, a Presbyterian minister, who, like all the rest, was astounded by what he saw, and described it in the funeral sermon.

A distinguished medical friend furnishes the following statement: "Human phosphorescence is a rare phenomenon. It is due to a disordered secretion of sweat, producing phosphorescent perspiration of the skin, and has been seen in miliaria, an inflammatory disease of the sweat glands. It has been known to follow eating phosphorescent fish, and a case has been reported in which the body-linen was made luminous by the perspiration after any violent exercise. It has also been noticed in dying persons, especially those dying of consumption, and has been observed in the human body after death. Cases also of luminous breath have been reported." See Buck's "Reference Handbook of the Medical Sciences," vol. v. p. 641; also "Index Catalogue of the Surgeon-General's Library," under titles "Body, Human, Light from," and "Phosphorescence."

We are concerned, not with explaining the occurrence, but with the side-light which it throws upon the candor of Dr. Robinson, who could accept duly attested facts without accounting for them. A certain openness, however, to mystical impressions, not uncommon in minds habitually sceptical, may be surmised from the footnote with which he closed his discussion of angels: "No one may positively and safely assert what even now is, or is not, the connection of supernatural beings with the mental and physical diseases whose seat is in a moral obliquity of the will." (Christian Theology, p. 115.) — ED.

II.

THE WESTERN THEOLOGICAL INSTITUTE OF COVINGTON, KENTUCKY.

THE curious history of this once very promising but most unfortunate of theological schools has been recovered by the painstaking researches of Professors B. O. True and A. J. Sage. The following sketch is made up almost wholly from materials that these gentlemen found in official reports of fifty years ago, supplemented to some extent by personal recollections. In a few cases I have pretty closely followed their words.

A General Convention of Western Baptists, held at Cincinnati in November, 1833, led to the formation of the Western Baptist Education Society a year later. The Executive Committee of this Society, acting on their own responsibility and accepting for themselves all risks, hit on the plan of endowing the school without an appeal to the churches for money, by means of a speculation in land. Their plans were sagaciously matured, and culminated in the purchase of an estate of some 370 acres situated in the rear of Covington, Kentucky, and overlooking the city of Cincinnati. The price agreed upon was $32,250, but only a small part of this amount was paid at the time of the purchase. The expectation of a rise in value sufficient to pay for the estate and provide an endowment for the future school was not disappointed. During the summer of 1835 some 90 acres were sold for $22,500. For a time the prospects were not altogether favorable, but in 1838 the measures necessary to the financial success of this venture were adopted with energy. Twelve acres were reserved for the school buildings, the remainder was platted, streets graded, and lots on this attractive site were offered for sale. By 1843 lots to the value of $62,000 had been sold, a four-story building 120 × 46 feet had been erected for the future school at a cost of about $25,000, and the assets were estimated at $126,000, while the indebtedness was only $17,000. So rapid the rise in value of these lands had now become that, although portions were sold from time to time to provide for improving the rest and to meet expenses of the school, the property retained was reckoned in 1848 to be worth, with its improvements, $200,000. Two years later the estate of 370 acres, which had been bought in 1835 for $32,250, was estimated at more than a million dollars, and since that time has probably trebled in value.

It is a curious feature of the successful management that less than $5,000 in all, perhaps not more than $3,000, were ever contributed in money for this school; and this estimate includes $500 given annually for about three years toward the President's salary. Of the amount actually paid in to purchase the land, all but $15 was raised north of the Ohio River; and ten of the fifteen dollars was contributed by a Northerner, Rev. Thomas S. Malcom, who was then pastor in Louisville. About ten thousand dollars were subscribed in the South, but no part of this subscription was ever paid. In fact, the institution was founded by Northern enterprise, and was located across the Ohio chiefly because here was a specially favorable opportunity for the land speculation on which the whole scheme was based; but partly because the founders were not without hope of Southern co-operation.

The enterprising managers of this investment postponed opening the school until their operations had provided a sufficient sum for carrying it on. The Institute was opened at length in the autumn of 1845, and was kept open until the disruption in 1848, of which Dr. Robinson speaks. It had both a literary and a theological department. Dr. R. E. Pattison was President, while E. G. Robinson and Ebenezer Dodge were Professors in the theological department, and Asa Drury, earlier a Professor in Cincinnati College, had charge of the literary department. Dr. A. J. Sage, who as a lad attended the literary department for three years, says it was an excellent school of about forty pupils, many of them connected with the theological department.

But the fair prospects of the Institute were wrecked by the storm of dissension which arose over slavery, and which reached its crisis as between Northern and Southern Baptists at precisely this juncture. The Baptist State Convention of Alabama demanded of the Board of the Triennial Convention whether a slaveholder would be appointed as missionary to the heathen; and the Board, located at Boston, — which the distinguished Southern Baptist, Dr. Jeter, declares, in his " Recollections of a Long Life," to have been "the most conservative of all our boards," — plumply replied in the negative. This was in 1844. In May of the next year the Southern Baptist Convention was formed; and it was in the autumn of this year that the Institute was opened in Covington. The Southern friends of the Institute wished Dr. Pattison to define his position. He had tried to be prudent, with the result that in the North he was called proslavery, and in the South denounced as secretly an abolitionist. His opinions, when disclosed, proved to be unsatisfactory to the Southern friends of the school.

The control of the school was vested in sixteen Trustees, nine of them living north and seven south of the Ohio River. The Kentuckians demanded equal representation; but this demand was rejected on the ground that the institution had been founded by Northern men with Northern funds, and that it was enough for Southern interests that it stood on Southern soil. The Southern party next required that the Trustees should declare in favor of slavery. Some question exists as to the form of words in which the demand was couched, but there is no question as to its purport; the Trustees were asked to affirm that slavery had the support of the Bible. But the Trustees declined, on the ground that their business was to conduct a theological school, not to pronounce on slavery, *pro* or *con*.

The next step made disruption inevitable. A report had got about that the Northern Trustees secretly designed to sell the property in Covington and transplant the institution to Northern soil. The Northern Trustees indignantly denied that they entertained any such secret design; but the Southern Trustees determined that the opportunity for it should be destroyed. The charter of the Institute authorized the Legislature of Kentucky to alter, amend, or repeal at pleasure. The Southern Trustees took advantage of this provision to apply to the Legislature, without knowledge of their Northern colleagues, for an amendment to the charter; and an Act was passed raising the number of Trustees to thirty-two, naming the additional sixteen, and providing that thereafter no one residing north of the Ohio River should be eligible. The Southern members of the reconstituted Board now claimed possession of the property, and, when the claim was rejected, took possession by force. They obtained an order from court that the Rev. O. N. Sage, Financial Agent and Manager of the Institution, should deliver to them the account books; but Mr. Sage slipped across the Ohio to Cincinnati with the books, and remained there to avoid proceedings for contempt of court. The decision being against him in the lower courts, the case was carried to the Court of Appeals of Kentucky, where it was decided that the amendatory act was unconstitutional, inasmuch as it undertook, by naming the Trustees, to exercise a corporate franchise, and not merely to amend the charter. This court also decided that the original Trustees had a right to reject the amendment and to wind up the corporation, thus according to them the right to do the very thing which the Legislature had been appealed to to prevent. The case is reported in 15 Ben Monroe Reports, under the title "Sage v. Dillard."

The Southern party moved that the case be reopened in the Court of Appeals, and pending further litigation proposed arbitration. The Northern party assented. Justice McLean, of the Supreme Court of the United States, sat as arbitrator, — whether with or without colleagues is not recalled, — and, after full hearing, decided that the property should be divided, one half going to the North, one half to the South. The Southern half was used to found a theological department or chair at Georgetown College in Kentucky; the Northern share was mainly expended in the Fairmount enterprise, of which Dr. Robinson speaks; but the library went to the college in Granville, Ohio.

The financial management of the venture had been upon the whole thoroughly successful, and the school during the brief period of its existence did excellent work. Professor True states that among the most efficient members of the Board of Trustees were Mr. Ephraim Robins, uncle of Rev. Dr. Henry E. Robins, to whose unwearied and unrequited work the business scheme and its success were largely due; Professor John Stevens, father of Professor William Arnold Stevens; and the admirable financial agent, Rev. O. N. Sage, father of Hon. George R. Sage, judge of the United States Court for the Southern District of Ohio, and of Rev. Dr. A. J. Sage. Judge Sage was of counsel for the Northern party before the Court of Appeals.

Of the thirteen years during which the Covington enterprise was on foot, the first ten were taken up in the development of a business scheme, while the last three, during which alone the school existed, were distracted by the "irrepressible conflict." The Western Baptist Education Society unquestionably expected to establish a theological seminary in the usual way; but when their own Executive Committee had once embarked upon the plan of setting up such a school without cost to any one, the Society was naturally willing to wait even ten years for so pleasing a scheme to realize itself. The project of founding a school for the ministry on a land speculation would never have been conceived outside the United States, and hardly in behalf of any but a "Western Theological Institute;" but once entered upon, the project was cared for with the same unselfish devotion, and with maybe more than the intelligence, that so many schools of the sort have enjoyed. Yet not all the sagacity and devotion of its founders could save it from being one of the most pitiful failures brought about by the slavery conflict. Still the history of the enterprise, from the original conception of it, through the long prenatal period of financial nursing, and the brief tale of its life among men until its final collapse, although a painful story, and once the theme of mutual reproaches, is not without its humorous aspects. The notion of basing a school of divinity on what in these days would be styled "a boom;" the threatened burst of the boom until, as one who then lived in Kentucky had to say when his advice was asked,[1] the lands were worthless ; the subsequent brilliant recovery of values ; the painful but unrelaxed devotion of the projectors ; the future distinction of the corps of teachers whom a project of this kind was able to secure ; the seizure of the infant establishment almost as soon as the breath of life was known to be in it, under what proved to be a false color of legality, by some whose only claim to seize it was that they had a chance ; and, to end with, the impartial and equal division of the proceeds among all claimants, — is a satire upon the state of things in the churches of those days a little wilder than any humorist outside this land of liberty would venture to invent. But good Christians conscientiously took care that it should all come true.

The foregoing sketch has been drawn from materials supplied for the most part by Northern men ; but I believe they spared no pains to get at the entire truth and to do exact justice. The writer alone is responsible for the use made of these materials, and for the interpretation put upon events. — ED.

[1] This was in 1842, when the gentlemen spoken of spent some days at Covington in company with Deacon Robins, and came away with the impression that "everything was lost." It was a period of general prostration. It is recollected that bacon and ham sold that year in Cincinnati for one cent and a half a pound. — ED.

III.

GRADUATING ADDRESS AT NEWTON.

August 24, 1842.

ECCLESIASTICAL HISTORY AS A SOURCE OF INFIDELITY.

UNBELIEVERS have resorted to Ecclesiastical History as supplying them with materials for argumentation. Arraigning Christianity at the bar of human judgment, they have entered the dark, silent archives of antiquity, and, arousing from their long sleep the witnesses of former ages, have summoned them to the stand, and suborned them to utter a testimony against her. They have sought to make the history of the Church an enemy of the Church, a foster-mother of scepticism, an abetter of infidelity. Thus did Gibbon; and who shall tell how many hearts have been blighted and made desolate forever by the pestilential influence of his labors alone?

But infidelity in later days has found aid for itself in the ecclesiastical histories of writers professedly religious. Their histories, it is true, have been made to render a reluctant and unnatural service; they nevertheless have rendered it. They have nursed — they are nursing still — many a feeble, stammering sceptic into a full-grown, dogmatizing infidel; and what is yet more painful, they are at the present moment furnishing the enemies of the cross with some of their deadliest weapons.

But why is this so? Has the career of Christianity in the earth been such as to bring reproach on its character? Has its influence been such as to render it unworthy of our love and respect? Or has history been made to misrepresent it?

The duty of the ecclesiastical historian is to give us a faithful picture of the Church as it has actually existed in successive ages and among different nations. To write a true history, he must be a true artist; skilful in selecting and grouping, skilful in sketching and shading, and possessed of that intuitive sense of propriety which shall perceive at a glance the impression of the whole picture. He must be one who, in his study of the Church in any particular period of the past, has traced the effects of Christianity through all the diversified channels of society. He must be, it is true, a faithful recorder of dates, a correct describer of persons and actions, but he must be something more than these, to write a truthful history. He must be wise in his selections from the wide fields of materials through which he passes, and he must be skilful in his use of them, or the history he shall write may be as false as if the persons selected had been imaginary beings, and the facts recorded the merest fictions. The truth of a history depends, not on the number or the importance of the facts recorded, or of the persons introduced, but on the use that is made of them.

But this is a principle which most ecclesiastical historians have strangely neglected. They have too often written as if their only business was to tell us of dignitaries, of important transactions, and of long disputes; of popes, cardinals, archbishops, and bishops, with their military, political, and religious actions, and of subtle disputants and their protracted controversies; but of what the transforming power of Christianity wrought among the people, they have seemed to regard it as not their concern to speak. The aspirants after fame, who, overleaping the more conscientious and devout, seated themselves in the highest offices of the Church, — the slimy serpents of ambition, that, winding their loathsome track up its lofty columns,

> "Hung hissing at the nobler men below," —

these are made to occupy the most conspicuous places in history, these are taken as the representatives of the spirit of Christianity in the age in which they lived. But the faithful pastors and teachers who toiled in obscurity, and led the people on to heaven, are left in obscurity to die and be forgotten; their names are interred with their bones. The Johns, the Gregories, the Benedicts, the Innocents, and the Leos that sat in the papal chair, and the Richelieus and the Woolseys that wore the cardinal's cap, all are embalmed in history; but the Oberlins, the Neffs, and the Richmonds, the Brainerds, the Pearces, and the Martyns, both of earlier and of later times, receive not so much as a passing notice. Hence has resulted incalculable mischief. The holy altars of the Church have seemed to be the nestling-places of ambition; its turrets and towers, the places where cawing rooks and sometimes birds of prey have built their nests unscared.

And so it is with the controversies of the Church. To these is given, in some ecclesiastical histories, a prominence to which they are by no means entitled; while the silent, regenerating influence of Christianity among the people is forgotten or passed over in silence. In this way, too, by partial statements and by unjust coloring, historians of the Church have defamed Christianity. They have made her, not an angel of mercy diffusing light and life through the earth, but a fiend scattering apples of discord and enkindling perpetual strife among all who bear the Christian name.

Suppose an author like those we have spoken of, five hundred years from this, to write the ecclesiastical history of the United States for the first fifty years of the nineteenth century. He will tell of controversies and convulsions. He will rehearse the contentions of Unitarians with Trinitarians, and of theologians of the old school with those of the new. He will speak of the theology of Andover, the theology of Princeton, the theology of New Haven, and, maybe, of the theology of Newton. He will allude to the bitterness and wrath displayed between Christians at the North and their brethren at the South, and to churches and general assemblies convulsed by angry discussions. Every word he shall utter shall be a word of truth. But to the reader of history in the distant future, there will be given an impression respecting our times as wide from the truth as the east is from the west. To such a reader, sitting in his silent study and reflecting on what he has read, the influence of Christianity in our day shall appear to have been disastrous in the extreme. He shall look back over the past, but see not one of the hundreds of thousands of humble worshippers that crowd the temple gates of our land on a Sabbath morning; he shall hear not one of the pungent heart-searching sermons we hear, not a word of the ten thousand prayers that daily ascend from as many altars like grateful incense up to God, not a syllable of the triumphant utterings of Christianity on the death-beds of departing Christians. He shall see nothing but high, thick, whirling clouds of controversial dust; shall hear nothing but the loud and angry words of heated disputants; and shaking his head with a melancholy air, he shall mournfully murmur to himself, " If this be Christianity, talk not to me of its divinity."

But every one knows that such a reader's impressions respecting our times would be utterly false. Every one should know that similar impressions respecting the past are equally false.

IV.

LECTURE-ROOM SAYINGS.

THE curt sentences with which Dr. Robinson enlivened his discussions sometimes overstate his meaning. This is not merely incidental, but it is a considerable part of the merit of his aphorisms. They struck and stick because they were shot with such excess of vigor. Just this merit belongs to many sayings of Paul and even of Jesus, and makes them so memorable. But allowance must in all cases be made for the hyperbole. The specimens from the theological lecture-room were mostly supplied by Professor T. W. Hopkins, of Auburn Theological Seminary, and by Professor B. O. True, of the Rochester Seminary; those from Brown University were furnished by the Rev. W. H. P. Faunce, of New York, A. G. Langley, A. M., of Newport, Rhode Island, and Rev. M. F Johnson, of Middleborough, Massachusetts. — ED.

AT ROCHESTER.

Never study theology in cold blood.

When a scientific man comes along, I say, Tip up your cart here, and let us examine what you have.

Gentlemen, if any of you have Barnes's Notes, don't give them away; burn them.

Physical science will undoubtedly smash some of our crockery gods.

The verbal theory of inspiration is a gigantic swindle, which has been carried on long enough, and must be riddled through and through.

We have a clearer idea of the scope and range of Christianity than any of the Apostles had.

The existence of God is one of those old truths that become new in the whirligig of time.

If God exists, he must be somewhat corresponding to our consciousness.

The German phrase " God consciousness " rightly means the response of the mind to the evidence of a Divine existence and will.

The doctrine of the Trinity is not to be preached formally. It is like the primitive rocks : sometimes they lie very deep; sometimes they are so near the surface that they may be scratched by the ploughshare.

It is nonsense to say that God hates sin but loves the sinner.

Logic leads to necessitarianism; consciousness attests free agency.

A man is bound to obey his conscience at the peril of his soul's salvation.

By the very nature of evil it is inexplicable.

There is a good streak left in the devil yet.

In the incarnation Christ became as nearly related to us as in his pre-existent state he was to the Father.

To say that sin is an infinite evil, and therefore only an infinite being could make atonement, is infinite nonsense.

We put our trust in one who has proved himself able to save himself and every one who trusts in him.   This is the gospel in a nutshell.

We are saved through the enforcement of law, every mother's son of us.

Every man honest with himself knows pretty well where he is going to.

Judgment is an eternal process.

Probably, like scarred twigs, we shall forever bear the traces of our sins.

Mercy never cheats justice.

The fundamental argument for eternal punishment is the reproductive power of evil.

Moral penalty is through the moral constitution.   Torments of conscience will alone be as a sea of fire.

Heaven is not a place of inactivity : it is not to be compared to a grasshopper on a shingle, floating down-stream on a bright summer day.

Every Christian man has power to bind and loose men's consciences.

Churchism keeps up the middle wall of partition which God has abolished forever.

AT BROWN.

(From Mr. Faunce's Memorial Address.)

Deity need not send a policeman after the sinner; the sinner carries the policeman inside.

Man without religion is a barrel without hoops.

Soul-liberty is not toleration; it is a natural right.

You cannot change a man by offering him a reward. You cannot make sheep love stones by shaking them in a basket.

The glory of Christianity is the boundless reach of its motives.

No man begins his life utterly anew; he finds himself like a top already spinning.

There has never been a great nature without reverence for God.

As soon as any church says that it alone is the true church and there is no other, take your hat.

Disciplined intellect, gentlemen, asks no favor but that of God.

(From Mr. Langley's collection.)

From Locke's time no treatise on Theology has been written in England worth turning the pages of.

All the assumptions of pantheism arise from misunderstanding of the mind's limitations.

A man's mind should be like an elephant's trunk, strong enough to root up an oak, delicate enough to pick up a needle.

The man who makes up his mind to believe only what can be scientifically proved might as well pack up.

Byron's " Don Juan " smells of gin all the way through.

The whirligig of thought has brought us around to the original dunghill on which Lucretius founded his philosophy.

[Panspermism is] not Minerva from a living brain, but Venus from the foam of the sea.

A man's principles and emotions come out and sit on his features.

You can rip through an Oriental language in a very short time.

All attempts to stimulate the brain [by liquor, etc.] come back with tremendous discount.

There is a root of truth in old realism. Nominalism throws two or three pebble-stones into the cog-wheel of thought which continually make some creaking.

Happiness is consciousness of unimpeded movement.

The religion that finds you will hold you, if you are an honest man.

Alexander's and Wayland's idea is that conscience carries a sort of locomotive head-light which throws light on its own path. *Es geht nicht.*

You cannot accept any authority unless it vindicates itself in your moral consciousness.

If you have not mind, you cannot have morals.

Conscience is the invisible police that you can't bribe.

Conscience is not a special kind of cork-screw on the side of an old jack-knife.

A crow from feeding on carrion comes to regard it as the greatest delicacy in the world.

A man is afraid of his conscience just as an old duck is afraid of a gun. The duck pops under the water and remains there as long as he can; so man keeps out of the way of his conscience as long as he can.

Many a man suddenly cries out, "Cursed be the day that I saw the man who has led me astray."

The constituent laws of personal being antedated the laws of Moses.

If the ethical teachings of the Bible were made, then we should outgrow them. They simply unveil what the moral nature is, or ought to be.

If you give all hell the freedom of the universe, will it make hell any better?

An idea is quite prevalent that moral law is a sort of scarecrow which Deity has set up in the cornfields of this world, and which he will take down whenever he thinks it safe to do so.

If a man controls himself, he goes through the world singing like a lark, singing all the time ; and God made it to be so.

If you assume that each volition has a precedent and causative volition, you are on a stairway with no end to it.

Many a man is moral who has no virtue.

The highest emblem of heaven is a happy home.

Never seek a place; seek preparation.

Christianity will digest the other religions.

The best evidences for Christianity have been disclosed by its enemies.

A man is hardly better than a heathen who will sneer at a heathen before his idol.

I should not want to sit in judgment on the heathen.

Authority and faith are totally irrelevant terms.   There may be authority for a certain course of conduct; but for a belief such authority is impossible.

Authority cannot compel assent to evidence; much less consent to dogma.

Truth always takes care of itself, and does this simply because it is a revelation of what is.

Modern atheism is largely due to the use in modern science of the word " law " in the sense of " cause." . . . Law is not force.

Not hope of heaven but fitness for heaven is the idea of Christianity.   God is not the caterer of the universe, as the governmental theory of atonement virtually makes him.

(From Mr. Johnson's collection.)

One form of the Anselmic theory, — so much merit spooned out.

A boy backs up into a corner, and calls the corner the beginning of all things.

A man lived by rule, weighing out his food; and when he took cold, he collapsed like a cabbage-leaf.

The whole soul is wrapped around a cut finger.

A smutty idea is connected with divine words; and when these are recalled, this imp peeps over the shoulder and says, " I 'm here."

Consciousness is like the ocean, ever restless; but, like the river, ever running.

I feel no sensation; but the sensation feels me.

V.

PUBLISHED WRITINGS.

THE titles which follow are of all the known published writings of Dr. Robinson, except book-notices and articles in the daily or weekly press.

BOOKS.

Revised translation of Neander's Planting and Training of the Christian Church: Sheldon & Co., New York, 1865.

Yale Lectures on Preaching: Henry Holt & Co., New York, 1883.

Principles and Practice of Morality: Silver, Burdett, & Co., Boston, 1888.

Christian Theology: E. R. Andrews, Rochester, 1894.

Christian Evidences: Silver, Burdett, & Co., Boston, 1895.

ARTICLES.

" Theology," — " Johnson's Encyclopedia," first edition; revised for last edition by Pres. A. H. Strong, D. D., LL. D.

" Experimental Theology," Inaugural Address at Rochester, — " Christian Review," October, 1853; also in appendix of " Christian Theology."

" The Relation of the Church and the Bible," — " Madison Avenue Lectures," American Baptist Publication Society, 1867.

" Ritualism in the Church of England," — " Baptist Quarterly," January, 1869.

" The Kind and Extent of Ministerial Culture demanded in our Time and in our Churches," — Proceedings of National Baptist Educational Convention, 1870, pp. 139–149.

" Reminiscences of Dr. Hackett at Providence, Newton, and Rochester," — " Memorials of Horatio Balch Hackett."

"The Sabbath and Free Institutions," — "Sabbath Essays," Boston, 1879, Congregational Publishing Society.

" Moral Law in its Relations to Physical Science and to Popular Religion," — Boston Monday Lectures entitled " Christ and Modern Thought" : Roberts Brothers, Boston, 1881.

" Men, Made, Self-made, and Unmade," — Phillips Exeter Lectures," 1885–86.

"The Inspiration of the Apostles," — "Baptist Quarterly Review," January, 1886.

" How I was Educated," — " Forum," December, 1886.

In " Homiletic Review " : —

"The Holiness of God," a sermon, May, 1884.

"Ministerial Education," May, 1885 ;

" How may the Ministry Raise its Efficiency and Usefulness ? " September, 1886.

" How can the Pulpit Best Counteract the Influence of Modern Scepticism ? " March, 1887.

"Training Men to Preach," December, 1891.

" Training Men to Preach," February, 1893.

"Mr. Hazard's Philosophical Writings," in " Life and Services of the Hon. Rowland Gibson Hazard," LL. D., pamphlet, J. A. & R. A. Reid, Providence, 1888.

INDEX.

BY REV. ROBERT KERR ECCLES, M. D.

www.ingramcontent.com/pod-product-compliance
Lightning Source LLC
Chambersburg PA
CBHW032147110726
47902CB00003B/725